M

O. HENRY MEMORIAL AWARD

PRIZE STORIES

OF 1943

Twenty-Fifth Anniversary Edition

O. HENRY MEMORIAL AWARD

PRIZE STORIES OF *1943*

Card filed under:
Society of arts and sciences.

SELECTED AND EDITED BY

HERSCHEL BRICKELL

ASSISTED BY

MURIEL FULLER

DOUBLEDAY, DORAN AND COMPANY, INC.

GARDEN CITY *1943* NEW YORK

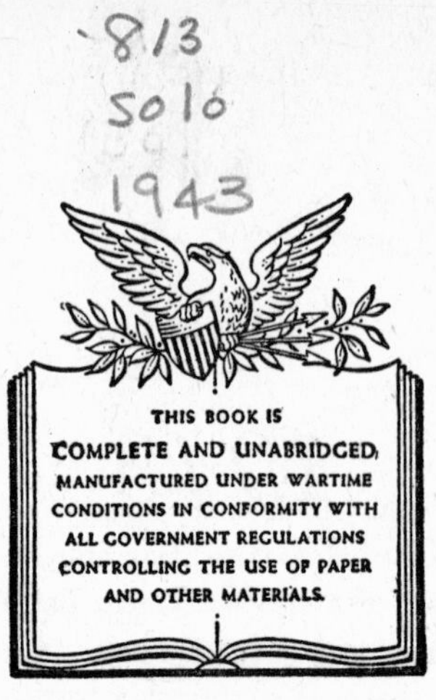

PRINTED IN THE UNITED STATES
AT
THE COUNTRY LIFE PRESS, GARDEN CITY, N. Y.

FIRST EDITION

This, the twenty-fifth anniversary edition of the O. Henry Memorial Award Prize Stories, is dedicated to the memory of Stephen Vincent Benét, good poet, good short-story writer, good American. In its quarter century of existence Mr. Benét's name adorned the collection three times as winner of the first prize, an unequaled record. The winning stories were "An End of Dreams," 1932; "The Devil and Daniel Webster," 1937; and "Freedom's a Hard-Bought Thing," 1940.

CONTENTS*

*After the prize stories, the order is alphabetical by authors.

INTRODUCTION

THIS YEAR the O. Henry Memorial Award Prize Stories anthology rounds out its first quarter century of existence. Its three editors—first Blanche Colton Williams, then Harry Hansen, and, since 1941, the incumbent—have never forgotten that the book was established to honor and preserve the memory of the master of the brief narrative whose world-famous pseudonym is a part of its title. William Sydney Porter was born in 1862 and died in 1910, after a life that at times resembled some of his own stories. Of these, he wrote some two hundred, averaging fifteen pages in length, and at the very least half a dozen of them are as certain to live as are any short stories of any period.

The fashion in the brief narrative has changed completely since O. Henry gave overwhelming popularity to the surprise ending, sometimes called "reversal of situation." But he had many other excellent qualities as a writer, in addition to his ability to trick the reader and make him like it, and he fully earned his place among the immortals.

The stories appearing in this collection are chosen from the hundreds written by American authors and published in American magazines between July and July. The book is regularly published in November. This year, for example, some six hundred stories were read and studied, in addition to scores that were scanned by the editor and his assistant. Thus simple inclusion means that a story has gone through innumerable screenings and that it has finally been judged to be of sufficiently high quality to fit into the annual mosaic which is a recurring reminder of O. Henry's contribution to our literature.

The prizes for 1943, following a time-honored custom, have been awarded on the responsibility of the editor, with the advice and assistance of the following judges, whose names appear in alphabetical order:

Esther Forbes, noted novelist and biographer, teacher at writers' conferences, and publishers' reader.

Wilbur Daniel Steele, many times O. Henry prize winner, and one of the most distinguished short-story writers of the past quarter century.

Carl Van Doren, critic, lecturer, biographer, and historian, as well as author of the standard work on *The American Novel.*

THE AWARDS FOR 1943

First prize of $300 for the best short story: To Eudora Welty, of Jackson, Mississippi, for "Livvie Is Back," published in the *Atlantic Monthly.*

Second prize of $200 for the next-best short story: To Dorothy Canfield, of Arlington, Vermont, for "The Knot Hole," published in the *Yale Review.*

Third prize of $100 for the next-best short story: To William Fifield, of Hollywood, California, for "The Fishermen of Patzcuaro," published in *Story.*

Special prize of $100 for the first published short story: To Clara Laidlaw, of Mount Morris, Michigan, for "The Little Black Boys," which appeared in the *Atlantic Monthly.* Previous winners of this recently established prize were Andy Logan in 1941, with "The Visit," from *Redbook,* and Jeanne E. Wylie in 1942, with "A Long Way to Go," from the *Atlantic Monthly.*

For the third year in succession Eudora Welty is a prize winner, and for the second year running she has been adjudged the author of the best story of the twelvemonth. In 1941 her "The Worn Path" came in second, a close contender with Kay Boyle's blue ribbon entry, "Defeat," and last year her "The Wide Net" was given first prize. It is a curious coincidence, no doubt noted by the skeptical, that a young woman from the home state of the editor should break the O. Henry record of twenty-five years by winning two first prizes in succession, although Mr. Steele was awarded a special prize in 1921 for "the best work in 1919, 1920, and 1921," a public acknowledgment that the early system of making the awards—a complicated adventure in mathematics—did not function satisfactorily. Other writers were given the "first" prizes for the three years in question. Later on Mr. Steele was ruled *hors concours,* which deprived him of another first.

Miss Welty's prize-winning story was chosen for inclusion in the volume against the stiff competition of two other examples of her work, "Asphodel," from the Fall 1942 number of the *Yale Review,* and "The Winds," from *Harper's Bazaar* of August 1942. All three stories possess the peculiar Welty magic to a striking degree and seem to the editor to rank high among her finest productions to date. "Livvie Is Back" was finally settled upon because of its greater originality, with the definite feeling that any one of the three might have been a source of pride to the best of Miss Welty's contemporaries.

This year, as in the other two mentioned, the judges bear the real responsibility for Miss Welty's deserved good fortune, and they must be free from any accusation of local pride or prejudice, since all three are Easterners. Mr. Van Doren placed the Welty story first, and both Mr. Steele and Miss Forbes put it in second place, thus giving a clear lead on points. Since the editor felt far less of an inclination to quarrel with this decision than he did with the final vote of a year ago, the award was made without a struggle. Mr. Van Doren said of the story: "It is beautifully written. The characters have dimension and substance, the locality is presented with vividness, and there is in the story—short as it is—a convincing sense of the passage of time, which gives body to the narrative." Miss Forbes added: "I am voting 'Livvie Is Back' second best. I like all Miss Welty's stories, but this one belongs close to the top, far ahead of 'The Wide Net' of last year." With this opinion the editor is in full agreement.

Miss Forbes continued: "I should have put William Faulkner's 'Two Soldiers' in first place in last year's voting"; an interesting comment, since a number of people have written in to say the same thing. "What I like so much about 'Livvie Is Back' is the author's ability to see life as it seems to the people who are living it, not as it might seem to a social worker. Old Solomon's three-room house, with its neat mousetraps inside and its bottle trees outside, seems as marvelous to us as it did to Livvie, and old Solomon as kind, and Cash as beautiful. Even that dreadful Baby Marie becomes an exciting apparition. This is pure magic." The editor agrees again with Miss Forbes, who has hit upon one of Miss Welty's most notable abilities, her complete identification with her characters, the sure mark of genuine talent in fiction, short or long. Mr. Steele wrote that he did not know why he liked anything, and did not care to try to rationalize his emotional reactions, but that he rated the Welty story second.

There was less agreement among the judges with respect to the second prize, and the editorial ballot was necessary to tip the scales in favor of Dorothy Canfield's extraordinary story of war-torn France, "The Knot Hole." Mr. Van Doren gave this story second place, saying of it: "Next to the Welty, I put the Canfield. It is not so beautifully written as the other and lacks a certain light of genius, I suppose. This has caused me to rate it second. But it has great power in an honest, downright way, and I was much moved by it. Stories of such timeliness as this are always hard to judge dispassionately. But if the other judges favor 'The Knot Hole' for first place, I shall not be disappointed." And Miss Forbes: "When I first read the stories through very fast, I was quite ready to give 'The Knot Hole' a place very near the top. I think it has the most emotional appeal of any of the stories. I shall not quickly forget those men in their boxcar, the legs of the guard, and their tiny view of France. But is it too long, or does one need the leisurely pace to get the impact at the end? In any case, its tremendous honesty and deep sincerity of feeling are very moving."

Mr. Steele, who wrote excellent stories of the first World War, did not mention this one, but Miss Fuller, the editor's experienced assistant, put it first on her list, saying of it: "I think this is one of the finest stories to come out of the war. I sat still for quite a while after I had read it. Even though Mrs. Fisher (Dorothy Canfield has written much under her married name, but dropped the Fisher this time. H.B.) uses the device of being told the story, one has the sense of being present—that the story has not gone through a third person. I believe this is a story which will live." These comments leave little to be added. The story is far more moving than any factual account of French suffering could be. It is a pleasure to have among the prize winners this year the name of one who for so many years has been an honor to American letters and American life, and always a devoted friend of the French. Obviously, part of the emotional impact of "The Knot Hole" derives from its relation to fact, but the short story has its topical element and is no more to be judged in a vacuum than any other work of art. (Never mind eternity, so long as our judgments can be justified within the contemporary frame, saith the editor.)

Mr. Fifield's "The Fishermen of Patzcuaro," which brings another young short-story writer into this collection, always a happy event, is one of the editor's special favorites. Mr. Steele gave it first place without elaborating on his judgment. Mr. Van Doren, raising a point that is never to be forgotten—namely the impossibility of drawing fair comparisons between stories of entirely different varieties—bracketed it with William White's "Pecos Bill and the Willful Coyote," and Miss Forbes rated it below her first six, with this comment: "Have you ever noticed how hard it is to write a short story with a background strange to the average reader? Here, as in 'Death and My Uncle Felix' (Alison Stuart's story of a child and her bullfighter uncle. H.B.), I was more conscious of background than of character and story. This, to my mind, is a common fault of short stories with a foreign or historical background. But it never bothered Steve Benét, nor does it bother Pearl Buck." Nor did it bother Kipling or Conrad, thought the editor, as he found it somewhat difficult to admit the point raised by Miss Forbes, although confessing that in the two stories mentioned the purely personal equation enters very obviously. For example, as a resident of Latin America, the background of the Fifield story does not seem foreign to him any more than, as an *aficionado* of bullfighting, does the background of Miss Stuart's well-done story. Actually the background of Miss Welty's "Livvie Is Back" is completely foreign to the experience of most Americans, and yet the strangeness of the setting does not seem to detract from the artistic merit of the tale at all.

Anyway, some of us are xenophiles by nature, and so the exotic has an intrinsic appeal which balances Miss Forbes's objection to unusual backgrounds. Miss Fuller was never a proponent of the Fifield story, although admitting that "the author did atmosphere well—you remember the scenery and the landscape detail." In other words, neither Miss Forbes nor Miss Fuller felt any emotional reaction to the story, while Messrs. Steele, Van Doren, and the editor did. This is a sharp and significant cleavage along sexual lines, which the reader may ponder at his leisure, although the reasons why the story appeals more to men than to women ought not to be too difficult to discern.

In the award of the special prize for the best first published short story, the judges made things as easy as possible by voting unanimously for Clara Laidlaw's "The Little Black Boys," a touching tale of race prejudice. Miss Fuller's ballot went to Elmer Grossberg's remarkable treatment of the same theme, "Black Boy's Good Time," which the editor would also have been inclined to favor if room had been left for discussion. That the problem of race prejudice is in the minds of many people at the moment is evidenced by the unusual number of stories on the subject that have appeared in the last year. Of Miss Laidlaw's story Miss Forbes said, having rated it among her top half dozen: "It has great charm and pathos. A great many writers can handle tragedy, even within the confines of the short story. Pathos is very hard and usually very bad. Miss Laidlaw seems to sense that the death of her two little black boys is hardly tragic, only very sad. I like the ease and naturalness with which the story is told, the feeling she is able to give the reader of participating, not merely being an onlooker." Mr. Van Doren wrote: "I rank the Clara Laidlaw story as third in the whole book, as well as best among the firsts, easily best. It is clearly conceived and freshly executed and of an exquisite and moving pathos. I do not know whether the little twins are drawn from life or not—I rather suppose they are—but the story is half a dozen times better than if the victim had been only one child. This is the kind of trick arithmetic plays on us in the moral and emotional universe." Mr. Steele contented himself with voting for the Laidlaw story.

Miss Fuller said of the Laidlaw and Grossberg stories: "I think the Laidlaw story is written with more artistry, but the Grossberg is more of a story. No matter who wrote 'Black Boy's Good Time,' or at what age (Mr. Grossberg was sixteen when he wrote the story a year ago. H.B.), it is memorable. I found it much easier to remember than the other, but the decision was a difficult one." Thus the Laidlaw award becomes the most clear-cut of this year's lot, and the special prize goes to a new writer already able to hold her own with the veterans. Also, as occurred last year, it goes to an *Atlantic Monthly* story, one more decoration for an ancient Boston bosom already bestrewn and bedecked with medals of this kind.

Judges agree and judges disagree, and the editor likes it both ways, because he does not admit the existence of absolutes in the criticism of the short story, and because he believes firmly that arguments and discussions are both desirable and useful. This year, for example, Miss Forbes voted for Bessie Breuer's "Pigeons en Casserole" as the best story in the collection, and it happened that this small masterpiece had been held over from the end of the last anthology year, so that it had to survive competition with everything that came between. It simply would not be denied. Miss Forbes wrote of it: "I can't see but that it has everything. Suspense, clear, brilliant writing, and for a short story not only remarkable characterization, but even character development. The narrator not only draws a perfect portrait of himself, but shows what he is and what he will become. The wife, too, is completely drawn, so also the boy. I can think of few short stories where so much is told in such brief compass, although one never feels the narrative is overcrowded, or would be better if expanded."

The editor feels that this is one of the best stories the *New Yorker* has ever published, and this is high praise indeed, for the magazine has brought a great deal to the short story, even to the extent of developing a fresh and recognizable type of compressed, very human tale, as often pathetic, or even tragic, as humorous, and with this development has arisen a whole school of exceptionally skillful writers. The editor's wife, Norma Long Brickell, his patient first-line assistant, also liked the Bessie Breuer story better than any other, saying that a dozen rereadings in the course of the year had only increased her respect for the masterly handling of the material. She cast her second vote for "The Knot Hole" and her third for "Livvie Is Back," explaining that she thought the Welty story one of the most finished ever done by its author. She admitted freely that her rating of the three stories had been influenced by the fact that two were related to the war, but thought that on its purely artistic merits alone the Breuer story could stand up to any in the volume.

Miss Forbes also like Pearl S. Buck's "The Enemy" and gave it third place, thus agreeing with the editor's own high opinion of this story. She wrote: "The situation is so naturally appealing to the reader today, I cannot but wonder if one was judging the story twenty-five years hence, it would seem so good. I think so. One quality I admire is its simplicity, a classic simplicity. The plot, and this is the most exciting plot in the collection, is open to a great variety of treatments. It could have supported a third-rate adventure story. This does not mean that it is a third-rate plot, but it does emphasize Mrs. Buck's skill. As in the Breuer story, I admire the economy with which an entire civilization is suggested, the primitive superstitions, the passionate love of country, and the hatred of everyone else."

Miss Forbes's top six stories included, among those already discussed in some detail, Kay Boyle's "The Canals of Mars," the story of a woman's good-by to her soldier lover. In the editor's judgment this is one of Miss Boyle's best stories. Of it Miss Forbes said: "This story is very beautiful, very skillful, and sad with a queer muted sadness of tears swallowed and not shed. I feel that it is as good as any in the collection, but the very intricacy of the patterns gives it a fragility, even as the reader delights in these patterns." The editor also admired very much Miss Boyle's "This They Carried with Them," from the October 1942 *Harper's Bazaar,* another of the memorable stories of stricken Europe, one of which, "Defeat," won first prize in 1941, and another of which, "Their Name Is Macaroni," was reprinted last year.

The only other story to receive special mention by the judges was Mr. White's tall tale, "Pecos Bill and the Willful Coyote," which Mr. Van Doren, as already indicated, placed with "The Fishermen of Patzcuaro" in third position, and which Mr. Steele also thought was third best. It is always satisfactory to the editor to see a humorous story thus recognized, and especially when it is so typically American as this one. Mr. White has made a notable addition to the saga of Pecos Bill, sometimes called the seagoing cowboy, and one of the most far-ranging and diverting of all our folk heroes. The editor wishes there might be a special prize for tall tales, but is delighted, in any case, to have the excellent storytelling company of Mr. White. Miss Fuller gave special consideration to Austin Strong's delicately beautiful story, "She Shall Have Music," and to Whitfield Cook's "The Unfaithful," two more of the editor's favorites. Of the first she wrote: "This is one of the most beautiful stories I have ever read. It stays with one like music; even when time blurs the detail a little, the impression of beauty remains." Of the Cook story: "This picture of a soda jerker will remain fresh in my memory a long time, his emotions, what he went through with his wife and the girl friend from his home town whom he met. It seems to me honest and sincere, as well as deeply moving."

The editor will not undertake to comment separately upon the rest of the stories except to say, which ought to be obvious, that he thinks them all outstanding. The amount of time and prayer that goes into the final selection of twenty-odd stories from more than half a thousand may easily be imagined, and there is always the lingering doubt, in some cases, that the decisions may not be wholly just. This year Mary Lavin's "The Will," another of the many fine stories to appear in *Harper's Bazaar,* remained to the very last, Miss Lavin being a talented young story writer who is much admired by some of the editor's most trusted lieutenants. Miss Fuller had special admiration for "Routine Case," a *Mademoiselle* story by Alis de Sola about a dictator-to-be, and the editor debated long over Maritta Wolff's "This Was the Day," also from the *Bazaar*. Also there was a Sherwood Anderson piece in *Twice-a-Year,* an exceptionally interesting publication, half magazine and half miscellany, called "When We Care." It was labeled "story" in the index, and the editor thought it very beautiful and very moving and very Sherwood Anderson, but he was unable to persuade himself that it could properly be called a story. Rather, it seemed a prose poem, or an essay, or a soliloquy. Many times during the editor's months in South America he has thought of how popular Anderson's warmth of human sympathy and love of people would have made him among the Latins. There was a peculiar irony in his death on the way to a part of the world where he would have been fully understood and appreciated for the first time.

Among the familiar contributors to this volume may be found this year Nancy Hale, for whose "Who Lived and Died Believing" the editor has a great respect, especially as a magnificent fictional treatment of a new scientific discovery, the shock treatment for insanity; Walter Van Tilburg Clark, whose past stories, "Hook" and "The

Portable Phonograph," have been much liked by the readers of this anthology, many of whom would have given either or both stories first prize, and whose acid satire, "The Ascent of Ariel Goodbody," reveals another aspect of his fine talent; Josephine Johnson, whose "The Glass Pigeon" is so delicately and surely done; and Carson McCullers, whose "A Tree. A Rock. A Cloud" is so peculiarly her own. In this quarter (personal, not geographical) William Saroyan is not regarded as any part of a genius, even with *The Human Comedy* thrown into the balance, but his "Knife-Like, Flower-Like, Like Nothing in the World" proved somehow irresistible. The only comment from a judge was the story "could not be remembered twenty-four hours after it had been read." It is also pleasant to have a second good story by Alison Stuart, whose "The Yoodeler" made a good run for the first-story prize of last year. Miss Stuart's "Death and My Uncle Felix" is a remarkable feat of the imagination, since she knows the ancient ritual ballet called tauromachy only at second-hand.

As indicative of the relative standing of current magazines in the publication of short fiction of high quality, the figures that follow will be of interest: *Harper's Bazaar,* from which five stories were taken last year, furnished six this year, in addition to several strong runners-up. The *Atlantic Monthly,* with three stories last year, all of which won prizes, this year supplied four stories, two of which received awards. *Harper's Magazine,* which supplied five stories last year, including the winner of the first prize, yielded only one this year, Mrs. Buck's "The Enemy," and obviously placed the principal emphasis of its editorial policy on articles. *Story* yielded three stories for this year's collection. The other magazines from which more than one story was taken were the *Yale Review,* the *New Yorker,* and *Mademoiselle.* The concentration of interest on the war and the decline of enthusiasm for the realistic, proletarian type of story have combined to make the little magazines less fruitful hunting ground recently than they were a few years ago, although they are still being faithfully read and appreciated, always with the hope that they will be able to struggle through these dark days and to continue, after peace has returned, to serve a useful purpose as laboratories for new and untried writers.

Some Short Story History

A backward glance at the twenty-five years covered by the life of this collection seems appropriate on the occasion of its silver anniversary. In her Introduction to the first book, that of 1919, Dr. Blanche Colton Williams gave a brief history of how the anthology came into being. The movement for a memorial to O. Henry, who died in 1910, actually began in April 1918, or about the time the first large bodies of American troops were moved up to the Western Front. The Society of Arts and Sciences of New York City sponsored the memorial, and in December 1918, shortly after the Armistice, a committee called together by John F. Tucker, managing director of the society, decided to offer a prize for the best short story published during the year by an American author in an American magazine. Later two prizes were settled upon, and the idea was fairly launched.

An honorary committee of writers and editors was formed to assist the Committee of Award, and the result of the deliberations was the selection of thirty-two stories from which the prize winners were to be chosen and the book composed. The winner of the first prize was Margaret Prescott Montague, with "England to America," a war story, published in the *Atlantic Monthly,* a noteworthy award, since an *Atlantic* story is the winner this year also. Wilbur Daniel Steele had three entries in the competition, the prize-winning "For They Know Not What They Do," "Contact," and "La Guiablesse," all from *Harper's Magazine*. The prizes were awarded on a complicated point system, which never worked satisfactorily and which was finally abandoned in favor of a less mathematical and far fairer method of choice.

The year that saw the publication of the first O. Henry volume also witnessed the publication of Sherwood Anderson's "Winesburg, Ohio," destined to be an important influence on the short story. It also saw, incidentally, the publication of James Branch Cabell's *Jurgen,* which aroused the fury of the censors. It was the year of the first flight of the Atlantic by Alcock and Brown, who made the crossing from Newfoundland to Ireland in sixteen hours, twelve minutes. This flight had a curious significance for the O. Henry collection, because for two years now the appearance of the volume has depended upon the air-mail service (born, incidentally, in 1928) between New York City and Bogotá, Colombia, the present home of the editor. The year also witnessed the foreshadowing of the defeat of the League of Nations plan, and saw, therefore, the first faint beginnings of the present holocaust. The next year came Sinclair Lewis' epoch-making *Main Street.*

Actually the modern history of the short story began about this time, although Edward J. O'Brien had started his pioneering in the field as early as 1916, when the first volume of *Best Short Stories* appeared, an event of great importance in American literary history because of its emphasis upon the original and the experimental. But dating from 1919 one may list the real masters of the brief narrative and, without discounting the work of writers like Poe, Hawthorne, Ambrose Bierce, Sara Orne Jewett, Mary E. Wilkins Freeman, or of our patron saint, O. Henry, assemble a collection of names that is impressive in length and quality. After Anderson came Hemingway, whose volume *In Our Time* made a deep impression in 1925 and started a fashion. And of Hemingway's generation is William Faulkner, who works with equal skill in the short story and the novel.

Other masters of this period were Ring Lardner, Erskine Caldwell, and F. Scott Fitzgerald, none of whom, as it happened, ever won an O. Henry prize, although each has more than one of the best American short stories to his credit. John Steinbeck is another of the younger writers who does well in both long and short fiction, which has not by any means always been the case. Wilbur Daniel Steele, who was for the first decade of the anthology's existence undoubtedly the most consistent performer among all our short-story writers, never had any luck with his novels. Thomas Wolfe also wrote a few good short stories, although it is hard to imagine his torrential talent cribbed and confined within such limits. Stephen Vincent Benét ranked with the very best we have ever produced. In recent years Jerome Weidman, Irving Shaw, John Cheever, William March, and many others have written notable stories.

Among the many admirable women authors of the quarter century, Willa Cather produced several fine short stories, published in her volume *Youth and the Bright Medusa.* Of the long short story no one in the course of American literature has produced more first-rate specimens than Katherine Anne Porter. Ellen Glasgow's single volume, *The Shadowy Third and Other Stories,* has notable tales in it, and Elizabeth Madox Roberts' highly poetical talent resulted in several memorable stories. Dorothy Parker has been responsible for a few classics, such as "Big Blonde," and Nancy Hale, Sally Benson, Josephine Johnson, and lately Eudora Welty have made notable contributions in this field. Kay Boyle, often included in the O. Henry volume, is better known for her short stories than her novels, and deservedly so.

These lists are not at all complete, but from the stories of the writers mentioned an anthology could be made up which would easily rank with the best of any other country of the world of any other period.

The short story flourishes in America as it does nowhere else, the primary and very practical reason being that our magazines need brief fiction and are willing to pay for it. The bulk of such material is completely conventional, machine-made stuff, but the simple fact that year after year this book is made up of stories from reasonably popular magazines is all the indication needed that the so-called artistic short story has its market and is profitable to write, as well as agreeable and satisfying to read.

A study of this collection for the twenty-five-year period would reveal the short story as a fair mirror of the times. And what times they have been! A World War, the development of the airplane, the radio, the automobile, television, the talkies, Prohibition, woman's suffrage, the Boom, the Crash, Wilson, Harding, Coolidge, Hoover, and Franklin Delano Roosevelt, the third term, and a global war to close the chapter! Also the coming of age of our literature in all fields, and its preponderant lead in the novel.

The Fashions Change

What has happened to the short story in all these stormy years? Wilbur Daniel Steele, asked this question, replied: "That the short story has changed there can be no question. It would be strange if it had not, and also it would be dead. As in any other form of creative art, the story writer is bound over to root-hog-or-die in the stuff of his own time, which is to say a time and a way of seeing things gone a while before, the world of his parents' prime, and his own young youth and early maturity.

"Let us take it at twenty-some years, a rough approximation, this lag between seeing and telling. The world which is being pictured by the story writers of today (as in this volume, for instance) is, by and large, and vividly, this day's, this troubled minute's, world. But vision is in eyes, not in objects. And it is eyes that are getting their lives' stocks of images together in the early twenties, say, that are doing the bulk and perhaps the best of the creative imagining of right now.

"What then of the stories (the bulk, not the best) that were being printed in those early twenties? Their world and way of seeing must have belonged away back around the turn of the century. Farther back, indeed. For the form of then, the so-called 'plot story,' was old in its kind, on its last legs, getting ready to pass over Jordan (and find the land of murder-mystery fabulous with grapes). But that story in its kind had nothing to be ashamed of, it had served its country well, depicted the America of its youth as no other shape of literature (or of any art perhaps) could have done so authentically.

"U.S.A., of the Golden Age. . . . Life skipping pages in its eagerness to know, of anything, what came of it; the Happy Ending. And the happy ending was no mere catchpenny escape mechanism of those days. It was solid realism. It was such matter-of-fact in the faith of then, that most men discover gold mines on grubstakes and die wealthy, as it came to be in a later faith, that most men buy utilities on margin and live unhappily ever afterward. It was the age of foreign concord and domestic doing-things. And there, it seems to me, lies the salient and inevitable difference between the stories that were that America, and the stories that are this America now. The short story of today strikes me as essentially a matter of seeing and feeling, akin to poetry in that. The older story was more nearly related to drama, melodrama if you will; how else could it have dealt with a life almost wholly preoccupied with doing? It is possible to feel without too fixed a pattern. But you can't do without a 'plot.'

"Another gulf between the two generations is shown by the changing need of appreciation by which a tale will feel itself rewarded.

The accolade was once 'How extraordinary,' and now it is 'How true.' That this has made for a deeper, wider, more mature and abundant literature of the short story seems to me, on the evidence of this volume, beyond question. Just as it is beyond question that no story was, nor ever can be, truly extraordinary, without first and foremost being true."

There is much to ponder in these words of a master of his craft, because they are thoughtful and true words. To them Miss Forbes, who has written a few short stories of the highest quality, has added her opinions:

"Short stories in America early tended toward two types, even in the nineteenth century. There was the 'straight' story, in which all was forgiven if only the plot could be sufficiently ingenious. In these, all the emphasis was on the skeleton, which often protruded indecently. In the other group the flesh received the emphasis, concealing the skeleton. These might be quite formless, as formless as some of Renoir's nudes. In the Victorian nomenclature they were often called sketches. During the last twenty-five years the stock of the straight story has been steadily sinking. The writer's ingenuity is less used, and his power to see and to feel, and to translate the seeing and feeling to the reader, has risen. What started out in this country as the 'sketch' has developed immensely and has become the typical 'perceptive' story, as I call it.

"The perceptive story stands and falls by the illumination it throws. It sees only what is there, but with an artist's vision, for it sees much more than is discernible to the average eye. The painters and the photographers have done much the same thing for us. They, like many of our best writers, will take scenes so commonplace most of us would pass them by as uninteresting, see them and record them in such a way as to make them become downright exciting; I am sure this type of story has been on the ascendancy for the quarter century under discussion. But note: Dreiser and Anderson were at work twenty-five years ago, and wasn't Sara Orne Jewett dead by then? (She was. H.B.) Of this perceptive school Chekhov was the past master and principal influence.

"But the desire to be perceptive, the anxiety to see the unseen in everyday occurrences, has led many writers to disaster. Clifton Fadiman, in his introduction to *War and Peace,* puts it neatly. He is speaking of the scene where Dolokhov gets drunk and sits on the window sill and has another drink: 'Imagine one of our more sophisticated novelists or short-story writers handling this scene. What subtle emotions that aren't really there he would put into it! What unnecessary underwriting, what overtones! But Tolstoy gives us only the scene itself, simply and vividly, yet with every desired effect obtained.'

"The effort of certain writers in the past to see more than there actually was sometimes gave an effect that was curiously itchy and irritating. It seems to me that that particular danger of overdoing a good thing has passed. Because the 'commercial' short story was too overplotted and because both Mansfield and Chekhov could get along very well with a minimum of plot or structure, too many of our writers came to think that any sort of foundation or skeleton for a short story was bad art. In their honest desire to get away from artificiality suspense was too often sacrificed completely. I think it is a German saying, but I like it still: 'They threw out the baby with the bath.'

"But I notice the stories you have selected this year all have form and structure, and most of them have plot in the strictest sense of the word.

"In closing, I should like to say that I do not believe the short story is in any danger of being forced into a mold. Writers to whom it is not a natural thing are not forced to cudgel their brains for ingenious plots with surprising (and unlikely) endings to get an audience. Neither do they have to sit about and appear much more perceptive than they really are. They can in our United States, and perhaps to a greater degree than ever before, be themselves, see the world honestly in their own terms, and so describe it. What more can any writer ask?"

The answer, Miss Forbes, in a word, is "Nothing," and on this cheerful note the editor would like to end his introduction. But not before expressing his renewed gratitude to the judges, to his assistants, and most of all, to the writers and publishers who generously make this volume possible once a year.

For the ailurophiles, or cat-lovers, who will remember from last year that there was then a feline helper named Federica García Lorca

Uribe White Brickell, it has to be announced that this black, slender, beautiful, intelligent, and most affectionate small cat died during an enforced absence of the editor and his wife from Bogotá. She was completely dependent upon human companionship from the day she opened her eyes upon this sad world, and when it was withdrawn she did not care to live any longer. So now she is a ghost cat, with all the others that have come into the editor's life and gone out again, all remembered as if they were still alive.

Herschel Brickell

Bogotá, Colombia,
August 5, 1943.

LIVVIE IS BACK*

By Eudora Welty

From the *Atlantic Monthly*

*This story is included in Eudora Welty's new book *The Wide Net,* and is reprinted by permission of Harcourt, Brace and Company, Inc.

EUDORA WELTY

won first prize in the O. Henry Memorial Award Prize Stories of 1942 *with "The Wide Net," from* Harper's Magazine. *The year before she won second prize with "A Worn Path," from the* Atlantic, *and was represented in the 1939 volume with "Petrified Man," from the* Southern Review. *She was born April 13, 1909, in Jackson, Mississippi, where she makes her home, of Scotch-Irish and Swiss ancestry. She attended the Mississippi State College for Women, and received her Bachelor of Arts degree from the University of Wisconsin in 1929. She went to the Columbia University School of Advertising the following year.*

Her first story appeared in Manuscript *in 1936, and later stories in the* Southern Review *attracted the attention of Katherine Anne Porter, who wrote the introduction to Miss Welty's first book,* A Curtain of Green, *published in 1941. Her second,* The Robber Bridegroom, *was published in 1942, and her third, a collection of short stories, appeared this fall under the title* The Wide Net.

Miss Welty has been a Fellow at Bread Loaf Writers' Conference, and has worked at Yaddo. She is also a painter, water colors being one of her hobbies, and is noted as a photographer of Negroes. Her other hobby is gardening. She likes to paint the countryside of Mississippi, which she finds full of color and beauty. She has earned her living by writing publicity and advertising, radio scripts, feature stories and society news for the local papers, and taking publicity photographs. She is now devoting herself entirely to writing, and insists good luck has been with her since the start. She was awarded a Guggenheim Fellowship in 1942 for a project to write a series of short stories centering around the Natchez Trace.

SOLOMON carried Livvie twenty-one miles away from her home when he married her. He carried her away up on the Old Natchez Trace into the deep country to live in his house. She was sixteen then. People said he thought nobody would ever come along there. It had been a long time, and a day she did not know about, he told her himself, since that road was a traveled road with *people* coming and going. He was good to her, but he kept her in the house. She had not thought that she could not get back. Where she came from, people said an old man did not want anybody in the world to find his wife, for fear they would steal her back from him. Solomon had asked her before he took her, "Would she be happy?"—very dignified, for he was a colored man that owned his land and had it written down in the courthouse; and she said, "Yes sir," since he was an old man then and she was young, and just listened and answered. He asked her, if she was choosing winter, would she pine for spring, and she said, "No indeed." Whatever she said, always, was because he was an old man, while nine years went by. All the time he got old, and he got so old he gave out. At last he slept the whole day in bed, and she was young still.

It was a nice house, inside and outside both. In the first place, it had three rooms. The front room was papered in holly paper, with green palmettos from the swamp spaced at careful intervals over the walls. There was fresh newspaper cut with fancy borders on the mantelshelf, on which were propped straight-up photographs of old or very young men printed in faint yellow—Solomon's people. Solomon had a houseful of furniture. There was a double settee, a tall scrolled rocker, and an organ in the front room, all around a three-legged table with a pink marble top, on which was set a lamp with three gold feet, besides a jelly glass with pretty hen feathers in it.

The room behind the front room had a bright iron bed with polished knobs like a throne, in which Solomon slept all day. There were snow-white curtains of wiry lace at the window, and a lace bed-spread belonged on the bed. But what old Solomon slept so sound under was a big featherstitched piece quilt in the pattern Trip Around the World, which had twenty-one different colors, four hundred and forty pieces, and a thousand yards of thread; and that was what Solomon's mother made in her life and old age. There was a table holding the Bible, and a trunk with a key. On the wall were two calendars and a diploma from somewhere in Solomon's family, and under that Livvie's one possession was nailed, a picture of the little white baby of the family she worked for, back in Natchez before she was married.

In the kitchen beyond there were a big wood stove and a big round table always with a wet top and with the knives and forks in one jelly glass and the spoons in another, and a cut-glass vinegar bottle between, and going out from those, many shallow dishes of pickled peaches, fig preserves, watermelon pickles, and blackberry jam always sitting there. The churn sat in the sun, the doors of the safe were always both shut, and there were four baited mousetraps in the kitchen, one in every corner.

The outside of Solomon's house looked nice. It was not painted, but across the porch was an even balance. On each side there was one easy chair with high springs, looking out, and a fern basket hanging over it from the ceiling, and a dishpan of zinnia seedlings growing at its foot on the floor. By the door there was a plow wheel, just a pretty iron circle nailed up on one wall, and a square mirror on the other, a turquoise-blue comb stuck up in the frame, with the washstand beneath it. On the door was a wooden knob with a pearl in the end, and Solomon's black hat hung on that, if he was in the house.

Out front was a clean dirt yard with every vestige of grass patiently uprooted and the ground scarred in deep whorls from the strike of Livvie's broom. Rosebushes with tiny blood-red roses blooming every month grew in threes on either side of the steps. On one side was a peach tree, on the other a pomegranate. Then coming around up the path from the deep cut of the Natchez Trace below was a line of bare crape-myrtle trees with every branch of them ending in a colored bottle, green or blue. There was no word that fell from Solomon's lips to say what they were for, but Livvie knew that there could be a spell put in trees, and she was familiar from the time she was born with the way bottle trees keep evil spirits from coming into the house —by luring them inside the colored bottles, where they cannot get out again. Solomon had made the bottle trees with his own hands over the nine years, in labor amounting to about a tree a year, and without a sign that he had any uneasiness in his heart, for he took as much pride in his precautions against spirits coming in the house as he took in the house, and sometimes in the sun the bottle trees looked prettier than the house did.

But there was nobody, nobody at all, not even a white person. And if there had been anybody, Solomon would not have let Livvie look at them, just as he would not let her look at a field hand, or a field hand look at her. There was no house near, except for the cabins of the tenants that were forbidden to her, and there was no house as far as she had been, stealing away down the still, deep trace. She felt as if she waded a river when she went, for the dead leaves on the ground reached as high as her knees, and when she was all scratched and bleeding she said it was not like a road that went anywhere. One day, climbing up the high bank, she had found a graveyard without a church, with ribbon grass growing about the foot of an angel (she had climbed up because she thought she saw angel wings), and in the sun, trees shining like burning flames through the great caterpillar nets which enclosed them. Scarey thistles stood looking like the prophets in the Bible in Solomon's house. Indian paintbrushes grew over her head, and the mourning dove made the only sound in the world. Oh, for a stirring of the leaves, and a breaking of the nets! But not by a ghost, prayed Livvie, jumping down the bank. After Solomon took to his bed she never went out, except one more time.

Livvie knew she made a nice girl to wait on anybody. She fixed things to eat on a tray like a surprise. She could keep from singing when she ironed; and to sit by a bed and fan away the flies, she could be so still she could not hear herself breathe. She could clean up the house and never drop a thing, and wash the dishes without a sound, and she would step outside to churn, for churning sounded too sad to her, like sobbing, and if it made her homesick and not Solomon, she did not think of that.

But Solomon scarcely opened his eyes to see her, and scarcely tasted his food. He was not sick or paralyzed or in any pain that he mentioned, but he was surely wearing out in the body, and no matter what nice hot thing Livvie would bring him to taste, he would only look at it now, as if he were past seeing how he could add anything more to himself. Before she could beg him, he would go fast asleep. She could not surprise him any more if he would not taste, and she was afraid he was never in the world going to taste another thing she brought him—and so how could he last?

But one morning it was breakfast time, and she cooked his eggs and grits, carried them in on the tray, and called his name. He was sound asleep. He lay in a dignified way with his watch beside him, on his back in the middle of the bed. One hand drew the quilt up high, though it was the first day of spring. Through the white lace curtains a little puffy wind was blowing in as if it came from round cheeks. All night the frogs had sung out in the swamp like a commotion in the room, and he had not stirred, though she lay wide awake and saying, "Shh, frogs!" for fear he would mind them.

He looked as if he would like to sleep a little longer, and so she put back the tray and waited a little. When she tiptoed and stayed so quiet she surrounded herself with a little reverie, and sometimes it seemed to her, when she was so stealthy, that the quiet she kept was for a sleeping baby, and that she had a baby and was its mother. When she stood at Solomon's bed and looked down at him she would be thinking, "He sleeps so well," and she would hate to wake him up. And in some other way, too, she was afraid to wake him up because even in his sleep he seemed to be such a strict man.

Of course, nailed to the wall over the bed—only she would forget who it was—there was a picture of him when he was young. Then he had a fan of hair over his forehead like a king's crown. Now his hair lay down on his head; the spring had gone out of it. Solomon had a lightish face, with eyebrows scattered but rugged, the way privet grows, strong eyes, with second sight, a strict mouth, and a little gold smile. This was the way he looked in his clothes, but in bed in the daytime he looked like a different and smaller man, even when he was wide awake and holding the Bible. He looked like somebody kin to himself. And then sometimes when he lay in sleep and she stood fanning the flies away, and the light came in, his face was like new, so smooth and clear that it was like a glass of jelly held to the window, and she could almost look through his forehead and see what he thought.

She fanned him, and at length he opened his eyes and spoke her name, but he would not taste the nice eggs she had kept warm under a pan.

Back in the kitchen she ate heartily, his breakfast and hers, and looked out the open door at what went on. The whole day, and the whole night before, she had felt the stir of spring close to her. It was as present in the house as a young man would be. The moon was in the last quarter, and outside they were turning the sod and planting peas and beans. Up and down the red fields, over which smoke from the brush burning hung, showing like a little skirt of sky, a white horse and a white mule pulled the plow.

At intervals hoarse shouts came through the air and roused her as if she dozed neglectfully in the shade, and they were telling her, "Jump up!" She could see how over each ribbon of field were moving men and girls, on foot and mounted on mules, with hats set on their heads, and bright with tall hoes and forks as if they carried streamers on them and were going to some place on a journey—and how as if at a signal now and then they would all start at once shouting, hollering, cajoling, calling and answering back, running, being leaped on, and breaking away, flinging to the earth with a shout and lying motionless in the trance of noon. The old women came out of the cabins and brought them the food they had ready for them, and then all worked together, spread evenly out. The little children came too, like a bouncing stream overflowing the fields, and set upon the men, the women, the dogs, the rushing birds, and the wavelike rows of earth, their little voices almost too high to be heard. In the middle distance like some white and gold towers were the haystacks, with black cows coming around to eat their edges. High above everything—the wheel of fields, house, and cabins, and the deep road surrounding like a moat to keep them in—was the turning sky, blue with long, far-flung white mare's-tail clouds, serene and still as high flames. And sound asleep while all this went around him that was his, Solomon was like a little still spot in the middle.

Even in the house the earth was sweet to breathe. Solomon had never let Livvie go any farther than the chicken house and the well. But what if she would walk now into the heart of the fields and take a hoe and work until she fell stretched out and drenched with her efforts, like other girls, and laid her cheek against the laid-open earth, and shamed the old man with her humbleness and delight? To shame him! A cruel wish could come in uninvited and so fast while she looked out the back door. She washed the dishes and scrubbed the table. She could hear the cries of the little lambs. Her mother, whom she had not seen since her wedding day, had said one time, "I rather a man be anything than a woman be mean."

So all morning she kept tasting the chicken broth on the stove, and when it was right she poured off a nice cupful. She carried it in to Solomon, and there he lay having a dream. Now what did he dream about? For she saw him sigh gently as if not to disturb some whole thing he held round in his mind, like a fresh egg. So even an old man dreamed about something pretty. Did he dream of her, while his eyes were shut and sunken, and his small hand with the wedding ring curled close in sleep around the quilt? He might be dreaming of what time it was, for even through his sleep he kept track of it like a clock, and knew how much of it went by, and waked up knowing where the hands were, even before he consulted the silver watch that he never let go. He would sleep with the watch in his palm, and even holding it to his cheek like a child that loves a plaything. Or he might dream of journeys and travels on a steamboat to Natchez. Yet she thought he dreamed of her; but even while she scrutinized him the rods of the foot of the bed seemed to rise up like a rail fence between them, and she could see that people never could be sure of anything as long as one of them was asleep and the other awake. To look at him dreaming of her when he might be going to die frightened her a little, as if he might carry her with him that way, and she wanted to run out of the room. She took hold of the bed and held on, and Solomon opened his eyes and called her name, but he did not want anything. He would not taste the good broth.

Just a little after that, as she was taking up the ashes in the front room for the last time in the year, she heard a sound. It was somebody coming. She pulled the curtains together and looked through the slit.

Coming up the path under the bottle trees was a white lady. At first she looked young, but then she looked old. Marvelous to see, a little car stood steaming like a kettle out in the field track—it had come without a road.

Livvie stood listening to the long, repeated knockings at the door, and then she opened it just a little. The lady came in through the crack, though she was more than middlesized and wore a big hat.

"My name is Miss Baby Marie," she said.

Livvie gazed respectfully at the lady and at the little suitcase she was holding close to her by the handle until the proper moment. The lady's eyes were running over the room, from palmetto to palmetto, but she was saying, "I live at home . . . out from Natchez . . . and get out and show these pretty cosmetic things to the white people and the colored people both . . . all around . . . years and years . . . both shades of powder and rouge . . . it's the kind of work a girl can do and not go clear 'way from home. . . ." And the harder she looked, the faster she talked. Suddenly she turned up her nose and said, "It is not Christian or sanitary to put feathers in a vase," and then she took a gold key out of the front of her dress and began unlocking the locks on her suitcase. Her face drew the light, the way it was covered with intense white and red, with a little pattycake of white between the wrinkles by her upper lip. Little red tassels of hair bobbed under the rusty wires of her picture hat, as with an air of triumph and secrecy she now drew open her little suitcase and brought out bottle after bottle and jar after jar, which she put down on the table, the mantelpiece, the settee, and the organ.

"Did you ever see so many cosmetics in your life?" asked Miss Baby Marie.

"No'm," Livvie tried to say, but the cat had her tongue.

"Have you ever applied cosmetics?" asked Miss Baby Marie next.

"No'm."

"Then look!" she said, and pulling out the last thing of all, "Try this!" she said. And in her hand was unclenched a golden lipstick which popped open like magic. A fragrance came out of it like incense, and Livvie cried out suddenly, "Chinaberry flowers!"

Her hand took the lipstick, and in an instant she was carried away in the air through the spring; and looking down with a half-drowsy smile from a purple cloud which floated above a chinaberry tree, dark and smooth and neatly leaved, neat as a guinea hen in the dooryard, she saw again her home that she had left. On one side of the tree was her mama holding up her heavy apron, and she could see it was loaded with ripe figs; and on the other side was her papa holding a fish pole over the pond, and she could see it transparently, the little clear fishes swimming up to the brim.

"Oh no, not chinaberry flowers—secret ingredients," said Miss Baby Marie. "My cosmetics have secret ingredients—not chinaberry flowers."

"It's purple," Livvie breathed, and Miss Baby Marie said, "Use it freely. Rub it on."

Livvie tiptoed out to the washstand on the front porch and, before the mirror, put the paint on her mouth. In the wavery surface her face danced before her like a flame. Miss Baby Marie followed her out, took a look at what she had done, and said, "That's it."

Livvie tried to say "Thank you" without moving her parted lips where the paint lay so new.

By now Miss Baby Marie stood behind Livvie and looked in the mirror over her shoulder, twisting up the tassels of her hair. "The lipstick I can let you have for only two dollars," she said, close to her neck.

"Lady, but I don't have no money, never did have," said Livvie.

"Oh, but you don't pay the first time. I make another trip, that's the way I do. I come back again—later."

"Oh—*then.*"

"But if you don't take it now, this may be the last time I'll call at your house," said Miss Baby Marie sharply. "It's far away from anywhere, I'll tell you that. You don't live close to anywhere."

"Yes'm. My husband, he keep the *money,*" said Livvie, trembling. "He is strict as he can be. He don't know *you* walk in here—Miss Baby Marie!"

"Where is he?"

"In yonder, sound asleep, an old man. I wouldn't ever ask him for anything."

Miss Baby Marie took back the lipstick and packed it up. She gathered up her jars and got them all inside the suitcase, with the same little fuss of triumph with which she had brought them out. She started away.

"Good-by," she said, making herself look grand from the back, but she could not help turning around in the door. Her old hat wobbled as she whispered, "Let me see your husband."

Livvie obediently went on tiptoe and opened the door to the other room. Miss Baby Marie came behind her and rose on her toes and looked in.

"My, what a little tiny old, old man!" she whispered, clasping her hands and shaking her head over them. "What a beautiful quilt! What a tiny old, old man!"

"He can sleep like that all day," whispered Livvie proudly.

They looked at him awhile so fast asleep, and then they looked at each other. Somehow that was as if they had a secret, for he had never stirred. Livvie then politely, but all at once, closed the door.

"Well! I'd certainly like to leave you with a lipstick!" said Miss Baby Marie vivaciously. She smiled in the door.

"Lady, I told you I don't have no money and never did have."

"And never will?" In the air and all around, like a bright halo around the white lady's nodding head, it was a true spring day.

"Would you take eggs, lady?" asked Livvie softly.

"No, eggs I have plenty of," said Miss Baby Marie.

"I still don't have no money," said Livvie, and Miss Baby Marie took her suitcase and went on somewhere else.

Livvie stood watching her go, and all the time she felt her heart beating in her left side. She touched the place with her hand. It seemed as if her heart beat and her whole face flamed from the pulsing color of her lips. She went in to sit by Solomon, and when he opened his eyes he could not see a change in her. "He's fixin' to die," she said inside. That was the secret. That was when she went out of the house for a little breath of air.

She went down the path and down the Natchez Trace a way, and she did not know how far she had gone, but it was not far, when she saw a sight. It was a man, looking like a vision—she standing on one side of the Old Natchez Trace and he standing on the other.

As soon as this man caught sight of her, he began to look himself over. Starting at the bottom with his pointed shoes, he began to look up, lifting his peg-top pants the higher to see fully his bright socks. His coat, long and wide and leaf-green, he opened like doors to see his high-up tawny pants, and his pants he smoothed downward from the points of his collar, and he wore a luminous baby-pink satin shirt. At the end he reached gently above his wide platter-shaped round hat, the color of a plum, and one finger touched at the feather, emerald green, blowing in the spring winds.

No matter how she looked, she could never look so fine as he did, and she was not sorry for that, she was pleased.

He took three jumps, one down and two up, and was by her side.

"My name is Cash," he said.

He had a guinea pig in his pocket. They began to walk along. She stared on and on at him, as if he were doing some daring spectacular thing, instead of just walking beside her. It was not simply the city way he was dressed that made her look at him and see hope in its insolence looking back. It was not only the way he moved along, kicking the flowers as if he could break through everything in the way and destroy anything in the world, that made her eyes grow bright. It might be, if he had not appeared the way he did appear that day, she would never have looked so closely at him, but the time people come makes a difference.

They walked through the still leaves of the Natchez Trace, the light and the dark falling through trees about them, the white irises shining like candles on the banks and the new ferns shining like green stars up in the oak branches. They came out at Solomon's house, bottle trees and all. Livvie stopped and hung her head.

Cash began whistling a little tune. She did not know what it was, but she had heard it before from a distance, and she had a revelation. Cash was a field hand. He was a transformed field hand. Cash belonged to Solomon. But he had stepped out of his overalls into this. There in front of Solomon's house he laughed. He had a round head, a round face; all of him was young, and he flung his head up, rolled it against the mare's-tail sky in his round hat, and he could laugh just to see Solomon's house sitting there. Livvie looked at it, and there was Solomon's black hat hanging on the peg on the front door, the blackest thing in the world.

"I been to Natchez," Cash said, wagging his head around against the blue sky. "I taken a trip, I been to Natchez, I been today. I am ready for Easter!"

How was it possible to look so fine before the harvest? Cash must have stolen the money. He stood in the path and lifted his spread hand high and brought it down again and again in his laughter. He kicked up his heels. A chill went through her. It was as if Cash were bringing that strong hand down to beat a drum or to rain blows upon a man, such an abandon and menace were in his laugh. Frowning, she went closer to him, and his swinging arm drew her in at once and the fright was crushed from her body, as a little match flame might be smothered out by what it lighted. She gathered the folds of his coat behind him and fastened her red lips to his mouth, and she was dazzled at herself then, the way he had been dazzled at himself to begin with.

In that instant she felt something that could not be told—that Solomon's death was at hand, that he was the same to her as if he were dead now. She cried out and, uttering little cries, turned and ran for the house.

At once Cash was coming, following after; he was running behind her. He came close, and halfway up the path he laughed and passed her. He even picked up a stone and sailed it into the bottle trees. She put her hands over her head, and sounds clattered through the bottle trees like cries of outrage. Cash stamped and plunged zigzag up the front steps and in at the door.

When she got there he had stuck his hands in his pockets and was turning slowly about in the front room. The little guinea pig peeped out. Around Cash the pinned-up palmettos looked as if a lazy green monkey had walked up and down and around the walls leaving green prints of his hands and feet.

She got through the room, and his hands were still in his pockets, and fell upon the closed door to the other room and pushed it open. She ran to Solomon's bed, calling "Solomon! Solomon!" The little shape of the old man never moved at all, wrapped under the quilt as if it were winter still.

"Solomon!" She pulled the quilt away, but there was another one under that, and she fell on her knees beside him. He made no sound except a sigh, and then she could hear in the silence the light springy steps of Cash walking and walking in the front room, and the ticking of Solomon's silver watch, which came from the bed. Old Solomon was far away in his sleep; his face looked small, relentless, and devout, as if he were walking somewhere where she could imagine the snow falling.

Then there was a noise like a hoof pawing the floor, and the door gave a creak, and Cash appeared beside her. When she looked up Cash's face was so black it was bright, and so bright and bare of pity that it looked sweet to her. She stood up and held up her head. Cash was so powerful that his presence gave her strength even when she did not need any.

Under their eyes Solomon slept. People's faces tell of things and places not known to the one who looks at them while they sleep, and while Solomon slept under the eyes of Livvie and Cash his face told them like a mythical story how all his life he had built, little scrap by little scrap, respect. A beetle could not have been more laborious or more ingenious in the task of its destiny. When Solomon was young, as he was in his picture overhead, it was the infinite thing with him, and he could see no end to the respect he would contrive and keep in a house. He had built a lonely house, the way he would make a cage, but it grew to be the same with him as a great monumental pyramid, and sometimes in his absorption of getting it erected he was like the builder slaves of Egypt who forgot or never knew the origin and meaning of the thing to which they gave all the strength of their bodies and used up all their days. Livvie and Cash could see that as a man might rest from a life labor he lay in his bed, and they could hear how, wrapped in his quilt, he sighed to himself comfortably in sleep, while in his dream he might have been an ant, a beetle, a bird, an Egyptian, assembling and carrying on his back and building with his hands, or he might have been an old man of India or a swaddled baby about to smile and brush all away.

Then without warning old Solomon's eyes flew wide open under the hedgelike brows. He was wide awake.

And instantly Cash raised his quick arm. A radiant sweat stood on his temples. But he did not bring his arm down—it stayed in the air, as if something might have taken hold.

It was not Livvie—she did not move. As if something said "Wait," she stood waiting. Even while her eyes burned under motionless lids, her lips parted in a stiff grimace, and with her arms stiff at her sides she stood above the prone old man and the panting young one, erect and apart.

Movement, when it came, came in Solomon's face. It was an old and strict face, a frail face, but behind it, like a covered light, came an animation that could play hide-and-seek, that would dart and escape—had always escaped. The mystery flickered in him and invited from his eyes. It was that very mystery that Cash with his quick arm would have to strike, and that Livvie could not weep for. But Cash only stood holding his arm in the air, when the gentlest flick of his great strength, almost a puff of his breath, would have been enough, if he had known how to give it, to send the old man over the obstruction that kept him away from death. If it could not be that the tiny illumination in the fragile and ancient face caused a crisis, a mystery in the room that would not permit a blow to fall, at least it was certain that Cash, throbbing in his Easter clothes, felt a pang of shame that the vigor of a man would come to such an end that he could not be struck without warning. He took down his hand and stepped back behind Livvie, like a round-eyed schoolboy on whose unsuspecting head the dunce cap has been placed.

"Young ones can't wait," said Solomon.

Livvie shuddered violently, and then in a gush of tears she stooped for a glass of water and handed it to him, but he did not see her.

"So here come the young man Livvie wait for. There was no prevention. No prevention. Now I lay eyes on him and it come to be somebody I know all the time, and been knowing since he were born in a cotton patch, and watched grow up year to year, Cash McCord, growed to size, growed to come in my house in the end—ragged and barefoot."

Solomon gave a cough of distaste. Then he shut his eyes vigorously, and his lips began to move like a chanter's.

"When Livvie married, her husband were already somebody. He had paid great cost for his land. He spread sycamore leaves over the ground from wagon to door, day he brought her home, so her foot would not have to touch ground. He carried her through his door.

Then he growed old and could not lift her, and she were still young."

Livvie's sobs followed his words like a soft melody repeating each thing as he stated it. His lips moved for a little without sound, or she cried too fervently, and unheard he might have been telling his whole life, and then he said, "God forgive Solomon for sins great and small. God forgive Solomon for carrying away too young a wife and keeping her away from her people and from young people who would want her back."

Then he lifted up his right hand toward Livvie where she stood by the bed, and offered her his silver watch. He dangled it before her eyes, and she hushed crying; her tears stopped. For a moment the watch could be heard ticking precisely in his proud hand. She lifted it away. Then he took hold of the quilt; then he was dead.

Livvie left Solomon dead and went out of the room. Stealthily, nearly without noise, Cash went beside her. He was like a shadow, but his shiny shoes moved over the floor in spangles, and the green downy feather shone like a light in his hat. As they reached the front room he seized her deftly as a long black cat and dragged her hanging by the waist round and round him, while he turned in a circle, his face bent down to hers. The first moment she kept one arm and its hand stiff and still, the one that held Solomon's watch. Then the fingers softly let go, all of her was limp, and the watch fell somewhere on the floor. It ticked away in the still room, and all at once there began outside the full song of a bird.

They moved around and around the room and into the brightness of the open door, then he stopped and shook her once. She rested in silence in his trembling arms, unprotesting as a bird on a nest. Outside the redbirds were flying and crisscrossing, the sun was in all the bottles on the prisoned trees, and the young peach was shining in the middle of them with the bursting light of spring.

THE KNOT HOLE

By Dorothy Canfield

From the *Yale Review*

DOROTHY CANFIELD

or Dorothy Canfield Fisher, as she is also known, is one of America's best-known novelists. She was born February 17, 1879, in Lawrence, Kansas, daughter of James Hulme Canfield, a prominent educator, and Flavia Camp Canfield, an artist. When she was ten she was sent to Paris for a year, where she learned to speak fluent French. She was graduated from Ohio State University in 1899, while her father was president. She studied later at the Sorbonne, and took a Ph.D. in French at Columbia University. She married James Redwood Fisher in 1907, and they have a son and a daughter.

While known best as a novelist, the teaching profession and education in general have always interested Mrs. Fisher. She has never taught but was secretary of the Horace Mann School in New York for three years, and before World War I she became very much interested in the work of the Italian educator, Dr. Maria Montessori, founder of the teaching system that bears her name. During the first World War, Mr. and Mrs. Fisher spent three years in France, he in the ambulance service, she working with blinded soldiers. Later she established a Convalescent Home for refugee French children. These years in France form a background for some of her fiction. While she later traveled extensively in Europe, Mrs. Fisher has spent most of her time since 1920 on her farm near Arlington, Vermont. Her father's family were pioneers in that state.

Her first novel to gain recognition was The Squirrel Cage, *in 1912.* The Deepening Stream, *published in 1930, is acclaimed as her best novel. Others that have been popular are* The Bent Twig, The Brimming Cup, Raw Material, *and* Understood Betsy, *classed as a juvenile but beloved by many adults. Her best-known translation is Papini's* Life of Christ. *She is a fine speaker, much in demand, and has managed any number of careers, while carrying on the business of being a wife, mother, grandmother, and homemaker. Her most recent book,* Our Young Folks, *was published this fall.*

Up to the invasion of France I had heard, with the taken-for-granted regularity of the twentieth-century postal service, from my dear goddaughter, Emilie-Anne—we who love her have called her, since her babyhood, Lianne. Those letters, safeguarded by the still-intact framework of civilization, had told us of the usual happy life of a happy young wife, scarcely touched by the odd, static war going on. Her lusty little four-year-old son was well; her adored husband, Jean-Jacques, came back from his artillery battalion for an occasional furlough (in peacetimes he taught physics in the local high school); she was joyfully expecting a second baby, due to arrive in the late summer of 1940.

When, in June, the German motorized army crashed through France, one more letter came from Lianne. It had evidently been posted on one of the last days before windowless walls shut half of a great nation into prison. Scrawled in pencil, this last brief note was written from a cowshed, where she and her little boy had taken refuge for the night. They had been bombed out of their home and town, and were trying to reach—on foot—Lianne's mother in the South. "Little Jacqui is being brave," she wrote. "He is his father's son. Of Jean-Jacques himself I know nothing—nothing—nothing!" . . .

But two years later I knew something. No letter from Lianne ever came. An American relief worker returned from France and brought me the story I have set down here. He got it, bit by bit, from a Frenchman who had escaped from a trainload of prisoners. The man who got away had been asked by a fellow prisoner to try to send news of him through some American to me, because I am his wife's godmother.

This is how my informant pieced together the fugitive's story. . . .

I thought it was probably by accident that I was among those in the boxcar. I never knew why I was. Perhaps there had been room—if you can call it room—for one more. Perhaps the official intention in my prison had been to send me out to be shot in reprisal for something done somewhere. There were always reprisals of this kind. And someone in the prison office might have picked up the wrong dossier from a desk. Such things were always happening in the tangle of orders and counterorders. All I knew was that I and twenty others were taken from our prison in a closed truck. When it halted, and we were herded out, the truck was beside a train, at a railway siding. In the open country. I thought the train was a long one. But it was black night. I could see only the boxcar into which I was pushed. I had no idea what happened to the other prisoners with me in the truck.

One armed guard unlocked the door to the car, opened it a crack, and two others shoved me in. The door was slammed shut behind me. I felt that the blackness was full of men, but I did not—not so strongly as in the prison where I had been for two years—smell them, for there was a sizable opening in the roof of the car and from it a current of fresh spring air poured down, which diluted the prison stench of unwashed bodies in dirt-encrusted clothes. I could not see the opening in the roof, but as I strained my eyes through the darkness to get some idea of where I was, I caught a glint of distant stars immeasurably high above us. Nearer, seen through the same roof opening, a yellowish glow. I recognized what that was—a guard's lighted cigarette.

I put one arm up to shield my face from blows and tried to get my back to the wall—prison technique. But the shove which had pushed me in had sent me stumbling several steps from the door, and when I tried to step back, I felt human bodies there.

Then a voice spoke in my ear. It was a French voice. It said neutrally, "We are from *Oflag*——" (the man gave a number of a prison camp) "confined there since June 1940. For the last four months we have been told every day that we would be sent back to France. We have now been two days and three nights in this car. Of that time it has rolled for about eleven hours. We do not know where we are."

The voice trembled, muttered, *"We think we are being repatriated."* I heard the men about me breathe deeply. There was a silence. The voice went on, "My name is Bergeron. High-school teacher of physics. Of the —— Field Artillery Battalion. Will you tell us who you are?"

I had been in prison for two years, and I knew before the end of the first sentence that Bergeron was the man who set the tone for the group. I knew, too, that I was safe from violence. I drew a long breath, dropped my arm, gave my name, the number of the prison camp I came from, the regiment to which I had belonged, my occupation in civilian life.

The rules of the place were explained to me. There were too many in the car for all to lie down at the same time. So they took turns in sleeping. The sick and crippled ones had twice the lying-down time allotted to the others. I would be put into the third division. Their time for lying down for rest came after the morning meal. When it was not your turn to lie down, you had your choice of sitting on the boards of the floor, or standing. The best sitting places were those around the edge, where you could lean back against the side wall of the car. These were also shared, turn and turn about. So far, the guards on the roof had allowed them to talk—at least most of the time. Silence was enforced when, as nearly as they could judge, the train was near a railway station of a town, where their voices might be heard. But where they were allowed to talk freely, as now, they supposed——

I broke in to tell them, "The train is standing on a siding in the midst of the empty country."

Yes, that was what they had guessed. Bergeron's voice went on, explaining the organization of the day. "One of us is a priest. There are morning and evening prayers in a corner of the car. No talking by others at that time. One of us was a medical student. He does what he can for our sick and makes a health inspection each morning. Four buckets make up the sanitary arrangements for forty men. *With covers,*" said the voice ironically. "They are, you know, a very cleanly nation. These buckets are emptied each day. After dark, four of us, each one roped to a guard and carrying a spade take them out, dig a hole, and empty them. They are never washed out, there is no water for that. Only a cupful for each man, night and morning."

"Roped?" I asked quickly.

"Roped."

"But while four guards are out with men from one car, there must be four cars without guards? And did you say a *spade?*"

There was a silence. I felt the men move closer to me. Then Bergeron's low voice said—and now it was not quietly firm, it was rough, agitated, terribly anxious—"You understand—didn't you hear me?—*we think we are being repatriated*—on our way home. Our release will be, of course, conditional on absolute obedience to rules. There must be no—no——" I felt a threatening movement toward me, and hastily assured the invisible men that I understood. There would be no——

Toward the end of this talk, the car had begun to roll again. I had to raise my voice to make my pledge heard above the clatter of the freight-car wheels. There was a muffled stirring as of animals at night, in a barn. We sat down as best we could. Someone near me coughed rackingly, and from among those lying down at the other end of the car came other dreadful, shattering coughs. Tuberculosis, I thought. I was given one of the favored places where I could lean my head against the side wall. As I relaxed against it, I said to the darkness, *"Thanks."*

Bergeron's voice answered, steady and grave, "It is your turn."

(At this point in my informant's retelling of the fugitive's story I broke in with a wondering question, "How did he happen to tell you about it in such detail?" My informant had been speaking as tensely as I had been listening. Before he answered me he shifted his position and drew a long breath. Then he explained, "Of course, he did not tell it to me, as I am telling it to you now, all in one piece. But he spoke of it incessantly. It had shaken him to the heart. Everything he saw or did when we were together seemed to make him live the experience over again. I told you how I happened to be with him so much—how we spent many long nights together near the frontier, waiting for—well, waiting. Not once did he see the blackness of the night fade to gray without telling me once more about the first dawn in the boxcar. He would go on like this"—)

First I noticed that the hatchway was gray. I looked up at it. And when I looked down, dawn had brought light enough into the car to see the men. There was no surprise for me in what I saw. I had known what they would be. I had been with men like that for two years, gray-faced, thin, their clothes faded, stained, patched, ragged, a stubble of beard on their sunken cheeks. They were sitting or lying down.

The bare boards of the floor transmitted to them every jar of the freight car. Yet many, even of those who were sitting up, were asleep, sagging to and fro, their heads fallen on their chests. Those who were awake braced themselves against the constant shaking by locking their hands around their knees. A rank stench came from the four buckets at the end of the car.

Yet when my eye caught that of Bergeron—I knew at once which one he was, a tall, gaunt, big-boned man, his eyes gray-blue—he saluted me from across the car with a nod, and a brisk wave of the hand. He was standing, wide-awake, an alertness in his face very different from the sodden dullness of the usual prisoner's expression. For the moment, he said nothing, not to disturb those who slept. But later, when those who had been sitting through the night were on their feet, yawning and stretching their stiff arms and legs, Bergeron came over to me to say, "One more night gone. Every one brings us nearer home—we hope." I noticed that no sour snarl rose from the other men, such as, in the prison I had come from, had instantly stopped any attempt to speak cheerfully about their situation. All of them, even the sick ones, hoped. . . .

The day began. Those which followed were exactly like it. The only variation was the color of the sky up there above the hatchway, which we saw beyond the rifle butt and the gray-green trousers of the guard seated in a sort of sentry box on the roof. Sometimes that bit of sky was blue and sun-flooded. Sometimes it was covered with lowering gray clouds. Once in a while the slow, rattling car jolted for a time under green tree branches. When this happened, every man clutched at his neighbor and pointed to make him look up. Even the sleepers, by rule never to be disturbed during their turn to lie down, wanted to be awakened to see this. Sometimes rain poured in streams down through the hatchway. This, as far as possible, we used hastily, as it fell, to clean the skin on our faces and hands and feet. It was not only the fresh air from the roof opening which lessened the fetid prison smell. Sometimes a square patch of real sunshine lay on the floor, big enough for several men to sit in. This privilege was shared in turn by all, with a double turn for the sick. Some of them, at the suggestion of the medical student, took off their clothes when their turn came for the sun bath. The white bodies they showed then were thin, but except for the six or seven really sick and crippled men, not strengthless.

This was probably because of the twice-a-day exercises. These were compulsory. As Bergeron had explained, the prisoners were never let out of the crowded car (except for the nightly sortie of the four who emptied the soil buckets). They would all have been half paralyzed if they had not taken some exercise. That lasted half an hour, twice a day, for each of the three squads into which the men were divided. There was no room to take more than three or four steps in what space could be cleared. But they were determined to be able at least to walk steadily on their own feet out of the car for their first steps as free men on their own soil. The coats were laid down—the thin, threadbare coats—to soften a little the boards of the floor, and the men, by fours, rolled, stretched, kicked, did somersaults (those who could), walked on their hands, "made a pyramid," or did simple bending exercises, rhythmic, taken in time to an accompaniment of folk tunes whistled by the spectators. A squad of helpers, directed by the medical student, massaged the sick, carefully flexed and gently moved the arms and legs—what there was left of them—of the crippled.

The food was—well, everyone now knows what prison food is—a little bread, often moldy, floating in what looked and tasted like tepid dishwater. Sometimes a few "eyes" of grease floated on the water. The prisoners, especially the sick ones, mortally dreaded the coming of these sickening rations. But we were so famished that when the food appeared there was always a deadly moment when we became starving animals—the frantic reflex instinct to fight for all we could grab barely held in check by the rigid self-discipline of the group. At such instants, when the ground swell of bestiality rose under our feet, Bergeron stopped it—"Now! Now! Turn and turn about is the rule here!" . . .

(I had not meant to interrupt the narrative again, but I could not help asking here, "Is it often that such self-control, such group discipline——?" My informant said, "I asked him that question too. He scorned me for not knowing the answer. 'That depends, of course,' he said impatiently, 'on who sets the tone. When those who do are like animals, then the troop is like a pack of wolves—or hogs. When the leaders are human—— Why should prisoners be different from other men? It's always that way, everywhere.' ")

What the men in the boxcar liked best were the long talks between those who were awake, sitting or crouched near each other. This talk was personal, casual, wandering—just what came into our heads. Mostly it was of what we would do when we were home again. As the car jolted slowly on, most of us were surer and surer we were being repatriated. Not all. The coughing, sweating sick did not hope to live till they were free in France. Several older men of the kind who always believe the worst insisted, like men biting on a sore tooth, that they were being taken to the Russian front, where they would be forced into front-line fighting. The trip was taking far too long, they said, for the journey into France. This point was frequently argued. A younger man, a university undergraduate, figured out from the stars wheeling over the open hatchway that the general direction of our course was south. There was a great deal of wrangling about this.

Two or three times we could not keep ourselves from thinking over what the chances of escape would have been—if we had not been going home anyhow—for at least one or two of us, during the night sorties with the soil buckets. Those ropes—a spade in each prisoner's hand, a spade has a sharp edge—the darkness—quick, concerted action—— Of course, it could have been done only once, would have meant a chance for only one or two men. And reprisals for the others. Yet it would have been worth it. But all this whispered talk was only speculation. As it was, it would only spoil the chances for all of us.

But mostly we talked as if we were certain that we were being taken back to France. Had they not been told over and over at the *Oflag* that any day we were likely to start home? Had not the *Oflag* been full of widespread rumors of this or that astute way in which *Le Maréchal* would secure the return of the prisoners? Most of us pushed away our doubts and sent our hearts flying forward.

A favorite subject for these endless rambling talks was the manner of each one's homecoming as it would be if he could have that as he wished. One man would send word ahead, and have all the village at the station to meet his train. With the band. He had played the piccolo in the band. Another young fellow would not let his parents know he was coming. He had planned to take the night train to his town, slip away from the station by the back road, and turn up the lane to his father's barn, where he would step in, take a milking stool, and be there, milking, his head dug up against the cow's flank, when his father opened the door and came in for the morning chores. The farm boy's dreamy description made them, even the city gutter sparrows, even the death-struck sick, feel against their cheeks that warm, living, hairy flank, and made them smell the barn odors—straw, milk, earth, manure, fresh hay.

Another man said, "All I want is to get drunk—one long, glorious, blind drunk after another. It would be like heaven to be drunk-sick again."

"A hot bath—a hot bath a week long!"

"Girls! Girls! Girls!"

"The heel of a loaf of real white bread, French bread, and a whole Brie cheese!"

The young priest saw himself walking up the steps to his country church and into its incense-fragrant dimness. A mechanic murmured, "To stand in my own garage again, to lift the hood of a car brought in for repairs, to lean over the engine, listening to hear what's the matter with it——"

A young research worker from the botanical laboratory of the Jardin des Plantes tried to make us feel how it would be to lean once more over his high-powered microscope. At this, someone said with the acrid savagery that was like the usual prison-camp talk, "Boy, you won't find any high-powered microscope there. It'll be in Berlin."

But Bergeron had quickly broken in to describe yet one more time what his own homecoming would be. Not in his cottage, which had been home. That house, like all that town, was only bombed, burnt rubble cinder now. But he would be going home, although to a wholly unknown place, because his wife and little son were there. He knew from his wife's telegraph-brief messages through the Prisoner-of-War postcard service just where he would find her—in a town in the South, with thirty or forty children in a kindergarten improvised in an old high-school building, crammed with refugees.

He described over and over just how he would open the door to that crowded room. Quietly, without knocking. Then he would stand there, looking at his wife and his son and those French children she had been taking care of, keeping them decent, saving them from becoming little animals. At first, she would think the door had been opened by one of the children. She would not turn her head. And then. . . .

Bergeron talked a great deal about his wife. He was proud of her.

All of us were unnerved with the incredible prospect of seeing our own again after two years of prison, none more so—in spite of his self-control—than Bergeron. Whenever he spoke of his family, his voice roughened and shook, and sometimes broke.

One of the other men explained to me one day, in a whisper, that Bergeron had had a baby daughter born seven months after the battle of Flanders. He had been taken with an almost dreadful affection for this child of his he had not seen—his wife wrote that the baby was like an angel—but, of course, all women thought that. Night after night the man in prison had waked up wild with a joyful dream that he had held his little daughter in his arms. When his wife had to wean her he had worried frantically lest she suffer from the poor, coarse, scanty food. Madame Bergeron had nursed her as long as she had any milk. His fellow prisoners had heard all about this again and again, till no one but other family men would listen.

When the rumor had begun to circulate in the *Oflag* that the prisoners were to be sent back to France, Bergeron, they said, had almost gone off his head at the thought that he would see his baby girl. But three weeks before they had been put on the train a telegram had been handed him—yes, a telegram!—they did not know why this was allowed—saying the little girl had died.

He had been broken by this. Could not eat, could not sleep, never spoke, kept his hands clasped over his eyes. His fellow prisoners had thought he would die. He seemed dying before their eyes. But ten days before their departure he had received from his wife one of those brief, officially allowed messages, "I promise you I will be here with Jacqui when you come back to me."

Then he rose and lived again. He had not been broken. He had been like a tree cut down. But the root still lived.

He used to say to us in those long rambling talks in the boxcar, "I always knew my wife was lovely. I never knew she was so strong." He used to say, "My wife does honor to humanity by her work with those homeless children. What she does is called kindergarten work.

What it really is is teaching French children to live together like civilized beings, not like wild beasts. She upholds human dignity, my wife does, by what she does for the future of France." He often said too, "She would not be allowed to put among the few words of those weekly Prisoner-of-War messages the three words—*'never give up!'* But really that is what I have heard her say, all these two years, in everything she writes me."

No matter how deep we were in these memories, Bergeron never forgot when the time came to get stiffly to his feet, motioning those with him to rise and let the waiting ones move to the better places where they could lean back against the wall.

Then one night the car came to a halt, and did not go on. For two days it was stationary, longer than ever before. The sky seen through the hatchway was gray-blue, with small clouds. Several men said it looked to them like a French sky. A graybeard, with one arm amputated, answered grimly, "Or Russian."

The guards on the train became bored with nothing to do. We could hear them calling idly back and forth to each other. Sometimes the gray-green trousered legs of the guard at our hatchway disappeared for a few moments. We could hear him clambering down the ladder at the end, and then a sound of several men talking and laughing together, as if he had been joined by others from other cars. Sometimes there was the measured sound of counting—*ein, zwei, drei*—the numbers pronounced in louder and louder voices, ending in a great burst of laughing and hooting, as though some kind of game were being played, watched from above by those who stayed on guard on the roof, rifles cocked.

During those two days inside the boxcar we went through the routine, planned to keep us alive till we were freed. We ate the dreadful daily slop; we exercised; we played what finger and guessing games we could invent. With no tools but our cups, which were examined and checked every time the food was handed in, we could construct nothing. We took our turns at lying down. We said our prayers or were respectfully silent when others prayed. We told the same stories over and over. We imagined again and again what we would do on the day we reached home. A few of the most thoughtful men talked about plans for serving their country and their country's youth more creatively than ever before—once they were free to do something creative. We ground our teeth in our struggle to remain human.

Over and over someone would say, in our rising and failing hope, "It *may* be only a little longer now——"

Every hour was exactly like the one which preceded it. In that windowless prison how could there be anything to make one hour, one minute, different from another? . . .

And then one of the men came darting from the other end of the car with the quick, astonished step of a man to whom something has happened. He put his lips to Bergeron's ear, whispered, and turned back to where he had been. With a startled look Bergeron sprang up and followed him.

In a rush we were all on our feet. There was nothing to be seen different from what had been there from the first. There could be nothing different. We knew that. But we were like stampeded cattle just the same. The break in the dragging monotony of our changeless days beat on our strained nerves as if a trumpet had shouted, as if— we did not know what, only that one among us had moved suddenly and swiftly as if—incredibly—something had happened.

Crowding, pushing, shoving to see what it was, the stronger ones using their fists to be ahead of the others, we were a mob. Dehumanized. Bergeron turned and held us back with an upraised arm. "Turn and turn about is the rule here," he said sharply, in a phrase so thickly encrusted now with associations of order that we halted. With a cautious glance up at the guard's legs and the rifle butt at the hatchway's edge, he said, "Before I take another step I will tell the man nearest me what Carrière said to me. He will tell the next man. And so on. Till we all know. It may be nothing, you understand. Nothing. If it is anything, we will all share it alike. Don't let the guard suspect anything." He leaned to whisper in the ear of the nearest man, who turned to whisper to the next one.

When it came to me I heard: "Carrière thinks he has found a knot in one of the planks of the wall, loose enough to work out of its hole. He came to ask Bergeron if he thought it safe to do this. We might look through it and see something. But a guard may be standing just outside. It may be a trap. Or the sides of the car may be double-planked. In that case the hole would not go through to the outside."

I passed this on to the man back of me. We were all on our feet craning our necks, even those whose turn it was to lie down. We watched Carrière stooping, the fingers of one hand picking slowly, delicately, at a place on the plank siding. After a time he looked around at Bergeron, asking a question with upraised eyebrows. Bergeron assumed the responsibility, gave a nod of assent. Carrière brought his fingers together and slowly drew out the knot. The sunlight shone through in a long beam. The hole was not much bigger than a man's thumb. Seen in that light, Carrière's pale face was chalky. He looked at Bergeron for orders.

Bergeron turned his face to glance up at the hatchway. At the end of the car where they were they could not be seen by the guard unless he stooped his head down through the hole. There was not a sound inside the car. Bergeron motioned the men to make a screen with their standing bodies around Carrière, said to him, all but soundlessly, "You were the one who found it. The first look belongs to you."

Carrière stooped and put his eye to the hole. The silence in the car was so entire that we could hear the guard on the roof clear his throat raucously and spit. Our hearts rose at the casual, ugly, unselfconscious sound. It could mean nothing but that there was no guard waiting outside. We gazed tensely at the back of Carrière's bent head. Would he never look away? What was he seeing?

Then he stood up and turned toward us. Tears were streaming down his cheeks. His mouth worked convulsively. He put his bent arm up before his eyes and stumbled away to lean against the wall, his shoulders shaking.

"Your turn next, Fayolle," said Bergeron steadily, motioning to the man who stood nearest.

So all of us looked in turn. I had not liked Carrière's crying. It made me sick to see one of us, who had endured so much, in tears. But every man was half blinded by tears when he turned away to let the next one see. I was resolved to be calm.

But when my turn came, what I saw—oh! it was France I saw there under the gentle French sunshine—a narrow green meadow; next to it, on one side, a rolling, half-plowed brown field, two great work horses, nodding their heads as they stepped strongly forward, throwing their shoulders against the tall collars; on the other side, a long, straight, white road bordered with slim poplar trees leading to a gray village in the distance, with red roofs and a white church tower; on the road a farm cart with two high wheels slowly approaching, the metal trimming on the harness winking in the sun; between the railroad tracks and the meadow, a slow-moving, dark green little brook bordered with silvery, pollarded willows—the earth, the grass, the water, the very sky of home. . . .

Bergeron was the last one to take his turn to look at France. We watched his tall form stoop, we gazed at the back of his head, seeing through it what he saw. We stood in a long orderly file beside him, eager for our second look at France.

When Bergeron stood up and turned toward us his face was white. His lips moved. In a rhythm we all knew as we knew our own pulses, his hand began to beat time. He began to sing in a low clear voice—we knew the words—we sang with him in the same hushed voice: "*Amour sacré de la patrie*"—and "*Liberté, Liberté chérie*——"

"*Nicht singen!*" shouted the astounded guard, shoving the barrel of his gun down the hatchway.

We gave a convulsive start. We had not known we were singing. We were like men wakened roughly from a dream, who for an instant do not know where they are. Bergeron motioned for silence. He looked as startled as we. He, too, had not known what he was doing. For an instant even he had forgotten the taut self-control which had focused all our faculties on one thing—to do nothing which might risk losing our release. . . .

Carrière, who had been stooping at the knot hole to look, stood up now, and again whispered into Bergeron's ear. Bergeron whirled, stooped, looked out through our tiny window, and continued looking. Carrière tiptoed around our circle, telling us in a whisper, "I was looking out while you were singing. An old man sitting in that cart beside the driver stood up and looked this way, as if he had caught the sound."

We were terribly affected by this. To have made ourselves known to a fellow countryman, not a prisoner, still living on the sacred soil! But Bergeron turned back to us, shaking his head. "It couldn't have been," he said. "We were singing too low. Nobody could have heard.

They were still a long way off. I watched closely as the cart jogged by. Neither of them so much as turned his head this way." . . .

For the next day there was not one hour of the twenty-four when one of us was not feasting his eyes on the look of France. Even at night someone was watching the golden lamps in the village, or the French stars in the French sky. The car had now stood still for three days.

Small as the hole was, it was possible, by shifting one's position a little lower, higher, to one side or the other, to take in perhaps a quarter of what we could have seen through a window. The far end of the car where the hole was, and where one man after another was perpetually stooping to look out, was not visible to the guard up at the edge of the open hatchway. We always kept a cluster of sitting or lounging men directly under him. Of course, twice a day when the slop food was brought in, the gnarled wood-brown knot, preciously preserved, was carefully inserted into the hole. Since only one could look at a time, we shared with the others whatever we had seen. "An old woman pushing a wheelbarrow was going along the road when I was looking out. The way her black headkerchief was tied made me think we are in the *Ile de France*." Yes, the others who had seen that stooped old figure agreed that the kerchief's twist did look like the center of France. "My grandmother tied her kerchief on with that knot at the back."

The first morning the watcher at the hole whispered, "School children," and stood back to let the fathers among us take quick looks at five little boys and girls in black aprons, clattering along in their wooden-soled galoshes, their leather schoolbags swinging. There was something special about the way those children stepped, set their feet down on the ground—we felt it in our own feet. They were our children; we were again children clattering to school along a white, straight, poplar-shaded road. Thus to possess with our eyes the longed-for home scenes swept us beyond what we knew was real. We were not prisoners; we were out there, walking freely on the French road as the early sun sent long rays down through the thin mist.

An hour or so after they had passed, something exciting began. An old workingman, very shabby, his shoulders stooped under a faded blue blouse, carrying a long-handled spade, plodded his way slowly out from the village along the road. When he reached the sagging, weather-beaten gate to the meadow just across the little stream from the tracks, he stopped and pushed it open. How many times had each of us in imagination laid his hands on that gate to push it open! We touched, handled, smelled, felt everything we looked at, as we pored over that piece of our home country, framed in the knot hole. The man at the lookout reported the arrival of the old man. Each one of us, as we took our turn to look, told what he did. "He is going into the meadow. He has shut the gate behind him. He has stopped, as if to get his breath. He has his lunch with him in a package. He has put his package down on a stone. He is going to stay all day. He has begun to spade. To turn under the sod."

At first we wondered at anyone, let alone an old man, spading away in the open country, in a meadow. That was land for plowing, not spading. The guards evidently wondered, too. Presently, one of our watchers at the knot hole reported that a green-gray uniform went out from the train toward the meadow, stood on the side of the little stream, and shouted something across to the old workman. The words were French, but the heavy voice sounded as writing looks which is done with a coarse pen in thick ink. But as we listened tensely, holding our breaths, we heard another voice—purely French, the clearly spoken vowels, the resonant consonants, the rise and fall of the familiar speech tune as accurate to our ears as, to our eyes, the tracing of fine lines made with a drawing pen. The sound of it was music, poetry. It took an instant for us to hear the prosaic words it uttered. "Potatoes," it explained. He was preparing a patch of ground to plant potatoes.

The watcher of the moment whispered back to us, "The guard isn't satisfied. He keeps standing there. He is going to order the old man off."

But he did not. He stood uncertainly for a while, calling something back to—we supposed—another guard on the train. There was an exchange of hoarse German. A moment of suspense. Finally, so our watcher reported, the guard came back, leaving the old man there. A long breath of relief went around the car. "What is he doing now?" we asked the watcher.

"He has gone back to spading. He is shaking out the earth from a sod." We felt, sifting through our own hands, the soil of our motherland. We smelled the fresh healing fragrance of earth newly turned over.

All day we shared what that free man did out there under the gray-blue home sky. Through that hole, which any one of us could have closed by putting a thumb into it, we flung our hearts, our senses, our souls. We stooped stiffly with the old man, we slowly spaded with him. With him we turned under what was alive, so that that something of more value could take root and grow. We stopped with him to rest, sitting down on a stone sucking a cold pipe meditatively. He evidently had no more tobacco than we. The stone happened to be so placed that when he dropped down on it to rest, he faced the railway track. Several times that day we saw his lifted glance run along the roofs of the cars indifferently and drop from there to the ground, to his work, to his shoes, to the grass. He leaned to knot a loose shoelace, to finger a clod, and he sat up again, looking off toward the horizon. He yawned, took his dead pipe out of his mouth, lifted his faded blouse to stuff it into his pocket, took up his spade again.

He did not get on very fast with his work, it seemed to some of us who knew about farm work. The farmer's son, every time it was his turn to look, whispered to us, "Listen, fellows, I don't believe he *is* a workingman. I never saw anybody try to spade with that kind of a push from the shoulders. You do it with your back and legs."

At the end of the first day he had only spaded one strip across that narrow field. But he was old. How old? We all made a guess. Sixty, perhaps? Probably had served as Territorial in the last war. "I've got an uncle sixty-one, looks about like that." . . .

The next morning began the fourth day since the car had stirred. Bergeron had insisted it would do no good to question the guards, since they probably knew no more than we. But on this fourth day he was overborne, and a man who spoke a little German was delegated to ask the guards who brought in the morning pail of food, "Why? Why so long waiting?"

The guards looked at each other, hesitated, said nothing, turned back to the door. The older one went out. The younger one went after him, stopped, said in broken French, "Not know. Hear that——"

The older guard shouted at him angrily. He stepped out and began to slide the door shut. Through the crack he pronounced one more word, "Laval."

We sat frozen. We looked down fixedly at our cups, at the drops of grease congealing on the pale brown liquid.

One man started to his feet and was sick, vomiting into one of the stinking soil buckets. His cup fell over. He trampled on the pieces of water-soaked bread. When he could vomit no more he lay down with his face to the wall.

Bergeron lifted his cup and began resolutely to eat. "We have no idea what that word means—for us here," he said firmly. "There is no reason to——" But he was breathing very fast as though he had been running with all his might. He swallowed down what was in his cup and got up. "If no one else wants a turn at our lookout, I'll take mine now," he said.

He stooped to look. Over his shoulder he whispered, "The old man is certainly looking at our car. He *keeps* looking. He darts his eyes up and down the train. Perhaps the guards are all down on the ground on the other side playing that gambling game." We looked up at the hatchway. Our guard was not there. A whisper ran about from mouth to mouth, "Make him a signal! Let the old man know——" One of us went close to Bergeron and whispered this in his ear. He looked up at the hatchway, saw that it was still empty, nodded to us, put his thumb through the knot hole, and slowly turned it up. Everyone's heart began to pound fast and hard. Bergeron withdrew his thumb, stooped again to look, and gave a great start. "The old man is starting to run this way," he reported on a sharply indrawn whisper.

There was an instant in which we did not breathe. Then Bergeron let his breath out in a gasp and murmured, "He has turned back. He evidently saw a guard. He has picked up his spade. He has gone back to spading."

We pulled Bergeron back to whisper urgently, utterly at a loss, "What does it mean—what do you think——?" His gaze was darkly inturned in thought. "Perhaps he *did* hear us singing. And he must have seen my signal," he said. And then, shaking his head, "But there is nothing he—nothing anyone can do. He will be shot if he tries."

"Tries what?"

He lifted his shoulders. "There is nothing he could even try."

After that we never took our eyes from the old man in the blouse. Late that day the watcher at the hole reported, "He has taken out a white handkerchief. He is unfolding it to wipe his forehead."

"A *white* handkerchief?" went rapidly around among us. "That's no workingman."

But what—what——? We could not think what.

We only never took our eyes from him. . . .

Late that afternoon our guard was again not at the hatchway. We had for some time heard the thick voices talking and laughing together down on the side of the train away from the road. Then, as sometimes happened, the brawling sound of a quarrel broke out. One of the players had perhaps cheated. We had heard them before this, shouting angrily at each other. Now the noise was louder than usual, more voices joining in, as if the guards still up on the cars were leaning over the side and taking part in the row.

"Bergeron! Quick! Here!" the man at the knot hole called in a loud whisper. Bergeron sprang to the hole. He saw the old man in the field racing toward us. He had something white in his hand. He sprang across the little brook. Looking fearfully up and down the train, he darted to our car. A paper, rolled up, was pushed through the knot hole. We rushed to see.

Bergeron unrolled it and held it up to the ten or eleven men near enough to see. It was a question in one word, "French?" Bergeron scribbled on it, *"French,"* and thrust it back. The man outside darted a look up and down the train, took the paper, and wrote feverishly. The tiny white roll came back through the hole. Bergeron held it up. On it was written, "Courage, Faith, Hope."

The thronging men leaning over Captain Bergeron's shoulder read the words at a glance and motioned him fiercely to send an answer. "Tell him——" "Say that we——" Their pulses pounded like thunder with the answer that must go back, to say what must be said. "Tell him that we——" There were no words.

Bergeron was stretched on the rack with them, brains and hands paralyzed by the longing to speak, by the need for haste. The pencil in his hand hung suspended over the paper while his eyes plunged into those around him, tense, strained.

From somewhere in the car a voice—we never knew whose—perhaps several at once—called hoarsely, *"Never give up."*

Bergeron's hand set the three words down all in one rushing line and pushed the paper through the hole.

He saw the old man read it at a glance, look up, his face convulsively working. He nodded over and over—his lips said soundlessly, "Yes, yes, yes, yes." He thrust the paper in under his blouse and clasped one hand closely on it over his heart. With his other arm he made a long gesture toward the town. He was gone, racing back to the field.

The brawling voices were dying down. We heard our own guard climb up to the roof of our car. We saw his legs and the rifle butt. He hawked and spat. We sank back limply. The man at the knot hole reported in a whisper, "He is sitting on the stone. He keeps his left hand pressed closely over his heart. He is looking straight at us." We took hasty turns at our lookout to meet that long gaze.

When twilight began to fall he went away toward the village, taking his spade with him.

The next morning before dawn the man who was at the lookout said, *"Pst! Pst!"* Several of us went at once. "It seems to me I make out people walking by on the road," he said.

We all looked in turn. Yes, people were certainly passing there, dim shapes at first, which might be of anything. As the light grew stronger the shapes became men—old men—and women, boys, more women —children, big girls, little boys, small girls. They did not come together or abreast. Sometimes singly, sometimes by family groups, sometimes two or three together. At times the road would be quite empty all the long way to the gray houses with the red roofs. Then from the end of the village street we would see a group or a couple of people coming out toward us. They did not look—not more than once—at the train. They only walked by on the long white road bordered with poplars. As they approached the train each one looked at it once, turning his full face toward us. Then as they passed on, everyone pressed his left hand over his heart and held it there. Even the little children.

Not one of us needed to be told what it meant. The old man had answered "Yes!" to our message. He had understood it. He had pointed to the town. He had meant he would tell them. They were telling us that they understood, that they would not forget.

We saw that our guard stood up several times as if to look. We heard the others shouting questions back and forth. But there was nothing for them to see except groups of quiet people—men, women, children, blacksmith, priest, shopkeeper, fine lady, old farmers—quietly walking along a dusty white country road, their eyes straight before them. They were still passing when twilight thickened so that our eyes could no longer see them.

None of us slept much that night. It would have been a waste of the first moments of happiness we had known for two years. We talked in low tones, each one adding to the common store what he had seen of the procession. "There was a little girl with curly fair hair exactly like my Claire. The old blacksmith with the leather apron—my grandfather looked like that." "The tall, dark-haired, good-looking girl in the blue dress—one of my girls at home walks just as she did."

Would we see them again, we wondered, the next day when dawn came?

About midnight the door to the car slid open a little—yet it was long before the time for food. And the soil buckets had long ago been emptied. A flashlight played on us, sitting there, silent, our hands clasped around our knees. We were counted. The alien voices mechanically pronounced the numbers, *ein, zwei, drei*—— The alien hand turned a flashlight on the paper and made a check mark.

The flashlight was held to another paper. The voice began to read aloud rapidly, rattling off the words drily. But they were not of the alien tongue. They were our own. We heard the words, "Sabotage. Reprisals." The door slid shut with a bang. In the smothering black stillness the lock rattled loudly.

We were being sent back.

We were being sent back to prison.

We were being sent back to Germany.

One of us began to shriek out curses as if he had been stabbed. His screams stopped with a strangling choke. Bergeron had sprung upon him. Bergeron's voice sounded out in a cry as sharp as if he also had been stabbed, "Order! No screaming. We are men!"

We heard the other man struggling frantically to breathe through the hand pressed over his mouth. We heard Bergeron, too, fighting to breathe, when, after an instant, his voice came—breaking, dying, as he tried with long gasps to draw air into his lungs, "We have pledged ourselves to—" he said, "all those people. We gave them our promise. They promised us——" He gave up trying to speak. We heard his panting—loud, rough, strangling, as if he had been struck a terrible blow in the chest. Or was it our own struggle to breathe that we heard?

When he spoke again his voice was under control. "We have been home," he said. "We have been home to France. We have made a promise to France."

The car jolted to and fro and began to roll slowly. On each side of me in the dark I could hear groaning. But not loud. . . .

After a long time Bergeron's voice said in my ear, in a faint whisper, "Now about those ropes——"

THE FISHERMEN OF PATZCUARO

By William Fifield

From *Story*

WILLIAM FIFIELD

is twenty-seven years old and comes from a family of Congregational ministers. He was formerly a radio director at Columbia Broadcasting System, in New York, but is at the present time in Hollywood. Before that he sold soap, watches, and cereal, and wrote scripts for the major radio networks. His stories have appeared in Story *and the* American Mercury.

About "The Fishermen of Patzcuaro" he writes: "It was written in the Hotel Reforma in Mexico City a day or so after a terrible and wonderful ride in from Guadalajara by bus. We left Guadalajara about ten in the morning and arrived in Mexico City just before dawn the next morning. The ride cost me about three dollars in American money." (*It was worth much more because it produced an excellent story.—H. B.*)

THE SYRIAN waved away the woman with the flat, jellylike slabs of candy. He watched her move on along the side of the comical little bus, holding up the wooden tray to each passenger in turn, and at the same time supplicating them with her eyes. A boy hurried out to the road swinging two buckets of clear water from a shoulder yoke. *"Agua! Agua!"* the boy called, lifting up the two buckets for the people at the bus windows to see. The farmer at the second window from the front stopped him and bought a cupful. He leaned out to pay, and the Syrian saw the long arms and the narrow, monk-bearded head outside, and the rest of him inside, only partly visible over the high backs of the seats. A woman came up with oranges in a basket balanced on her head.

"Cuanto vale?" the Syrian asked her.

The woman steadied the basket with her hands and looked up. The oranges were three for ten centavos.

"Three, then," the Syrian said.

He had to turn back a little to reach into the basket for his oranges, and as he was selecting them he saw the girl. She was standing near the entrance door at the rear of the bus. That was why he had not noticed her until now. She was talking to someone, to a thick-bodied man who stood with one heavy hand grasping the pommel of his burro's saddle, and the Syrian saw her soft, dark face and her small figure. The smooth skin of her face, framed in the hood of her dark blue *rebozo,* seemed to have a sort of glow under it, and her eyes were black and large. Her heavy skirt spread out over the underskirts beneath it formlessly, but her blouse was of a lighter material and her arms and throat were bare, so that you could see she was small-boned and young-breasted. These things the Syrian noted in an instant, then went back to choosing his oranges.

Two of the oranges he put in the pocket of his suit coat, which was on the vacant seat beside him. The skin of the third he cut into eight parts, running the blade of his clasp knife once around the middle and then four times down from end to end. He was careful to cut only the peeling and not break the juicy pulp inside. Then, one at a time, he loosened the eight segments with his knife, took them between the knife blade and his thumb, pulled them off, and let them fall to the floor between his feet. Then, dividing it into quarters, he ate the orange. When he had finished he took out a soiled handkerchief from his hind pocket. He rubbed his hands dry of juice, took off his hat, and wiped the sweat from his forehead.

It had been cold when they left Guadalajara in the morning, but now it was hot. Coming down through the maguey fields of the State of Jalisco and into the more rolling country of Michoacan, it had grown warmer and warmer, and the sweat had begun to form on his high, back-sloping forehead, drops of it standing out along the prominent frontal ridges over his eyes, and thin, dust-laden rivulets of it staining his face in the deep grooves between his nose and cheekbones. And now, in the early afternoon sun, it was hot. It was more noticeable when the bus was stopped. The Syrian left his hat off and opened his shirt collar.

The girl he had seen outside the bus came up the narrow aisle. She was holding a large bundle before her, leaning backward to balance the weight of it. At the next seat ahead a tall basket of vegetables blocked the way so that it was impossible for the girl to pass with her burden. She put it down, stepped over it, and sat down on it.

"Do you wish this seat?" said the Syrian. He lifted his coat from the vacant seat beside him and put it across his lap. The girl said nothing, only looked straight before her at the basket of vegetables in the aisle.

"It will be more pleasant for thee," the Syrian said. Still the girl did not look at him.

The bus started forward with a jerk, and the gears clashed as the driver shifted into second. There was a second jerk when the clutch was released. The bundle under the girl shifted and almost unseated her, and the Syrian caught her arm. She looked at him, her large eyes frightened, then turned away. Still holding her arm, the Syrian drew her toward the seat, and because she was even more weary than she was afraid, she did not resist.

It was not only the physical weariness from the long trip down to the highway, four hours walking in the sun beside her father's burro —and from the sleepless, excited night before that. It was also the sickness from what her mother had told her in the morning, told her secretly and weeping, just before the father had found them.

"What are you saying to her?" the father had demanded, coming on them suddenly after having gone off to saddle the burro and lash the bundle of clothing behind the saddle.

The mother had left off abruptly from telling her what it all meant, from telling her what it would be to live on the hacienda of Angel Castro, from telling her how it was with scullery girls who were virginal, and who also were young and pretty to look at and touch. She dropped her daughter's hand and stepped back from her as though the affection between them were sinful.

"What have you told her?" the father said again, coming close to her. The mother drew back into herself as she always did before him, seeming almost to contract bodily.

"I was asking the grace of Our Lady," she answered quickly, knowing it would satisfy him. He was religious, brutally so.

"Very well." He walked away from them and squatted on the dirt floor of the room. "When we have eaten we will go," he said.

They sat on straw mats on the floor eating the putty-colored tortillas and saying nothing. Paco, the brother, was off in the hills somewhere, so there were only the three of them at breakfast. In the night, when the father had gone outside to relieve himself, Marta, the girl, had drawn her sleeping mat close to her brother's and whispered to him excitedly about the wonderful fortune that had come to her. The father had come back from his weekly trip to sell skins and leatherwork in the village, and he had told her of his arrangement for her to leave the next day to live on the great hacienda of Angel Castro almost at the very edge of the fine city of Morelia. The city of Morelia was a wonderful place of cathedrals and splendid houses, and people riding about in motorcars. These things she had been told many times by friends. And the hacienda of Angel Castro was the most splendid of the entire countryside.

Paco had grunted something and turned away from her.

"Will it not be something splendid, Paco!" she had exclaimed, snuggling close to him again and hugging him in her excitement.

"Leave me alone," he had said. "Go to sleep."

But nothing could repress her. She had only giggled at him and kissed him behind the ear. Then the father had come back and she had had to lie quiet, but she had lain there for hours staring into the darkness and imagining the great sights of Morelia and the magnificent estate where she was to live. In the morning, after they had gotten up, and Paco had gone sullenly off into the hills with his gun, she had begun to be frightened. She had never been beyond the village at the opening of the valley before, never even been so far as the highway, but today . . .

Then her mother had told her what it was to be, and the father had returned, and they had sat down to eat. The eating finished, the father stood up.

"We go now," he said without expression.

As they started away, the father astride the burro and the girl walking beside him, the mother stood just outside the door of the adobe hut. She stood there heavily and wearily, her legs apart and her splayed, calloused feet in the red dirt. She had scarcely dared say good-by to her daughter. Now she stood watching, and she was very tired. From a distance she was a lump of earth before the earthen house, but Marta, looking back from time to time, did not think that. She saw only the familiar shape and the familiar place becoming smaller and smaller, and she felt a sickness.

The sun rose higher and it became very hot in the narrow defile that led down between the hills to the village, and thence to the trail to the highway. The pine needles on the ground smelled resinous and scorched. The father, slumped in the saddle with his belly thrust forward and his hands folded on the pommel, whistled through his teeth. He was thinking of the money. Some of it he would use for himself, he decided, and some of it he would spend for candles at the church. There was, of course, no question of atonement for this thing he was doing. His wife had wept, that was true; but a woman's tears are to be expected, and to be repaid with contempt. Still, in a general way a man must repent, and, moreover, it was pleasant to kneel in the quiet church in front of the beautiful altar and talk with Jesus.

Thinking of Jesus, and thinking of the money, the father decided against stopping in the village. He would stop on the way back to go to the church, and later to join friends and play dominoes in the cantina.

They went on through the village and down the trail to the highway. The man with whom he had contracted was waiting. Sending Marta away—she was tired from walking and sat down in the narrow band of shade at the side of a house—he talked with the man and received from him the money. In turn he pledged that he would put his daughter on the bus, that she might be taken off when the bus arrived at the property of Angel Castro.

When this was finished the father went over and sat down beside his daughter in the shade. For fear of what he might do to her mother later, she said nothing about what she knew. She wanted to pretend to be happy and excited to carry off the part, but this she was too weary and sick to do. She said nothing. The father said nothing. Merely sat complacently, fingering the purse at his belt and occasionally picking something from between his teeth. After some time the bus arrived.

The father went over to where his burro was munching at a dusty clump of grass. Slapping it, he drove it to a place near the rear of the bus and stood beside it ready to mount and ride back up the trail to the village.

"You will find a happy life at the hacienda," he said. "It is better than we have in the hills."

She said nothing, and so he added rather awkwardly, "You know that is true?"

She nodded, not looking up.

The vendors were clearing away now: the water seller and the two women, the one with the oranges and the one with the yucca candy. It was clear the bus was about to depart.

"Go with God," the father said.

The girl picked up her bundle and, holding it before her, climbed into the bus. The father turned his burro's head uptrail and settled heavily into the saddle.

"Where do you go?" the Syrian asked her. The bus was moving along rapidly now, stirring up a breeze that felt good in the thick heat. It swayed from side to side as it went downhill, and the two red lanterns that hung in the upper corners over the windshield swung back and forth.

The girl looked up quickly but did not answer. Something in her fright, in the way it clung to her smooth cheeks and made her eyes wider, stirred the Syrian. He had a trick of lowering his lids over his pallid blue eyes and at the same time seeming to thicken his lips that gave him a sensual expression. He did this now.

"You need not fear me," he said. "Where are you going? To Uruapan, or perhaps Morelia?"

"To Morelia."

"That is my home. I live there."

"I go to the estate of Señor Castro."

"You are a relative of his?"

"I go there to do service."

The Syrian looked at her more closely. Her coarse hair was in two pigtail braids tied together at their ends. Thus her hair was parted down the middle of her head, the hair going to the two braids. She had let the *rebozo* slip back because of the heat.

In the lobes of her ears were two small circles of silver. They were like plain silver wedding bands, broken and separated, with a tiny wire connecting the broken ends. This wire pierced the lobe of the ear. All these things the Syrian noticed, and, noticing them, he noticed she was younger than he had thought at first.

"You are young for service," he said.

She said nothing.

"How many years do you have?" he asked.

"I have fourteen, but soon I shall have a birthday."

Taking his handkerchief from his hind pocket, the Syrian wiped the sweat from his face: from along the sides of his bony nose, from behind his ears, from under the collar of his shirt. He ran the cloth back along the slope of his forehead and over his ridged, almost hairless skull. Then he coughed suddenly and drew in air through his nose, dilating the wide-flanged nostrils.

"Mucho calor," he said only half aloud.

Unexpectedly, the girl smiled at that. He had looked so funny wiping the sweat from his face, and now the unnecessary way he added, "Very warm," made her smile. Partly, too, it was reaction. She was still only a little girl, and even under the circumstances it was hard to feel sick and like crying all the time.

"Very warm," the Syrian repeated, smiling back. The sensual look was gone now. This girl was a mere child. And besides, she was somehow very soft.

"You see, I am not so frightening, child. You do not fear me now, do you?"

Now that she dared look at him closely, she wondered at him. In all her fourteen years the only men she had known were her father and brother, and men of the village who were like them. And of course the round little *muchachos* with their shirts coming only to their middles and their plump brown bottoms naked. But this man could never have been round, not even as a baby. He was angular; the bones jutted out. And his eyes! His eyes were blue. Marta had never seen anyone with blue eyes before.

"Why do you stare at me?" the Syrian asked.

"The eyes," she said. "They are blue."

"Does that amuse thee?" he asked.

"Yes," she answered frankly. She giggled. "You have a funny nose!"

Now the Syrian laughed. The nose was like a scimitar. With a sudden comic gesture he folded his hand over it as though to hide it, letting only the highest part of the hooked ridge remain in view. They both laughed.

"Where I was born," the Syrian said, "many have noses like this one."

"That must be far away."

"It is. It is across the ocean and across a great sea."

"The ocean is near Morelia," the girl said.

"Not the ocean, child."

"Paco said so. Paco is my brother. He saw it."

"That is the Lake of Patzcuaro."

"It is not the ocean?" she asked. Her eyes were disappointed.

"No," the Syrian replied, "but it is much bigger than the ocean."

Suddenly the little girl sat straight up in her seat. *"Mira! Mira!"* she sang out. "There it is!" She shook her head back and forth in her excitement, and the silver earrings jiggled.

The Syrian looked out the window. The twin spires of a church could be seen over a clump of trees down the road.

"Is it Morelia?" the girl asked excitedly.

"No," the Syrian smiled, "not until two hours more. That is Zacapu."

The bus turned off the highway and circled the plaza of Zacapu. It came to a stop in front of a row of buildings across the square from the church. Several of the passengers got off. Marta had to lift her bundle and hold it in front of her to let them by, and all the while looking eagerly out so as not to miss anything. Other passengers crowded up the aisle and took the vacated seats. One woman was carrying a child in the sling of her *rebozo*. It began to cry, and as soon as she was in her seat she swung it around to her breast and it was quiet again.

"Dulces?" the Syrian asked, leaning out his window. *"Hay dulces?"*

The vendors had come hurrying out, followed by the dogs of the village. They stood beside the bus holding up their wares, and the gaunt yellow dogs rooted in the dust for what scraps might be thrown down. The Syrian leaned out, asking for sweets.

A woman heard him and trotted over; made the sale. The Syrian sat back in his seat.

"Is Morelia as big as this?" Marta asked him.

"It is more than a thousand times as big," the Syrian replied. "Much more than a thousand times."

The girl's eyes darkened in wonder. "But this is so big," she said.

"Well, Morelia is even more so."

Now it was all a great adventure. The bewhiskered *garrotero* herded in the last of the passengers and, shouting, *"Vamanos! Vamanos!"* and slapping the rear of the bus to tell the driver everything was closed and ready, took his place in the small niche made by the back door. He stood there in his dirty coveralls, hanging onto one of the bars that ran down the length of the ceiling, and joked loudly with the men who were smoking. The hacienda, and Angel Castro, and what the mother had said, and how the father had been—these things were forgotten. Marta bounced up and down in her seat; tried the leather headrest, tilting back her head all out of position to do it; gazed out at the painted houses that lined the street leading out of Zacapu; noticed the cutout of the Virgin of Guadalupe thrust in the lining of the top over the bus driver's head; smiled up at her new friend, the Syrian.

"I have a gift for thee, child," the Syrian said.

"A gift!"

He brought out the chocolate. It was in a brown wrapper with tin foil underneath and said "Made in Mexico" on the reverse side.

"It is a chocolate," he explained.

She looked up at him and then down at the candy again, but she did not reach out to touch it.

"It is a gift for thee," the Syrian said gently.

She took the sweet and slowly unwrapped it. It was intensely hot in the bus and the bit of chocolate emerged soft and shapeless, most of it sticking to the foil.

"You must eat it," the Syrian said, when she merely sat holding it in her hand. "It will melt and be spoiled."

She began to eat it then, holding it flat on one hand. She laughed just for the joy of the sweet taste, and the Syrian, watching her, laughed to see her laugh, and laughed to see her greedy mouth with the melted chocolate smeared around it.

Beyond Zacapu the road began to circle down, working gradually into the basin of Patzcuaro. Most of the pines were stunted now, and they stood looking hunched and uncouth on the dry slopes. The bus crossed a bridge, crossing a small stream that sprang from out of a divided place between the hills. The stream turned abruptly and followed along beside the road. Along the banks of the stream the undergrowth was greener, and sometimes there would be a yellow splash of goldenrod or a cluster of morning glory like white trumpets. The pine smelled good.

They crossed another bridge. The stream was larger now, the second branch joined with it.

Suddenly, the driver stamped down on the brake pedal. The rubber tires whined as the bus careened to a stop; the two red lanterns over the windshield danced dangerously. Everyone sat forward in his seat. Several said something out loud.

"What is it?" Marta gasped. She took the Syrian's hand.

The Syrian gripped her hand to reassure her, half rising meantime to see what it could be. Up ahead he thought he saw smoke. There was something wrong up ahead.

"It is the bridge!" someone exclaimed. "The bridge is burning!"

The driver came down the aisle from the front of the bus. "The bridge is on fire," he called to the *garrotero*.

"We cannot pass?" someone asked.

"No," the driver answered.

"What are we to do, Pepe?" the *garrotero* called, coming up the aisle to hold consultation with the driver.

"It is impossible to pass," the driver said.

"Clearly. Since the bridge is afire."

"Then we must leave this car here."

"Clearly."

"You," the driver said, "will walk ahead to the house of Miguel Vargas at the shore of the lake. You will telephone for a car to come from Patzcuaro."

"And you, Pepe?"

"I will see that we are all on the other side, with the baggage, when the car comes."

The bridge was a charred ruin; there was nothing to be done there. When the *garrotero* had gone, the bus driver had the men unload the bus. Then, everyone taking something, all of them started across the stream. It was not deep, and the cold water felt pleasant in the heat. Most of the women did not even lift their skirts, preferring to have them damp and thus retain some of the coolness. The men did not trouble about their white cotton trousers. They walked through the stream bed, stepping on the rough rock of the bottom impassively with their leather feet. Only the bus driver and the Syrian winced at the rocks. They rolled up their trousers, each of them, and waded across barefooted, carrying their shoes so as not to spoil them.

"It will be an hour until the car arrives," the driver announced.

Some of the men gathered in a circle to tell stories and gamble.

Others were already stretched on the ground, hats over their faces. The women sat at the edge of the stream with their feet in the water.

"Come," said the Syrian, "I will show thee Patzcuaro."

She took his hand and they walked off together.

"Is it truly bigger than the ocean?" she asked.

"Truly it is."

The hill sloped gently, and after a little while they could see blue through the trees. When the blue was plainly the water of the great lake, the girl could walk slowly no longer. She tugged at the Syrian's hand but he could not keep up with her, and so she ran ahead and was standing there at the edge of the cliff when he came up to her again.

"Does it please thee?" he asked.

She nodded slowly, still staring out over the lake.

The green-blue water lay in the bowl of the hills; brown and green-brown hills all around it. The long end thrust away almost out of sight, narrowing gracefully, and beneath the great end curved out vastly, rounding the two long sides together so that the lake was like an enormous teardrop. There were green islands in the lake.

"Come here," the Syrian said. He crouched down on the very edge of the cliff, pointing.

"What are they?" she asked.

"Houses."

The girl laughed aloud at that. They were so tiny. They were so small they were just white marks on the shore, and yet they were houses. Houses where people lived.

"It is true," she said, still laughing with delight. "It is bigger than the ocean."

"The fishermen live in those houses," the Syrian said. "In the day they sail on the lake in their boats, and at night they spread the long nets on the shore to dry."

"I would like to do that," the girl said.

The Syrian smiled at her. Then he sat back in the grass, taking off his coat and making a pillow of it. He closed his eyes and then opened them again. The girl was looking at him, but when he opened his eyes she looked away quickly, shyly. He unknotted his tie and opened the first several buttons of his shirt. The lake breeze felt good where he had been sweating under the shirt. Then he saw that she was staring at his throat, but now her eyes were not soft. She was staring.

"What is it, child?"

He sat up.

She looked up into his eyes, unbelief in her eyes. Then again she was looking at the place at his throat. He lifted his hand. Felt at his throat.

"Is it this?" he asked, holding the holy medal between his fingers.

Mutely, she nodded.

"What is it? It is only the medal of St. Francis."

She looked into his eyes again.

"What is it, child? Why are you troubled?"

"It is the same as the medal of my father," she said slowly.

"Your father?"

"Yes."

"It is only the medal of St. Francis."

"There are many?"

"Yes."

"I did not know."

"Why are you afraid of it, child?"

"It is the medal of Jesus."

"But that is no reason to fear it."

"Jesus tells my father we have sinned. He tells him we have sinned and that he must punish us. Then he beats us." The girl looked away, looking quickly away from the dangling holy medal. "Jesus hates us because we sin. And after we have been punished we must kiss the medal and say we repent our sins."

The Syrian sat still, saying nothing.

"Jesus told our father to send me to the place of Señor Castro, and I was happy and loved Jesus, even though he had made Father punish me many times. And then Mama told me how it would be!" She looked up, her face black with defiance.

"You will have need of Jesus," the Syrian said softly.

For a moment she still glared at him, withstanding his gentle look, hating him for wearing the medal of Jesus, hating him because he wore the medal her father wore. But then his compassion touched her—he had given her the chocolate—and she began to cry. He took her in his arms and laid her face against his.

"What you know of Jesus is not true," he said softly. "Jesus has much love for you, child."

She was not comforted. She began to tremble.

Pulling his coat from under him to cover her, the Syrian felt something heavy in the pocket. He reached in and touched the smooth, cool skins of the two oranges he had bought from the roadside vendor. He had quite forgotten them.

"Do you wish an orange?" he asked her. She did not stop crying.

Sitting back so that he could support her with his shoulder but have his hands free, he brought out the clasp knife. Opening it, he picked up one of the oranges and began to slit the skin. Once around the middle went the blade, then four times down from end to end. Carefully the Syrian loosened the eight segments of peel. He seemed completely engrossed with his work, but he noticed that she had stopped crying. Making more of it than was necessary, he removed the yellow bits of peeling. Then, using the knife again for show, although it would have been easier to do it by hand, he began to divide the pulp into neat little pieces. These he laid side by side along his leg. When the last piece was down, he began to count them in a strange, clownish tone.

"Uno, dos, tres, quatro——"

He glanced up at the girl. The black eyes were still shiny with tears, but there was a bit of sparkle back in them somewhere. Slowly the Syrian winked one of his blue eyes. Marta tried not to, but she smiled.

"His friends were like these fishermen," the Syrian was saying. "They loved Him, and He them."

The bus that had come for them was a peculiar one. It had evidently been intended for use as a street bus, and so the aisle down the center was almost wider than the seat room at the sides. The girl sat in her narrow seat at the window, and the Syrian looked out across her. The bus was rounding the end of the lake.

"Those are the houses we saw from the cliff," the Syrian said.

"They are nice houses," the girl said, "but I like better to see them from the cliff."

"You do?"

"They are so small from the cliff."

"He lived in such a house as one of those," the Syrian said.

She looked at him. "Did Jesus live in a house?"

The Syrian nodded.

"As we do?"

"Of course."

"I did not know that."

They passed the last of the group of houses, and there beyond were a number of men gathered on the beach. They were stretching the fishing nets on the water grass, pegging them down with wooden stakes.

"He helped the men with their nets, and fished with them," the Syrian said.

"I would like to fish," she said.

The Syrian pointed toward an opening through the clump of trees that now stood between the highway and the water. "There. Look! There is one of the boats."

There it was. White belly of sail startling in the falling afternoon sunlight.

"It was a boat like that that Jesus sailed," the Syrian said. "It was on a sea very near where I was born."

"That is far away."

"Yes. But the people are the same."

The tall, fine-limbed Tarascan men looked up as the bus passed. Their faces were friendly. Among them were a father and son.

"Did Jesus have any children?" the girl asked.

"Many children. Many."

She looked at him, and the question was there in her eyes.

"And He loved them greatly, and they loved Him," the Syrian said. "He would take them with Him in the boat, and they would fish together. And He let them help Him with the nets in the evening."

"I did not know that," she said.

They had come to the end of the lake and turned inland. Now it was but a few kilometers to Morelia. The Syrian, thinking now that they would soon come to the estate of Angel Castro, found no further words in his mouth.

The road curved up a shoulder of hill, and behind the lake fell away, dropped down and down, growing smaller. The houses were again mere strokes of color at the edge of the water. The girl looked back at the houses. The bus reached the crest of the hill; swung to the left toward the pocket of smoke on the horizon; moved faster now that the road was straight. Ten minutes. Then, far ahead, there were the first buildings of the city under the fan of smoke.

"That is Morelia," the Syrian said quietly. The girl seemed not to hear him. "That is Morelia," he repeated.

"I was thinking of what you have told me," she said.

The bus slowed to a stop. Looking out, they saw the arched gateway and the columns of trees that lined the roadway leading up to the group of houses. They both knew what place it was.

A man in *charro* costume was sitting astride a white horse at the side of the highway. The stirrups were of silver, and there was much silver on the saddle and on the bridle. One with such wealth could be no one less than the *patrón* of the hacienda himself. His face was pudgy and of a putty complexion. His eyes were froggish behind his thick-lensed glasses. As the bus came to a stop, it backfired. The wonderful white horse reared suddenly. Señor Castro reined him in. He had risen with the abrupt movement of the horse easily and almost carelessly, for all his pasty appearance. He had only seemed slightly annoyed. Now he watched the exit door of the bus.

"You must not be afraid," the Syrian said.

"I am not afraid," she answered.

She stood up, and he stepped out into the broad aisle to let her go by him. As she stooped to pick up her bundle, he reached inside his shirt and jerked at the medal of St. Francis, breaking the thin chain on which it was suspended. He was about to give it to her, but just then she straightened and looked into his eyes, and her eyes were large. "I thank thee for the sweet you bought me," she said earnestly. Then she started away from him down the aisle, and it was too late to give her the medal.

The bus started up again, and the driver ground the gears as he shifted. He was not used to the new machine. The Syrian sat with his eyes closed and did not open them until he heard the street sounds of Morelia around him. The bus rounded the end of the *zocalo* and pulled up beside the long line of red coaches waiting to leave for Mexico City.

"Mexico?" one of the hostlers asked him as he stepped out into the street. He shook his head.

"Tacos? Tacos? Quieres tacos?" The Syrian did not even notice the vendor with his cart of hot *tacos*.

He found a taxi and, slumped back in the seat, watched the familiar buildings pass. He had lived in Morelia twenty years now. Come over from Europe in the war years. Gone back for a wife. Then settled in Morelia. Well, the wife would be waiting for him.

The taxi turned into his street. Opposite the flat bank of houses was a parkway. At the end of it was a blockish, ugly equestrian statue. But along the parkway were rows of jacaranda trees in bloom. The petals had drifted to the ground, so that each tree stood in a pool of blue snow.

The cab stopped and the Syrian looked quickly away from the parkway and at the expressionless houses again. He was home. This house was his house, and inside it she would be waiting.

He gave the driver a peso and went up the steps and into the house. She was not in the front room. Then she would be in the bedroom.

Going to the bedroom, he noted mechanically the slovenly, disordered appearance of things. It was usual; it no longer troubled him. She was in the bedroom sitting on the bed; she was wearing the blue wrapper with the big butterflies embroidered on it. He had known she would.

He went over to her and kissed her. The wrapper slipped open a little and he saw her breasts. Sensing that he saw them, she pressed her hand harder against him as she gave him back the kiss. The breasts moved slightly. They were like fat, veined gourds.

"It is good to be home," he said in a flat tone. He walked away from her and went to the window. Looking out, he saw again the blue petals of the jacaranda trees along the parkway.

"The jacarandas are blooming," he said.

Then she began to speak, and he knew he would have to turn

around and face her, go to her. He had been away from her, and so he knew what he must do. He gazed at the jacarandas hopelessly. Now he would have to turn around. Now—or her voice would go high and querulous.

Turning, he thrust his hands down into his pockets. One hand encountered something small and cold. Metal. He fingered it quickly and then remembered. It was the little medallion of St. Francis. Holding it in his hand, he felt strengthened and made braver and he looked up and smiled at his wife.

THE LITTLE BLACK BOYS

By Clara Laidlaw

From the *Atlantic Monthly*

CLARA LAIDLAW

was born in Gladstone, Michigan. She has lived there all her life, "between a wooded bluff and the waters of a bay of Lake Michigan," except for her college years in Marquette, Michigan, at Northern Michigan College of Education, and the year she taught away from home. She calls herself "the world's most persistent letter writer," and says most of her writing has been in that form. In the summer of 1941 she was in the class in creative writing at the University of Michigan taught by Professor Carlton F. Wells. With his help she won a Hopwood award that year, though none of the stories she wrote then have been published. She writes: "Last summer my luck held, and Professor R. W. Cowden, director of the Hopwood awards, under whose direction most of the successful Hopwood novelists and poets have written, permitted me to work with him. 'The Little Black Boys' was one of a group of stories which won first prize in the Avery Hopwood Contest of 1942, though then it was called 'The Cloud Will Vanish.'" Miss Laidlaw is completing her work for a master's degree in English at the University of Michigan. She hopes to be in Ann Arbor during the present school year, teaching and also writing.

THE LITTLE BLACK BOYS, Samuel and Hamuel, were the first, indeed the only, Negro children I'd ever had in my classes in Northford. I remember very well the first time I saw them, on Wednesday, the second day of school, when my freshman math class assembled for the first time.

They sidled into the room shyly, after all the white children had rushed in to begin disputing noisily over the choice seats in the back of the room. The black boys hesitated just inside the door, looking around in a bewildered way, and then they slid quickly into two empty front seats. I couldn't help noticing how bent and shriveled and small their bodies were. Obviously they were twins, but even the usual physical retardation of twin children did not explain all their difference from the robust white children. There was hunger in the shallowness of their chests, and their thin, bent shoulders told of hard work beyond their years. When they sat down the seats were almost ludicrously large for them.

The white children buzzed and tussled until I called them to order, but the little black boys sat like twin statues, their eyes gleaming white as they stared at me, their round, fluted lips sober and still. They had cheap new dime-store tablets before them on their desks, and penny pencils, the dull brown ones with pointed erasers wedged into the tops.

When I asked them, as I had the others, if they wanted to be called by their full names or by nicknames, the frozen stillness of their faces broke for the first time, and the one nearest the blackboard said, his white teeth flashing, "I'm Sammy. He's Hammy."

Some of the little girls behind him began to giggle. I nodded hurriedly and said, "All right, boys. Sammy and Hammy it shall be," and turned quickly to take up the first lesson.

As the days and weeks went by I paid little attention to the twins.

They were quiet and sober and good. They never whispered to anyone and no one whispered to them. I grew used to seeing their black faces staring blankly up at me, or their kinky black heads bent laboriously over their work. With diminished penny pencils clutched tightly in skinny black fingers, they worked hour after hour to produce grubby papers covered with painfully worked problems, all wrong. The class was a slow one; but of all the group, Sammy and Hammy were the slowest. If, after weeks of work, they became finally convinced that if A and B, working alone, could each do a piece of work in six days, working together they could do it in three, then the next day they would be equally certain that, if one tablet cost ten cents, two would cost five.

I used to find myself scolding them occasionally, and they would look up at me with remorse in their liquid black eyes, their mouths drawn down into a mask of guilty grief.

Once I said, "Oh, Sammy and Hammy, what am I to do with you?" and Hammy said, "We're sorry we's so dumb, Miz Carey." Then he smiled and Sammy smiled, like two bad little dogs trying to be ingratiating. So we were friends again, and I began writing on their papers, to their innocent delight, "This is better than yesterday's paper," or "Fine! You had two problems right today," instead of the bare 0's and 20's they really earned.

One day I found a paper of Hammy's from which the comment I had written had been neatly cut.

"We saves them," Hammy said shyly when I questioned him. "Our mammy pastes 'em in a big book we got from the tailor shop. She say —'tain't every boy gets him so many nice words said to him—least, not every black boy."

"Those twins!" the other teachers groaned. Poor little black boys, they couldn't do anything at all. The other children shunned them too, it seemed, and their days would have been sad indeed had they not had each other for company. Each day they brought their dinners and sat alone on the steps eating their plain bread from a paper sack, while the other children ate and played noisily in the lunchroom.

Sammy and Hammy would sit watching the antics of their fellows with eager interest and delight, whispering to each other, chuckling companionably at whatever pleased them, but never offering to join the fun. Their apparent contentment in their isolation puzzled me until one day Sammy said, concerning another matter, "Our mammy say—you twins, so you be twins together," and I understood what the mother was doing for them: making the gulf between white and black be their choice, guarding them thus from fear and from desire for what they couldn't have, making them self-sufficient in their two-ness.

Still, their aloofness bothered me. I didn't want to make an issue of it, but when two or three boys or girls would come in to discuss class politics or the play, or to get news for the paper, or just to visit, I'd begin in a roundabout way to talk about democracy and the American dream and the Golden Rule, and finally, as offhandedly as I could, by way of illustration, I'd bring in Sammy's and Hammy's need of friends. The boys and girls would say, "Yes, Miss Carey," "Of course, Miss Carey," but the shadow would come down over their faces. They would look secretive and stubborn, and I knew they'd been talked to at home.

In a way, you couldn't blame their parents. The twins lived alone with their mother in an old shack 'way down at the shore. At first the black woman had gone about asking for work for herself and her boys, and she had done washing for a few ladies until it had got around that Cash Benson, the town's ne'er-do-well, had been seen hanging around the shack. Now she and the boys managed to live with no apparent means of support, and lately when the woman came to town everyone could see that she was visibly big with child. "Cash's nigger woman," the men on the street corners called her, guffawing as she passed. No wonder white parents kept their children from making friends with her boys.

She had gone to the Swedish Baptist Church twice when she had first come to town, taking the boys, stiff and clean in their patched Sunday suits. "I been baptized and bred up pure Baptist," she had told Reverend Swanson proudly, hesitantly accepting his proffered hand as he had bade her good day at the door of the church. Behind her the Swedish Baptist ladies had whispered and stared. The next Sunday, when she and the boys had taken their seats humbly in the last pew, there had begun a rustling as, one by one, some irately, some shamefacedly, the white ladies had risen and left the church. The black woman had stayed for the service, though Sammy and Hammy, watching her face, had begun to cry. She had never come again.

The way things were, there didn't seem much I could do except be especially nice to Sammy and Hammy, and that was hard too, because I certainly couldn't praise their work, and to treat them differently from the others would have antagonized the white children and made things still harder for the twins.

Toward spring it came time to have the annual freshman party. We had a class meeting, and the youngsters decided to charge twenty-five cents a ticket to pay for the lunch, and to have dancing and a program. Miss Carey, of course, was to help with the program. I always got that!

"Mr. President," I said. (We try to teach them to observe parliamentary procedure, heaven help us!) "Mr. President, may I say a word?"

"Keep still, you kids," the class president yelled gallantly. "Miss Carey's got sumpin to tell you."

When approximate quiet had finally been achieved I said, "The program committee and I are going to need help, so if you can play a musical instrument, or sing, or dance, or recite, or stand on your head"—(Hoots from the class. "Miss Carey made a joke! Listen to her!")—"why, come and tell us. We need talent for our program."

Then, before the tumult could get under way again, I added, remembering the time I had missed the eighth-grade picnic because my mother had been away visiting and I had been too proud to borrow from the neighbors, "And another thing—sometimes twenty-five cents is hard to get hold of, so if there's anyone who wants to go to the party but who hasn't the money at the time, why, you just come to me, privately, and we'll see if we can't fix it up."

The next day, after school, I was correcting papers when the door opened and the twins sidled in. My heart sank. After all, did it matter what one apple cost if a dozen cost twenty-five cents?

Sammy's black face glistened, and he moistened his lips with a pale tongue. "Us—us——" he whispered.

"We's got us each a box," said Hammy quickly from over Sammy's slight shoulder. His eyes rolled toward his brother fearfully. Obviously it was not what they had intended to tell me.

"A box?" I echoed, a little relieved that the bewildering price of apples was not in question.

"A gittar," explained Sammy, his black face deadly serious. "We each got us a gittar. We plays us gittar music."

"Also, us—we sings," nodded Hammy enticingly. They obviously wanted me to say something. Their eyes begged me to say it, but I could not imagine what it was. It somehow never occurred to me that the two black boys would be coming to see me about the party.

But that was it. Sammy and Hammy wanted to go to the party, and, moreover, they wanted to be on the program.

"But I ain't got no two bits," said Sammy, his mouth drooping sadly.

"Nor me," echoed Hammy. "You said—come to you, Miz Carey . . ." His voice died away plaintively.

"We'll work for you—hard," offered Sammy.

Their eyes held mine apprehensively, like spaniels' eyes, hoping for a kind word.

"That's fine," I said with unnecessary vigor. "Fine! I'll put you down for the program. And don't you worry about the money. Your music will pay your way."

It was the wrong thing to say. I knew it when the boys stiffened into black statues and their faces hardened into expressionless masks.

"Our mammy say—work for what you gets," Hammy said at last, adding with sober dignity, "So we works for you."

"Yes," I said quickly, "maybe you'd better, so the others won't be jealous and think I like you best."

A look of blind adoration came into Sammy's face, and Hammy grinned in a pleased sort of way.

So it was fixed. I gave the boys the tickets, ostentatiously taking fifty cents out of my purse and putting it ceremoniously into the "party box." The work was to be done later, when I needed something done.

As the day for the party approached, excitement began to run high in the freshman class. The twins whispered to me that they had been "practicing up," and the sight of their raptly pleased faces intensified in me a little feeling of doubt I'd been trying to suppress. What,

I thought, if the white children should be unkind to the black boys? What if the others on the program should refuse to appear with them? And what about the dance? What little girl would dance with them —and would I want her to, if she would?

I needn't have worried about the program. Apparently no parental ultimatum had been laid down. Perhaps no one had mentioned that the black boys were to make music, or perhaps the hours of the party were to be a sort of secular Truce of God wherein even black boys with a bad mother could have their hour of fun.

The party was to begin at eight, and at seven-thirty the gym was almost filled with children, all the little girls in bright new party dresses, with their hair tortured into elaborate beauty-parlor curls, sitting shyly on one side of the decorated gym, while all the little boys, dressed uncomfortably in new suits, with their damp hair brushed to alarming neatness, were seated on the other. The problem of the first half of the evening, as far as we teachers were concerned, was to coax the two groups, much against their wills, to consent to dance together, while the problem of the last half was to pry them apart and get them home before irate parents began telephoning.

But first came the program. Promptly at eight, since everyone had already been there for at least a half hour, the curtain went up, after several false starts and muffled grunts from the laboring stagehands.

Mary Ellen Adams and Jo Anne Merrill gave their usual military tap dance, which, since Mary Ellen is short and fat and lazy, and Jo Anne tall and thin and active, was rather far from the military effect desired. Little Genevieve Johnson sang "Ciribiribin," which she pronounced "See-ree-bee-ree-bean" for some unknown reason, and, with practically no encouragement, graciously added the encore "Blues in the Night." Glen Tillman played an excruciating violin solo, during which, mercifully, one string broke, so that the rest of the solo was, by anybody's mathematics, only three fourths as bad as the first. Benny Norton gave a reading in Swedish dialect with occasional lapses into Irish, Yiddish, and just plain American.

Then the twins came out from the opposite side of the stage, hesitating, looking dwarfed and lonely under the floodlights, black faces glistening and fearful, patched Sunday best pressed within an inch of its life. They clutched their cheap "gittars," looked out uncertainly at the darkened gym, struck a few chords, and then they sang.

I don't remember much else, not even what they sang. There was stamping of feet when they finished, and shouting. They sang song after song. They sang as the class danced, when it did dance. They sang with the Capehart and without it. They sang while the lunch was passed out until the class president himself brought them two heaped plates and clapped each of the boys on the shoulder by way of congratulation, while the class cheered through mouthfuls of sandwich and cake and waved pop bottles in the air.

They never left the stage all evening. Now, at last, something was well with them: the little black boys, for whom 3×8 was a variable, could sing.

After that, school was their heaven. Boys and girls who couldn't play with them outside of school never failed to call: "Hi, Ham! Hi, Sam!" in school. Math homework papers grew mysteriously accurate though tests still revealed the most abysmal misconceptions concerning mathematical practice. Even the seniors had them sing at their class party. They made the senior glee club, though they had feared before to try out for the junior one.

And they haunted my footsteps with a doglike persistence that came near to wearing me out.

"When we going to work out that fifty cents, Miz Carey, ma'am?"

"When the frost is out of the ground," I explained for the tenth time. "I want you to spade my flower garden."

A day later: "When that frost get outa that ground?"

"Not for two weeks, at least."

Two days later: "That frost gone yet, Miz Carey?"

"Not yet," patiently.

"My! My! Sure stays a long time—that frost!"

When at last the frost did depart the two black boys attacked my little garden spot with a vigor it had never known before. They trailed quack-grass roots to their remotest hiding places and exterminated them forever. They spaded and weeded and spaded again.

"That's a great deal of work for fifty cents," I teased at last, a little troubled at the sight of their thin bent backs stooping over my garden so long.

"Our mammy say—work good," Sammy said firmly, and Hammy's monkey-thin face echoed the stubborn set of his brother's jaw.

"You give us those seeds—we plant 'em," Hammy called pleadingly.

They planted my seeds, they hovered over the new little shoots, they weeded and watered and tended. I tried to give them extra pay, but they stiffened with hurt pride.

"Our mammy say—you take good care o' Miz Carey's garden, for she been purely good to you."

So I gave up in despair and let them do as they wished. I did all I could to get my neighbors to give them odd jobs, but only a few did, for the black boys' mother had had her baby, a girl baby, almost white, old Dr. Bates said, with hair like Cash Benson's.

In school the boys still haunted my room after class. They'd sit staring at my face, saying never a word until I had finished my work, and then not much unless I set the pace.

One afternoon I'd been reading a volume of Blake's poems, and on an impulse I asked them if they'd like me to read them a poem about a little black boy. I didn't think they'd understand a word of it, but I love to read poetry aloud, even if it's only to myself. Only after I had started to read did it occur to me that the black boys might read into it something that Blake had never intended, that I might be shaking their protective unawareness, might be emphasizing their difference in a way bad for them. But I had started and I had to go on.

They sat still as statues while I read:

"My mother bore me in the southern wild,
And I am black, but oh, my soul is white!
White as an angel is the English child,
But I am black, as if bereaved of light.

"My mother taught me underneath a tree,
And, sitting down before the heat of day,
She took me on her lap and kissèd me,
And, pointing to the East, began to say:

" 'Look on the rising sun,—there God does live,
And gives His light, and gives His heat away;
And flowers and trees and beasts and men receive
Comfort in morning, joy in the noonday.

" 'And we are put on earth a little space,
That we may learn to bear the beams of love;
And these black bodies and this sunburnt face
Are but a cloud, and like a shady grove.

" 'For, when our souls have learned the heat to bear,
The cloud will vanish, we shall hear His voice,
Saying: "Come out from the grove, My love and care,
And round My golden tent like lambs rejoice." '

"Thus did my mother say, and kissèd me;
And thus I say to little English boy.
When I from black, and he from white cloud free,
And round the tent of God like lambs we joy,

"I'll shade him from the heat, till he can bear
To lean in joy upon our Father's knee;
And then I'll stand and stroke his silver hair,
And be like him, and he will then love me."

I watched their faces as I finished. They were still and solemn, but radiant.

"Our mammy say—heaven's like that," Hammy said softly at last.

"Who that man say all that?" Sammy whispered in an awed voice.

"William Blake, a very great poet."

"He a preacher, Miz Carey, I bet?" Hammy asked, looking at me hopefully.

"No, not exactly," I answered, and saw the radiance in their faces dim at my words. Impulsively I added, "But he was a man who thought he spoke with angels, and—and he wrote 'as one having authority, and not as the scribes'!" And I found myself telling them how Blake, dying, sang of the glories of heaven opening before his dimming eyes.

Hammy's face shone, and his teeth flashed in a grin of solemn delight.

"He sure knew—that white man!"

"God sure told him sumpin," Sammy affirmed, nodding deeply.

"Read it again, please, Miz Carey," said Sammy suddenly.

I read it again, and they both sighed with one accord.

"That's better'n music," Hammy whispered. "Read it once more again? Huh? Please?"

I laughed and shut the book. "No, twice is enough. Some other day, perhaps."

But I never read it to them again.

As he went out of the door Sammy turned. "You like rock gardens, Miz Carey?"

"Why, yes, of course," I said, "but if you're thinking—— You've done altogether too much——"

"We knows a place," Hammy was saying dreamily, "a place where there's moss like a feather bed an' little white violets that's sweet as Jesus' breath——"

That was the last I was ever to see them. They rowed across to the place they knew after supper that night, a marshy island not very far offshore. Folks who saw them start said the water was choppy as they were going over. Coming back the boat overturned, and before the men could get to them they were drowned.

I heard the next morning in school.

The late May sun was warm on my hair that day, when school was over and I was plodding along the beach toward the Negro woman's shack. The silvery sand filtered into my slippers and dribbled out with each difficult step. Under the slanting sun the smooth blue waves lapped the shore and retreated in little slipping movements, as if they had never known storms or death.

Around the shack the rank shore grasses had been cleared away with scrupulous care, and in the shifting sand a few drooping plants gave evidence of the twins' efforts to make a garden of their own.

She opened the rough, tar-paper-covered door when I knocked—a thin, worn woman of about forty, with the fine features and liquid eyes one sometimes sees in people of her race. Her lined black face was masklike in its calm, but the eyes themselves were alive and tragic.

I don't remember what inadequate thing I said to her, but she must have felt my sorrow reaching out to hers, for she thanked me with something of the boys' doglike look in her eyes.

"They loved you so, Miz Carey," she said strangely, and I had the feeling that behind her simple words there was something strong and seeking, something she wanted of me—wanted badly, if only I could find out what it was.

She asked me in with homely courtesy and pulled out a rough chair for me to sit on.

The one room was painfully neat and bare. In a broken tumbler on the table a small bunch of short-stemmed white violets was beginning to droop, and on the ledge of the one window I saw the purple tulips I had given Hammy two days before. A table, three old chairs—one with no back—a small camp stove, and two camp cots were the only furnishings. The floor, rough and splintered from much scrubbing, was immaculate.

That space of floor seemed to me that day to be waiting mutely—waiting for the boys, who hadn't yet been brought back in their cheap little coffins. People never knew until long afterward that it was Cash Benson who had paid for it all, giving them the best funeral he could afford. That, at least, is to his credit, though he went off the next week and never came back. Reverend Swanson, too, came, the good old man, although he had to face the disapproval of the Swedish Baptist ladies to do it. I've thought of it often since and blessed the kindness of his gentle old heart.

But that day there were just the two of us. I sat by the table, and the afternoon sun through the only window threw the shadow of Hammy's tulips across the bare floor.

The boys' mother stood by the other side of the table, black and monumental and unweeping, staring at me with that queer tense look, seeming about to speak and then closing her lips gravely.

The baby began to cry, and she went over and picked the little thing up from the bed, blindly, as if she hardly knew what she did. After a moment she sat down opposite me, rocking the child gently in her arms.

Awkwardly I tried to comfort her, saying it was good she had the girl baby to fill a part of her heart. She looked at me strangely across the sun-mottled oilcloth, her ugly black face sharp with pain.

"But they was my true-born child'en," she said, as if reasoning with one who was dull of understanding. Slowly she looked down at the whimpering infant in her arms. "She white man's child, poor little thing."

Then she looked me straight in the eyes, not doglike but womanlike.

"I was all alone," she said simply.

I tried to speak, but there was nothing to say now.

When I started to go at last, it was with the feeling of how very futile my visit had been, of how empty sympathy and words of sympathy were to this woman.

She rose reluctantly when I did, saying softly, "You was good as they said you was to come." Then she added pleadingly, as if she feared I would misunderstand, "But it ain't fitten you come no more. Besides——" Her voice caught, but she swallowed and went patiently on, "Besides it be best you remember Hamuel and Samuel as they was—yestiday."

I nodded mutely, and she seemed satisfied that I had not misunderstood or taken offense.

But on the doorstep she stopped me again, hesitating, uncertain, and I knew that the thing that was haunting her was still unsaid. I could feel the conflict of urgency and fear in her, the tension and the longing, but I had to watch her helplessly, hoping she would speak, afraid to ask for fear what I might say would be wrong.

She drew a deep breath then, throwing her head back nervously. Her eyes were shining and fearful, and the words, when they came, were slurred and hurried, breathless.

"Last night—suppertime—Hammy 'n Sammy, they full of some word song you read 'em. They say—it better'n music. They go away singin' it to them two—— Something about—black boys? You remember, Miz Carey, ma'am?"

Her breast rose and fell in agitation, and the child, awakening again, began to cry.

"I'll send you a copy," I said thickly. "A poem I read to them."

She shook her head. "You say it to me, please? I never did learn book reading."

I turned my head away, thinking of the scrapbook of "nice words" she had kept for her boys.

What I could remember, garbled, imperfect, half forgotten, I tried to say, remembering the two thin black faces lifted to mine in the quiet of the dusty schoolroom.

She was very still when I had finished, but her face was bright with a faith I could never know.

"My Hammy and Sammy?" she said wonderingly. "Maybe they God's white lambs today?"

And then she wept, putting her face down against the baby in her arms. "Oh, bless God," she whispered brokenly. "Blessed God, make it so. Sweet Jesus, make it so."

I touched her hand silently in farewell and went away. At the gate, when I turned and looked back, she had lifted her head, and I saw that she was looking far out over the water, gazing across at the distant shore line of that green, marshy island where the moss is like a feather bed and the little white violets are as sweet as Jesus' breath.

THE CANALS OF MARS

By Kay Boyle

From *Harper's Bazaar*

KAY BOYLE

began writing very early, and by the time she was seventeen she had written hundreds of poems, short stories, a novel, and an outline of history, the latter for children. She was born February 19, 1903, in St. Paul, Minnesota, but much of her childhood was spent in Europe—summers in France, winters in Switzerland—among people who painted, wrote, and composed. She has lived in Washington, D. C., and in Cincinnati, but at eighteen she married a French engineer and in 1922 went with him to France, where she remained until 1941, when she returned with her four children, two stepchildren, and her second husband, Laurence Vail, on the Clipper.

Miss Boyle has twice won the first prize in the O. Henry Memorial Award Prize Stories: *In 1935 with "The White Horses of Vienna," from* Harper's Magazine, *and in 1941, with "Defeat," from the* New Yorker. *She was represented in the 1939 volume with "Anschluss," from* Harper's Magazine; *in the 1940 book with "Poor Monsieur Panalitus," from the* New Yorker; *and in the 1942 collection with "Their Name Is Macaroni," also from the* New Yorker. *She is the author of a dozen books, the most recent of which is* Primer for Combat, *published last fall. A novel,* Avalanche, *was published this September. She has also written one book for children,* The Youngest Camel. *She now has five children of her own, and in February of this year was married to Joseph M. Franckenstein, formerly of Austria, now a private in the American Army.*

SHE WAS SITTING on the bench, waiting under the park trees, when he came out of the draft-board office on the other side of Columbus Avenue and made for the curb. He had the whitish raincoat on, and his head was bare, and he started to cross at once, not even looking at the lights, stepping between the cars and the careening taxis with his eyes fixed on her as he came. The first time she had seen him—five years ago at the other end of the Sacher bar in Vienna—she had thought at once the same thing of him as she was thinking now: that he couldn't be anything but English. In spite of the purely Austrian blood in his veins, she had kept on thinking it of him in ski huts in the Alps when he would come in and brush the fresh snow from his shoulders, with his eyes looking for her; or in restaurants, or in city swimming pools, or on Mediterranean beaches; or when she had waited for him on café terraces, and seen him coming at last down the streets of Geneva or Paris or Marseille. The mustache was clipped short and straight as the English military wear them, the cheekbones were narrow and high with the color of weather on them, and he made his way now through the traffic with the same degree of casual pride as would an Englishman better than six feet tall and with broad, sensitive shoulders and the traditional reticence in his bones. When he reached the bench where she waited, he sat down quickly.

"I've got until half-past three," he said. On the street before them the rain was just beginning to fall.

"And then where do you go?" she said. She looked at the side of his face, at the hair a little light with sunburn above the ear, and the lean, shaved cheek, and the pulse that beat incredibly soft and tender in his throat beneath the jaw's straight bone. Five years, she thought, and I'll never get over it, never. Every time I look at him I know I wasted twenty years of life because I wasn't sitting somewhere waiting for him to cross a street or a glacier or a mountain and sit down.

"Then I check in at store seven at Pennsylvania Station," he said. He looked at his watch. "It's just eleven. That gives us four and a half hours," and he shook the cuff of his raincoat down across his wrist again.

"Perhaps we should do something special. I mean, perhaps we ought to do something rather important," she said. She watched the rain falling fine as mist before them in the street. "I mean, like going up the Statue of Liberty, or something. You've had your two weeks' furlough, and now you're going to be a soldier, so there we are. If you make a sort of ceremony out of the last hours together, it usually makes it go better." If I just don't look at him, she thought, I can go on forever talking like this. "The time you took the boat for Casablanca, there was the night before," she said.

"Yes," he said quietly. "I know."

"There were the perfumed sheets," she said. "There was the orange satin cover on the bed. She wanted transient trade. She didn't like married people at all except for the price they'd pay to have a place to spend the night."

"All the way to Trinidad, whatever wind was blowing, I smelled that violent perfume," he said.

"But still it was something special," she insisted.

"Yes," he said, looking at the rain, "it was something special."

"Can you only go as far as her wrist, or can you go up inside her palm and into the torch?" she said. She looked at his hand with the blue veins and the sunburn on it, lying bleakly on the raincoat's cloth on his knee.

"You mean in the Statue of Liberty?" He turned his face to hers, and, as their eyes met for a moment, she saw the look of despair upon his brow. "Four hours go so quickly. Perhaps we could just sit and have a drink somewhere," he said.

Yes, we could do that, we could have a drink, she thought. We could face each other across the half dark of an alcove's table, and after a scotch the words would start crying out loud like the drowning to one another. There's certainly nothing to stop us from sitting down and having a drink or two somewhere together, and then simply letting it begin. For a little while we could stave it off by talking about the glass sticks that nobody wants to disturb the heart of his drink for him, or we could put nickels into the juke box and talk about last year's tunes. Or else we could stop the travesty of uproariousness at once by starting making plans together, plotting the precise design to defeat the absolute muting of each other's voices, contriving a way to go on saying the things we haven't said often enough in five years of time.

"Perhaps we ought to try doing something better than that," she said, and she felt the rain on her hair now. "The planetarium's behind us. We could go in and have a look at the stars."

"Yes," he said, but he was watching the two soldiers who were coming toward them, his eyes fixed closely on them as they passed the bench. "They have shoes like mine on," he said, "so perhaps they'll let me keep mine." He thrust one leg out from under his coat and looked down at his shoe with the strap across the tongue of it and the buckle on the side. "I want to keep them. I don't want to have to wear shoes without memories," he said.

"The heels are worn sideways," she said. "That wouldn't be regulation."

"I like them that way," he said, still looking at his shoe. "I like the things we did to wear them sideways."

"All around the edge," she was saying, "you can see the skyline of New York exactly as if it were the skyline, and as if it were early dusk, with no lights in the windows yet." He was running one finger along the thinning sole. "And after a while, whichever would be the first star at this time of year, that star comes out, and the sky goes slowly darker the way the sky would go tonight if the rain stopped." And to herself she said in silence: There isn't going to be any tonight; everything that has been night and day or summer or winter is going to end at half-past three. "And you sit there in the dark," she said, "and the constellations come out in their proper order."

"All right," he said, and he stood up and looked across the bright green grass at the back of the museum, his eyes on the planetarium's dome. He turned the whitish coat collar up against the rain, and then he drew her arm through his arm. "It's quite a monument," he said as they started off along the path with the rain falling on them. He looked ahead at the museum. "It's quite a memorial to my going away," he said.

"We'll see the dead green canals of Mars," she said, and she felt his arm lying in peace and quiet against her.

"They'll be something special to take to Australia or Alaska all right," he said.

"The other times you went away you didn't have anything half as good to take with you," she said in rebuke to him. "The time you went to concentration camp you had nothing but the bad coffee at five in the morning."

"I had a waltz," he said. "I had a waltz the night before with you. Perhaps I ought to go out waltzing this time," he said, "the way all good Austrians go."

"Where would they put a waltz in the Pennsylvania Station?" she said. She thought of the people that might be there, the mothers, the wives, the sisters, the girls, with their handkerchiefs held against their mouths. I'm not just one woman taking it alone, she said in silence. I'm a lot of women closing their teeth hard on what they're not going to let make any sound.

"That time I had a waltz," he was saying as they walked, "and because they wouldn't let you on the platform, I made up a little group to see me off. I had Héloïse and Abélard," he said, "and King Arthur in tourney dress." There was the planetarium's dome and the closed glass doors before them. The sign on its pedestal said: "Next performance at two-thirty," and they walked away. "I had Aldous Huxley," he said. "I had him walking down the platform, just tipping his hat and smiling slightly through the window at me. But underneath that correct manner there was something else: there was an acute expression of grief in his eyes."

"I don't think he's capable of it," she said as they crossed the street. "How was King Arthur taking it?"

"He had what I should have liked to borrow to go off with," he said. "He had all his nobility showing in his face. When the train started going off with me and the other prisoners and the gendarmes in it, his lips didn't move, but his whole face seemed to alter, you know, the way a statue's does when the light changes on it. Have I told you all this before?"

"No," she said. "You simply went through the gate with the gendarmes. For me, it ended there——"

"I don't know why I wanted Héloïse and Abélard to be there," he said, "but I wanted them badly. I kept watching through the window of the compartment for them, just wanting to see them come, holding arms like we are, maybe as some kind of proof that, in spite of the *Historia Calamitatum,* people do manage to survive. Even as brother and sister, I wanted them, I mean, even with the other feeling gone, and only the tomblike devotion left. But they didn't get there until the last minute," he said. "She came running ahead of him down the platform, looking in the car windows for me. Abélard was terribly nervous; I think he was really annoyed at having to be associated with anyone in my position. He stood back, away from the train, distinguished and embittered looking, snapping at her from time to time. I didn't have handcuffs on, of course, but still he didn't like the situation." They had turned down Broadway now, and the rain was falling hard. "I thought until the very end that he might forget his pride and look at me for a moment as one doomed man at another, but he was past that, he was even past that. I should have known him in the Notre Dame period," he said, and then they saw the moving-picture theater before them.

"It's *Pépé le Moko,*" she said quickly, and they stopped and looked at the face of Jean Gabin in the frames. "It's in French," she said. "I saw it in Toulon after you went away. It's like walking into a *bistro* and sitting down and hearing all the right things said. It's something you ought to take to Alaska with you. It's even better than the canals of Mars," she said.

He paid the money out, and they walked abruptly into the dark together, feeling their way into seats at the back; and they sat down with their coats on still and looked at the illuminated screen. They sat there silent a little while, watching the canoe trip through the Adirondacks unfold before them, the waterfalls drop without hope to the sun-dappled basins, the needled branches hang low upon the moss, the rapids pass, the pines stand up in melancholy.

"It's a quarter past twelve," he said in a low voice to her, and their shoulders were touching in the dark.

"In just a minute it'll come," she said in a whisper. "When this thing's finished, you'll see. I walked in off the quays at Toulon one afternoon when I didn't know whether the Germans had caught up with you yet or not, and there it was," she said. "The speech and the characters are so good that it couldn't matter when you came in on them—I mean, the same way it doesn't matter when you come into actual people's lives because you always know right away, even if you come into the middle of people's lives, exactly what they are and what they've always been."

"This," he said in the darkness, "is the picture about canoe trips which should put an end to all canoe trips."

"In just a minute," she said in a quick whisper, "you'll see. Pépé's the tough guy, the bad egg, the *maquereau* who knows all about love from the beginning. He's out of Montmartre, serving a life term in prison in Algiers. Or perhaps it's Morocco, or perhaps not quite a term for life. But it's the shape of love you get. I don't know how you get it. Perhaps there isn't any love in it, but still something like it is there."

"What if we just went somewhere quietly and had a drink?" he said to the sight of the man and woman stroking the canoe across the sunlit screen.

"In just a minute it will change," she said softly. "It's something you can take away with you and keep under glass. Pépé escapes, he hides in the Casbah, and there's one line you can keep forever with you. It's when he's kissing the girl who's come from Paris, and he knows he never can go home. He doesn't tell her that she is the lilacs in the Bois," she whispered, "or the *marronniers* along the boulevards. He says, '*Tu es le métro,*' and he says it the way no one's ever said anything before."

"It's one o'clock," he said in the dark, "and they haven't reached civilization yet."

"This can't go on forever," she said.

"It can go on until they pitch camp," he said. "It'll have to go on until she's made the coffee and cooked potatoes in the ash." He had got to his feet now, and he said: "You wait here while I ask. I don't want to have to see them paddling into the sunset." She watched him going, the silhouette tall and somehow vulnerable against the rapids' brilliant summer light. When he came back he leaned over her in the darkness. "We'll go to the Pennsylvania Station and have a drink," he said. "Gabin goes on at half-past two."

The bar there was shaped like a clover leaf, and men were thick around it, army men and navy men with their packs at their feet. There was one table left, a small one by the plate-glass window that looked on the arcade, and they sat down and ordered sandwiches and scotch, and their eyes met suddenly, and he reached over and took her hand.

"I know it's impossible to make any plans ahead," he said, "but if there's any way to telephone, I will. If you'll just be there almost all the time, I'll try to get through to you. Maybe they let visitors come on Sunday," he said, the conniving against silence and time and distance, as they had known it in other countries, beginning stubbornly again.

"Don't make yourself write too much," she said, and she watched the people passing in the arcade. "I mean, the routine will be hard. Don't feel you have to do it."

The food and drink had come now, and they bit into their sandwiches and drank the scotch and soda fast.

"I'll try to telephone or telegraph at once," he said. "Only don't expect it." It was only when he glanced down for a moment that she could bear to look now at his forehead and his eyebrows and his hair.

"This isn't like the other times," she said, and the first scotch was spreading its weakness in her. "This time you're not just one man bearing the burden alone of what you've decided to do. There's a national sanction to it. This time you're not an outcast any more."

"Two more," he said to the waiter, and he pointed to the empty glasses.

"This time it's different for me, too," she said. "I'm not just one woman keeping her mouth shut about what her husband's doing. I'm Russian women and English women and French women," she said, and she heard the sound of it rising foolish and high.

"You're the canals of Mars and the Casbah," he said, and because she could not look at him, she closed her hand tight in her pocket and looked straight at the shaved neck of a sailor who stood drinking at the bar. "I don't know exactly at what age one starts putting the thing together," he had begun saying across the table to her, and now there was something else in his voice, and she knew it was this he had been wanting a long time to say. "Perhaps we began putting it together younger over there," he said, "because over there you had to know it young in order to know by what means you could survive. You decided young, and when you were young still you put that kind of armor on you, link by link—I mean, the sort of contraption of ideals, or dreams, or merely exact distinctions, and once you had it clear, you had it for life, and there was no way to get from under it or to set it aside."

The second scotch came, and he took a swallow of it, and his eyes were fixed, grave and deliberate, on her face. "And then the real trouble began," he said. "I mean, the real struggle was to get it out of the realm of vision or poetry, and give it an act at last. You could write things about what you believed, or dream things about it, and there lay the idea so pure and remote in you that you could deceive yourself into thinking that it would survive alone. But it can't survive alone, and for a long time you can't find the act to give it for survival. But now suddenly it's happened," he said. "It happened to me the way it happened to everybody else standing up there having a drink in uniform—we were suddenly given the outer trappings for the thing in which we had believed. It's something like kneeling down and being knighted," he said, saying it quietly and soberly, and he ordered two more drinks for them. "It'll be a quarter to three in a minute," he said.

They went down the first flight on the escalator, and the second flight they walked down, and there they saw all the other men with the zipper canvas satchels in their hands. He went through the door of store seven, and it closed behind him, and through the top pane of glass she could see his head and shoulders moving across the room. Beyond the store, five or six hundred men were standing behind the iron fence, and in a moment he too was there among them, with his little bag hanging in his hand. He put the bag and his raincoat down, and his eyes went quickly over the people outside the barrier, looking for her, and then he walked across to the edge, where some of the other men stood already, saying the last words to the families that had come to see them go. He put his hand through the bars and touched her sleeve, and the things the whisky was murmuring in them were the things they did not say.

"I don't see Aldous Huxley around anywhere," she said in a bright, strange voice to him. He stood close, with the bars between them, twisting the ring on her finger and looking at her face.

Behind him a draftee in a gray, silky, summer suit got up on a bench in the enclosure, wavering uncertainly above the humbly standing or seated others, and began to speak. He was not a young man, and his paunch was large, and the drink was hot and tight in his face, and as he swayed above them he cried the words of his farewell speech aloud.

"Friends, countrymen, and slackers!" he cried. "There aren't five ways of doing your duty, there aren't even four ways, there's only one way! You take a drink, and then you do it! You take a drink——" he shouted, but now the sergeant had put his hand up and helped him down.

"This time there'll be furloughs," she said through the bars. "You'll have good food—and then they have musical shows, you know, they have famous actresses and dances and things."

"Yes," he said quietly on the other side. "I know." Behind him in the enclosure the men were forming into lines, and he turned his head and looked at them. "This must be it," he said.

He looked for his raincoat and bag again, and he picked them up, and then he set off with the others walking two by two. The waiting families had not begun to move yet, but the woman pressed close beside her called out in a strong, fearless voice:

"Good-by, Mike! You show them what you're made of!" She turned, with her head up, and looked quickly at the other women. "That's my little brother," she said, and tears were standing in her eyes.

And now the women and the men started walking along each side of the iron bars, the women walking at the same pace the coupled men walked toward departure with their satchels in their hands and their eyes turning back to see. As they rounded the pillar at the corner before the descent, the families ceased to call aloud; there was no sound left but that of the men quickly marching. It was not until they reached the head of the stairs that the three Italian women broke through the line and flung themselves forward—perhaps grandmother, wife, sweetheart, sister, or mother—shouting aloud their pain. They fell upon the little man in the summer suit as he passed, short, heavy women in silk dresses and high heels, with no hats, no veils, no gloves to mask their anguish, not whisky but merely the passionate flesh betraying the grief of nights and days they could not and would not bear. The little man flung out his short arms in one ludicrous, despairing gesture to them, and then he went suddenly down the stairs with the others. And perhaps it is like that, she thought as she ran on, dry-eyed among the women, perhaps it is like that that men want their women to roar out their good-by.

He was just ahead now, with his height and the weathered look of his skin singling him out, and the raincoat slung white across his shoulder, and they were going fast. He looked back once, and the lips did not move, and she ran futilely and wildly as the others ran, tripping in haste across their feet. She thought of King Arthur, and the face altering like a statue's face when the light changes on it. This time it is different, she thought; this time it isn't just one man taking nothing but his own lonely honor with him; and then he too went down the stairs.

PIGEONS EN CASSEROLE

By Bessie Breuer

From the *New Yorker*

BESSIE BREUER

was born Freedman, October 18, 1892, in Cleveland, Ohio, and christened Elizabeth. Her father was a composer. Her early ambition was to be a reporter, and accordingly she went to the School of Journalism at the University of Missouri. From the St. Louis Times *she went to the New York* Tribune, *where she edited the women's department, and later, at twenty-two, was Sunday editor for six months. She has also been director of magazine publicity for the American Red Cross, and was on the staff of the* Ladies' Home Journal. *She wrote many articles for various magazines and spent a number of years in France. While there,* Harper's Magazine *and* Story*—then in Vienna—accepted her first short stories. Her two novels,* Memory of Love, *in 1934, and* The Daughter, *in 1938, followed.*

Miss Breuer's second husband was Carl Kahler, and she is now married to Henry Varnum Poor, the painter. She has a son and daughter, and lives near New York in the country. She likes to ride, walk, and swim, and also to cook. At present she is doing a special series of states and cities for overseas broadcasts for the Office of War Information, and hopes soon to be finished and back at an uncompleted novel.

FROM THE FIRST I felt uncomfortable. I thought it was the unpleasant news I must break pleasantly to her, but then I am always so nervous now. To live in New York, to earn a living from its neurotic, unstable women—that is work for a Tantalus; for a refugee, a man who has literally, but literally, nothing but his manners and a little talent, *petit tout petit,* it is more disgusting than a concentration camp. There, I think, one's honor sustains one, come what may. But to be always at bay, like a cunning animal, a little animal, in a jungle of devouring women—that she could never understand.

I telephoned her—I detest writing letters—to say I would meet the boy at the Grand Central station and bring him up on the first train to her in the country. It was his summer holiday.

Her voice over the telephone was so warm, so gay and fresh. "How kind of you!" she said. "How very wonderful of you!" It was always like that whenever I called her up, most of the time to say I could not come up to see her. Sometimes for months on end I was unable to come, and always she answered in that fresh, happy voice, "Yes, darling, I understand."

When we finally got to her station on one of those villainous local trains, there she was, running toward us, her face aflame with such joy that it was, in a way, terrible to see. The boy stood slightly to the rear of me, as if he were afraid of it, almost.

Yet any mother would stare at a son who left her a little boy and returned, after eight months, a head taller and the bony structure of a man's head already changing the baby face. I too had stared when I first saw him.

"Mon petit!" she exclaimed. *"Comme tu as grandi!"* In her excitement at seeing him she had forgotten he had begged her never to speak anything but English to him, especially in public. People passing us looked around curiously, hearing the foreign sounds, and Kurt frowned. To remind him of anything that makes him different

from an American boy is a great pain to him. When he did not step forward to embrace her, she turned toward me, nonplused.

It is something to handle an adolescent boy. The primitives do that very well. Take him away from the women and when he returns from the ordeals and the rites he is a man and there's an end to all this oppressive mother love. I took her on one arm and Kurt on the other—a boy has enough to contend with in his own self—and I marched them along fast to the house down at the other end of the village street.

The village had had some charm in the early spring, with its white painted fences and houses and blossoming trees, but that day when we walked up the street there was so much green everywhere, such rank growth, lilac and honeysuckle both past their period of flowering, and the sky partly overcast so there was neither sunlight nor sharp shadow. In the corners of her little yard around the house, the weeds were knee-high. (Having lent us a farmer cottage, you would think my client's generosity would extend to sending a gardener twice a year to keep the weeds down, but no.)

However, once inside the house, it was really most astonishing how pleasant Eugénie had managed to make that shabby little room with bouquets of grasses, wild flowers, and whatnot. She ran and lit the kerosene lamps. Then she turned to us, smiling now, for she could see Kurt's stiffness softening out of his face. As his mother helped him off with his topcoat, he could, without loss of that precious dignity of an adolescent, quite naturally embrace her.

Ah, that was much better. She became her old self. "Go upstairs with the bags," she said. "Although I should send them up, somehow. For you are my guests. Especially this first day you are not to lift a finger," she called after us, again the woman whose endless courage gave one the strength to go on. In all the years there had never been a word of complaint from her, even in that first, that frightful year when we finally reached New York without money, without friends or acquaintances. For months I walked the streets of New York without success, and always she would welcome me back to that miserable little hole of a room in which we all three lived, with such grace of spirit that I could go on.

The only things I really knew were how to run a car and fly an airplane. I answered every advertisement, went to every kind of garage —in New York, Brooklyn, across the river in New Jersey, anywhere. But to no effect. Everywhere gruffness and terror. Naw, naw, naw. Then—ah, God, it is really fantastic, this country—I, an amateur, a patron of artists at home, unable to earn a living at motors, which I knew even in my dreams, I became an interior decorator! And to whom do I owe this belief in me, this beginning of a whole new life, I, a monarchist and a Black of Vienna? To a Jew! The ignominy, the humiliation! Yes, only from Jews in New York, from their organizations, did I get help. A Jew lent me the money. Lent, did I say? Pressed it into my hand, the check for two thousand dollars. "You!" he stuttered. "That you should go begging for work! It must never be!" You see, in his mind was still fresh the memory of that old Vienna he had left as a poor ghetto boy. "A count," he said. "It's simple. You must become a Park Avenue decorator."

For herself, for Kurt, Eugénie would take little of the money. I remember he had only one pair of woolen stockings that first winter, they were so expensive, and when she told how she had washed and darned them she would say that she was a costly luxury—fifty dollars a month just to keep those stockings in order. Then she would laugh. "Really, I am of no earthly use to you," she would say. "Even Kurt does not need me. He's taken to getting his own breakfast not to disturb me when he knows I have a migraine on, the dear." So she would go on making light of everything so that I might not have her on my conscience, with all that I had to worry about and the great outlay that was necessary in this new profession of mine. The studio rent alone was two hundred dollars, the butler seventy-five. That was before I even started to pay for food and drink for the parties I had to give. As Eugénie herself pointed out, it was a double economy for her and the boy to live in the country while he was young. He could go to the village school, she would need no elaborate wardrobe, and I wasn't—a man alone—under endless social obligations. Had I introduced a wife into such a milieu, it would have been complicated and boring. We could not afford to bore anybody. Since I quite definitely had the social flair of the two and she was the solitary, the *spirituelle,* it seemed the only solution for us. She simply would not take one penny more than that fifty dollars, though how she managed I hardly knew, for although it was only fifty miles from town, I didn't get out there more than twice that whole winter. It was such a cold and lonely house, and bad enough that she should have to live there. I simply could not relax out there, and I needed frightfully to relax, I was so nervous all the time. So it was better to go to someone's place on Long Island and have breakfast brought to one's bed and good food and drinks and no responsibility and feel really refreshed, and unexpectedly make a really valuable connection—one never knows. Eugénie understood all that, understood that no person must be unexplored, no time must be lost. She seemed never to mind when I saw them so rarely in that first winter.

But one year, two years, and now things were much better. Through an influential client (always a woman; one steps ahead on the breasts of women, so to speak), Kurt received a scholarship at this truly magnificent boarding school.

I saw the way he looked around at his bare bedroom, as if it were a strange place, opening his bag so slowly, as if he regretted to take up this life again. It was, indeed, a pity he must return to this forlorn little house, but even that would not be for long, as he knew. "So brace up," I told him. "Smile and make your mother happy. She has such a little while with you," I said, and going down the stairs with him, I wondered how to break the news of this to Eugénie. It must be managed carefully, I knew.

But how to describe that table? So charming! And done with what? Colored paper napkins, kitchen oilcloth, a pair of scissors, and candles, and whatnot from the ten-cent store. In the center of this delightful array, a casserole, the veritable French *cassoulet,* and inside, glazed with judicious cooking, squabs and tiny vegetables.

"But really, Eugénie!" I exclaimed. "How did you manage that? A *cordon bleu* could do no better! And squabs! Where did you get squabs out here?"

She was very pleased at this tribute. "Then I really did surprise you? I am so happy! You know your friend, that Johnson boy, Kurt? He has a new rifle and was most anxious to use it. So I paid him.

Six cents for the BB shots and ten cents to clean them, and a blessing to be rid of the wild pigeons, his mother said. So, you see, I am learning to be an American. Also a *cordon bleu*. Please taste it, Kurt, taste my *chef-d'œuvre*." She leaned over and joggled his elbow to get him started.

It is not a food a growing boy enjoys—a bite of bird flesh in wine sauce—and in any case neither she nor Kurt got very far with their meal, because, during the small talk of passing this and that, most casually I said we had only this day with her, the Vanderdorn boy having invited Kurt for a summer of travel. She dropped her hands from the table.

"Impossible!" she said to me. "He cannot go!"

Just like that, without preamble or softening or grace. Kurt stopped eating and, like any man, began to shift in his chair and look anywhere rather than at her.

"Please, Eugénie," I begged. "It's most wonderful, really. First they go to the plantation near Charleston, and then the whole family goes to the Rocky Mountains. Kurt will see the whole of America. Marvelous. And such valuable connections for his future. Congratulations are in order. But really, Eugénie."

"No, no, no," she went on monotonously, as if to herself alone. "No, he can't. Kurt must not—he can't." Kurt's eyes grew wide with fear. Nothing in his life had prepared him for this, his mother, who had always been so gracious, now with a face like death. I begged her to be sensible, but she shrugged off my words and leaned toward Kurt.

"Kurt! You won't leave me? You don't want to, do you, Kurt?" Kurt could not meet her eyes, naturally not. The boy had made his first friend, an American, and he was happy at this, his first step, his own, in a strange land.

"I don't care," he mumbled, ashamed of the tension, ashamed to look at his mother.

She could not even read the disappointment in his face, so happy was she for the bare, unwilling words. "You see?" she said to me. "Kurt does not wish to go."

If he could not face his mother, I, his father, must and could. "I'm afraid it's too late for Kurt to change his mind. I accepted for him,"

I said. "They leave in a few days from the Vanderdorn estate outside of Philadelphia. It is my fault, I know, but I had not the time to consult you, and so I took the responsibility in my own hands."

"No, no. This is my time with Kurt," she began all over again. "You promised it when I allowed you to take him away to school. Don't you remember, Richard? You promised me the summer with him!"

Of course I had promised it. But that was before he went off to school, before he knew any boy his own age. Would she never realize that we were beggars, opportunists, who must seize every advantage as it comes?

"That's all I asked of you—this summer," she went on, her voice rising. "I must, I must have something!"

I really could not understand her. So suddenly had this happened, so completely without cause this hysteria. How could she, his mother, be anything but happy that her son at last had an opportunity and a friend of his own in this strange land? It is hard enough for him. He speaks English with an accent and all that. Why burden him further with father, mother, with love? Women have the greed of spoiled children. They will break the world rather than yield this self-centered thing they call happiness. The senseless, the insane ego! Even revolution, homelessness, the death of a whole world teaches them nothing! Ah, what a business I went through with her.

"It is only this summer, a few weeks," I said. "Why take it so seriously?"

"Oh no. I know better," she said, staring away with a terrible sadness in her eyes. "I have lost him. I have lost him forever."

"He is only going away for a few weeks of fun," I said. "You would not deny that to Kurt, would you? What else is there for him this summer? Be sensible," I urged her. "You were not brought up to be a housekeeper. It will be much more comfortable for you not to have to prepare meals on time for a big, hungry boy. And it will be better for Kurt. He could not possibly bring a friend here." To all that she nodded an abstracted agreement, for even she knew that his social life must never enter this house, with its kitchen filled with old golf bags, gloves, hats, junk; in summer, flies, soiled dishes always standing about. Kurt must go on with the life he had started so well in boarding school. I would see ahead and work it out for him. All that would in any capital of Europe be his by right of birth and family connection for hundreds of years back must be carefully managed in America. Eugénie and I had come through the first part—the homelessness, the despair—in agreement and fortitude; now, if only I could persuade her to be reasonable about Kurt's future!

"Boys need lots of good food," I said. "At regular intervals. You can't even cook, and why should you?"

"But I am learning," she said, and brightened up. "The squabs—aren't they delicious?"

"My poor Eugénie," I said. "That is once in a life. But string beans in the pot without water—remember?" I laughed. "No, no. You are neither housekeeper nor cook, thank God."

I saw immediately that I had gone too far. Her eyes filled with tears. She looked across at the remains of the bird on my plate, at the bird untouched on Kurt's, and hers also barely stabbed at, and then she turned her head away.

I did not dare look toward Kurt. Too bad that he must see and hear all this. But what is one to do? That is life. And what could I say? Sometimes it is easier to say soothing words to a stranger than to a woman you have been married to so long that certain kinds of sentiment are false, no matter how much you love her. We sat there, all of us, carefully not looking at each other.

"I am utterly to blame," I said, "and I am sorry. It would be most embarrassing, because of certain business plans, to withdraw Kurt now. I cannot, I dare not, afford such whims. After this I swear to you I will make no more plans without consulting you. After this we will all be together. Always. Trust me, Eugénie."

"Trust?" At last she looked directly into my eyes. "Trust you?" she said, with her eyes blazing. "You *boulevardier!*"

It was frightful. In all these years, whatever she knew or guessed, it had never been acknowledged by word or glance. No matter what the provocation. Then, suddenly, this! How could she do it to Kurt? Or to me, for that matter? Sometimes people go away right in front of you. Their eyes turn inward and go staring within and you cannot tell what land they are living in or what thoughts make their mouths twitch in that strange way. When they look out at you again, it is with the eyes of a stranger, an implacable enemy. So now Eugénie turned from Kurt to me and back again to Kurt.

It must have been something that happened during that long winter when, for the first time in her life, she had been without Kurt. Because she had been so humble, really, and willing when he went away to the school in the fall. She knew it was bad for him to be lying late in bed reading or mooning and saying "What's there to do?" all the time, and doing nothing, not even helping her with the dishes. She saw as clearly as I that it was no good for a boy to be cooped up with his mother after a certain age. "And after his schooling, Kurt will marry," she said then, "and I'll be left alone anyhow."

"But you like it, don't you, up here, Eugénie?" I asked her at that time. "Or would you prefer to come in and stay at the studio, perhaps for a month?"

"Oh no, not at all," she said. Sometimes, when I think I must be to blame, I remember that answer. "I should only be in the way," she said. And that would have been true. I could leave her in the country with a clear conscience, for she had none of the petty lonelinesses of the immature. Occasionally, when I did run up, I would walk into the house and find her, broom in hand, reading, lost to everything. She would come awake with a start when I called out. "There is not enough time in a day," she would say, and tell me about her reading, her painting, her long walks. So, naturally, I thought she would be all right. But perhaps the loneliness of an American village—no cafés, everyone shut tight to himself, and she an alien—perhaps it was too much even for her.

Yet what could I possibly have done? Introduce her suddenly, a wife, into my social life? To those steel-thin, shiny women? Isn't it enough that *I* must live with them? Something one must keep.

So here we were, Eugénie, Kurt, and I, sitting at a festive table in tragic silence. Quickly, quickly, a diversion, anything to bring a light back into their sad faces. I remembered the photographs of me taken by that millionaire girl Millicent, who wants—ah, they all want, all of them—to be a creative artist. "Here, Eugénie, look," I said as I returned to the table. "Please choose the one you like best." I spilled the large, shiny proofs under her eyes. "It is to illustrate an article about my work."

Kurt's hand stretched out quickly for them. He was of an age, you know, when a boy turns to his father. The way he wound his arm around my chair, leaned over me—it was almost tactless in its neglect of her. She took up the photographs as he dropped them to the table. Slowly she ruffled them.

"It comes clear in a photograph, the first signs of corruption," she said bitterly. "Your mouth, your eyes. Like a movie actor." She stared into my face. "America has done this to you."

The boy caught his breath. No one moved. No one spoke. She stared at her little gala dinner, and sighed. Then she arose, removed the plates, and brought in an apricot tart. At any other time it would have been something to exclaim about. I managed to compliment her on it and urged Kurt to taste it. She, also, urged him to eat. Her voice now was overquiet, humble, but the boy shook his head. She saw that what Kurt had just witnessed could not be sweetened with an apricot tart.

To run away then, the woman's way; to run away when she is crossed or defeated, like a spoiled child. She excused herself. "It's really been too much of a day for me. Do you mind if I clear the table now?" she asked. "Please, nobody move."

After she went upstairs the boy and I were free. We could look at each other. At first with a feeling of guilt; then our voices rose more certainly. Kurt struck the match for my pipe. Ah, it was good. At last we had conversation, and all the stories of his year at school came out—the friends, real friends, Americans, his so thrilling life at school, his teachers, the young man who took him bird hunting. Everything that Eugénie must have been waiting to hear he told me now. I knew that she must be hearing his voice—not the exact words, only the happy, assured tones that were rolling up the staircase to her avid ears. Ah well, it could not be helped, her suffering. He would come back to her when he was more certain of himself. She was too hasty. *Kurt is lost to me forever*. That was nothing to say before a growing boy. That sort of bitter looking into the ultimate future is something one keeps to oneself, out of self-respect, out of respect for the other, out of respect for life.

But there it was. Whatever she had lost for the time being, I had gained a son, a big, fine boy. We went upstairs when he was all talked out, arms around each other, the blood flowing from one to the other, strong and assured. What a moment that is for a father! I hoped she was asleep, that she need not hear, like an outcast, the boy talking to me drowsily while I sat on the edge of his bed. At last, under cover of the darkness, he threw his long, bony arms around my neck and kissed me. "Father, Father," he murmured. "Oh, Father . . ."

When I turned toward Eugénie's bedroom, it was with a feeling of guilt. With her usual tact, however, she had withdrawn to the far side of the bed and turned her back to me, so that I had privacy. Whether she was asleep or awake I could not know, she lay so still.

But for me there was no sleep. The lumpy mattress, the miserable thin sheets, the narrow blanket, the wind roaring like waters in the flood, the whole thing so strange; to be lying in a hard bed in a strange land and all the smells and sounds strange, and even the sky weird and violent and the livid moon bright on my face—no curtains, of course. How could she sleep in such a place? Somehow it had never affected her, judging by the letters she wrote me. I would get a letter almost every day, and many of them would be sent special delivery—that was her one extravagance—although they were about nothing, a bird she saw, or something she read, nothing of importance. And I lay there cold and unsleeping, but not moving nearer her, because—ah well.

I must have drifted off to sleep despite the cold, for something, a movement, awoke me. She was slipping out of the covers. I lay still and listened to the swishing sound of her in Kurt's room. When she returned and stood over the bed ready to slip into it, her face was so gray and terrible that I sat up and cried out, "What is it? What's happened, Eugénie!"

"Nothing. Sh-h-h. Nothing," she whispered. "I thought Kurt might be uncovered."

Ach, the endless dumb obstinacy of women!

"Eugénie!" I said. Now I was really annoyed. "What in God's name do you think will happen to him? He's been away from you all winter and look at him, a head taller and strong as an ox! You cannot go around wiping his nose forever!"

No answer.

I said nothing more. Of what use? Her sorrow was really all she had. Kurt would escape today. From now on his life must be healthy, I thought, steeling myself against this woman by my side. I, his father, am responsible to him and to my ancestors for him. About this there can be no sentimentality.

In a little while she arose. I heard the rumble of ashes being shaken out of the kitchen stove, and I must have fallen asleep again, for when Kurt and I got downstairs a delightful breakfast was already prepared. She shared in the conversation at the table and she was her sweet, gracious self again, our departure taken for granted, and after breakfast she helped Kurt with his packing.

He had picked out the few things he wanted to save and all about him in his room lay books he would no longer read, a broken model airplane which had taken a whole winter to build, all the oddments and junk a boy collects whether he has money for toys or not. He was finished with all that childishness now, the chrysalis outgrown, and stepping out to his larger youth. She was being so nice about it, bringing him his gun, everything, and as we sat eating sandwiches and milk at noon, there was an atmosphere of something finished, of farewells made and the air empty and strained, although we were not leaving until the evening train.

"There's the two-forty," said Kurt. It slipped out, showing how anxious he was to be off.

"Of course," Eugénie said quickly. "An hour more or less. Really, why not take it, Richard? Dinner, a movie in New York—it would be so jolly for Kurt."

It was enough to look at Kurt's glowing face to see what pleasure it would give him.

"But are you sure you won't mind?" I asked her.

Now I realize the smile on her face was too extravagant. Only now.

We all walked to the station together. When the train drew in she stood there, profoundly still. She did not put up a hand to touch Kurt or me. Only that upward-looking, radiant, sweet face. I kissed her, but Kurt was too embarrassed to make the first move of emotion. He stood frozen, and then finally he looked down at her.

I am glad his eyes were full of the love he could not express. His hand just brushed over her arm, but, you know, in such a way—gentle, loving. And still she did not move; only her lips began to flutter when his hand tentatively, softly, brushed along her arm.

As nearly as I can find out what happened, she never went back to the house. Straight from the station she must have started off on one of those long walks of hers. The pond was ten miles away and it had a long, sloping beach. She must have walked straight into it, gloves, cane, and all, as some fishermen found her the next day, fastidious to the end.

As for Kurt, it was good he was with strangers. I went immediately to see him. He was immobile. Not now, I told him. Someday we will both try to understand. Now it is only necessary to know that she wished it so.

No more was said. One must grow, one must experience many things before one can taste the true bitterness of death. To a boy, it is still only a fact. Someday he will need to know, to understand. Then the day of reckoning. Of explanation.

Until then everything is finished. I might as well go on the trip to Idaho. I have never seen a ranch or the West, and it isn't as if they knew her. I shall go to Amelia's at Shinnecock Hills and we are to meet Geoffrey and take the plane at LaGuardia Field. After all, why should their plans be spoiled? My relations with them are, in a way, professional, and a man cannot, simply cannot, telephone as late as this and say "I had a wife." That would be most embarrassing. I might even get to do Maggie's new ranch house if I handle her impressively. Kurt is settled for the summer in a way that is most fortunate, and I, of course, shall get through somehow, though I can't stop thinking about it.

What I cannot get over is that I, who am so clever, should not have sensed that something was wrong. I reconstruct the whole day over and over again; I go over that whole visit to see where I might have stopped the thing. But it was like any other day in a country village—nothing happening with the sharp form in people or event that gives such style to city life. Except for that outburst at table, quite natural in any mother. Why didn't she give me a hint? Why didn't she say what was really the matter? On the contrary. Walking toward the station, I asked, "Are you all right?" meaning about Kurt. "Yes, my darling," she answered, her eyes profoundly tender, looking into mine the way they did when we first fell in love. Who, looking into that worn face, could possibly suspect what must have formed already in her mind? "I'll try to run up if you like," I told her, walking along with Kurt on my other arm, so content with my whole family. "No. On no account. No," she said. And then she whispered, "I'm ashamed. I'm ashamed, Richard, of the way I behaved." Then later, apropos of nothing, "Do you think, because you are so clever, you can escape all the consequences?" I looked at her, bewildered, and she said, "Oh, I'm so sorry I said that, Richard. Forgive me for everything." Her face, as the train slipped by, was so sweet and virginal, looking toward us, that I was completely reassured.

And it was immediately after that—think of it!—that she turned and went off on that walk. What is one to think or say about a thing like that? She, who was always so considerate!

THE ENEMY

By Pearl Buck

From *Harper's Magazine*

PEARL BUCK

was born Pearl Sydenstricker, June 26, 1892, in Hillsboro, West Virginia, the daughter of missionary parents. She spent the first part of her life in China, returning to America at seventeen to attend Randolph-Macon College. After graduating from there she went back to China, and two years later married Dr. John Lossing Buck, an agricultural missionary. In 1932 she returned to America, the year after her best-selling novel, The Good Earth, *had appeared. Her first novel,* East Wind, West Wind, *was published in 1929, but attracted little attention.* The Good Earth *won the Pulitzer Prize, was made into a play and later into a moving picture. It won for Mrs. Buck the Howells Medal of the American Academy of Arts and Letters, in 1935, and helped her become a Nobel Prize winner in 1938.*

In 1933 Mrs. Buck returned to China with her husband, although due to a controversy she had resigned as a missionary. The following year she returned to America for good and became an editor for the John Day Publishing Company. After her divorce from Dr. Buck she married Richard J. Walsh, president of John Day and editor of Asia, *of which magazine Mrs. Buck is also an editor, as well as editor-in-chief of John Day. She and Mr. Walsh live on a farm in Bucks County, Pennsylvania, with Mrs. Buck's two daughters and their four adopted children. She has written eight novels about China, two biographies of her father and mother—*Fighting Angel *and* The Exile*—and numerous books about America, both fiction and non-fiction. Her most recent book is* What America Means to Me. *She has also translated a number of books from the Chinese.*

Mrs. Buck won second prize in the 1933 O. Henry volume with a story from the Woman's Home Companion, *"The Frill," and was present in the 1934 book with a short-short story, "Shanghai Scene," from* Asia.

Dr. Sadao Hoki's house was built on a spot of the Japanese coast where as a little boy he had often played. The low square stone house was set upon rocks well above a narrow beach that was outlined with bent pines. As a boy Sadao had climbed the pines, supporting himself on his bare feet, as he had seen men do in the South Seas when they climbed for coconuts. His father had taken him often to the islands of those seas, and never had he failed to say to the little grave boy at his side, "Those islands yonder, they are the steppingstones to the future for Japan."

"Where shall we step from them?" Sadao had asked seriously.

"Who knows?" his father had answered. "Who can limit our future? It depends on what we make it."

Sadao had taken this into his mind as he did everything his father said, his father who never joked or played with him but who spent infinite pains upon him who was his only son. Sadao knew that his education was his father's chief concern. For this reason he had been sent at twenty-two to America to learn all that could be learned of surgery and medicine. He had come back at thirty, and before his father died he had seen Sadao become famous not only as a surgeon but as a scientist. Because he was now perfecting a discovery which would render wounds entirely clean he had not been sent abroad with the troops. Also, he knew, there was some slight danger that the old General might need an operation for a condition for which he was now being treated medically, and for this possibility Sadao was being kept in Japan.

Clouds were rising from the ocean now. The unexpected warmth of the past few days had at night drawn heavy fog from the cold waves. Sadao watched mists hide outlines of a little island near the shore and then come creeping up the beach below the house, wreathing around the pines. In a few minutes fog would be wrapped about the house too. Then he would go into the room where Hana, his wife, would be waiting for him with the two children.

But at this moment the door opened and she looked out, a dark blue woolen haori over her kimono. She came to him affectionately and put her arm through his as he stood, smiled and said nothing. He had met Hana in America, but he had waited to fall in love with her until he was sure she was Japanese. His father would never have received her unless she had been pure in her race. He wondered often whom he would have married if he had not met Hana, and by what luck he had found her in the most casual way, by chance literally, at an American professor's house. The professor and his wife had been kind people anxious to do something for their few foreign students, and the students, though bored, had accepted this kindness. Sadao had often told Hana how nearly he had not gone to Professor Harley's house that night—the rooms were so small, the food so bad, the professor's wife so voluble. But he had gone and there he had found Hana, a new student, and had felt he would love her if it were at all possible.

Now he felt her hand on his arm and was aware of the pleasure it gave him, even though they had been married years enough to have the two children. For they had not married heedlessly in America. They had finished their work at school and had come home to Japan, and when his father had seen her the marriage had been arranged in the old Japanese way, although Sadao and Hana had talked everything over beforehand. They were perfectly happy. She laid her cheek against his arm.

It was at this moment that both of them saw something black come out of the mists. It was a man. He was flung up out of the ocean—flung, it seemed, to his feet by a breaker. He staggered a few steps, his body outlined against the mist, his arms above his head. Then the curled mists hid him again.

"Who is that?" Hana cried. She dropped Sadao's arm and they both leaned over the railing of the veranda. Now they saw him again. The man was on his hands and knees crawling. Then they saw him fall on his face and lie there.

"A fisherman perhaps," Sadao said, "washed from his boat." He ran quickly down the steps, and behind him Hana came, her wide sleeves flying. A mile or two away on either side there were fishing villages, but here was only the bare and lonely coast, dangerous with rocks. The surf beyond the beach was spiked with rocks. Somehow the man had managed to come through them—he must be badly torn.

They saw when they came toward him that indeed it was so. The sand on one side of him had already a stain of red soaking through.

"He is wounded," Sadao exclaimed. He made haste to the man, who lay motionless, his face in the sand. An old cap stuck to his head soaked with sea water. He was in wet rags of garments. Sadao stooped, Hana at his side, and turned the man's head. They saw the face.

"A white man!" Hana whispered.

Yes, it was a white man. The wet cap fell away and there was his wet yellow hair, long, as though for many weeks it had not been cut, and upon his young and tortured face was a rough yellow beard. He was unconscious and knew nothing that they did to him.

Now Sadao remembered the wound, and with his expert fingers he began to search for it. Blood flowed freshly at his touch. On the right side of his lower back Sadao saw that a gun wound had been reopened. The flesh was blackened with powder. Sometime, not many days ago, the man had been shot and had not been tended. It was bad chance that the rock had struck the wound.

"Oh, how he is bleeding!" Hana whispered again in a solemn voice. The mists screened them now completely, and at this time of day no one came by. The fishermen had gone home and even the chance beachcombers would have considered the day at an end.

"What shall we do with this man?" Sadao muttered. But his trained hands seemed of their own will to be doing what they could to stanch the fearful bleeding. He packed the wound with the sea moss that strewed the beach. The man moaned with pain in his stupor but he did not awaken.

"The best thing that we could do would be to put him back in the sea," Sadao said, answering himself.

Now that the bleeding was stopped for the moment he stood up and dusted the sand from his hands.

"Yes, undoubtedly that would be best," Hana said steadily. But she continued to stare down at the motionless man.

"If we sheltered a white man in our house we should be arrested and if we turned him over as a prisoner, he would certainly die," Sadao said.

"The kindest thing would be to put him back into the sea," Hana said. But neither of them moved. They were staring with a curious repulsion upon the inert figure.

"What is he?" Hana whispered.

"There is something about him that looks American," Sadao said. He took up the battered cap. Yes, there, almost gone, was the faint lettering. "A sailor," he said, "from an American warship." He spelled it out: "U. S. Navy." The man was a prisoner of war!

"He has escaped," Hana cried softly, "and that is why he is wounded."

"In the back," Sadao agreed.

They hesitated, looking at each other. Then Hana said with resolution:

"Come, are we able to put him back into the sea?"

"If I am able, are you?" Sadao asked.

"No," Hana said. "But if you can do it alone . . ."

Sadao hesitated again. "The strange thing is," he said, "that if the man were whole I could turn him over to the police without difficulty. I care nothing for him. He is my enemy. All Americans are my enemy. And he is only a common fellow. You see how foolish his face is. But since he is wounded . . ."

"You also cannot throw him back to the sea," Hana said. "Then there is only one thing to do. We must carry him into the house."

"But the servants?" Sadao inquired.

"We must simply tell them that we intend to give him to the police—as indeed we must, Sadao. We must think of the children and your position. It would endanger all of us if we did not give this man over as a prisoner of war."

"Certainly," Sadao agreed. "I would not think of doing anything else."

Thus agreed, together they lifted the man. He was very light, like a fowl that has been half starved for a long time until it is only feathers and skeleton. So, his arms hanging, they carried him up the steps and into the side door of the house. This door opened into a passage and down the passage they carried the man toward an empty bedroom. It had been the bedroom of Sadao's father and since his death it had not been used. They laid the man on the deeply matted floor. Everything here had been Japanese to please the old man, who would never in his own home sit on a chair or sleep in a foreign bed. Hana went to the wall cupboards and slid back a door and took out a soft quilt. She hesitated. The quilt was covered with flowered silk and the lining was pure white silk.

"He is so dirty," she murmured in distress.

"Yes, he had better be washed," Sadao agreed. "If you will fetch hot water I will wash him."

"I cannot bear for you to touch him," she said. "We shall have to tell the servants he is here. I will tell Yumi now. She can leave the children for a few minutes and she can wash him."

Sadao considered a moment. "Let it be so," he agreed. "You tell Yumi and I will tell the others."

But the utter pallor of the man's unconscious face moved him first to stoop and feel his pulse. It was faint but it was there. He put his hand against the man's cold breast. The heart too was yet alive.

"He will die unless he is operated on," Sadao said, considering. "The question is whether he will not die anyway."

Hana cried out in fear. "Don't try to save him! What if he should live?"

"What if he should die?" Sadao replied. He stood gazing down on the motionless man. This man must have extraordinary vitality or he would have been dead by now. But then he was very young—perhaps not yet twenty-five.

"You mean die from the operation?" Hana asked.

"Yes," Sadao said.

Hana considered this doubtfully, and when she did not answer Sadao turned away. "At any rate something must be done with him," he said, "and first he must be washed." He went quickly out of the room and Hana came behind him. She did not wish to be left alone with the white man. He was the first she had seen since she left America and now he seemed to have nothing to do with those whom she had known there. Here he was her enemy, a menace, living or dead.

She turned to the nursery and called, "Yumi!"

But the children heard her voice and she had to go in for a moment and smile at them and play with the baby boy, now nearly three months old.

Over the baby's soft black hair she motioned with her mouth, "Yumi—come with me!"

"I will put the baby to bed," Yumi replied. "He is ready."

She went with Yumi into the bedroom next to the nursery and stood with the boy in her arms while Yumi spread the sleeping quilts on the floor and laid the baby between them.

Then Hana led the way quickly and softly to the kitchen. The two servants were frightened at what their master had just told them. The old gardener who was also a house servant pulled the few hairs on his upper lip.

"The master ought not to heal the wound of this white man," he said bluntly to Hana. "The white man ought to die. First he was shot. Then the sea caught him and wounded him with her rocks. If the master heals what the gun did and what the sea did they will take revenge on us."

"I will tell him what you say," Hana replied courteously. But she herself was also frightened, although she was not superstitious as the old man was. Could it ever be well to help an enemy? Nevertheless she told Yumi to fetch the hot water and bring it to the room where the white man was.

She went ahead and slid back the partitions. Sadao was not yet there. Yumi, following, put down her wooden bucket. Then she went over to the white man. When she saw him her thick lips folded themselves into stubbornness. "I have never washed a white man," she said, "and I will not wash so dirty a one now."

Hana cried at her severely, "You will do what your master commands you!"

"My master ought not to command me to wash the enemy," Yumi said stubbornly.

There was so fierce a look of resistance upon Yumi's round dull face that Hana felt unreasonably afraid. After all, if the servants should report something that was not as it happened?

"Very well," she said with dignity. "You understand we only want to bring him to his senses so that we can turn him over as a prisoner?"

"I will have nothing to do with it," Yumi said. "I am a poor person and it is not my business."

"Then please," Hana said gently, "return to your own work."

At once Yumi left the room. But this left Hana with the white man alone. She might have been too afraid to stay had not her anger at Yumi's stubbornness now sustained her.

"Stupid Yumi," she muttered fiercely. "Is this anything but a man? And a wounded, helpless man!"

In the conviction of her own superiority she bent impulsively and untied the knotted rags that kept the white man covered. When she had his breast bare she dipped the small clean towel that Yumi had brought into the steaming hot water and washed his face carefully. The man's skin, though rough with exposure, was of a fine texture and must have been very blond when he was a child.

While she was thinking these thoughts, though not really liking the man better now that he was no longer a child, she kept on washing him until his upper body was quite clean. But she dared not turn him over. Where was Sadao? Now her anger was ebbing and she was anxious again and she rose, wiping her hands on the wrung towel. Then lest the man be chilled she put the quilt over him.

"Sadao!" she called softly.

He had been about to come in when she called. His hand had been on the door and now he opened it. She saw that he had brought his surgeon's emergency bag and that he wore his surgeon's coat.

"You have decided to operate!" she cried.

"Yes," he said shortly. He turned his back to her and unfolded a sterilized towel upon the floor of the *takonoma* alcove, and put his instruments out upon it.

"Fetch towels," he said.

She went obediently, but how anxious now, to the linen shelves and took out the towels. There ought also to be old pieces of matting so that the blood would not ruin the fine floor covering. She went out to the back veranda where the gardener kept strips of matting with which to protect delicate shrubs on cold nights and took an armful of them.

But when she went back into the room she saw this was useless. The blood had already soaked through the packing in the man's wound and had ruined the mat under him.

"Oh, the mat!" she cried.

"Yes, it is ruined," Sadao replied, as though he did not care. "Help me to turn him," he commanded her.

She obeyed him without a word, and he began to wash the man's back carefully.

"Yumi would not wash him," she said.

"Did you wash him, then?" Sadao asked, not stopping for a moment his swift concise movements.

"Yes," she said.

He did not seem to hear her. But she was used to his absorption when he was at work. She wondered for a moment if it mattered to him what was the body upon which he worked so long as it was for the work he did so excellently.

"You will have to give the anesthetic if he needs it," he said.

"I?" she repeated blankly. "But never have I!"

"It is easy enough," he said impatiently.

He was taking out the packing now and the blood began to flow more quickly. He peered into the wound with the bright surgeon's light fastened on his forehead. "The bullet is still there," he said with cool interest. "Now I wonder how deep this rock wound is. If it is not too deep it may be that I can get the bullet. But the bleeding is not superficial. He has lost much blood."

At this moment Hana choked. He looked up and saw her face the color of sulphur.

"Don't faint," he said sharply. He did not put down his exploring instrument. "If I stop now the man will surely die." She clapped her hands to her mouth and leaped up and ran out of the room. Outside in the garden he heard her retching. But he went on with his work.

"It will be better for her to empty her stomach," he thought. He had forgotten that of course she had never seen an operation. But her distress and his inability to go to her at once made him impatient and irritable with this man who lay like dead under his knife.

"This man," he thought, "there is no reason under heaven why he should live."

Unconsciously this thought made him ruthless and he proceeded swiftly. In his dream the man moaned, but Sadao paid no heed except to mutter at him.

"Groan," he muttered, "groan if you like. I am not doing this for my own pleasure. In fact, I do not know why I am doing it."

The door opened and there was Hana again. She had not stopped even to smooth back her hair.

"Where is the anesthetic?" she asked in a clear voice.

Sadao motioned with his chin. "It is as well that you came back," he said. "This fellow is beginning to stir."

She had the bottle and some cotton in her hand.

"But how shall I do it?" she asked.

"Simply saturate the cotton and hold it near his nostrils," Sadao replied without delaying for one moment the intricate detail of his work. "When he breathes badly move it away a little."

She crouched close to the sleeping face of the young American. It was a piteously thin face, she thought, and the lips were twisted. The man was suffering whether he knew it or not. Watching him, she wondered if the stories they heard sometimes of the sufferings of prisoners were true. They came like flickers of rumor, told by word of mouth and always contradicted. In the newspapers the reports were always that wherever the Japanese armies went the people received them gladly, with cries of joy at their liberation. But sometimes she remembered such men as General Takima, who at home beat his wife cruelly, though no one mentioned it now that he had fought so victorious a battle in Manchuria. If a man like that could be so cruel to a woman in his power, would he not be cruel to one like this for instance?

She hoped anxiously that this young man had not been tortured. It was at this moment that she observed deep red scars on his neck, just under the ear. "Those scars," she murmured, lifting her eyes to Sadao.

But he did not answer. At this moment he felt the tip of his instrument strike against something hard, dangerously near the kidney. All thought left him. He felt only the purest pleasure. He probed with his fingers, delicately, familiar with every atom of this human body. His old American professor of anatomy had seen to that knowledge. "Ignorance of the human body is the surgeon's cardinal sin, sirs!" he had thundered at his classes year after year. "To operate without as complete knowledge of the body as if you had made it—anything less than that is murder."

"It is not quite at the kidney, my friend," Sadao murmured. It was his habit to murmur to the patient when he forgot himself in an operation. "My friend," he always called his patients and so now he did, forgetting that this was his enemy.

Then quickly, with the cleanest and most precise of incisions, the bullet was out. The man quivered but he was still unconscious. Nevertheless he muttered a few English words.

"Guts," he muttered, choking. "They got . . . my guts . . ."

"Sadao!" Hana cried sharply.

"Hush," Sadao said.

The man sank again into silence so profound that Sadao took up his wrist, hating the touch of it. Yes, there was still a pulse so faint, so feeble, but enough, if he wanted the man to live, to give hope.

"But certainly I do not want this man to live," he thought.

"No more anesthetic," he told Hana.

He turned as swiftly as though he had never paused and from his medicines he chose a small vial and from it filled a hypodermic and thrust it into the patient's left arm. Then, putting down the needle, he took the man's wrist again. The pulse under his fingers fluttered once or twice and then grew stronger.

"This man will live in spite of all," he said to Hana and sighed.

The young man woke, so weak, his blue eyes so terrified when he perceived where he was, that Hana felt compelled to apology. She served him herself, for none of the servants would enter the room.

When she came in the first time she saw him summon his small strength to be prepared for some fearful thing.

"Don't be afraid," she begged him softly.

"How come . . . you speak English?" he gasped.

"I was a long time in America," she replied.

She saw that he wanted to reply to that but he could not, and so she knelt and fed him gently from the porcelain spoon. He ate unwillingly, but still he ate.

"Now you will soon be strong," she said, not liking him and yet moved to comfort him.

He did not answer.

When Sadao came in the third day after the operation he found the young man sitting up, his face bloodless with the effort.

"Lie down," Sadao cried. "Do you want to die?"

He forced the man down gently and strongly and examined the wound. "You may kill yourself if you do this sort of thing," he scolded.

"What are you going to do with me?" the boy muttered. He looked just now barely seventeen. "Are you going to hand me over?"

For a moment Sadao did not answer. He finished his examination and then pulled the silk quilt over the man.

"I do not know myself what I shall do with you," he said. "I ought of course to give you to the police. You are a prisoner of war—no, do not tell me anything." He put up his hand as he saw the young man about to speak. "Do not even tell me your name unless I ask it."

They looked at each other for a moment, and then the young man closed his eyes and turned his face to the wall.

"Okay," he whispered, his mouth a bitter line.

Outside the door Hana was waiting for Sadao. He saw at once that she was in trouble.

"Sadao, Yumi tells me the servants feel they cannot stay if we hide this man here any more," she said. "She tells me that they are saying that you and I were so long in America that we have forgotten to think of our own country first. They think we like Americans."

"It is not true," Sadao said harshly, "Americans are our enemies. But I have been trained not to let a man die if I can help it."

"The servants cannot understand that," she said anxiously.

"No," he agreed.

Neither seemed able to say more, and somehow the household dragged on. The servants grew daily more watchful. Their courtesy was as careful as ever, but their eyes were cold upon the pair to whom they were hired.

"It is clear what our master ought to do," the old gardener said one morning. He had worked with flowers all his life, and had been a specialist too in moss. For Sadao's father he had made one of the finest moss gardens in Japan, sweeping the bright green carpet constantly so that not a leaf or a pine needle marred the velvet of its surface. "My old master's son knows very well what he ought to do," he now said, pinching a bud from a bush as he spoke. "When the man was so near death why did he not let him bleed?"

"That young master is so proud of his skill to save life that he saves any life," the cook said contemptuously. She split a fowl's neck skillfully and held the fluttering bird and let its blood flow into the roots of a wistaria vine. Blood is the best of fertilizers, and the old gardener would not let her waste a drop of it.

"It is the children of whom we must think," Yumi said sadly. "What will be their fate if their father is condemned as a traitor?"

They did not try to hide what they said from the ears of Hana as she stood arranging the day's flowers in the veranda near by, and she knew they spoke on purpose that she might hear. That they were right she knew too in most of her being. But there was another part of her which she herself could not understand. It was not sentimental liking of the prisoner. She had come to think of him as a prisoner. She had not liked him even yesterday when he had said in his impulsive way, "Anyway, let me tell you that my name is Tom." She had only bowed her little distant bow. She saw hurt in his eyes but she did not wish to assuage it. Indeed, he was a great trouble in this house.

As for Sadao, every day he examined the wound carefully. The last stitches had been pulled out this morning, and the young man would in a fortnight be nearly as well as ever. Sadao went back to his office and carefully typed a letter to the chief of police reporting the whole matter. "On the twenty-first day of February an escaped prisoner was washed up on the shore in front of my house." So far he typed and then he opened a secret drawer of his desk and put the unfinished report into it.

On the seventh day after that two things happened. In the morning the servants left together, their belongings tied in large square cotton kerchiefs. When Hana got up in the morning nothing was done, the house not cleaned and the food not prepared, and she knew what it meant. She was dismayed and even terrified, but her pride as a mistress would not allow her to show it. Instead she inclined her head gracefully when they appeared before her in the kitchen, and she paid them off and thanked them for all that they had done for her. They were crying, but she did not cry. The cook and the gardener had served Sadao since he was a little boy in his father's house, and Yumi cried because of the children. She was so grieving that after she had gone she ran back to Hana.

"If the baby misses me too much tonight send for me. I am going to my own house and you know where it is."

"Thank you," Hana said, smiling. But she told herself she would not send for Yumi however the baby cried.

She made the breakfast and Sadao helped with the children. Neither of them spoke of the servants beyond the fact that they were gone. But after Hana had taken morning food to the prisoner she came back to Sadao.

"Why is it we cannot see clearly what we ought to do?" she asked him. "Even the servants see more clearly than we do. Why are we different from other Japanese?"

Sadao did not answer. But a little later he went into the room where the prisoner was and said brusquely, "Today you may get up on your feet. I want you to stay up only five minutes at a time. Tomorrow you may try it twice as long. It would be well that you get back your strength as quickly as possible."

He saw the flicker of terror on the young face that was still very pale.

"Okay," the boy murmured. Evidently he was determined to say more. "I feel I ought to thank you, Doctor, for having saved my life."

"Don't thank me too early," Sadao said coldly. He saw the flicker of terror again in the boy's eyes—terror as unmistakable as an animal's. The scars on his neck were crimson for a moment. Those scars! What were they? Sadao did not ask.

In the afternoon the second thing happened. Hana, working hard on unaccustomed labor, saw a messenger come to the door in official uniform. Her hands went weak and she could not draw her breath. The servants must have told already. She ran to Sadao, gasping, unable to utter a word. But by then the messenger had simply followed her through the garden and there he stood. She pointed at him helplessly.

Sadao looked up from his book. He was in his office, the outer partition of which was thrown open to the garden for the southern sunshine.

"What is it?" he asked the messenger, and then he rose, seeing the man's uniform.

"You are to come to the palace," the man said, "the old General is in pain again."

"Oh," Hana breathed, "is that all?"

"All!" the messenger exclaimed. "Is it not enough?"

"Indeed it is," she replied. "I am very sorry."

When Sadao came to say good-by she was in the kitchen, but doing nothing. The children were asleep and she sat merely resting for a moment, more exhausted from her fright than from work.

"I thought they had come to arrest you," she said.

He gazed down into her anxious eyes. "I must get rid of this man for your sake," he said in distress. "Somehow I must get rid of him."

"Of course," the General said weakly, "I understand fully. But that is because I once took a degree in Princeton. So few Japanese have."

"I care nothing for the man, Excellency," Sadao said, "but having operated on him with such success . . ."

"Yes, yes," the General said. "It only makes me feel you more indispensable to me. Evidently you can save anyone—you are so skilled. You say you think I can stand one more such attack as I have had today?"

"Not more than one," Sadao said.

"Then certainly I can allow nothing to happen to you," the General said with anxiety. His long, pale, Japanese face became expressionless, which meant that he was in deep thought. "You cannot be arrested," the General said, closing his eyes. "Suppose you were condemned to death and the next day I had to have my operation?"

"There are other surgeons, Excellency," Sadao suggested.

"None I trust," the General replied. "The best ones have been trained by Germans and would consider the operation successful even if I died. I do not care for their point of view." He sighed. "It seems a pity that we cannot better combine the German ruthlessness with the American sentimentality. Then you could turn your prisoner over to execution and yet I could be sure you would not murder me while I was unconscious." The General laughed. He had an unusual sense of humor. "As a Japanese, could you not combine these two foreign elements?" he asked.

Sadao smiled. "I am not quite sure," he said, "but for your sake I would be willing to try, Excellency."

The General shook his head. "I had rather not be the test case," he said. He felt suddenly weak and overwhelmed with the cares of his life as an official in times such as these when repeated victory brought great responsibilities all over the south Pacific. "It is very unfortunate that this man should have washed up on your doorstep," he said irritably.

"I feel it so myself," Sadao said gently.

"It would be best if he could be quietly killed," the General said. "Not by you, but by someone who does not know him. I have my own private assassins. Suppose I send two of them to your house tonight—or better, any night. You need know nothing about it. It is now warm—what would be more natural than that you should leave the outer partition of the white man's room open to the garden while he sleeps?"

"Certainly it would be very natural," Sadao agreed. "In fact, it is so left open every night."

"Good," the General said, yawning. "They are very capable assassins—they make no noise and they know the trick of inward bleeding. If you like I can even have them remove the body."

Sadao considered. "That perhaps would be best, Excellency," he agreed, thinking of Hana.

He left the General's presence then and went home, thinking over the plan. In this way the whole thing would be taken out of his hands. He would tell Hana nothing, since she would be timid at the idea of assassins in the house, and yet certainly such persons were essential in an absolute state such as Japan was. How else could rulers deal with those who opposed them?

He refused to allow anything but reason to be the atmosphere of his mind as he went into the room where the American was in bed. But as he opened the door, to his surprise he found the young man out of bed, and preparing to go into the garden.

"What is this!" he exclaimed. "Who gave you permission to leave your room?"

"I'm not used to waiting for permission," Tom said gaily. "Gosh, I feel pretty good again! But will the muscles on this side always feel stiff?"

"Is it so?" Sadao inquired, surprised. He forgot all else. "Now I thought I had provided against that," he murmured. He lifted the edge of the man's shirt and gazed at the healing scar. "Massage may do it," he said, "if exercise does not."

"It won't bother me much," the young man said. His young face was gaunt under the stubbly blond beard. "Say, Doctor, I've got something I want to say to you. If I hadn't met a Jap like you—well, I wouldn't be alive today. I know that."

Sadao bowed but he could not speak.

"Sure, I know that," Tom went on warmly. His big thin hands, gripping a chair, were white at the knuckles. "I guess if all the Japs were like you there wouldn't have been a war."

"Perhaps," Sadao said with difficulty. "And now I think you had better go back to bed."

He helped the boy back into bed and then bowed. "Good night," he said.

Sadao slept badly that night. Time and time again he woke, thinking he heard the rustling of footsteps, the sound of a twig broken or a stone displaced in the garden—a noise such as men might make who carried a burden.

The next morning he made the excuse to go first into the guest room. If the American were gone he then could simply tell Hana that so the General had directed. But when he opened the door he saw at once that it was not last night. There on the pillow was the shaggy blond head. He could hear the peaceful breathing of sleep and he closed the door again quietly.

"He is asleep," he told Hana. "He is almost well to sleep like that."

"What shall we do with him?" Hana whispered her old refrain.

Sadao shook his head. "I must decide in a day or two," he promised.

But certainly, he thought, the second night must be the night. There rose a wind that night, and he listened to the sounds of bending boughs and whistling partitions.

Hana woke too. "Ought we not to go and close the sick man's partition?" she asked.

"No," Sadao said. "He is able now to do it for himself."

But the next morning the American was still there.

Then the third night of course must be the night. The wind changed to quiet rain and the garden was full of the sound of dripping eaves and running springs. Sadao slept a little better, but he woke at the sound of a crash and leaped to his feet.

"What was that?" Hana cried. The baby woke at her voice and began to wail. "I must go and see."

But he held her and would not let her move.

"Sadao," she cried, "what is the matter with you?"

"Don't go," he muttered, "don't go!"

His terror infected her and she stood breathless, waiting. There was only silence. Together they crept back into the bed, the baby between them.

Yet when he opened the door of the guest room in the morning there was the young man. He was very gay and had already washed and was now on his feet. He had asked for a razor yesterday and had shaved himself, and today there was a faint color in his cheeks.

"I am well," he said joyously.

Sadao drew his kimono round his weary body. He could not, he decided suddenly, go through another night. It was not that he cared for this young man's life. No, simply it was not worth the strain.

"You are well," Sadao agreed. He lowered his voice. "You are so well that I think if I put my boat on the shore tonight, with food and extra clothing in it, you might be able to row to that little island not far from the coast. It is so near the coast that it has not been worth fortifying. Nobody lives on it because in storm it is submerged. But this is not the season of storm. You could live there until you saw a Korean fishing boat pass by. They pass quite near the island because the water is many fathoms deep there."

The young man stared at him, slowly comprehending. "Do I have to?" he asked.

"I think so," Sadao said gently. "You understand—it is not hidden that you are here."

The young man nodded in perfect comprehension. "Okay," he said simply.

Sadao did not see him again until evening. As soon as it was dark he had dragged the stout boat down to the shore and in it he put food and bottled water that he had bought secretly during the day, as well as two quilts he had bought at a pawnshop. The boat he tied to a post in the water, for the tide was high. There was no moon and he worked without a flashlight.

When he came to the house he entered as though he were just back from his work, and so Hana knew nothing. "Yumi was here today," she said as she served his supper. Though she was so modern, still she did not eat with him. "Yumi cried over the baby," she went on with a sigh. "She misses him so."

"The servants will come back as soon as the foreigner is gone," Sadao said.

He went into the guest room that night before he went to bed and himself checked carefully the American's temperature, the state of the wound, and his heart and pulse. The pulse was irregular, but that was perhaps because of excitement. The young man's pale lips were pressed together and his eyes burned. Only the scars on his neck were red.

"I realize you are saving my life again," he told Sadao.

"Not at all," Sadao said. "It is only inconvenient to have you here any longer."

He had hesitated a good deal about giving the man a flashlight. But he had decided to give it to him after all. It was a small one, his own, which he used at night when he was called.

"If your food runs out before you catch a boat," he said, "signal me two flashes at the same instant the sun drops over the horizon. Do not signal in darkness, for it will be seen. If you are all right but still there, signal me once. You will find fish easy to catch but you must eat them raw. A fire would be seen."

"Okay," the young man breathed.

He was dressed now in the Japanese clothes which Sadao had given him, and at the last moment Sadao wrapped a black cloth about his blond head.

"Now," Sadao said.

The young American without a word shook Sadao's hand warmly and then walked quite well across the floor and down the step into the darkness of the garden. Once—twice—Sadao saw his light flash to find his way. But that would not be suspected. He waited until from the shore there was one more flash. Then he closed the partition. That night he slept.

"You say the man escaped?" the General asked faintly. He had been operated upon a week before, an emergency operation to which Sadao had been called in the night. For twelve hours Sadao had not been sure the General would live. The gall bladder was much involved. Then the old man had begun to breathe deeply again and to demand food. Sadao had not been able to ask about the assassins. So far as he knew they had never come. The servants had returned and Yumi had cleaned the guest room thoroughly and had burned sulphur in it to get the white man's smell out of it. Nobody said anything. Only the gardener was cross because he had got behind with his chrysanthemums.

But after a week Sadao felt the General was well enough to be spoken to about the prisoner.

"Yes, Excellency, he escaped," Sadao now said. He coughed, signifying that he had not said all he might have said but was unwilling to disturb the General further. But the old man opened his eyes suddenly.

"That prisoner," he said with some energy, "did I not promise you I would kill him for you?"

"You did, Excellency," Sadao said.

"Well, well!" the old man said in a tone of amazement, "so I did! But you see, I was suffering a good deal. The truth is, I thought of nothing but myself. In short, I forgot my promise to you."

"I wondered, Your Excellency," Sadao murmured.

"It was certainly very careless of me," the General said. "But you understand it was not lack of patriotism or dereliction of duty." He looked anxiously at his doctor. "If the matter should come out you would understand that, wouldn't you?"

"Certainly, Your Excellency," Sadao said. He suddenly comprehended that the General was in the palm of his hand and that as a consequence he himself was perfectly safe. "I can swear to your loyalty, Excellency," he said to the old General, "and to your zeal against the enemy."

"You are a good man," the General murmured, and closed his eyes. "You will be rewarded."

But Sadao, searching the spot of black in the twilighted sea that night, had his reward. There was no prick of light in the dusk. No one was on the island. His prisoner was gone—safe, doubtless, for he had warned him to wait only for a Korean fishing boat.

He stood for a moment on the veranda, gazing out to the sea from whence the young man had come that other night. And into his mind, although without reason, there came other white faces he had known—the professor at whose house he had met Hana, a dull man, and his wife had been a silly, talkative woman, in spite of her wish to be kind. He remembered his old teacher of anatomy, who had been so insistent on mercy with the knife, and then he remembered the face of his fat and slatternly landlady. He had had great difficulty in finding a place to live in America because he was a Japanese. The Americans were full of prejudice and it had been bitter to live in it, knowing himself their superior. How he had despised the ignorant and dirty old woman who had at last consented to house him in her miserable home! He had once tried to be grateful to her because she had in his last year nursed him through influenza, but it was difficult, for she was no less repulsive to him in her kindness. But then, white people were repulsive of course. It was a relief to be openly at war with them at last. Now he remembered the youthful, haggard face of his prisoner—white and repulsive.

"Strange," he thought, "I wonder why I could not kill him?"

THE ASCENT OF ARIEL GOODBODY

By Walter Van Tilburg Clark

From the *Yale Review*

WALTER VAN TILBURG CLARK

was born August 3, 1909, in Maine. His first published short story was in the O. Henry Memorial Award Prize Stories of 1941, *"Hook," from the* Atlantic. *The 1942 volume included "The Portable Phonograph," from the* Yale Review. *Mr. Clark was brought up in West Nyack, New York, and later in Reno, Nevada, where his father was president of the State University of Nevada. After being graduated from there Mr. Clark received a fellowship for two years at the University of Vermont. He taught one year at the College of the City of New York, but since that time has taught in Cazenovia, New York, where he coaches sports and dramatics. He is married and has two children.*

His first work was mainly poetry. His first novel, The Ox-Bow Incident, *in 1940, received high critical praise and was also a movie. He has just finished a new novel,* The City of Trembling Leaves.

Ariel goodbody spent his boyhood with protruding ears and a fervid imagination in the region depicted by Charles Burchfield and among the people of Grant Wood. This setting, and the fact that his father spoke seldom and loudly and his mother never, drove him early into dreams, and these, in turn, to an outlet through his pencil. At six he made a realistic sketch of a barbed-wire fence. At eight he portrayed a sleeping cat, showing nearly every hair. At twelve he painted a portrait of his favorite mare, which had in the eyes something of the luminous appeal of an Italian Madonna, and at fourteen he began to put forth an endless flow of adolescent female figures, reduced in years and slightly reduced in garments from originals in the *Police Gazette*. Clearly, he hungered to escape from arid realism, although nothing in his surroundings encouraged this urge. His father tolerated his work because, as he often said, "The brat will never be fit for an honest day's work anyway," and, "Who cares what happens to such a no-good anyway?" and his mother never noticed what he was doing. It is true that his latter works would have won popularity with his contemporaries, but his instinctive sense of their detestably academic nature is indicated by the fact that he kept all the drawings under the shirt in his bureau drawer, and took them out only at night, in order to be moved toward something better. He even slept with them under his pillow, that they might instruct his dreams, in which he had the faith of genius. In this spiritual isolation he was physically lonely also, and took a morbid delight in going out alone to watch clouded sunsets or at night to keep trysts with imaginary, gauze-clad nymphs in the bushes by the creek.

He might never have surmounted this environment had it not been for an accident, painful at the time. Mr. Goodbody discovered him one day in the hayloft, completing a nude proportioned somewhat after a news photo of Sally Rand, but reclining in a stimulating position in the hollow of a familiar wood lot and wearing the mistily recognizable features of the neighbor's sixteen-year-old daughter. Mr. Goodbody said rather critically, "What the hell kind of filth is this?" and after some uneasy preliminaries learned of the previous studies and took them off to determine the extent of his son's default—a matter so intricate that he retained the evidence for re-examination. He had never expected intelligent counsel from his wife, so he merely remarked to her, in effect, that if that Brown girl, who had premature inclinations, appeared again, he would take active measures following an exposure of her outstanding characteristic. His wife supported him more ardently than usual, saying, "Yes, Albert."

Ariel, unable to rest after his father's rebuke, went for a walk. It was a sullen, windy day in November. The road stretched direct and rolling before him, and flocks of migratory birds swept over with plaintive sounds. Cheered by the agreeable accompaniment, Ariel walked farther than ever before and, arriving at a strange crossroad, stood to gaze up at its finger post. NEW YORK 1542 mi., said the most entrancing pointer.

"May I be subject to a violent physical abuse if I remain here longer," Ariel said in his own way.

"You are evidently a man of strong passions," remarked a deep voice.

The stranger, who had come up unheard in the wind, was as tall and thin as Ariel, and resembled a projection of the boy thirty years into the future, providing he should become so immersed in his work as to neglect all else save a few basic physical necessities. There were the same intense, protuberant eyes gazing inward, the same thin, white, triangular face, the same stooping shoulders and pendulous, unquiet hands. This likeness at once established a bond between them, in spite of a few superficial differences, Ariel's hair being merely uncut, while the stranger's was deliberately combed to his shoulders and mated by a thin beard set off by a broad-brimmed black hat, a long black cloak, and a black leather portfolio.

"In fact, a young man of genius," the stranger said, staring. "I am drawn to you. Our blood is akin in this unlivable place, in an undying pact against ugliness." He swept his bony hand scornfully across prairie and sky.

Then he poked Ariel suddenly in the chest with a forefinger. "You are an artist."

"Don't talk," he said when Ariel tried to answer. "You are also a fool, since you live here. Your conversation would be idiotic."

He flung his portfolio upon the roadside and ferociously extracted paper and charcoal.

"Draw something. Anything," he ordered, glaring.

Ariel worked carefully upon the scene before him, which included a windmill, a dead tree, and some grass. He had not completed the outline when the stranger snatched the paper.

"Atrocious," he said. "Abominable.

"Still," he said, "there is the desire, though your soul is still a camera.

"Look," he said, crumpling the drawing, seizing the charcoal with one hand and another piece of paper with the other and beginning to make rapid, sweeping strokes. "It is only a note, a suggestion," he said, "but I know my own soul. Nothing I do is without the touch. To capture the abstracted spirit of the subject, entirely in the tone of one's own inimitable soul, that is everything. And with haste, haste, haste. Give the psyche wings." And he blocked in the last angular area with the side of the charcoal.

"What do you see?" he roared, holding up the composition.

"Well——" Ariel began.

"Never mind," said the stranger quickly, carefully inserting the drawing into the portfolio. "You have the soul of a photographer, and labor in dung. Children are nasty things, the vile result of their parents' disgusting urge to perpetuate themselves, being unable to conceive anything less ugly. I would be wholly unable to reconcile myself to children, excepting beautiful girls of fifteen or more, if their appalling numbers were not necessary in order to produce, once in a century, a soul like mine.

"Don't become angry, you yokel," he said. "Would I waste wisdom if I did not perceive in you the nucleus, infinitesimal and revoltingly gelatinous, but a nucleus nonetheless, which, nurtured in the glorious plasma of life, may in time swell to a soul?

"How," he asked, rising with the portfolio under his arm and sweeping the dismal horizon again, "how, even with the inclinations of a saint, would a soul flower in this ordure?

"It makes me unhappy," he stormed.

He grasped Ariel's arm and began to walk him rapidly along the road. "You can't stay here," he yelled. "You must come with me and swim in life. We will create you a soul. I will fill your mind with little bright angels and introduce you to women who don't have to be kept in a sty. I will teach you to see the thing itself, not its stupid manifestations.

"Do you know anything about color?" he bawled. "Do you know anything about the impression? Do you know anything about pure form, rescued from all vulgar similitude? Do you know anything?

"Of course you don't," he interrupted furiously. "You even believe other people have a right to be alive. You will learn. They are all fools. They do not even know the difference between civilization and culture. Nobody since primitive man has had any culture. Now everything is a ghastly academic brown. Turner used color, they say. Bah. Like a painter of barns, but his soul still saw brown. El Greco created original forms, they say. Contamination. Mere vulgar distortion."

He continued to talk torrentially, jerking Ariel's arm around with his gestures. He condemned a thousand painters by name, as academic, and proved that a thousand different theories of art were degenerate. There was nothing, he said, between the primitives and himself which counted, and the primitives deserved no credit because they were naturally childish. Rembrandt was abominably black; Michelangelo, grossly realistic; Leonardo, a dull technician. Even Picasso believed he had to look at something, and Braque was a queasy sentimentalist.

This flood of revelation dazed Ariel's mind. He remembered only one statement, because it was repeated innumerable times. "Only one artist counts, the artist who will have nothing to do with the past, the artist who does not fiddle with technique, the artist who is impelled to ascend immediately into a heaven of his own and work dangerously, the artist who will work so far into the unknown that even he is in constant doubt as to what he is doing. The rest are nothing. They are dirt. They are disciples. I trample on them." Ariel did not fully comprehend this at the time, but he remembered it because it was in keeping with his own mood at the moment.

He became an ardent disciple of the volcanic stranger, whose name was Christopolus, and went with him to Paris, where they lived in an interesting attic, supported by innumerable less talented disciples and a few stupid purchasers, whom Christopolus loved to gather around him for hours so long as they did not talk also. There they explored not only the trackless empyrean of freed art, but also the whole life of the world for hours at a time with cigarettes and wine in all the studios, cafés, and bedrooms of the neighborhood. "To live," Christopolus often bellowed, "to delight in all the intricacies of pornographic abominations as much as in the purer elixir of an unphilosophical metaphysic, that is the only way to freedom," and they would pursue this theory with fiery practice for weeks together rather than become enslaved by their materials. Ariel was so thoroughly converted that when he was twenty he let his hair and beard grow and thinned them with tweezers. He chose, however, rather than become a mere imitator of even so great a master as Christopolus, to populate his conversation with fiends and scenes from the inferno instead of the angels and saints in which Christopolus delighted, and to turn for inspiration to the African primitives and brunettes in place of the pre-Inca stone sculptures and blondes which Christopolus preferred. He also constructed a metaphysic founded on the pleasures of sin to oppose to Christopolus' metaphysic of the sinlessness of pleasure, and drank whisky instead of port. All of these tendencies Christopolus berated as misanthropic, but secretly they pleased him, since they did away with conflict in several fundamental experiments. In only one important principle did Ariel never depart from Christopolus. The master thus stated this principle: "When anyone likes your work, throw it away. They are all cows, bourgeoisie. They have the gray middle minds, and can never hope to ascend to pure light and the music of angels. Besides, they will love you all the more, and buy everything." Ariel rephrased this principle: "When anyone is fascinated by your work, throw it away. They are all swine, guzzlers of German beer. They think in middle-class morals and dread the secret light of hell. Besides, they will be more than ever in awe of you, and buy everything." But these differences, naturally, did not split them in their pursuit of an almost identical ideal.

When Ariel was thirty, Christopolus died from the fever of his explorations. The attic became unbearable without him, and Ariel went to New York. This seemed at the time an unfortunate move. He was shortly discovered by a middle-aged brunette, a Mrs. Blacklane, who was really glad of his companionship, having been lonely sometimes since her last husband had jumped off the George Washington Bridge, leaving only a cryptic message to the effect that he was sick to death of her damned chatter. And Mrs. Blacklane finally permitted him to move into an interesting warehouse by the East River, and set a schedule for her visits which left time for the somewhat younger brunette who came in to do his dishes and other things. So materially he was well fixed. But in the gloom and uproar of New York, and without the dynamic presence of Christopolus, he became mired in doubts as to the originality of his work, though none of it sold, and at last he ceased painting altogether, and spent his time pacing about the warehouse, wrestling with his spirit. At the end of a year this frustration was so advanced that he dismissed the younger brunette and even succeeded in making an arrangement, with a slightly diminished stipend, whereby he saw Mrs. Blacklane only once a week at her own home. He moved from the warehouse, which began to seem forbidding, into a single room in an old brownstone house, where he pursued his flagellations in peace. Here he finally became so enraged at the influence of Christopolus, which he began to see in everything he had done, and to believe an impure abstraction anyway, with detestable remnants of recognizable form and even of intellectual implications, that he shaved off his beard and hair, undertook a diet of black beans and German beer, attired himself in a rough black robe, and, barefooted before his easel, set about discovering an entirely new style, far beyond Christopolus, in a realm of which he was himself in doubt.

He experienced more success than might have been expected in this quest. It is true that he still endured long hours of misery, when he would sit in a corner gnawing his knuckles or make a penitential pilgrimage of his pacing, further tormented because he kept finding no hair or beard to pull. But he also had periods of illumination, when the vision, in its perfectly abstracted form, and with a rhythm and palette entirely new, would appear before him complete, and he could not work fast enough. In searching the elaborations and profundities of his psyche, he came to credit these inspirations in part to the room in which he worked, where he had felt peculiarly at home from the first. Other influences loosed their hold upon him there, and for the first time he felt roots of his own creeping down into truth and expanding to suck up the moisture of life. It was a simple chamber, containing only his working materials, a couch, a washstand, an old tapestried spring rocker, and a small coal stove, the long black neck of which reached nearly to the ceiling and then plunged into the wall.

All these things, though actually strange, were spiritually familiar. The stove was much like the one over which his mother had dreamed. The couch was akin to an abandoned one on the back porch of the farmhouse. In his own room there had been a similar washstand, with an identical flowered pitcher and basin. The rocker, so worn that its colors were nearly one, had a brother on the front porch in the summer, from which he had watched the chickens scratch the dirt of the front yard. Even the high windows, threadbare carpet, and faded wallpaper of allover pattern, had their counterparts in the home living room. The wallpaper, of an elaborate combined geometrical and floral design, must once have been much different from that of his home, but now that it had been faded by years to soft pinks and tans, lighted by only flecks of the original gilt, and transfigured by smoke, the innumerable stains of living, and many intriguing sepia tentacles and blotches due to moisture, this difference was negligible. To enter the room became so much like rediscovering himself that Ariel found it more and more difficult to leave it at all. He worked ever harder, constantly destroying, and changed his diet to an even more abstemious one of black coffee, gin, and Mexican cigarettes. He began to dream every night in a most fruitful manner, and to hold exciting conversations with himself during the day, which he recorded in purple ink in a small notebook.

Sometimes, fearing to seem ungrateful, he allowed Mrs. Blacklane to visit the room, and painted her unveiled in numerous positions on the couch, in the old chair, upon the table, surrounded, in good design, by any number of objects of pleasing differences in texture—apples, cracked pitchers, cups, tin forks, bananas, dead flowers, small black fiends, and always detached abstractions of the wallpaper design, of which he was very fond. All these compositions were, of course, marvelously abstracted, yet for Ariel they remained boorish potboilers, perpetrated for the sake of a connection which was actually becoming intolerable, for with advancing years Mrs. Blacklane waxed importunate and sometimes insisted upon staying to get his supper and even longer. Besides this, she was getting fat, and he could find no way to prevent her talking, so that after she left he would have to douse his head repeatedly in cold water to stop the ringing. When, at the end of five years, therefore, he felt his style maturing, and even, through the services of a dealer, Goldiron, whom Mrs. Blacklane had interested, began to sell a few paintings, he severed relations with his patroness and labored with furious contentment, never leaving the room. Those few services he could not render himself were supplied by a dull but full-bodied Irish girl, who acted as a kind of chambermaid to everyone in the decayed mansion.

Regularly, once in six months as prompted by his agenda, Mr. Goldiron paid a visit. He was a most agreeable, small, plump, bald man, and his refrain, invariable save for increasing intensity, was also agreeable.

"My dear Goodbody," he would say, balancing upon the toes of his spatted feet and holding his pince-nez glasses between thumb and finger while his keen eyes priced the display, "my dear Goodbody, you are really quite ready for a show. You have sold a number of excellent canvases. There is interest. My rooms are at your disposal. I assure you that with the impact of a full appearance your reputation will be established, and a very comfortable little sum realized into the bargain."

"I will never be known in my lifetime," Ariel would say harshly. "The world is not ready for me. They are all clods. They have the souls of timetables and drink seltzer water. Let me alone."

At the end of fifteen years of this devoted labor, however, he found himself one morning unable to rise when the Irish girl, now a very mature woman, wished him to rise, and became frightened. When, in the late afternoon, he managed to don his black robe and totter about the beloved chamber, he counted the canvases standing face to the wall, enumerated his years, examined his countenance in the piece of mirror over the washstand, and in the evening surrendered to Mr. Goldiron over the phone in the lower hall. "In six weeks," he said. "I must have six weeks to complete these last two, which are my best."

Mr. Goldiron was enormously enthusiastic. "You will come yourself," he added. "No, no, my dear Goodbody, you positively must appear. There are thousands of people simply wild to meet you. I could name six to you now." And he did. "Your appearance would be the event of the show, in fact, I may say, the apex of my own poor career of appreciation."

In the end Ariel promised to appear, and for the next six weeks found himself cheered by remarkable hopes for a man of his years. He refused to let the Irishwoman into the room for any purpose, painted assiduously, even into the night, dropped sweet gin from his menu, encouraged his beard and hair to resume their Parisian length and restored them to their natural color. At the end of the six weeks Mr. Goldiron himself arrived, with a van.

"I have borrowed your previous sales also," he announced while rapidly counting the canvases. "In all they will number one hundred and thirty-eight; a most impressive display; a massive impact. I have the highest hopes. And you will come with me, my dear Goodbody?"

"Not the first day. Certainly not the first day. Later, perhaps, when your kind illusions have been tested." They settled upon the third day, at a tea reception in the afternoon.

In the meantime Ariel prepared himself by purchasing a flat-brimmed black hat and a long black cloak, and by working gloomily at the account of his life which was now filling the notebook. He was a little disturbed on the evening of the second day to receive a telegram saying, "My dear boy, come home. Your mother has been dead ten years and I am sick.—Albert Goodbody." He did not understand this interest after so long a silence, but resolved it at last, as his notes of that moment prove. "My father," they say, "was never a good farmer, and probably, feeling his land slip from him now, has transformed, well enough to please himself, the fiends which have always been his servants into cupids of love and goddesses of forgiveness not unlike the angels of that vicious old egotist Christopolus, in order to bring home a son who can still plow. Well, forgiveness expands the soul. I will go to him when I have recovered from the animosity aroused by the show, if only to let him see I am no longer the frightened stripling he still conceives me to be. I have thought of much to say to him. My poor mother was an angel indeed, and of an elevation Christopolus never glimpsed. I am heavy with the sin of my negligence."

At three o'clock the next afternoon Ariel combed his thin hair and beard, donned the black hat and cloak, and took a taxi to Goldiron's. On the way he did not look into the street once, but fixed his hyperthyroid gaze before him upon the cruel indignity he was about to suffer. The sidewalk before Goldiron's appeared to have been a scene of violence. It was littered with programs, fragments of women's handbags, bits of canes, and even shreds of clothing and of bank drafts. Ariel steeled himself.

"Poor Goldiron," he said aloud. "I hope he has escaped with life."

He assumed a stern countenance, straightened his hat, and entered. At first, in spite of this preparation, he shrank, for the reception room was indeed a scene of utmost confusion to a man so long alone. When it resolved itself into details, his comprehension was staggered. It was an alarming assemblage, both men and women, all white-haired, comfortably abundant of body, and attired with a completeness and restraint reminiscent of the late nineteenth century. The uproar was a result of numbers only, accompanied by an incessant din of silver and thin china. Ariel recognized an influential, retired banker who was seen these days only in his portrait, a grandmotherly founder of a home for orphaned Siamese cats, an elderly scholar who wrote charmingly concerning Scott, a wealthy amateur who had once briefly championed Winslow Homer and Sargent but had written a delightful apologia and turned to restoring Watteau to favor, a railroad magnate who had barely survived the shock induced by streamliners, a lorgnetted spinster who supported forty-seven missionaries, and a once wealthy manufacturer of barouches. They gazed upon the apparition that was Goodbody with the uniform benevolence of seals basking in the sun. Goldiron appeared and strove toward him through the press, his round face beaming. "Mr. Goodbody," he cried, "Mr. Goodbody," in the accents of one giving thanks for perfect fulfillment, but got no further. The assemblage closed upon Ariel, piping and wheezing his name, and nearly suffocating him with praise, congratulations, and a scent of old lavender. He was faint when Goldiron reached him.

"My dear Goodbody," he said, pumping the long hand. "What did I tell you? An amazing success, even beyond my wildest expectation. Truly the fruiting of your great career and the crowning of mine. The newspapers are full of you from coast to coast. Your ten self-portraits will be reproduced by every photographic magazine in the country. *Zip* wants a full-page spread of you with the girl of the hour, the National will hang five paintings, and *Crown* will devote an entire issue to your work. London and Paris clamor. Every picture has been sold, and after the deduction of my little fee and a few minor expenses such as advertising, catering, flowers, and wires, you will clear nearly two hundred thousand dollars. You are made."

"I must get away," Ariel muttered. "I am unwell." He looked about nervously from under his eyelids for an opening. There was a swell of sympathetic sounds like the sea on a calm day.

"I do not understand," Ariel said. "I must be alone. May I be alone with my canvases, Mr. Goldiron?"

So he entered the back room by himself, in a hush of concerned worship. There he at once felt restored, as if by gentle magic. The gallery of Mr. Goldiron was an old and unpretentious one. The height of the walls and their general contours were not unlike those of Ariel's cell of unremitting labor. All of the one hundred and thirty-eight pictures hung there, and as Ariel moved softly across the worn carpet the profound reason of his content became clear. The one hundred and thirty-eight pictures were of all sizes, and, fitted together, so exactly covered the four walls that their uninterrupted effect made a perfect reproduction, save that the colors were somewhat restored, of the wallpaper of his room in the brownstone mansion, including the marks of time and the sepia tentacles.

Ariel stood with his face lifted and smiled.

"I am original," he whispered.

THE UNFAITHFUL

By Whitfield Cook

From the *American Mercury*

WHITFIELD COOK

was born April 9, 1909, in Bloomfield, New Jersey. He went to high school in Winnetka, Illinois, and to the Yale University School of Fine Arts. He has been writing off and on since childhood, and his first published story appeared in Story *in 1937. In addition to the* American Mercury, *his fiction has appeared in* Mademoiselle, *the* Woman's Home Companion, *and* Redbook. *He is the creator of a popular fiction character, Violet, and stories about her have been appearing in* Redbook *since 1941. A book of that title was published in 1942.*

While Mr. Cook grew up "in a whole series of Midwestern towns in Wisconsin and Illinois," he has lived in the East since 1930, dividing his time between New York and Old Lyme, Connecticut. He spent a little while in Mexico. He has done considerable work in the theater, for which he prepared himself by studying in the Drama Department of Yale. He has been stage manager of numerous plays for various New York producers and also has directed several plays himself. He is at present in Hollywood, writing for the movies.

HAMP had sometimes read about sin in the magazines. In those shiny women's magazines that Lola bought and left around the apartment. It was different when you read about it like that. It was like something out of another world. It was big and glamorous and wicked and soul-shaking. And when you saw sin in the movies it always seemed to go on in beautifully decorated rooms and the girl would be lighted so she looked like a dream, with her eyelashes casting shadows and her lips so perfect. It always seemed awfully important, sin in the movies.

It was not like that, though. Not with Hamp. It was just something that happened, like you caught a cold. And he still couldn't believe it. As he stood there behind the counter washing glasses he still couldn't believe that he'd been unfaithful. For the first time. And what would Lola say? Because she'd be sure to find out. He was no good at lying.

He rinsed a batch of glasses in the soapy, oily water, feeling the heat on his big red hands, feeling the ends of his fingers crinkling from the hot water. He stared over the counter as he worked, down the length of the narrow drugstore, his small, pale eyes unfocused, his thoughts on last night, and on the future, and on money. His forehead was wrinkled and his thin, brownish hair fell a bit down toward his eyes. A nerve in his thin neck kept twitching. Oh God, he thought, oh, my Jesus!

It was a quiet period after the breakfast rush. There were only two customers at the counter. He'd have about a half hour to do the dishes and get tidied up. Then the women would begin coming in, the housewives, plopping down for a soda in the middle of the morning, or for a cup of coffee. And that would go right into the noon rush. And the afternoon would be busy too. Saturday. Lots of kids. So he ought to do his thinking now.

But he couldn't seem to think straight. Everything was all confused. He kept thinking about things he didn't want to think about. Things about Lola. Like their marriage and their honeymoon. *Oh, my Jesus, was that a sweet time!* Like the magic of the first time he saw Lola dancing on the stage. She had a little moment when she danced all by herself and the spotlight was just on her. And Mike Lash said she had what it takes and she could go far. . . . Like when he heard Lola telling people he was a pharmacist. He frowned and plunged his hands into the dirty water. ("Well, Christ, I can't tell 'em you're a soda jerker, can I?")

After the noon rush, when he had a few minutes to eat, he'd call the hospital. He'd find out how Lola was. Then at six he'd go right up and see her. He'd sit with her awhile. He'd tell her not to worry. But what if she asked him what he did last night? He wouldn't want to lie to Lola. He had never lied to Lola. . . .

It was a funny thing—Lola wasn't really pretty, he guessed, but she always seemed pretty to him. On the stage she had always looked beautiful. And her legs were fine. Lola was proud of her legs. No wonder she was frightened by this accident. A girl like Lola, with those beautiful legs, to be lying up there in Roosevelt Hospital. . . . Hamp could remember so clearly how they used to go swimming when they were on their honeymoon. There was a little lake near the tourist cabin they had in Vermont. They'd drive over at noon and park by the shore. And Lola would dive right in and swim surely and steadily. When she swam back to him he'd smile at her and say, "Good girl." And then they'd kid around a little and Lola would pretend she was going to duck him because she knew he hated being ducked. But finally she'd kiss him instead, her face and lips all cool and sweet from the cold water. And then they'd get out and lie on the worn old canoe dock and dry in the sun. . . . *What a sweet time! What a sweet, faraway time! Four years ago . . .*

"Coffee and a custard roll."

Hamp automatically wiped a rag across the counter in front of a fat man with a weak voice. He drew the coffee and flipped a custard roll from the glass case onto a plate. He cut the roll in half. The man lifted a piece sullenly and looked inside. They usually complained because there wasn't enough custard. This fat man said nothing.

Hamp stared dreamily down the length of the store. He could think clearly about last night now. So clearly that it frightened him. . . .

He had gone home to the apartment at six and Lola hadn't been home. Maybe she'd gone to a movie, he figured. He turned the radio on and flopped down on the big double day bed. He listened to some swing and some news and to Lum and Abner. And then he opened the glass-paneled door that went into the tiny kitchenette. It had once been an entryway, but it had been converted into a kitchenette. He looked into the icebox. He wondered if maybe he should start something for dinner.

While he was standing there, wondering, the phone rang and it was Emily, Lola's sister. She said she was at Roosevelt Hospital and Lola had fallen down and broken her leg.

"My God, how? When? . . ."

"You just come on over," said Emily.

Hamp threw on his coat and ran out of the apartment and down the two flights of creaking stairs. He walked to the corner of Eighth Avenue and hailed a taxi. It would cost about seventy cents, he figured, but never mind.

Just after he had climbed into the taxi he remembered that he and Lola never had taken out that hospitalization insurance. Hamp felt sick to his stomach, and he started to bite the nails of his left hand. . . .

He could see again so vividly Lola's face as he came into her hospital room. She was in a semi-private room. That's what Lola said it was. It had three other beds in it. It was high and old and had dark wooden moldings. Lola was lying very still and the sheets were smoothed neatly across her breast. Her head was little against the pillows. And her black hair was flattened out around her in an odd way. Without make-up her face looked more pinched and tired than Hamp had ever seen it.

"Lola girl," he said, and went and stooped over her and kissed her. "Oh, my God, Lola girl, what happened? . . . You gonna be all right, huh?"

"Hello, Hamp," said Lola quietly, as if she were far away, as if all that had happened to her in the last hours had taken her far away.

"Emily said it was your leg."

"Yeah." Lola's lips quivered and her eyes were misty.

Hamp held her hand tightly. "It don't hurt, does it?" he asked, looking closely into her sweet, familiar face.

Lola moved her head no. "Not much. They fixed it. They gave me something. But, Hamp, my leg, . . . my dancing . . ."

"It's gonna be all right, honey. They fix broken legs up good as new."

"I don't know. . . ."

"Sure they do."

Lola drew in her breath as if she were going to sob, but she didn't.

"How did it happen, girlie?" said Hamp.

"I fell downstairs," said Lola. Then she turned her head a little, so she wasn't looking right at him. "I thought I'd go up to see Mike Lash. You remember, I used to dance with him. I just thought I'd go up and say 'Howdy.' And I did. And when I was leaving I fell down those goddam stairs in that crumby old rehearsal building."

She turned her head to the side, away from Hamp.

"Why didn't you send for me right away, honey? I'd have left the store."

Lola didn't answer for a moment. "Emily was nearer," she said then. "I had them send for Emily."

Hamp stroked her hand. He looked at her big dark eyes, which were staring off into space. He felt the tears coming into his own eyes. He felt he couldn't bear to see Lola look so worn and beaten. He wanted to pick her right up in his arms and make her leg well, make a miracle happen, and carry her out of that dimly lit room.

"I gotta be here quite a long while. Then I'll have the cast for three months. Oh, Christ, oh, why did it have to happen!"

"Now, Lola, don't. . . . It might have happened to anybody."

"Then why *didn't* it happen to anybody!"

"Now, Lola, don't."

"And how we gonna pay for it, how the hell we gonna pay?" she said in an agonized whisper.

"Now, Lola girlie, don't you worry. . . . Don't you worry now."

After a while a nurse came in and said Hamp had better leave. They wanted Lola to sleep. They were going to give her a sedative.

When he came out onto the street it was raining. Not hard, just a slow, misty drizzle. He started walking. He felt dazed and as if his movements were a little out of control. *How we gonna pay for it? Oh, my Jesus!* He looked down at his shoes and at the wet pavement, full of oily puddles. After a while his feet would get wet. No matter. He turned down Ninth Avenue and walked slowly along through the blur of rain and small neon signs.

He walked all the way home. Forty blocks almost, thinking and thinking, until he felt his brain would burst. The cold dampness was all over his face. And he kept stretching out his fingers nervously and then clenching them. And he realized he was holding his jaws tense, his teeth pressed together. He guessed he'd have to have a drink.

Below Twenty-second Street he went into a little bar. He put his foot on the rail and stared at the taffy-colored tin wall. He drank a straight rye. He could feel it nestling in a warm ball in his stomach. He could feel it spreading up into his chest and down into his loins. But it didn't seem to relax him any. He had another. Then he remembered he hadn't eaten yet and he paid for his drinks and went to a lunch counter.

It was steamy inside and the windows were dripping. The air was close with heat and smoke. The radio was moaning a blues song, the deep bass notes overemphasized. He kept thinking about the hospital bills and the doctors' bills and the way Lola looked, as if she was worrying her heart out. *How the hell we gonna pay?* What can a guy do on fifteen a week? How can he save? How can he be ready for emergencies?

The loud, vibrating, dreamy music sank into him. He felt empty and lonely. Not empty for lack of food. But just empty, all over. He bit his fingernails. Where would he get the money? What would he do?

He felt somebody touch his shoulder and he looked up.

"Hello, George Hampton!" she said.

It was a girl he used to know in his home town in New Jersey. Gertrude Brophee. She lived near by and he had run into her once before.

"Why, hello, Gertrude," he said.

They had gone to junior high school together in Red Bank. And Gertrude was the same Gertrude, with the broad mouth and warm, friendly gray eyes. Only she was bigger and sort of disappointed looking now. Hamp had always thought Gertrude was nice. And now they had a bond in a way, because Gertrude worked at a soda fountain too. At a Liggett's.

"Just come off the job?" said Gertrude.

"No, I just come from the hospital. My wife broke her leg."

"Oh, say, I'm sorry."

"Yeah."

"I sure am sorry."

Hamp looked down at his coffee. He picked up the spoon and started to stir it. "You eaten?"

"Just finished," said Gertrude.

"I thought we might sit together," said Hamp.

"Sorry. But I just finished," said Gertrude. She was buttoning her coat.

"How you been, Gertrude?" said Hamp with an effort.

"Fine."

And she was just standing there, pulling her collar up around her neck. Looking at Hamp's thin little face with the hurt blue eyes and untidy brown hair.

"You look like you need a drink, boy," she said.

"I've had one," said Hamp.

"You look like you need another."

Gertrude still looked at him. And the heavy, languorous music swirled around them and got into the mind. Maybe Gertrude decided he must be lonely. Or maybe she felt suddenly lonely herself. Or maybe it was just that she remembered Red Bank, New Jersey.

"Listen," she said, "why don't you come home with me and let me cook you up something decent. You can have a drink too. You don't want to sit here and eat alone. Not tonight."

"Well, Gertrude, that's awful nice of you. . . ."

"Come on. I'll love doin' it. And we can talk over old times. Huh? . . . Aw, come on, George Hampton."

There was something about the way she said George Hampton. Just the way she used to say it in high school. Somehow it made the years drop away and it almost seemed as if he was meeting Gertrude after school, the way he used to.

So he went. He flipped down a nickel for his coffee and went up to Gertrude's for sausages and scrambled eggs and homemade cake. "I love to make cake," Gertrude said.

They drank gin, because it was all Gertrude had in the house. And after a while Hamp began to feel lighter and less troubled and the hospital and Lola and the drugstore all seemed way off in another age. He felt good. And he and Gertrude talked about Red Bank.

Do y' remember . . . ? And the time we went . . . And old Beetnose Northrop with his funny hats? . . . Remember that class picnic . . . ? And the time Joe Gavin fought Joe Harrison over Milly Wicker? . . . Remember, huh? . . . Remember, remember, remember . . .

Time went flying by and the worry drifted off into nothingness. They were both sitting on Gertrude's ugly green studio couch and Gertrude had her head back against the wall. Her solid, rather heavy neck was nice, stretched back that way. Hamp looked at it. He just kept looking at it. And smiling, too, because he was dreamy and happy and the sharp, hurtful little thoughts had gone away.

Gertrude rolled her head a little against the wall. She turned it and looked at Hamp.

"Gee, I ain't had such a good time for . . . for a long time," said Hamp.

"Me too," said Gertrude.

Hamp looked at her. And then he put out his hand and rested it on her neck. It was warm and he could feel the big artery pulsing under his fingers. Gertrude didn't move. She just smiled gently at him.

"Oh, Gertrude . . ." And he moved closer and kissed her. And suddenly he felt warm and free and powerful. And Gertrude reached up and pulled off the light above them.

It was like something he'd always wanted. He'd known Gertrude since he was a boy. She was like his family and his old gang and his town. She was like home. . . .

Later they lay still and heard the rain falling in the narrow court outside Gertrude's window. They could see the grimy rayon curtains blowing a little. And then Hamp got up and went back to his apartment.

Well, that's how it had happened. Just as simply as that. And now he was an unfaithful husband. And, standing there, behind the drugstore counter, he could hardly believe it. He'd never had much to do with women. Lola had been almost the only one. And what would Lola think? Darling Lola, lying up there in that hospital, miserable and bitter. He'd treated her rotten. But maybe she'd understand.

"Chocolate malted," said a man sharply.

"An egg in it?" said Hamp.

"No egg."

The afternoon rush was starting now. It would keep up steady till six. Then Moe came on and Hamp could knock off.

When he left the drugstore at six-fifteen Hamp took a bus uptown to the hospital. In the main hall he met Lola's sister, Emily, on her way out. Emily looked a lot like Lola, except that no one would ever think her pretty, not even Hamp, or Everett, her husband. Her nose and chin were just too sharp and witchlike. And her rather gawky neck looked like fine gray sandpaper.

Her eyes snapped at Hamp, as if all this were his fault.

"How is she?" said Hamp.

"O.K.," said Emily sullenly.

"I'm so worried about her," said Hamp.

"I'm worried about how you're gonna pay for all this," said Emily, pulling on her gloves savagely. "You and Lola sure haven't got any money for hospital bills."

"No . . ."

"And *we* can't do anything for you. Everett's not doin' much business."

"Oh, I wasn't expectin' . . ." said Hamp quickly.

"Well, don't," cut in Emily.

"Don't act so cross, Emily," said Hamp.

"Well, I am cross. I told Lola she shouldn't try to go back on the stage. A wife's place is with her husband. If she hadn't begun rehearsing with Mike Lash this wouldn't have happened."

Hamp looked puzzled. Lola hadn't told him she was rehearsing.

"Why you'd be willing to let her take up her dancing again is more than I can see. You oughta have more backbone, Hamp."

"Look," said Hamp, looking past Emily, "just *how* did this accident happen?"

"Didn't Lola tell you? She was rehearsing with Mike Lash, and she took a spill doing a fancy turn and came down on her leg. Naturally she'd be stiff after four years of not dancing."

So Lola hadn't fallen downstairs. She'd been rehearsing with Mike Lash. . . . And she had never told him. She had lied to him.

"I'm goin' up now," said Hamp, fingering his hat uneasily.

"Yeah, you better."

He moved along the hall to the elevator. Maybe Lola wasn't ever going to tell him, he thought. Maybe she was just going to land a job with Mike Lash as a partner and leave him. He felt suddenly terrified, because he hadn't known what was in Lola's mind. Maybe he didn't know Lola at all. After four years even.

She looked just the same as she had yesterday, lying there unhappily between the neat sheets. Her hair had been combed and brushed. It looked awfully straight, somehow. She looked at Hamp a long time when he appeared around the end of the screen.

"Hello, Hamp."

"Hello, Lola girlie." Hamp kissed her tenderly.

It was quite dim in the room, and when Hamp sat down on the straight chair near the bed he was in the shadow. He could hear the faint voices of visitors at the other beds.

"How do you feel, Lola?"

"O.K."

Lola didn't seem to want to talk much. Her mouth looked more unhappy than ever. Hamp leaned over and kissed her a second time. She came to life a little then. "How'll you get along, Hamp? About meals and things?" she said.

"I'll get along," said Hamp.

"Did you get your own dinner last night?"

Here it comes, thought Hamp. Now Lola was going to find out. She'd know.

"I ran into Gertrude Brophee," said Hamp casually. "You know, that girl I introduced you to once? From Red Bank?"

"Oh."

"She cooked me a supper at her place."

"That was nice," said Lola. She meant it. Her voice sounded as if she really wasn't paying much attention.

"I—I stayed up there most of the evening."

"Uh-huh," said Lola. She *wasn't* paying attention. She didn't care. Hamp felt it like a blow. She didn't care what he'd been doing.

Lola turned her head away from him on the pillows.

Hamp swallowed. He wanted desperately to tell her about Gertrude. He wanted to explain it didn't mean anything. He wanted Lola to say, Never mind, baby. He wanted them to be close again. He didn't want to carry that secret around with him. Even if Lola had secrets from him, even if she lied to him. He didn't want to lie to her. Only by telling her could he make it all right.

He sat there for a long moment, saying nothing.

"Hamp," said Lola finally, staring up at the dim ceiling, "how we gonna pay for all this? What we gonna do?" Lola's forehead was all wrinkled, and she bit her lip.

"Now don't you worry, Lola girl."

Hamp leaned over her and touched her hair awkwardly.

Lola moved her head in a little gesture of irritation. "Don't," she said.

Hamp sat up straight in the chair again. And the room was very still. And then he knew that he wouldn't tell Lola about Gertrude Brophee. There'd be no point. Lola wouldn't even care. He would never tell her. And maybe it was only the first of many things he would never tell her.

Sitting there in the shadow, clutching nervously at his hat, he felt full of a nameless hurt. He felt his eyeballs beginning to sting. He blinked quickly.

Lola just stared up at the ceiling, her lips pressed together desperately.

It was so still Hamp could hear her breathing. His thoughts went back to their honeymoon. He couldn't help it. *Oh, my Jesus, what a sweet time. What a sweet, faraway time . . .*

STANDBY

By Sarah Grinnell

From *Harper's Bazaar*

SARAH GRINNELL

is a pseudonym. She insists that if one was good enough for O. Henry, it's good enough for her. She had her first story published in Harper's Bazaar *in 1938, and has sold stories to three other magazines. She says she is not a real writer, but one of those innumerable "Navy wives" who "chase up and down, and back and forth, across the length and breadth of the United States in not-too-successful attempts to be with their husbands when and if they are in their base port." She has lived in practically everything from cheap boardinghouses and WPA projects to the most luxurious hotels and tremendous houses. Once she lived alone on a private island in a house with seven bedrooms and five baths. In the past two years she has traveled about eleven thousand miles by plane, train, automobile, boat, bus, and bicycle. Once she hired a hearse as the only way to get where she was going.*

THE TELEPHONE WAS RINGING. She fought her way up through the layers of heavy, sickening sleep that was part of living here in the subtropics. It rang again and then again, shrill and insistent in the dark. The ship was on standby—was it going out? She suddenly was wide awake and fumbling frantically for the phone, but already John was leaning over her to lift it off the hook. "Hello, yes, all right, I'll be right down." His voice was very quiet, solemn, calm. Then he had hung up and both of them were out of bed. Neither said a word; there was nothing that needed saying. The important thing was to dress as fast as possible and drive to the Navy Yard. Once she groaned despairingly when she got her slip on backward, but even so she was ready as soon as he.

Now they were hurrying from the house, he striding swiftly down the walk to start the car, she running in the darkness right behind him. Then they were backing out of the garage. "All right, cramp hard," she said, and they were speeding through the dimmed-out streets. At one corner they barely missed another car with only slits for headlights, but swerved and drove on swiftly and in silence as before.

Finally she couldn't help it. "John," she said, "is it bad—is it a sub?"

"M-m-m-n-n-n." He made the noise that meant, I can't tell you even if I know. That made her ashamed of having asked, so she didn't speak again.

The sentries had the gates open: the ship was ready to sail at once. Already the crew had taken in the gangplank and were standing by the lines waiting for him.

"Good-by." He kissed her hurriedly, then jumped aboard. And then the ship was backing out, and—and well, there suddenly wasn't any hurry, there wasn't *any*thing any more. Nothing to do now but go home and wait until the ship came in again.

But, back in their hot little cottage, she couldn't go to sleep. She lay listening to the idiot recurrent whine of their electric fan, thinking of John upon the bridge, taking the ship out of the harbor, taking her out and out until . . . Where were they going—what was it this time that had called them out? In the case of larger ships with lots of officers, you could try to guess at such things with the other wives; but with a small ship like John's, you could only lie and worry all alone. Were they hurrying now to some torpedoed tanker, sinking in a sea of flaming oil? Were they hunting for an enemy submarine—and being hunted by it in turn? Or were they only on some routine job or some mysterious false alarm? She was still lying awake when the eastern sky turned pinkish yellow behind the tin roofs and the palm trees of the town. She turned face down upon John's pillow that still smelled faintly of Vitalis from his hair. Somehow that seemed to reassure her and finally she fell asleep.

At seven-thirty she was wakened by the whistle on the big white laundry down the street. "Who-o-o-o-o." It always sounded breathless, as if exhausted from the heat of the preceding night, wistful and yet patient, even philosophic at the prospect of another torrid day. On ordinary mornings when she heard it she'd get up and wash and dress and get John's breakfast ready. Then she'd kneel beside the bed and slip her arm beneath his neck. She hated so to have to wake him: the ship was out so much, at such strange hours of the day and night, that he was always nearly dead for lack of sleep. "Johnny, wake up, Johnny darling, I'm sorry but I *have* to wake you up." She'd keep repeating it, holding his head like a child's upon her shoulder, staring almost tearfully at the trusting utter relaxation of his face. Finally his eyes would open; he would moan and stretch and vaguely smile at her. Then with an almost superhuman effort he'd jump up from bed. And now today, when she could sleep all morning, she lay awake and wondered where he was. Perhaps the ship was back already. Perhaps the phone would ring sometime that afternoon and she would hear his voice, a little shy because of calling from the ship, saying, "Want to come get me in the car?" She got up quickly and began to dress. She'd go out to the commissary and get some nice lamb chops for supper. He'd be hungry by the time he got ashore.

But once out on the hot and glaring street, she hesitated. She couldn't resist the impulse to look and see if John's ship might just happen to be coming in. Of course she couldn't hang around the Navy Yard, but she could walk down the street until she reached the harbor. She could catch a glimpse of it from here: a stretch of jade-green water shading to vivid peacock blue farther out from shore. Sometimes she had seen destroyers pass across it on the way to tie up at the Navy Yard. They always glided by so slowly, silently, inexorably. There was something dramatic and unreal about them against the theatrically lurid background of the Southern seas. She wondered why so many things had seemed like that in the two weeks she'd been here. Perhaps it was the heat, the enervating dampness, or just because the subtropics were so different from her Northern home. Sometimes things seemed as in a nightmare or delirium: abnormal, sickly, tainted, slowly putrefying in an all-pervading, frightening sort of way.

She had that feeling now as she walked down the street past the shuttered houses rotten with dampness and with termites underneath the dingy paint. The yards were literally choked with exotic flowers, shrubs, and trees—periwinkle, croton, bougainvillea, red and pink and clashing purple, royal poinciana, banana and papaya trees, and palms, palms everywhere—all growing lush and strange and junglelike from the sandy coral soil. But the jungle vegetation grew densest in the vacant lots. It sprang up around the concrete steps where houses once had stood and round the rusty wrecks of old deserted cars. The sidewalks there were covered thick with brown decaying coconuts and palm stems, like the skulls and bones of prehistoric beasts. And as she passed, a multitude of little lizards striped with gold and turquoise blue darted frantically out from underneath her feet.

At last she reached the ruined warehouse at the harbor's edge. Just beyond it was a sagging wooden wharf; from there she could have a view of the whole harbor. Expectantly she hurried forward: perhaps John's ship was really coming in; perhaps she'd actually see it. But the harbor stretched empty, just one smooth sheet of beautiful translucent jade, zigzagged here and there with winy-purple streaks where seaweed grew upon the coral bottom. The only living thing that she could see was a single man-of-war bird hanging sinister and buzzard-like above the water in the bright blue sky. She stood a moment peering toward the Navy Yard, then searching the horizon in case John's ship was just appearing there. Suddenly she noticed a peculiar odor, a faint but sickening charnel smell. She saw that the pier was slippery with grease beneath her feet, and in the shallow water and all along the shore lay bare bones, yellowish with age and green with slime. Beef bones, she thought. Perhaps the ruined warehouse had been a storage place for meat, or perhaps the wharf here was a garbage dump. Hurriedly she turned to leave and saw a dead pig, half fallen from a wooden crate beside the pier. The flies that swarmed upon it rose in buzzing clouds as she walked past, then settled gluttonously again upon its lifeless flanks.

It's only a garbage dump, she kept repeating to herself, but even so she felt contaminated all the way until she came to the commissary with its spotless cleanliness and courteous white-coated clerks. The place was jammed with navy wives in slacks or shorts with gay bandannas covering the curlers in their hair. They rolled their wire self-service baskets madly up and down the aisles, with their babies sitting wide-eyed in them among the packages of food. They gossiped, giggled, grabbed for vegetables, made wisecracks to the clerks. They were most of them so young she could have been their mother, but that made little difference to her now. She felt inordinately grateful when two came up and spoke to her: she'd met them at the commandant's reception and now they asked her to come and call on them sometime. That's what I need, companionship, she told herself as she walked home; I just get morbid staying all alone. But after lunch she couldn't bring herself to leave the house. John might phone when she was out. He might be able to come home earlier than usual. Or perhaps he'd be calling hastily to say the ship was in but going out again and he wouldn't be home at all. What if she weren't there to answer? The phone would ring and ring till finally he'd have to give it up. She'd have failed him then; he'd have to sail without their even speaking to each other, without her even knowing he had called.

Four o'clock came and went . . . then five . . . then six, and still there was no word from him. She told herself that she was silly: what reason had she anyway to think the ship was coming in today? She remembered what he'd said to her so many times. "There's no sense worrying," he always told her gently. "It doesn't really do a bit of good, you know. Just don't expect me till you hear from me. You have to learn that in the Navy." By eight o'clock she knew he wasn't coming. Feeling as though it were a fateful action, she took the chops from the refrigerator shelf and wrapped them in waxed paper, then put them in with the ice-cube trays. They would freeze up solid there and keep for days and days. . . .

That night there was a tropic storm. Before it broke, the air was hotter, muggier, more unbearable than ever. No matter how she tried, she couldn't sleep. Even turning the electric fan directly on herself did no good. Her legs jerked convulsively in spite of all her efforts to relax them, and the bed beneath her became hot and sticky. In desperation she rolled over to the far side, then back again, then back and forth at intervals. Finally she got up and filled the bathtub with cold water and soaked herself till she was cool. She must have slept a little after that, for suddenly she was conscious of a roaring sound. A gale of wind was lashing at the sapodilla tree outside her bedroom window, bending its boughs over till it seemed that they would have to break. Then the rain came, tremendous sheets of it, slanting furiously past the single light that burned above the dimmed-out street. It hammered deafeningly on the windows which she hastily had closed, and flowed in a solid river down the panes. It swept across the roofs of near-by houses and blew from the eaves in clouds of mist; it leaped up in a million inch-high crystal fountains from the puddles in the street. Then the gutters overflowed till they formed one single torrent rushing down the street, while wrinkled wind squalls raced along it as if upon an inland sea. She could hear the church bell tolling. She knew it was the wind that rang it, but it seemed to be warning the town of danger just the same.

But the storm was frightening in itself: its hurricanelike fury seemed too great for mere men to withstand. When there was an especially violent gust of wind she actually moaned in protest. How could John see to navigate in such blinding squalls of rain? How could he control his tiny ship in so violent a wind? What if he had been torpedoed and was drifting helpless on a raft? *Stop it,* she told herself, don't start imagining things like that, you're getting hysterical, you fool. . . .

The morning came, the day dragged by, and still there was no word. And then another day and night . . . another . . . and another, till a whole week had passed. Every morning she woke up and thought, "He'll *have* to come today." The ship was too small, had too limited a cruising range, to stay out any longer. They'd be running out of water, out of Diesel oil. By nighttime she was almost frantic. I can't let things go on like this, she thought. Tomorrow I'll go down to N.O.B. and ask if they can't tell me something. But then she'd tell herself she mustn't. John would have a fit. The Naval Operating Base had more important things to do than reassuring nervous women.

Now the other navy wives began to drop in. They knew John's ship was overdue and she would catch them sometimes watching her with morbid curiosity. She realized each of them was thinking, this might happen to me, too; I wonder how it feels. But she was grateful to them for their friendliness, and when they asked her to their homes for bridge she forced herself to go. She got too panicky when she stayed home alone now: she knew she must distract her mind with other things. But even so she kept a constant lookout for the ship. She simply couldn't help it. Suddenly the thought would pop into her head: perhaps the ship is coming in this very minute. And she would have to go and see. She didn't go down to the harbor any more, but to the other end of town that faced out upon the open ocean. She walked so fast and eagerly that she passed everybody on the street: the Negroes in their bright print frocks and raffia scuffed shoes, the Cubans and the dried-up Yankee-looking natives, all strolling very slowly in the heat. She hurried to the beach and stared out at the varicolored sea. It was milky beige inshore where the surf stirred up the coral sand, then aquamarine with garnet seaweed stripes, then jade, then turquoise, then, far out, a deep and satisfying sapphire blue. But she didn't care how beautiful it was: the only thing she looked for was one speck that might become a gray ship, and that was never there.

When she started home at last she again had that feeling of decay around her everywhere. Sometimes she saw a scorpion or a whitish, crablike thing that scuttled quickly down a hole. Sometimes there would be a dead hen lying in the gutter, and once there was the carcass of a dog, all crushed and bloody, with its entrails spilling out. It lay there till it swarmed with flies, and the natives sat and fanned themselves quite unconcernedly on their piazzas just the sidewalk's width away. In this end of the town there were entire blocks of unsold real-estate developments and jungle growth. Past that she could see the swamp, an impassible expanse of mangrove thickets, scabrous coral rock, and stagnant pools where alligators and mosquitoes bred. It seemed to hem in the town almost completely excepting on the ocean and the harbor sides. And beyond it stretched a wilderness of other swamps and hammock, palms and mangrove thickets, coral rock and wide lagoons: one had to travel half a day to cross it on a line of bridges and a single narrow road. More than anything it made her feel that she was trapped, cut off from civilization and the safety of her Northern home.

One day she walked back up a different street that led past the cemetery. The sun was beating mercilessly down upon the coral street, but in the graveyard there were trees that cast a tempting shade and there was grass, real greensward as there was up North, instead of the coarse Bermuda grass that grew so sparsely here. She paused for just a minute at the gate with that peculiar hesitation people sometimes feel at going into graveyards. Was she getting morbid? Had she better keep on walking up the glaring street? Then she told herself that that was silly and went resolutely in. It was cool and peaceful inside. The tombs were built above the ground, ornate and lovely with stone crosses, angels, doves, clasped hands, or wreaths of flowers carved in bas-relief. She strolled along the grassy path and before her fluttered two white butterflies as if coquetting with her.

Suddenly she came upon a plot enclosed within a green and silvered iron fence, the gate of which bore two large navy eagles clasping shields and sheaves of flags. And in the center of the plot, upon a tall stone monument, stood the life-size statue of a sailor in antiquated uniform. Somehow his pose was touchingly old-fashioned too: one hand clasped an oar, the other was held above his eyes as if to shade them while he stared at something out to sea. She slipped inside the gate and up the walk of red, white, and blue concrete, inlaid with stars and anchors. Upon the statue's granite pedestal she read:

In Memory
of the Victims
of the
Disaster
of
U. S. Battleship
MAINE
In Havana Harbor
Feb. 15, 1898

Behind the monument were three long rows of small plain stones. Each bore a shield with lettering, a few with names but most with only the inscription, "One Unknown, U.S. Battleship *Maine* Killed in Havana Harbor, Feb. 15, 1898." They'd been blown to bits, she thought, literally blown to bits so that they couldn't even be identified. And suddenly she realized that John's quarters were right above the magazine. If a torpedo struck up forward . . .

Hastily she looked away, as if to turn her thoughts to other things. She fixed her eyes upon the beautiful wide-spreading gambalamba trees that grew in the two back corners of the plot. But their sap was poisonous, she remembered; again she had that nightmare consciousness of decay and deadliness around her everywhere. With a feeling of hysteria she saw the graves beneath the trees. Three of them had names and "U.S.T.B. *Winslow*" on them: they gave no other information, but she thought the *Winslow* had been shelled off Cárdenas at the beginning of the Spanish war. And in the center, a little farther forward than the other gravestones, was a small white marble obelisk with names upon three sides of it and "September 29, 1918, U.S.S. *Salem*" on the front. What had happened to the *Salem?* She didn't know, but the date stared back at her significantly. There's one ship here for every war, it seemed to say: in this war now, will it be . . . ? There was an empty space between the monuments; there still was room enough for . . .

She turned and ran back down the concrete walk. The eagle-crested gate clanged shut behind her, echoing like a tocsin in the silent cemetery. But she didn't pause to glance back toward it; she felt as if she couldn't bear to see those monuments again. She only ran on faster, ran until she reached the street. It was panic, hysterical unthinking panic: she couldn't stop to analyze it, she only knew she had to get away. All the fear that she'd been fighting for a week rose up inside her, magnified a hundredfold for having been suppressed so long. Those carved words on the monuments had done it. They had made the whole thing real. All those men had actually died; perhaps their wives had waited here and told themselves they mustn't worry till one day they'd learned their husbands had been killed.

Automatically she started up the street toward home, but suddenly stopped and looked around in desperation. She musn't go there now, not to the empty house where she and John had been together, where she had waited all this week beside the phone that never rang. She turned and started back the other way.

And then at last she saw it, far out on the ocean, just a blurred gray shape upon the outmost strip of sapphire blue. *Could* it be? She told herself she mustn't get her hopes up: so many times a ship that far away would look like John's and turn out not to be. But again she started running, ran and ran with pounding heart and aching lungs until she reached the shore. Oh, it *had* to be the ship: it was, *it really was*. She could clearly see the outline of it now, the streamlined sides, the superstructure and the sheerly curving bow. It seemed to dance a little on the swell as if excited to be coming home, and two white plumes of spray kept leaping gaily up beside its prow. With maddening slowness it came in, across the sapphire strip, the turquoise one, the jade, till finally it disappeared inside the harbor's mouth.

Then she turned and started home. She'd change her dress and get the car and drive down to the Navy Yard. If she hurried, she could reach the dock before the ship came in. The palm trees seemed to crackle gaily in the wind as she passed, the royal poincianas flamed above her all along the street, and suddenly she thought, How beautiful it is down here. I think I'm going to love it after all. And she began to run again.

BLACK BOY'S GOOD TIME

By Elmer Grossberg

From *Esquire*

ELMER GROSSBERG

was born November 18, 1925, in New York City, where his father was a shoe worker who died when Mr. Grossberg was eight years old. He has been writing for five years, and has written some fifty or sixty stories. Until he was about twelve he was undecided whether to be a writer, an artist, or a baseball player. He feels that if he had received the set of paints he asked for at that time he would have become an artist. He still draws caricatures of his instructors at Brooklyn College, where he is in his sophomore year. He lives in Brooklyn and was graduated from the Abraham Lincoln High School there in 1942. He edited their literary magazine, Cargoes, *and won three of the five prizes for essays—two of them city, the third state. In addition, on graduation he received the creative-writing award. He won a contest conducted by* PM. *He played basketball on the school team and remembers how the coach's eyes bulged on one occasion when he "threw in some twenty-odd set shots in a row in practice."*

His summers he spent peddling ice cream on the beach. He feels his greatest achievement to date was learning "to spot a dick in a bathing suit." He shined shoes, was a laundry-truck assistant, cleaned and plated jewelry, and picked berries in the country. He has always helped around the house and says there isn't anything connected with housework that he can't do. His favorite game is baseball, and he played varsity baseball, third base, .312, during his freshman year at Brooklyn College. He is majoring in English and says that, next to his writing, music is the greatest thing in his life. "I have been to California by rail and back by vibrant thumb," he adds. "My favorite writers are Saroyan, Steinbeck, and Sholom Aleichem."

The sheriff shoved him into the room and his face looked very pale under the yellow bulb. He had very light skin for a Negro . . . but the shadowy color of his skin was still there. There was a chair in the middle of the room and nothing else. The walls looked empty.

The tall, wiry fellow whom they called Slim just looked at him, and then his face broke into a slow grin and the grin, like his face, was hard.

"I thought mebbe y'had a big, tough nigger," he said. "Dis nigger looks weaker 'n drinkin' water." He laughed and it was the only sound in the room. The sheriff stood with his hands on his hips behind Johnson, who was motionless, though his eyes were very wide and wonderingly fastened on Slim.

Slim's sleeves were rolled up and he had on a closely knit slipover. His forearms were thick and strong, out of proportion with the rest of his body.

He took a few steps toward Johnson, looking him over carefully. "Kinda small," he said. "What'd he do?"

The sheriff's heavy lips opened sluggishly. "Crook," he said shortly. "Take ole man Dugan's Chevvy."

"You're sure he's the guy done it?"

The sheriff looked at him with annoyance. "That's my job—you got yours! Give 'im the works an' give it to 'im good." The sheriff's thick lips closed.

Slim grinned again. His knuckles moved under the rough skin as his fingers clenched and unclenched. "O.K.," he said. "I just wanted t'get good'n' mad at 'im. Do a better job that way."

The sheriff turned toward the door. "You'll do a good job anyway," he advised. "I can pick up any big tough bum outside any time I wanta fer a buck a job."

"Yeah," said Slim, his grin widening, "but not one who fought Lew Jenkins oncet."

The sheriff grunted as he opened the door and turned around again. "Any dumb bastard can get in a ring with Jenkins an' get the hell knocked out of 'im. Specially when Jenkins was jus' a fiel' hand that nobody heard of fightin' fer his stomick."

"Well"— Slim laughed—"Lew's champ now!"

"That's all! Give the black bastard a goin' over. Won't confess he robbed the car—get it out of 'im. An' don't spare the knuckles—this nigger's too damn fresh. Gotta put 'im in his place."

Slim spit in his hands and rubbed them.

"Sure," he said. "Now 'm in the mood."

The sheriff stepped out of the room. Before he closed the door he called, "Want 'im handcuffed?"

"Naw, this is too easy."

"O.K. Don't forget I wanta hear 'im." The door closed. There was a silence in the little room as Slim took his time to look at Johnson.

Johnson quavered and his brow was wet and gleaming.

"I didn't take the car," he fumbled. "I—I didn't——"

"Look, nigger boy," Slim said curtly. "When I hit a guy I hit 'im hard, see? Not because it's my job, but because I hate 'im . . . see?" He walked over close to Johnson.

Johnson's body shivered. "I—didn't take it—it's a lie—it's a lie . . ."

Slim grabbed his collar in his fist and twisted till it was like a tight rope around his neck.

"Know why I hate 'im?" Slim continued, grinning fiercely into Johnson's face. "Cause I see 'im like I see him in the ring. A guy wanta smash in the face . . . An' I hate crooks—especially a nigger crook . . . see? Difference is, in the ring I wanta knock 'im out—here I don't—here I jus' wanta sock 'im an sock 'im again, smash his damn face to a pulp . . . Keep 'im jus' 'live enough so's he can talk if he don't want no more . . . see? That's my job—can't knock 'im out. Guy can't talk if he's dreamin' . . . Ketch on?"

He waited for a response. The Negro's eyes were wide and his shady skin was paler than before. His lips trembled with fear. He tried to speak, but his mind could not think and his lips could not form words.

Slim did not wait too long for an answer. Johnson watched in a daze while Slim's fist drew back carefully over his shoulder. And he knew it was his last chance to think of something to say—anything . . .

He thought of home, and in the same terrified instant wondered why . . . He managed to see his skinny mother and little sister, while the fist drove forward. And as it crashed into his face just above his mouth, the figures exploded into spots and blurred rushing stars. The room rocked while he whirled around it furiously. And then a bright blinding light appeared in the middle of it. His eyes saw through a slit, and when his lips parted in pain, a trickle of blood ran in and painted his white teeth red. He blinked feebly and tried to lean back, and then he knew that he was against the wall and was on the floor. When the bright sun faded from in front of him he dimly saw Slim's face grinning at him from the middle of the room. And the grin of this man's face at such a time was the most terrible thing that Johnson had ever seen.

Johnson put one hand to his face to a spot that pained and whimpered when the spot could not feel the hand. Slim's legs moved under him and he was glaring down at Johnson, crouching over him.

"Had enough, nigger?" He was a fighter now and words came through his teeth.

Johnson stared at him through the wet, glistening film that covered his eyes. His mouth opened as if he would cry out, but no sound came out the quivering bloodstained lips. Slim muttered sharply, "All you gotta do is say 'yeah!' . . . " and then quietly, "Well, you took ole man Dugan's Chevvy, didn't ya?"

Johnson stared up at him. His hands felt the floor unconsciously. He co-ordinated his senses enough to wonder why his hands were feeling the floor; an idea condensed in his head and as it sank downward his brains managed to grasp it, and as soon as he understood it he relaxed his hands quickly . . . He wanted to get up—if he had he would have been smashed down again . . . God, what did they want from him . . . What did they . . .

Slim had yanked him again by the collar with both hands. Johnson was flat against the wall. Suddenly fear made him desperate, and in his desperation he became reckless. He put his hands on Slim's arms, persuasively, resistingly, and his voice sobbed.

"Please—don't hit me again—don't—I didn't take the car—I don't want a car—I'm sick—I'm very—weak—Please—don't——"

Slim breathed heavily with the excitement that came professionally.

"I'll give y'one more chance, nigger, an' that's all. You admit y'took that Chevvy from old man Dugan?"

"It's a mistake," sobbed Johnson. "Somebody else took it—I wouldn't take a car—I don't want a car—please—don't——"

Then the hard knuckles crashed into his mouth again. His head smashed up against the wall, and the force of the blow seemed to carry the fist deep into his face, crushing every bone in his head. His teeth felt as if bent inward and a pain shot through his head like a lightning bolt. His eyes closed. He felt the molten world pouring out into the universe. And a blinding sun flashed before him again. As he sagged downward the last thought he had was the intense desire to spit the taste of Slim's rough, dirty knuckles out of his mouth. Then a blackness like death passed over him. And it was a quiet, efficient blackness, allowing not a ray of light to filter through.

When his eyelids crept apart again he was surprised to see an unfamiliar gray wall in front of him. The gray color and the nakedness of the wall made it look cold.

Suddenly Johnson was aware that his face and neck were wet and that his shirt clung to his throat with persistency of cold, wet cloth. And then his eyes made out a large light bulb sticking straight out on a loose chain from the middle of the wall in front of him. He wondered vaguely about the gravity angle, and also about his peculiar feeling of wetness; as he lifted his arm it felt heavy. Very heavy. He let it drop. It banged against something, and the slight pain that resulted from his knuckles unexpectedly striking wood made him wince, and as his lips moved a river of pain ran around his mouth and up to his nose and cheeks and there it branched out. His whole face felt heavy and swollen; he struggled to remember.

Then a tall, lanky figure moved into view and came up to him. The figure looked familiar and it stood at right angles to him, and that was how Johnson knew he was lying down. Suddenly he recognized the face. It was Slim. His first impulse was to smile at him as though he were meeting an old friend in a foreign country, but then his brain functioned more sharply and he remembered . . . Everything jumped into place in his mind. His eyes widened again through fear, but he saw that Slim's face was relaxed, not hateful, and that he was bending over him.

"How d' y' feel, kid?"

Johnson stared at him. The voice had not been angry or threatening. His lips stretched wide over his mass of white teeth, though they ached, in a smile. "I—I feel better . . ." He was trying to figure it all out.

"Kin y' get up?" Slim asked.

Johnson sat up stiffly. The wall, with the bulb sticking straight out of it on the end of a chain, moved up over his head and became a ceiling, and he sat on the floor looking at the real wall, rubbing his eyes and trying to smile. He turned to Slim, smiling.

"I—I didn't take the car," he said, feeling kind of foolish as he said it, because he felt everything was all right.

"You'll be O.K.," said Slim. "I didn't hit you too hard. A little water woke ya up right away."

Johnson looked around and saw a red pail on the floor near him, with the word Fire painted on it in big black letters. There were little pools of water under the pail and on the floor around him. The water from his face and neck trickled down to his chest.

Behind Slim, he could see that the door was open. He was still a little dazed.

"I didn't take the car," he repeated. "I don't want a car. . . ."

"That's O.K.," said Slim. "You didn't steal it; we caught the real fellow that stole it. A mulatto . . . Looks a lot like you, that's how we made the mistake."

Johnson's smile widened as his bruised mouth got used to it. He asked, "Can I go home now?"

The door opened wider and the sheriff came into the room.

"How y' feel, kid?"

"He's O.K. now," Slim said. "Just got a bruised face, that's all."

The sheriff chuckled dully. "From the fist of the man that fought Jenkins! You ought to be proud, kid."

Johnson's gleaming teeth smiled up at him. "Stand up, Johnson—kin y' stand up?"

Johnson leaned on his hands and got painfully to his feet. He swayed a little, but soon was used to it.

He smiled at the sheriff.

"Can I go home now?" he asked.

The sheriff put a hand on his shoulder.

"Sure you're a good nigger. Got y' mixed up with another guy, that's all. They're bringin' him in now. Don't worry—we'll break his goddam neck. If he wouldn't stole Dugan's car, you wouldn't got into trouble. We'll give him hell for ya, don't worry, Johnson . . . Sure you'll go home. But first we're gonna give ya a good time—t' sorta make up for it. You're O.K. You got a nice face. Can tell it a mile off. . . . I was damn surprised when I thought you was the crook." He turned toward the door. "C'mon, le's go."

He moved off and Johnson followed him. "Better fill the fire pail up with water again," he said to Slim. "Get a rag and wipe up the water 'f y' got nothin' t' do."

Slim said angrily, "What the hell am I—your scrubwoman?"

"All right—y' don't hafta 'f y' don' wanta," the sheriff yelled back. Johnson was waiting outside. He scowled at Slim and went out. The door closed sharply behind him.

Slim growled, "Damn right I don't! Stinkin' liar—says, 'Mind my own business an' he'll mind his.' Poor ignorant nigger—'f I was him I'd poke that fat bastard straight in the puss!"

He picked up the pail and walked slowly toward the door. Outside a heavy door slammed, and a few moments later a car door echoed the sound. Slim listened, and then in disgust slammed his own door behind him.

"Where y' live, kid?" asked the sheriff, glancing casually over at him.

Johnson's smile seemed perpetually on his eager-to-please face. "Down in the old shack on the bottom of the Big Hill."

"That's Fowler's property, ain't it?"

"Yes—but he lets us live there. Says he don't care if we live in the old shack. We're clean. We don't want us trouble. We just want to live peaceful."

He smiled winningly and the sheriff turned his eyes back to the road.

The sheriff was silent a moment. Then he said dully, "You're a good nigger. I can see that. Wait'll we get that mulatto, we'll—— Shack on the bottom of the hill—the Big Hill—huh? That's four miles, twenny-minute ride . . . How'dya like t'have a good time, huh, kid? Have you ever seen a movie?"

"Yeah-h-h," breathed Johnson happily. "They're swell."

The sheriff's hands lightly persuaded the wheel. "O.K., we'll set ya in a movie—give ya a good time. We're sorry about that mistake, kid. This'll sorta make up for it. . . . How ya like ice cream?"

Johnson grinned with ecstasy at him. "Swell!"

"O.K. We'll give y' some of that too. How's y' face feel?"

Then Johnson remembered how he had been hit—how frightened he had been. And he didn't know why, but a sudden feeling of misery and unhappiness swept strongly over him. The smile faded as his lips came slowly back over his teeth and settled glumly together.

"It's O.K.," he said slowly.

The sheriff's eyes were interested in the road. A few buildings passed by them, and a tall black chimney came into sight over a low level of roofs in the distance.

"We're in town already," said the sheriff. "You're gonna have a good time now, kid."

Johnson couldn't explain it. He knew he should be happy now. It was a mistake—they weren't going to put him in jail, they weren't going to hit him any more . . . they were sorry about it, and they were going to give him a movie now, and ice cream . . . He had seen a movie only twice in his life, and it was a rarity, the highest of luxuries. And he could not explain the strong feeling of unhappiness that welled up in his breast. He longed to be home, home in the old shack with his mother and pig-tailed sister. . . . He wanted to see them again, and that desire became powerful although he had just seen them four or five hours ago. He remembered how he had stood in the little room with Slim clutching his collar and grinning into his face, and the long wait as he watched the fist draw back and come crashing into his face, and the thought that had been in his mind—the last curious thought—before the blackness had descended on him like a falling cloud and caught him up in the swirling midst . . . And he remembered the blow . . . Every tooth had felt as if it were being smashed in with a sledge hammer and the bones in his head had rattled like dice in the fast-shaking hand of a gambler.

And then Johnson knew that he was lonely. He had been hit that way before, and the feeling of loneliness in him was for his mother and the shack—where his own life was filled only with love for his family and a desire to help protect them from the fate that his father and brothers had met. And he knew they wanted the same thing.

The loneliness brought up a mist before his eyes.

"I—I want to go home," he said suddenly.

The sheriff looked at him. "What?—Yeah, sure—sure you'll go home, kid—that's O.K., you don't have to worry about that. Don't you wanta have a good time first?"

Johnson stared weakly before him. He didn't answer.

The sheriff looked at him and then broke out in laughing as he looked back to the road.

"I'll bet you're still scared, kid," he laughed. "Look—you don't hafta be afraid of nothin'. We caught the real thief—an' you're safe now. . . . 'Course if you wanta go home now it's O.K. Only I don't see what the hell's botherin' ya. Y'gonna see a swell piktcha an' you'll have some ice cream. Don't y' like that?"

Johnson wavered. "I—I——" he began.

"Forget about it, kid. Soon's y'see the movie house you'll be dyin' t' go in; swell piktcha playin', too. How ya like Buck Jones, kid?"

Johnson looked at him blankly and without change of expression. "Buck Jones?" he said.

"Never heard of him, huh, kid? Wait'll y'see him. He's terrific—totes two guns an' he don't spare the lead. Fights with the crooks on horses, jumps on 'em from a tree when they ride under him. Always wins, too. Wait'll y' see him." He glanced nervously over at Johnson and he saw Johnson was undecided. "Look, kid—I don't want ya to go away feelin' lousy. Y'don't hafta feel bad about this thing, see? It was a mistake can happen any time with anybody. You don't wanta go home an' feel bad about us an' hate us. That'll jus' make ya spiteful an' maybe get y' inta trouble again. An' listen, kid. Nobody don't hafta know about this, see? It's none of nobody's business. You go have a good time an' then go home an' forget about it. That's all, kid. You're a good li'l nigger. Well, stay that way. You don't wanta be mad at us an' then go tellin' stories. That'll jus' get ya inta trouble. You heard about these damn Reds that go around killin' people all over the country. That's the way they are—hateful and spiteful. Hate everybody an' then wanta kill ever' body. Don't get that way. It'll jus' get y' inta trouble. See?"

Johnson nodded. "Yes sir—I'm not mad. I don't want no trouble."

"O.K., Johnson. You're all right. I can see that. Jus' keep y'mouth shut, that's all, an' y' won't have no trouble. Nobody don't hafta know what went on, remember that."

The car had entered the town, and the bulb-studded marquee of a movie house appeared a block down from where they were. The sheriff drove slowly.

"Yessir!" he said, "this sure is gonna be a swell piktcha, all right. Gonna be the third time y'seen a movie, huh, kid?" He winked slyly at Johnson. "Ever see Mae West?"

Johnson smiled. He had never heard of Mae West, but he pieced together the sly wink with the grin and figured a smile would be the right answer—especially since it was about a girl.

The sheriff laughed loudly. "Haw—haw! You prob'ly got your own nigger idol, huh?"

Johnson smiled because he did not know what it was all about. The loneliness was disappearing and he began to feel happy again after all. It would be a thrill seeing a real movie—and ice cream too . . . !

The police car nosed in toward the curb in front of the movie house and stopped abruptly.

The sheriff and Johnson got out and the Negro followed the deputy to the box office.

"O.K., kid," said the sheriff, "go ahead in an' enjoy the piktcha." He handed him the ticket. "Here, wait a minute, Johnson. Take this half dollar an' buy some candy inside. Y'kin have some ice cream when y'get out, too. It's all on me. No hard feelings, kid, an' remember—what happened is nobody's business, see? So long, kid!"

He lumbered back to the car and bounced in under the steering wheel, slamming the door. The green car zoomed smoothly out from the curb, hesitated, and then blended into the single line of traffic.

Johnson looked at the ticket and at the half dollar. Then his teeth flashed again and he looked around for the entrance. He put the coin carefully into his pocket and went in, giving the ticket taker the whole ticket and looking amazed when the latter offered him back half of it. He took it and put it into his pocket to be saved as a treasure. Then, smiling at him and at the couple that came out through the other door, he disappeared into the darkness of the theater, smiling in the darkness.

Johnson sat on the edge of the first empty seat he found and stared breathlessly at the living screen for full three and a half hours. And when he saw the same part twice he did not know it until the feature was finished and the second picture that he had come in upon began. Then his eyes were tired and he felt dizzy and the stuffy air of the theater began to nauseate him. He went out smiling weakly at everyone he passed; he stood on the sidewalk and looked around uneasily. He spied a candy store near the theater and went over to get some ice cream. He waited patiently while the man prepared the cone, his lips twitching uncertainly around his mass of white teeth—not knowing whether to expand or recede.

Then Johnson found himself outside again, walking up a comparatively empty side street while he finished the cone. It was late in the afternoon; the fire in the sun was cooling slowly, and with it the earth cooled.

Johnson paused in the middle of the sidewalk and looked around. He had taken the advice of the sheriff: He had had a good time—ice cream and movies—and that had been more fun than he'd ever enjoyed before in his life.

It was time he went home. His mother would think that they had put him in jail, and she would worry and cry, and then his sister would cry too and she would be afraid—terribly afraid, like he had been before in the car . . . afraid and very lonely . . .

He was not mad or anything. He didn't want to get into anything; he didn't want to get into any more trouble, like those Reds the sheriff had talked about. . . . It was all a mistake, and now everything was all right. His bruised mouth still hurt a little, but it was all right. "A mistake can happen to anybody," he echoed.

Johnson snuggled his hands into his pockets. He turned around. There was a huge billboard behind him advertising the very movies he had just seen. His eyes passed over it uninterestedly, and he turned again and looked down the length of the street.

Yes, he would go home now. . . . He had had his good time—a swell time—and he was very happy. After all, he reasoned unconsciously, he wasn't in jail, he wasn't being knocked down any more—and on top of it all he had seen a movie for only the third time in his life, with an ice-cream cone and forty-five cents in his pocket to boot, and to persuade himself he fingered the forty-five cents in his pocket. . . .

But still Johnson was bewildered. He stood quietly on the partly deserted sidewalk and struggled hard with himself to understand what it was, and why.

And a great wave of loneliness and bitterness swept over him and took him with it. Soon it was all-powerful and he tried in vain to explain it to himself.

He was unhappy, very unhappy, and that was all that he knew, was how he felt.

Johnson's fortitude collapsed with this feeling; it was too strong for him. He moved slowly over the curb and sat down on it. Tears welled in his eyes and he looked down to hide his face from passers-by.

The tongues of flame from the edge of the sun lapped at the horizon. A chilly breeze took its cue and swept down from the hills into the town, across the valley.

Johnson sat in his torn shirt on the curb and cried to the dust that padded his feet, and the dust patiently absorbed the large drops that splashed into it. . . .

Johnson made no sound, but people walking by saw the wet face and perhaps the falling drops. They stared at him curiously and walked on.

. . . Just a little nigger crying on the curb.

WHO LIVED AND DIED BELIEVING

By Nancy Hale

From *Harper's Bazaar*

NANCY HALE

was born in Boston, May 6, 1908, of a distinguished American family. Her father was Philip Hale, the painter; her grandfather was Edward Everett Hale; and among her great-aunts were Lucretia Hale and Harriet Beecher Stowe. She was graduated from the Winsor School, in Boston, in 1926, and studied the following year at the Boston Museum of Fine Arts. She studied for a number of years in her father's studio and is a competent portrait painter. She sold a fairy story to the Boston Herald *when she was nine, and her first book, a novel,* The Young Die Good, *was published in 1932. She was assistant editor on* Vogue, *and later on* Vanity Fair. *She has been married twice and has two children.*

In 1935 Miss Hale won a special prize for a short-short story in the O. Henry Memorial Award Prize Stories *with "To the Invader," from* Modern Youth. *The following year she served as a judge, and the 1937 book included "To the North," which appeared in* Redbook Magazine *under the title "All He Ever Wanted." The 1938 volume contained "Always Afternoon," also from* Redbook; *the 1940 collection "That Woman," from* Harper's Magazine; *the 1941, "Those Are As Brothers," from* Mademoiselle; *and the 1942, "Sunday—1913," from* Harper's Bazaar.

Miss Hale's second novel was Never Any More, *and her third was* The Prodigal Women, *a best seller of last fall.* The Earliest Dreams *was a collection of short stories, and* Between the Dark and the Daylight, *also short stories, was published this spring.*

It was a strange, hot summer. The days throbbed and the nights were exhausted and melancholy. In August the temperature rose over ninety and hung there; the heat shimmered over the buildings and the streets of the town. Every afternoon at two Elizabeth Percy came down the steps of the house that was made into apartments for nurses. She walked along the burning pavements, around the corner, past the newsstand where the magazines hung fluttering on lines of wire, to Massey's Drug Store.

Her hair was very dark and as smooth as dark brown satin; it was combed back from her calm forehead and fell curving under at the back behind her ears. She wore plain uniforms with small round collars close about her neck, and she was all white and fresh and slender and strong.

From the heat outside she would walk into the dim coolness of the drugstore that smelled of soda and candy. There was a faint sweat upon the marble of the soda fountain; Mr. Massey and the other clerks stood about in their light tan linen coats, and they smiled at her without speaking. Dave was behind the prescription counter wrapping up a small package; first the white paper and then slowly the thin bright red string. He lifted his head as she walked down the center of the store to where the tables were, and his eyes met Elizabeth's. She sat down at the small black table, and one of the boys from the fountain came and took her order of Coca-Cola. Several electric fans whirred remotely, high on the ceiling. The door opened again at the front, and three interns from the hospital came in. They leaned together on the marble counter in their whites. Their faces were young and pale with heat.

Dave came around the corner of the counter and sat down beside Elizabeth. Mr. Massey walked slowly up toward the front of the store; he smiled absently at them; he always smiled at them as they sat together between two and three.

They never talked much. Elizabeth sucked the drink slowly through a straw and lifted the glass and let bits of crushed ice drop into her mouth; they melted on her tongue. She loved to look at Dave. He was very thin and tall and he had straight yellow hair that fell forward in a lock on his forehead. His eyes were restless. He would glance at her suddenly and smile.

"How you doing over there?"

"She's just the same."

"Long case."

"Unh-hunh. Going to be longer."

"Tough you have to nurse one of those cases. Beckwith have any idea how long it'll be?"

One afternoon Elizabeth said, "Grainger told me yesterday he said he was going to use shock. Maybe."

"Insulin?"

"No, I don't think so."

Dave raised his eyebrows and shook his head. The damp yellow lock trembled against his forehead. He had finished the second year of medical school and was working at Massey's during the summer months.

"Oh-oh. That won't be so good."

"Grainger'll have it, in the mornings."

"No, no fun," he said.

"I'm so sorry for Mrs. Myles."

Dave shrugged his shoulders.

"Don't get tough," she said. "You're not a doctor yet. Beckwith's sorry for her too. It's not the usual thing. She's gone through plenty."

"Sure," he said.

"Oh, real doctors have pity, you know; it's just you little boys."

She smiled at him, and he smiled back after a minute. He looked restless and impatient. He reached one hand under the table and put it on her knee and looked into her long, calm, dark blue eyes.

"Meet you at eleven?" he said. Elizabeth nodded. He took his hand away.

"She wants to see you again."

"Oh God."

"It doesn't hurt you any. Just go up there to her room for a minute and say good night. She gets so much out of it."

He gave a sort of groan and shifted in his chair.

"She's got those damned eyes. I don't *mean* anything, I don't like her looking like that."

"It's just because we're going together," Elizabeth said. "It's the only thing outside herself, you see, like the only thing that's outside and ahead, and she likes to think about our going together."

"Oh God."

"She asks me about you every day. Lots of times. I don't know whether she forgets she's asked before or whether . . . Come on, do it again once. It doesn't hurt you."

"All right. All right. Eleven."

"Eleven."

She got up and walked to the counter and laid the check down with a nickel. She went out into the heat, crossed the street, and walked up the wide steps of the hospital entrance.

In Copperthwaite Two the corridor was dim and hot. Elizabeth stopped at the desk and turned over the leaves of the order book. Dr. Beckwith had ordered the shock treatment for the morning; no breakfast. Elizabeth drew in her breath. Miss Grainger came out of the door of 53 and down the hall, without her cap.

"Hi," Elizabeth said.

"Hi."

"See you've got it ordered for tomorrow."

"Yeah, man."

"Does she know about it?"

"I'm not sure. He came up and went over her this morning, heart and all, before we went out. Told her, but not exactly; said they were going to give her a treatment and there'd be acute physical discomfort. I love Dr. Beckwith. Discomfort. I don't look forward to it, I tell you. Seems like there's some things you don't get used to, and I don't like shock."

"What have you all done?"

"About the same. Walked. This walking miles in this weather does me in. I'm going home and go to sleep."

Elizabeth flipped back the pages of the order book.

"What is this stuff, anyhow? We didn't have it, then."

"Oh . . . camphor derivative? . . . something. Reckon I'll know plenty in the morning. How's Dave?"

"Fine," Elizabeth said. They parted and went along the long corridor in opposite directions. Elizabeth pushed open the heavy door of 53.

Mrs. Myles sat beside the open window and in the vicious heat observed passing back and forth outside (along the pavement?), back and forth from Hell, the doughy and grimacing faces of the damned. And a little part of the rotted grapes that rolled about within her brain watched the faces with an abstracted care; each of the faces was forever familiar, a face seen before (where?), seen before and seen again, and where, where, had been the face before? In her brain the fruit gave out a stench that she could taste in her mouth, and with it came the horror; no, no, those faces she had never seen before; it only seemed that she had; and the seeming was wrong and she could not send it away, the seeming stayed, shaking its tattered locks and grinning; yes, these faces had been seen before. The faces passed, and none of them was his. Watch, watch, observe with shrinking but insistent care each hideous face that comes nearer and nearer with death in its eyes and the unbelievable humanity, the bigness, in the coming-nearer mouths, until each face passed and was not his, was never his.

Her heart that was no longer her friend beat frantically one two three four five six seven eight eighty is a normal pulse for a woman seventy for a man but this was—hundred and forty . . . MAD

The heavy-strained tension split with the scream of silk. The door opened and Miss Percy came in. So cool so calm so bright. With calm brow, with dark hair, and eyes like dark blue water. Cool as the little leaves that tremble in the tree. What thou among the leaves hast never known. This she has never known, with her calm eyes. Oh, reach to me, thou among the leaves, reach down to me in Hell with your cool hands, reach down to me.

She sees it all clean. The same world, clean. It is just me. I must remember that, it is just me; the world is cool and calm and bright. Not this. It is just me. Not mad, he said, just an exaggeration of your understandable state of tension, just an exaggeration of a normal point of view, just an exaggeration but not mad.

"Poor old Mr. Duggan next door's making quite a lot of noise," Miss Percy said, smiling. She stood before the mirror of the yellow-oak bureau and took her cap from the bureau post and pinned it to the back of her dark head. "I hope it doesn't bother you too much. Anyway, we'll go right out."

"Poor Mr. Duggan," Mrs. Myles said. "Is he getting any better at all?"

"I think they're going to give him some treatments that will make him all well."

The nurse glanced quickly at the patient.

She didn't mean to say that. She doesn't know if I know it too. They are coming.

"You'd better wear your wide hat," Miss Percy said. "The sun's real hot this afternoon."

Obediently she put the hat upon her head and tied the ribbons that held it on under her chin.

"Put a little lipstick on," the nurse said. "It's so becoming to you to have a little color in your lips. Don't you remember what Dr. Beckwith said when he met us outside the steps yesterday, how pretty you looked? You've put on a pound and a half in two weeks. It won't be long before we have you weighing what you ought to. Before you know it you're going to be right strong."

Now to smile. Now widen the corners of the mouth and look straight into Miss Percy's eyes and hold it for a moment. But no! This is no smile. This is the terrible and tragic shape of a comic mask. Thus grimace the damned, who burn in the fires and, looking upward to the cool hand that is stretched in kindness and impotence to meet their torment, try one last time and achieve the horrible stretch, the grin, of the comic mask.

They walked down the hot dim corridor and turned to the right.

"Can't we please go down in the elevator?" Mrs. Myles said.

Miss Percy's face looked troubled.

"I know," she said. "Only he wants you to walk through the hospital."

"All right."

So once again. Endure, endure. Endure to the end.

First they walked through the children's ward. Once it had not been bad; the universal slime had not had time to foul this too; she had seen them as children, delicate and pale and sweet. But then the tide of the slime had mounted here too, and ever since it had been this way. Student nurses, nurses, interns passed them. "Afternoon, Mrs. Myles." They all know me. Can they see it in my face? . . . In the little beds the children lay or sat, with their sick faces. Sickness was everywhere. This is the great house of sickness. The children's faces were greenish with the heat. Which among them is mine? He is dead. He is not dead; which among them is mine, not well and laughing, but sick, which among them is my sick, corrupted child, infected from me all its tiny beginnings with the worm of sick sick sick? I am sick and all of mine is sick.

And she smelled the sharp recurrent fear. Fear, that clawed at the ruin of her mind; fear that rattled in her chest about the flabby palpitating boundaries of her heart. This fear is wicked, she thought: I am not afraid *for* the children, I am afraid *of* them. I am afraid of everything. I am full of poison of wickedness and fear; cold poison.

"He wants you to face things," Miss Percy said as they passed through and beyond the men's ward. "You know. Not get so you think you couldn't do something, special."

"I know."

In the beds the men lay, with sickness floating in the pools of their eyes. They passed on through the women's ward. A woman looked up. One side of her face was swollen out to huge proportions and covered with bandage through which leaked sticky yellow stuff. There was the long ominous smell of sweet ether and they passed suddenly across the hall of the hospital and their feet sounded sharp and loud on the stone flagging, and they went out into the loud sad heat. They descended the steps and started to walk down the road away from the town.

Suddenly from behind in the sunshine blared a loud-speaker, carried on a truck painted silver, with huge letters advertising an air-cooled movie house downtown. Slowly, slowly, the truck crept along the hot street. The enormous screaming music shook the atmosphere:

"Fall in love, fall in love, says my heart. . . .
Fall in love, FALL IN LOVE . . ."

It swung slowly around a corner, out of sight. From far away in the afternoon the idiot voice still screamed:

"Fall in love, fall in love, says my heart. . . ."

They walked steadily on, the nurse with a secret little smile, the woman with a stiff and empty face.

The hours passed in gross and threatening procession. And with the hours the woman felt the always coming on, the rising walls, of the enclosing fear, like soundproof glass, shutting her away; the terrible pawlike hand fumbling with the cork to stopper her finally into this bottle of aloneness.

She sat beside the window in the decline of the afternoon, and her hand was too sick with fear to stretch out to the shade and pull it down against the sun. She did not dare to move her hand. And soon the sun had bobbled behind the dreadful mountains of the west.

The nurse spoke to her several times and at last in her closing bottle she heard the voice from far away and turned, and it was supper being put before her on a tray. In the bowls of all the spoons were faces that grinned at her and twisted their mouths into screams.

She ate, and then she was sick and the good food left her body in protest and she sat again by the window where the evening light now ran in around the edges of the shade like liquid poison, wet and lying on the floor and on the furniture of the room. The nurse put a table before her and laid out cards for a game upon its surface.

She looked down and saw the ferret faces of the kings and queens, the knaves; pinched and animal-like faces that whispered until the whispering was like a whistling in the room; and she turned her face away, but there was only the faraway flapping shade with the night running in around the edges, and she looked again at her hands but they were vast and swollen and she turned away and closed her eyes but within her was nothing but fear.

"How do you feel?" the nurse said in the evening room.

"How do you feel?" the nurse said.

"How do you feel?" the nurse said.

"HOW DO YOU FEEL?" the nurse said.

The nurse said, "Mrs. Myles, is there anything the matter?"

"It's as if," she said, "all the human things had been taken out of me and it left holes, like a cheese with great empty holes. And the holes have to be filled with something and they are all filled up with fear. So that where I had all sorts of things now I haven't got anything but fear in all the holes."

But that wasn't it at all, not only that; there was the bottle, how to tell someone of the bottle, glass and soundproof, where the stopper was being pushed tight home with her inside; not like a moth, no, not so clean, not like the souls in bottles, *animula, vagula, blandula*. No, like a festering purple lump of tissue.

Hell is not heat or cold, it is banishment to the ultimate ego. And in a few hours I shall be stoppered forever, she thought. I will not be able to speak, I will not be able to hear. I will be *mad*.

She asked for a pencil and paper. She wrote, and her handwriting was not her own; it was strange and inchoate like the sawings of the line of a fever chart. She looked at it with desperation. Will I scream? Will I groan? Will I grimace and mouth meaningless words? What will I do, with all of them watching me, crawling loathsomely inside the bottle, the face plastered on the purple stinking tissue like the fearful little faces in the spoons; while they watch, with their cool, well eyes, dressed all in white.

She tried to explain about the bottle on the paper with her failing handwriting, and then she folded it and wrote the doctor's name outside.

"Put it somewhere," she said urgently. "I want you to give it to Dr. Beckwith tomorrow if . . . if I . . ."

If I can no longer communicate what I feel, if I am mad.

"You're going to be fine," the nurse said. "You're going to be fine. Nothing's going to happen to you. Don't be afraid."

She thinks I mean die. No. Only the bottle. Or die?

Or die? For they are coming in the morning with something in their hands. For they are coming in the morning, footsteps measured, slow, down the corridor to me, bearing . . . the cross? . . . in their arms. No. No. You can still endure a little, do not think of Christ, that's the beginning. When the stopper is jammed at last deep into the neck of the bottle, then it will all be thoughts of Christ. Just with the last resisting inch, I can avoid the thought of Christ. . . .

But Christ. So cool, so calm, so bright. O Jesus, thou art standing outside the fast-closed door. Jesus with his mild face, his mournful eyes, the bright brown beard, the suffering. Oh no!

The minutes, the hours passed in ever-gathering procession. Miss Percy ran water and opened the high, narrow bed and helped the woman into it.

"Dave is coming to say good night to you," she said above the bed. "Dave is coming to say GOOD NIGHT TO YOU," she said.

Oh . . . Dave is coming to say good night to me. . . . Dave? I don't know what is that word: Dave. Something; once; better; but not now. Only the bones of ego smelling of fear and dirt.

"Mrs. Myles."

"Mrs. Myles."

"Mrs. Myles."

"MRS. MYLES!"

She turned her head and in the doorway, unreal, remote, beyond Hell, they stood, the nurse, white and slender, and the young man—he was Dave. They stood there, down a tiny vista beckoning, the last reminder. For they were love. It still endured, somewhere, upon the fading world. It was a flickering candle point upon the dark; flickering in the waves that even now, like the great winds of Hell, blew the candle flame, tiny, tiny.

The woman on the bed strained toward what she saw. Upon these bones of ego hangs one last shred of flesh, and as long as it hesitates there, gnawed by the mouths of cockroaches, so long that shred of flesh shall reach, shall strain toward what it sees, toward love. The shred is hanging by a nerve, and the candle point flickers and grows far, far away at the end of the cone-shaped darkness.

"Good night, Mrs. Myles."

"Good night," she said. "Are you going out somewhere together?"

"Unh-hunh," Miss Percy said. "Reckon we'll go for a drive in the country to find a breeze."

"Yes," the woman said. "I hope it'll be cool, in the country. I hope you have a lovely time. I hope you're happy."

She turned her head away from the door and closed her eyes, struggling to maintain that point of light somewhere in the darkness that was growing. As long as I can see it the bones will not be wholly bare, and the world not gone. I hope they will be happy. They love each other. Here I lie: in my sepulcher, and the stopper hovers, and the smell of brimstone everywhere. But while the candle flickers I will remember. When it gutters and goes out, I will go out, and the shred of flesh shall drop at last and the paw that reeks shall push the stopper down. . . .

"Well, if you need anything, you know you just have to ring and Miss Perley will get it for you, dear. Good night," the nurse said.

But that the woman did not hear.

After eleven the hospital was quiet and the lights along the corridors were turned out, so that only the light over the desks of the nurses in charge shone. The wards were dark and still; along some corridor could be heard occasionally the rattling trundle of a stretcher being pushed in a hurry, the stifled coming and going of a night emergency.

Elizabeth Percy went out through the hospital to the main entrance with Dave. A yawning nurse behind a desk raised her eyes and said "Hi!"; a doctor came hurriedly along the passage, wriggling his arms into a hospital coat as he went; his head was down and as Elizabeth passed he glanced upward from under his brows, nodded, and said, "Miss Percy. . . ." They came out on to the open stone flagging of the entrance hall where lights burned behind the admittance desk, and went down into the melting, melancholy night.

Elizabeth put her hand through Dave's arm and squeezed it; he glanced down at her and smiled.

"How you, babe?" he said.

"A little whipped. . . . That case is so hard, you can't do anything for her much and she's going through something awful."

"Forget it," he said. "You're off now. Climb in. Reckon it'll hold together a little longer."

She got into the old Chevrolet parked by the curb in the darkness.

They drove through the subsiding lights of the town, past the movie theaters with their electric signs turned off now; the few people in light clothes dawdling before the doors of ice-cream parlors; there was the faint occasional hoot of a motor horn, the slam of a front door. As they passed into the outskirts of the town the smell of the honeysuckle met them, drifting in from the country, and from far away the small sweet sawing of the crickets in the fields. They crossed a bridge and drove out along the country road, like a tunnel of darkness covered over with the branches of the trees. Their headlights made a white passage down the center of the tunnel. The smell of honeysuckle grew stronger, filling the whole night air, and sometimes they would pass a spot where the honeysuckle smell grew suddenly sharper, sweeter, bursting like fresh fountains into scent.

"My, this is nice," Elizabeth said. Her head was leaned back against the back of the seat.

He pressed her knee with his right hand and drew it toward his.

"Heat like we've been having can't last much longer," he said. "Registered over a hundred outside the store this afternoon. Got to crack sometime. May Leeds says her father and all the farmers are praying for rain."

"How's May?" Elizabeth asked in her low, quiet voice.

"Oh. . . . I just took her to a movie while I was waiting around for you. She just dropped in while I was finishing up. . . . I've got to do something with the evenings, haven't I?"

"Of course, darling."

"It was a lousy movie."

She said nothing.

Far out along the road Dave stopped the car off to one side, under the boughs of the trees, and switched out the lights so that nothing could be seen; only the wide dark; the smell of the honeysuckle quivered through the darkness, and in the field beside them a whippoorwill called. Dave lit a cigarette and put his arm around Elizabeth.

"God, it's good to get out of that hellhole," he said.

After a moment Elizabeth spoke.

"I can't get Mrs. Myles out of my head," she said. "She just doesn't get any relief at all."

"Oh, skip the hospital when you're out of it."

"I know. Only I keep thinking that's what love can do to you."

"Inability to adjust."

"Yes, I know. But I guess it isn't so easy to adjust when you're too much in love, and then everything sort of came on her. I can't help picking things up. She was just mad about him and apparently he never cared much about her and she knew it, and that must be just . . . awful. And then when she got pregnant he went off with this other woman, and when she had her baby it died right away. Placenta previa. It would take quite a lot of adjusting."

"Well. . . . Skip it. You can't go stewing about patients' problems. Leave that to Beckwith. How about kissing me?"

"You'd think she'd be through with love, wouldn't you? But she sort of hangs on to the idea of it. Like about . . . us."

"Yeah. Listen. I'm sorry, but I can't go up there any more and represent something for your patient. It just makes me feel too goddam gummy."

"You don't have to. You never had to, only she seemed to get so much out of seeing you and it's awful seeing her every day, so lost. Anyway, she's getting shock in the morning."

"She is?"

"Yes. I hope it'll do the trick."

"How about skipping the hospital, baby? You're supposed to be a nurse, not an angel of mercy. Quit brooding about work out of hours. Kiss me."

She put both arms around him and kissed his mouth. His arms came around her and she felt the restlessness, the impatience in his body, and the eagerness, the searching.

"Oh, darling," she said. "I guess I'm pretty much in love with you."

"I don't mind you one bit myself," he murmured.

She started to speak, checked herself, and then spoke.

"Dave darling, you wouldn't hurt me, would you?"

"Mmh-mmh."

"You could hurt me so easily. I'm so wide open to you."

"That's just the way I like you," he said, and he put his mouth down on hers, and his hands passed down her arms. Now they were close together, closer and closer in the satin darkness, and in the field the bird called at intervals and the smell of the honeysuckle came down in waves of shuddering sweetness. Over the country where they were the night sky seemed to brood, hanging soft and thick and vast over the land. Far away a train passed in the darkness, and across the fields Elizabeth heard its whistle cry three times, three times—ah, ah, aaaah.

When they drove back into town it was very late and the air had a false coolness; there was a little breeze that would go away with the dawn. Elizabeth leaned silent against the seat back. Dave sat up straight and drove, and talked about the coming year of work.

"We get Parsons in surgery and will that be something. You remember Jim Jencks from down Eliza County, he was a real nice guy, I used to see a whole lot of him; he just had one run-in with Parsons after another, and that's one reason, I guess, he isn't going to be able to come back this year. Hope I don't get fixed up wrong with the old bastard."

"What's Jim Jencks doing now?" Elizabeth said.

"He just went on home. The damn fool, he got married. That finished him. Reckon he'll be raising pigs the rest of his life."

"I didn't know he got married."

"Yeah. Lehman, Lemmon . . . ? Married a nurse, anyway. Never had good sense."

Elizabeth made a small noise with her lips.

"Oh! . . . Beg your pardon! Only *you* know, the business of guys marrying nurses, the way they do . . . You know just as well as I do."

"Yes."

He left her in the dark and empty street before the apartment house where she lived. In the silence of the town the car sounded noisily as he drove away. Elizabeth looked after the car for a moment and then she walked slowly up the brick steps to the house full of nurses asleep.

The woman in Room 53 was awake, passing from unconscious to conscious horror, as soon as the phlegm-gray dawn had filled the corners of the room. There was the relentless metronome beat of doom rapping everywhere. It could not be slowed, nor stopped, nor avoided, but beat faster minute by minute until at last the beat would fuse, would *be* the footsteps coming down the corridor outside, bearing the thing that would be borne. The woman turned her head in an old and useless reflex against horror and stared out of the window into the gray light.

On the bank opposite the hospital window there were a number of little things, moving about and pecking, and she knew that they were birds; but they were not birds, they were frightful lumps of mud, mud birds, that jerked about the dirt. She turned her eyes away from them in loathing, but there was nowhere else to look. She closed her eyes upon the horror of outside, to meet the inside horror.

The chorus sang the evil hymns. O Jesus, thou art standing outside the fast-closed door. O Jesus, thou . . . the bright brown beard, the promise that is stained and filthied with corruption, and where is there to fly to lose this wickedness? Abide with me; fast falls the eventide. The awful sweetish dripping of the notes in chorus; that seems to be a promise, that asks for comfort.

The panic grew and the metronome beat, a little faster; the tentacles within reached out in frenzy and there was nothing there to grasp, only abide with me; fast falls the eventide; the dim valley of sin, echoing in the shadows. Though I walk through the valley of the shadow of death, I shall fear no evil; for thou art with me; thy rod and thy staff. . . . Were those what they would bear? The rod and the staff? Though I walk through the valley of the shadow of death. . . . I shall fear this evil, spreading like phlegm along the valley, everywhere, and all is evil, abiding with me. . . .

Oh no! she cried inside herself with one last straining, no! But where was there to look? And in the ultimate necessity there flickered far off the pale point of the candle flame.

And then the footsteps down the corridor. And then the footsteps, am I dreaming them? The door opened and the priests and the acolytes came in—no, the doctor and the resident and the interns and the nurse—no, the white-robed priests of this obscene observance, this sacrifice, and I am the sacrifice that lies quite still upon the altar, and they bear the weapon in their hands: the huge, brutal, long syringe lying upon a bed of gauze, and I am Christ to meet their sacrifice, to give my life. Six people in the room, and the sacrifice.

"Good morning, gentlemen," the woman said.

The nurse, by the head of the bed, laid her hand upon the patient's hand. The three interns stood grouped at the foot of the bed. The doctor stood on the right of the bed and looked down into the patient's face. The resident stood halfway down the left side of the bed, and in his hands he held the syringe.

She looked up into the doctor's face and upon it lay his eyes, flat, like gray, wet, cold oysters laid upon a plate.

"Listen," the woman said hurriedly. "Tell me quick. Does it matter what thoughts I am thinking? I mean will this fasten them permanently this way? Because my thoughts are so bad, and I can't seem to think any good thoughts. . . ."

"It doesn't matter, kiddy," said the doctor. The eyes like oysters swam at her and spun a little round and round. He laid his fingers on her wrist. The resident took her left arm and felt with his fingers along the veins on the inside of her elbow. She closed her eyes. Now let me think one good thought, that my brain may be embalmed in this sacrifice with a good thought held in it like a fly in amber. Oh, stay with me, flame, the point before the eyes, the one last point. . . .

A wave from the outside of sick; of liquid; of shuddering horror ran up her veins.

"Thrombosed," the resident said. "We'll have to try another."

"Steady, kiddy," the doctor said.

Oh, flame, abide with me in the moment of dissolution. . . .

Then crashingly a thousand carmine circles spun in her brain and there were crashes and mad carmine and the dark.

"Look at that," the leftmost intern said as the figure on the bed sat straight up, clenched in convulsion.

"Patient down on G Ward fractured three vertebrae in one of those," the resident said, watching.

"You'll have your good days and your bad days." The nurse's voice came to her. "You'll have your good days and your bad days, Mrs. Myles."

She was eating lunch off a tray and it was lettuce that she was putting in her mouth. It was thin and crisp and very cold. The world around her was hot and the sun beat through the window beside her. Everything was fatigue, and pain in her back, but the lettuce on her tongue was cool, and the nurse's voice; her name was Miss Percy and she was always there, in the revolving mist, speaking to her out of the wilderness, cool and clear.

"You'll have your good days and your bad days, Mrs. Myles."

She was walking through the jungle of the world, and she was lost. She did not know where she was. It was an utterly strange, green jungle. Only the nurse, Miss Percy, was there beside her, and so she continued to walk through this land.

They came to a brook that ran through a shady hollow and they sat down on a large stone by the margin of the brook and the nurse took off the woman's shoes, and she put her tired feet in the brook. The water was warm and fresh and ran softly past her feet. Beside the brook stood tall green trees that she had never seen before. She kept her feet in the soft running water and listened to the rustling in the leaves of the strange trees.

"How did I get here?" she asked. "Where have I been?"

The nurse's voice came with the sound of the brook, cool and clear.

"You're taking a walk in the country. You're staying at the hospital for a while."

"I don't remember . . ."

"You'll have amnesia for a little bit. It's all right."

It's all right. . . .

Miss Percy stopped the doctor in the corridor.

"Dr. Beckwith, may I speak to you for a minute?"

The doctor stopped on one foot in his hurrying walk. The two horns of the stethoscope stuck up from the pocket of his white coat.

"My patient isn't getting hardly any sleep, Doctor. I wondered if you could order something."

"Can't give sedatives, you know, with the treatments. Has a counteractive effect."

"She just seems so terribly tired."

"Well, she didn't even feel tired before. . . . I'll order insulin tonight, Miss Percy. See whether that'll put her to sleep."

"Thank you, Doctor."

"You don't look as if you'd got much sleep yourself," the doctor said.

"Oh . . . it's just this heat."

"Got to break soon."

"Yes."

They were in a bowling alley, that was what it was, although she did not know where the bowling alley was or how she had got there. But the nurse was sitting on one of the wooden theater seats behind her. She herself was standing, facing the alley with a bowl in her hand.

She continued with the action that somehow she had begun. She neither felt the bowl with her hand nor felt the floor under her feet when she moved forward. It was like moving through air. She willed herself to make the gestures that somewhere inside she knew should be made now, and her body carried out the commands, but without sensation, without seeming to touch anything at all.

It just shows what you can do by will power, she thought, surprised. I can do anything I will myself to do, even though I am moving in air.

She let go the bowl and watched down the long straight alley where the bowl rolled, and heard the rumble of the falling pins.

She watched as the three black bowls came rolling up the wooden trolley to the side and came to a stop. She picked up one of them and although she had picked it up she felt nothing against her palm.

It's almost fun, she thought, seeing what you can do by will power.

It was night, and suddenly she could not bear to lie in bed any longer. Since the nurse had stuck the needle in her arm the strangest energy and slow hope had begun in her.

In the dim spaces of this room the nurse was moving about. She was taking off her cap.

"I want to get up," the woman said. "Can I get up? I want to talk."

The nurse turned and smiled.

"All right," she said. She pulled forward the big chair that was by the window and helped the woman into it. The nurse sat down on a small straight chair and smiled at the woman.

"But were you going away . . . ?" the woman said, puzzled. Something stirred in her head, faintly remembered.

"No," the nurse said. "I haven't anywhere special to go. I'd be glad to stay a little later, Mrs. Myles."

"You don't know," she said, "what hope can feel like. It's like running water. I mean freedom. Oh, you don't know what it's like! to be able to see freedom. Even just a little bit."

"You're going to have all the freedom in the world."

"I keep thinking of the loveliest things—long straight roads and driving along them fast in an open car. You don't know what hope can feel like. It's like the wind beginning to blow. Am I really going to be free?"

Suddenly the words of something whose origin she could not remember came into her head and she began to repeat them aloud: "That this nation, under God, shall have a new birth of freedom—and that government of the people, by the people, for the people shall not perish from the earth."

Shall not perish. . . .

"That's what I mean," she said. "That's the way it feels. I can't remember, but it wasn't that way before, it wasn't for the people, by the people, I mean as if I were the people, as if I were a nation. A woman like a nation."

"Yes," the nurse said. "I know. Instead of under a dictator, you mean. It's awful to live under a dictator and not belong to yourself any more, isn't it?"

"Yes," she said impatiently, pushing that part away from her, for now there was hope, forming like a five-petaled flower, like a star. Sitting forward on the edge of the chair in her excitement, she repeated the words again, whatever they were: "This nation, under God, shall have a new birth of freedom—and that government of the people . . ."

And after some time the nurse went away and came back with a tall glass that was filled with sugared water, flavored deliciously with lemon, and the woman drank it.

And on some mornings the doctor and the resident and three interns came into her room, and the resident carried the large syringe. He was always the one who inserted the needle into her vein. It was a thing that came suddenly on some mornings and it had to be faced, once more; endure, she thought, endure to the end. And always at the last she summoned to her the vision, with her eyes closed, of the candle flame that companioned her through the darkness, through the bad days, through it all. It did not leave her, it remained to fortify her in the last extremity, when they came and the needle went into her arm and in her head spun the carmine circles and the world crashed, and then the dark. . . .

"Don't think she'll have to have another," the doctor said as they watched the figure in convulsion on the bed. "This stuff certainly is magic in some cases."

On an afternoon in the yellow sunshine suddenly she was sitting under an apple tree in the yard beside the hospital, and the nurse, Miss Percy, was sitting on the grass beside her. Mrs. Myles turned her head slowly and smiled. The heat had gone; it was a cool and lovely afternoon; the leaves rustled in the tree above her and from its branches came the smell of apples.

On the grass further away some interns were playing baseball. Their voices shouted to one another, and the ball could be heard smacking their cupped palms. A breeze trickled along the air. The shadows were beginning to lengthen from the wall of the hospital, and in that light the interns, in their white clothes, ran and shouted. From a grass bank on the other side of the road from the hospital a bird called, suddenly, sweetly.

"Hello," Mrs. Myles said.

"Hello, dear. You're feeling much better, aren't you?"

"Yes," she said. Things were swimming back into her memory, the buildings here were taking their places in the world. And everything was very calm, very peaceful; there was no hurry. It doesn't matter.

She looked at the nurse, who had been there all the time. In the darkness and the long confusion, in that strange land where she had been, the nurse had been with her all the time. She studied the dark, smooth hair, the oval face, and the long, dark blue, quiet eyes.

"How is Dave?" Mrs. Myles said.

"You're remembering, aren't you?" the nurse said without looking at the patient. "I think he's fine. I haven't seen him for a while."

"But . . ."

That did not fit. She stayed silent for a little time, while the remembrances slowly rearranged themselves within her head.

"But you're in love with him," she said slowly. "It was you both. You are in love with each other."

"Well. . . . You see, we aren't going together any more."

Something was wrong. Wait while the sifting memory slowly settled. Her own life was dead, somehow she had learned that, someone had taught her that in the strange, twilight land. She knew that she had been reborn and that this was a new life. She could never have the things of her own old life, for they had gone and they were dead. But one thing only . . . a candle burning down a vista, some constant star that had companioned her through the dark valleys of the land she had left. . . . She remembered two figures standing in a doorway.

"You're not?"

"No," the nurse said. She looked tired. They stared at each other and then a new and curious thing happened, a wave swept upward and from her eyes the woman felt tears falling. It was not despair. It was only deepest sadness. The last thing had gone out of the old life. Now the past was wiped black and she was all alone and beginning a new life, reborn alone. The purest, quietest sadness swept her and she could not halt the tears that fell and fell.

"You mustn't mind at all, dear," the nurse said. But their eyes kept meeting: the nurse's quiet and dry, the woman's full of tears.

The baseball game had broken up, and a young intern came strolling by the apple tree and looked down at the two who sat upon the grass. His face Mrs. Myles knew. It had looked at her on many mornings.

"Afternoon, Mrs. Myles, Miss Percy," the intern said, and then stopped in embarrassment at the tears on the woman's face.

"Well . . ." he said. "Seems fine to have a good cry, doesn't it?"

"Yes," she said, crying quietly, for all that was dead now, forever, and could never be brought back. And it was fading fast. Fade far away, dissolve, and quite forget what thou, among the leaves, hast never known. It was all over; it was finished; the fight with death and sin, the wandering in the strange lost land. It was all gone, and love was gone too, and the candle flame had silently gone out. Above their heads where they sat upon the grass the little leaves in the apple tree whispered. It was all gone, and from now on the world was new, a page unwritten.

THE GLASS PIGEON

By Josephine Johnson

From *Harper's Bazaar*

JOSEPHINE WINSLOW JOHNSON

won a special prize in the O. Henry Memorial Award Prize Stories of 1935 *for the best short-short story with her "John the Six," from the* Atlantic. *In the 1934 volume her story, "Dark," from the* Forum and Century, *was included, and the 1942 book contained her "Alexander to the Park," from* Harper's Bazaar.

She was born June 20, 1910, in Kirkwood, Missouri, of Irish-Scotch-English ancestry, and went to private and public schools there. When she was twelve her family moved to a hundred-acre farm in Webster Groves, Missouri. She says she loves the country and nature more than anything else. After specializing in art and English at Washington University, she began writing short stories and poetry for magazines. She has traveled extensively both in this country and in Europe. She has exhibited her water colors and painted murals for two children's schools in St. Louis.

Miss Johnson's interest in social problems and her active social-service work is reflected in her fiction. Her articles on share-croppers, local strikes, and relief conditions appeared in St. Louis newspapers. She taught at the Bread Loaf Writers' Conference in Middlebury, Vermont, and at Iowa University. In addition to her love of books, especially poetry, she likes cooking, walking, and all kinds of animals. Her novels are Now in November, *which won the Pulitzer Prize in 1934, and* Jordanstown. Winter Orchard *is a book of short stories, while* Year's End, *published in 1937, is poetry. She has also written a juvenile. She has been married twice, has a son, Terence, and a daughter, Jane Ann, born on March seventh of this year.*

He sat on the blue chintz chair and waited for the two women, his son's wife and her mother, and observed the feminine whiteness and purity of these rooms. The white silk hangings striped in blue. The glass pear holding a pink rose, and the living roses, delicate and fragrant in their shallow bowls. On the mantel a strutting fantail pigeon in white glass, plump and translucent. On the walls were pictures of white lilies, immaculate, flat, and cool. Above him the small chandelier of uncut glass swung in the summer breeze.

He picked up the table book, a copy of *Sapphira and the Slave Girl,* and held it doubtfully in his hands, hands huge and pudgy like those of a giant child. He was an enormous man. Tall and enormously wide and fat like some great boulder, and his dusty clothes hung on him like old laundry. His hermit hair fell around his ears and turned up in little wisps, which gave his huge face a childish and naïve look under its high bald dome. He seemed to walk slumbering, but among a thousand men he was visible and majestic, moving thoughtfully and ponderously as a great gray elephant. In this chaste white room he seemed monstrous and static, like an abandoned packing case for the grand piano.

Slowly he lowered himself again in the wide armchair, and the chair seemed to vanish under him, to assume the frail and ridiculous dimensions of doll furniture. He could hear the women moving around upstairs. Moving and rustling about. Speaking to the child, running water, saying, "Stand still. Don't touch. Just a minute." In the kitchen the maid banged shut an oven door, and he could smell the warm quickening odor of hot bread.

He leaned painfully sidewise and peered into the dining room. The table was set for three, with a small side table for the boy. There were more roses in a bowl, and a rose in a little vase for the child.

He eyed the delicate chairs distrustfully. He had never been in this house before. Mike's mother-in-law's home. But he wanted to see Mike's boy again.

All the hour ride out on the streetcar, swaying and lurching toward them through the heat, his mind had been preoccupied, dwelling on his own matters, his troubles and the union's troubles, his memories and reflections rising and swelling like huge amorphic clouds, taking shape slowly; seeing masses of men, and then a very few men gathered around a table, and time running out and dying in a room bare and enormous, with a charter and a calendar on the wall. He had been so lost in memories and immediate matters that he rode four blocks beyond his stop and had to walk back down the unfamiliar summer streets, the sweat gathering and rolling in silver streams down his enormous cheeks, his collar soaked and briny. It was a nice section of the city Mrs. King lived in, he noticed idly. The houses small but new. He was grateful for the maple-shadowed sidewalks and the faint coolness from lawn sprays all up and down the block. Once he paused and stood still at a corner, and then moved ponderously on. He had been thinking of himself, John Powers, as a little boy selling ice-cold lemonade under a maple tree, and how the town cop had come along and drunk up a glass and paid him double. "The best I ever drunk, Powers," he had said. Times sure changed. He felt the old scar along his skull where the pistol butt had landed.

He had found the house number after a while and went up the walk. Mike used to come here once in a while after he and Libby got married and she had left the old lady all alone. John thought of Mike's death with a calm sadness. The things dearest to our hearts always drifted away or were cut off too soon. The strongest, the healthiest, the most vigorous. Somehow he had massed a great bulk of flesh and a great rampart of lives against death. He felt as though he had had many sons in his long life. But this year's hollow was still alive with pain.

The colored maid had let him in. Carefully, softly. "You is expected?"—a delicate balance between welcome and suspicion. She had taken his hat and left, and he felt like an elephant shaking a plump brown bee from its ear.

Alone in the room, he paused and looked around him slowly. Here in this strange and manless place with the flat lilies pure and immaculate on the wall, his curious and discerning senses stirred and were baffled. He had spent a long life with men, studying them, following them, leading them, watching them climb and crumble in a crisis, or climb and harden and smash the next man's face when he got too near up the ladder. Time and again over the littered conference table, over the beer-stained saloon table, over the unmade bed in the smoke-filled hotel room, he had seen the invisible boot swing and smash in silence over a man's heart, into his life. But women he saw only in relation to their men. What they did to a man, what they said in private, manifest in that man's relation to other men. Nothing in his long, violent, gargantuan life had prepared him for this room, this glassy pigeon, this fluttering silence.

He moved over to the piano and looked at a picture of Libby. It was a fancy photo and looked a lot like other girls, but he recognized her eyes. He hadn't seen her since Mike's funeral a year ago. In his vast impersonal way he had been fond of Libby. She did not nag and was cheerful and a fair cook. He had been aware happily that Mike loved her very much. He recalled with pleasure evenings in their kitchen, and the deep white coffee cups. He and Mike had done all the talking, but Libby had not seemed left out. She kept the cups filled and sewed on the boy's overalls. John was always aware, as though his great flesh were listening antennae, when those around him were with him or a long way off. And in that kitchen he knew they were all there, very alive and close. The boy he remembered distinctly. Even at three he had looked so much like Mike.

". . . What are you going to raise him to be, Mike?" ". . . Anything he wants to be. Anything he can make the grade of. . . ."

Jeff had wanted to be a lion tamer then. He and Mike made tents out of rugs and the kitchen table, roared around inside, and ate meat balls out of a frying pan on the floor. Then he wanted to be a baseball player, and they went to the Big League games on Sunday, and John lumbered along. He could hear the clean crack of the ball, that hard and satisfying sound, and Jeff's voice rising and curving with the arc of the ball. The splendid and shining excitement of his face! He saw them in his mind, climbing the steep evening stairs together, Mike with the groceries in one arm, and the boy with a little bag of crackers in his fist . . . climbing and vanishing together in the darkness of his memories.

He sighed enormously and clasped his hands. His need to see the boy was like a sharp hunger inside him now. After a while he heard their feet coming down the soft carpet, and lifted his chin sunken in reverie on his chest, lost in the folds of his open collar, and looked down his vast front to see if his shirt and trousers were still meeting. Down at the union hall they laid bets on this meeting, but he never found shirts that would stay tucked under. "The lugs," he murmured to himself. "The big lugs," and smiled mournfully, hitching his trousers up in front.

They were in the room. He roused himself with effort and waited like a great untidy rock for their ripples to flow over and around him. ". . . Father, this is my mother, Mrs. King. . . ." "Pleased to meetcha, Mrs. King. . . ." "So nice of you to come, Mr. Powers. So hot today, so awfully hot. . . ." He saw her faded Virginia elegance, her upright rigid figure with soft, extended hand.

"See my cowboy suit!" Jeff blurted loudly. "See my new suit, Grampaw!" He was dressed in a doll-like cowboy suit, his felt sombrero dangling from his fat brown fingers. The boots were rich and tooled in an intricate design, the shirt black silk. His freckled face looked plump and round under its halo of bleached hair.

He gets the eats, John thought. That's fine.

They sat down stiffly, facing each other. The boy circled around the room warily, whirling an invisible rope. John watched his radiant pride. "That's some outfit, Jeff!"

"I was afraid to give him the lasso part," Mrs. King said. "But all the rest is safe enough, I guess."

"If I had a lasso," Jeff said loudly, defiantly, "I'd get that there bird!" He whirled his arm at the glass pigeon. "Ping!—like that!"

"Be careful!" Mrs. King said. "Be careful, Jeff! Don't touch!" She laughed, gently, nervously.

The child retreated, watching her. His face was not angry, but tight and watching. John looked at Libby. In the whirlpool of the meeting he had not really seen her. Her face seemed plumper and her hair different. Smarter. *Fixed,* he supposed vaguely. She was dressed in white, with red shoes, and all her clothes were new. She was very quiet and glanced sidewise at him sometimes, but kept her attention on the child.

He felt alone.

They talked about how hot it was, and he asked Libby what she was doing now. She said, "Nothing now," but that she was going to teach in a girls' school next fall, an academy in Ohio. Merom. A very nice place.

He said that was nice, she would have a job. He knew some joes in the Braun, Beed and Shaffer Iron Works in Merom, but there didn't seem much point in mentioning it. "I hope you like it," he said.

Libby glanced at her mother, and Mrs. King smiled at John. "Libby is looking forward to it," she said pleasantly.

"What about Jeff?" John said.

"Jeff's going to stay with me." Her face was a quiet mask. "Libby won't have the time."

They went in to lunch, and Jeff darted ahead. "Don't touch anything on the table!" Mrs. King called softly. "Go sit down in your own little chair, Jeff."

Jeff stalked around the white lace cloth inquisitively, then sat down at his table. He seized the small rose and smelled it lustily and audibly. "Smells good!" he said. He was watching his grandmother.

"Be careful of the rose," Libby whispered. "You might break it."

Jeff plunked it back in the vase and reached for a muffin.

"Wait a minute," Mrs. King said. "No one *else* has begun to eat."

The maid passed them some cold meat and salad. "It's so hot," Mrs. King said, "I didn't think we would want very much."

There was a long silence, and John kept his eyes on his plate. He wanted suddenly to speak of Mike, but felt that the mention of his name was forbidden. Not in good taste. Something one didn't do; like lap off the plate.

He roused himself to hear Mrs. King speaking: "These are uncertain times," she was saying. "I notice the difference so much. Our carpenter, the one who worked for us on our Ozark place, is getting ninety-five dollars a week building an ammunition plant. Lima beans are thirty-nine cents a pound, and only last week they were twenty-nine. The Government is going to make us wear shorter skirts for defense. . . ." She ate a pickled mushroom and passed the muffins, but her eyes kept turning to Jeff, watching him with a nervous, hovering intensity.

John went on eating in his own way, very quickly, because he was hungry, and swallowed the blueberry muffins whole. He realized he was finished before anyone else, and curbed his impulse to shove back his chair and lumber away on business.

Jeff watched him in awe and, taking a small muffin in his palm, plastered it against his mouth and swallowed it whole.

"Don't do that, Jeff!" Mrs. King said sharply.

Jeff looked at his grandfather and smiled with his eyes, his mouth distorted with muffin. John waited for the accusing "Grampaw done it!" but it did not come. He wouldn't squeal, John thought with pride. . . . He's a chip off Mike.

For dessert they had macaroon ice cream and sugar cookies. Jeff spilled the ice cream down his black silk waist, and suddenly the tears came to his grandmother's eyes. John could see her hands shaking with anger. Libby mopped Jeff up with nervous fingers and there seemed about to be a moment of prayer, so pregnant was the silence. The child sat quite rigid, staring at his plate.

Then John mopped his great glittering head, and the silence was broken. "Shall we leave the table?" Mrs. King said, and they all pushed back their little chairs and stood up. John leaned over and took a final quick swallow of his tea, and moved enormously into the other room. Jeff followed in silence, fingering the stiff and sticky stain on his shirt. His chin was tucked down on his neck, and he looked strangely tired.

John heard the women murmuring to each other as they walked ahead of him: "When he goes, I want to go downtown. Is there anything I can get for you?" "Those beads," Libby murmured: "you might exchange them. They're too bright a green. . . ."

The phone rang, and Libby answered it. He heard her voice suddenly animate, bright, and cheerful: "I'd love to!—yes, I'd love to. No, this week is full, quite full and overflowing—could we see you Monday? Next Monday? . . . I'm sorry. I wish I had more time. . . ."

Filled and overflowing. John wondered idly: filled with what plans? what details? He thought with a mild horror of her future, teaching something or other in a girls' boarding school in Merom. What was

Mike to her now, he wondered, and did he mean more than the name of Jeff's dead father?

They sat again in a little circle facing each other. Light came in delicate bars through the Venetian blinds. Jeff was silent, staring through their pale slits of space, and then came and put his hand on John's knee. "I'm a cowboy," he said. He kept one eye on his grandmother's cold white face. "Sing me the song!"

"What song is that, Jeff?" Mrs. King leaned forward. Smiling. A terrible, inquisitional smile.

"The song about the cowboy."

John smiled. "I ain't much of a singer."

"Go ahead," Mrs. King said. "Libby never could keep a tune either."

"Oh, ma dadee was a cowboy——"

John began.

"A-ridin' the range——"

His voice was big, and beat like a drum:

"My chaps are wide, my shirt is red,
Ah'll wear ma Stetson till Ah'm dead,
Ah keep mah boots on the ta-bul——"

He paused awkwardly and flushed. "I need a banjo. I can't just sit here and beller."

"Libby could play the piano," Mrs. King suggested. "I try to make her keep up her music."

Libby turned away. "I can't," she said abruptly. "You go ahead and sing, Father."

John drew a great breath and went on chanting:

"A cowboy's life is mighty lean
When he ain't herdin' cows on the movie screen.
So hear what your dad-dee's advisin'——"

He paused and took his breath and launched ahead:

"When you swing your lariat,
You're one of the proletariat,

So get yourself a hoss and start organizin'!
Ah, I went down to the old corral
To pick me out a bronco.
I looked them over one by one,
And there was a great big stallyun!
And blazin' on his side was a union labul!
Ol' Paint, Ol' Paint,"

He sang softly:

"A prouder hoss there ain't
Than my Ol' Paint,
The hoss with the union labul!"

He paused and looked at Jeff. The child was leaning heavily against his knees and whispering the words with him:

"And I have a feelin'
Ol' Paint he'll never die,
He'll thunder on through the wild mesquite
To be on time at a union meet-in',
Strong and fearless and able——"

His voice cracked, and he stopped. A memory of Mike and Jeff together came before his eyes, so distinct and compelling that he almost put out his hand. "We ain't afraid. We're strong and fearless and able, ain't we, Dad?" ". . . That's right, Jeff. There's us. Just like it says. . . ."

He looked at Libby, but her eyes were on her mother's face, anxiously, apprehensively.

Mrs. King said nothing.

She wants me to get the hell out of here, John thought without passion. He was still lost in memory.

Jeff galloped suddenly around the room. "Paint, Ol' Paint!" he shouted. "I'm ridin' Ol' Paint!" He drew an imaginary bow and arrow and aimed it at the glass pigeon. "Ping!" he shouted. The glass and china vibrated on the mantel.

"Jeff!" His grandmother's voice was high and hysterical. The name came stinging through the summer air.

"Be careful," Libby said nervously, softly. "You might break something."

The child flushed and retreated across the room. He bent his head to one side and stared at his feet.

"The little bird was expensive," Mrs. King said. "I've had it a long time. I've always dreaded Jeff's beanshooter stage!"

Libby's fingers made a nervous pattern on the white camellias. She did not look up.

In silence John drew a long breath. The great bellows in his chest seemed to have stopped blowing. The immaculate walls drew in on him, shrinking cell-like around him; the quiet seemed filled with swarming gnats. Don't touch . . . Don't touch . . . Don't touch. . . .

With a great effort he rose from his chair, heaving upward like a sea elephant rising through warm transparent waters. "Well," he said heavily. "Well, I got to be going."

Libby gave him a swift, almost relieved look, and stood up softly. Jeff came and stood near him in silence.

"We're glad you were able to come," Mrs. King said. "Perhaps you can come again, sometime. . . ." She looked down at the child: "That is, if Jeff is a better boy than he was this time. Otherwise Grandfather won't want to see him."

The child shifted his feet unhappily, sullenly, and looked at his grandfather.

The big man stood still, trying to breathe again. His eyes rested on the glass bird, the fragile and pleasing pigeon, and a look of innocent delight came over his great face. He looked down at the child to see if Jeff was watching, and as their eyes met he made a great and deliberate gesture with his hand: "It was nice of you ladies——"

The dusty black hat struck the pigeon and swept it down on the hard blue tiles. A sharp quick crash, and white fragments flew like a small explosion. The hollow and crested head rolled to one side.

He heard the ladies' mournful and horror-stricken voices beating like wounded doves in his ears, and looked at Jeff's face, expecting a shameless joy and excitement at the long-desired and glittering explosion.

But the child's round pink face was only a mirror of maiden horror. "Oh, look!" he breathed. "Look what Grampaw done!" He turned and glared up at the big old man, his innocent, righteous face quivering. "You weren't supposed to touch that pigeon!" he said. "See what happened! It busted!"

John put on his black soiled hat. "So it did," he murmured. "So, by God, it did!"

He looked at the anxious little child in his false and shining cowboy suit, and a great sadness crept through his enormous flesh. All the bitterness in his life, all the contempt and grief, rose to his mouth:

"You poor little joe!" he said.

BLINKER WAS A GOOD DOG

By Ben Hur Lampman

From the *Atlantic Monthly*

BEN HUR LAMPMAN

was born August 12, 1886, in Barron, Wisconsin. Before he was twenty he had moved with his family to North Dakota, where at nineteen he founded, edited, and published the Michigan, North Dakota, Arena. *He also helped his father and brother publish a weekly newspaper, the Neche* Chronotype. *From there they moved to Gold Hill, Oregon, in 1912, where they published the Gold Hill* News, *and in 1916 Portland became his home, where he has lived ever since. Today he is associate editor of the* Oregonian *of that city, and in February of this year nineteen outstanding students of Lincoln, including Carl Sandburg and Ida M. Tarbell, voted an* Oregonian *editorial which Mr. Lampman wrote as the "most timely" one written on the subject.*

He is the author of several books of essays and stories: How Could I Be Forgetting? Here Comes Somebody, Tramp Printer, *and* At the End of the Carline, *the latter published in 1942. An editorial he wrote on war last year, "The Pack Beyond the Fire," was called the best short story of the year by Harry Hansen. He is married, and his only son died in June of this year. He is described as physically powerful and of excellent health. He wears flowing black ties and is a tireless fisherman. He is widely known as a poet, and in May of this year the University of Oregon bestowed upon him the degree of Master of Arts, "In recognition of his mastery of the art of distinctive literary expression; his deep and poetic insight into the mysteries of nature; and his undying devotion to the task of dignifying, through sympathetic understanding, the life and work of the common man."*

A MAN naturally disremembers—it all happened such a while ago—a good many the yarns that used to be told up river and down about him and her, and how they was always a-jowering and a-jawing one at t'other, come day, go day, the old man and the old woman. Them as knowed them never blamed them, on account of they was so all-fired alone on the home place, with the young ones growed up and gone, that him and her was sort of bound for to entertain theirselves, in times when there wasn't no mail in the country, and no radio.

So him and her taken to disagreeing, the whole eternal time, sort of to keep interested. All the while the old man would have give his last breath for the old woman, happen it would come in handy, and the old woman would have more'n died for the old man. Him and her was like that. Lots of folks is.

But of them times beyond reckoning when him and her was as cross as two sticks, one at t'other, in all them years at the old place on the upper river, a man recollects best of all the time the old man was plumb sot on having a regular Christian funeral for their old dog Blinker, so near as the old man could manage it. You knowed about how the old folks finally lost Blinker, him that they'd raised from a pup on the bottle—he growed old and gray with them two, him and her—but did ever you hear tell of how Blinker was buried?

By Godfrey, that time the old man and the old woman may have been nigh to a-splittin', because the whole p'int was religion—and the old woman, she sot great store by religion; she could be hard as a niggerhead when it come to the Word. Of course the old man, he knowed this to his sorrer, but when Blinker up and died on him, and laid there in the chips in the dooryard, stiff as a poker, and the old man was recollecting how the old dog used for to grin at him, dang him if he could see any way to get out of a-burying Blinker like a Christian. For the life of him, seemed like he couldn't.

So the old man, he come into the kitchen, and he seen right away that his old woman had been a-weeping whilst at her housework—but when he taken his courage in hand and told her what he had a mind for to do, told her as best he could manage, the old woman she give it some thought for a moment, and then she turned on him, clicking her store teeth. He knowed that for the worst sign of all. But danged if he didn't have for to admire her, like always, outfacing him like that—little and puny but bold as a bobcat, whilst she give him a piece of her mind.

When his old woman got her dander up, seemed like she looked like the girl he fetched home from the valley. She looked like the queen on a playing card. And she give him to understand that them two had buried their own, years past, and had sorrered over them, and though the old man might be sort of minded to forget, a woman she must always recollect. She wouldn't have spoke ary word such as that—if she'd rightly knowed how it hurt. But, howsoever, when a woman gets riled—— The old man, he stood there and blinked at her out of his whiskers, but he was as sot in his ways as she was in hern, and he knowed what he allowed for to do.

"It's mighty un-Christian to bury a dog like a Christian!" the old woman says. "You want me, your own wife, for to sing a gospel hymn over Blinker, whilst you pray? God is my witness I cared full as much for old Blinker as you ever did! Who redd up the kitchen after him, since ever he was whelped? Who seen to his platter? But I shan't have no part in mockery that's fit only for heathens. Nor shall you!" says the old woman. "It ain't fitting for Christians!"

And up come her apron whilst she cried her eyes out. She fair twisted the old man's heart—but you know how it is. There's times when a man is just bound not for to give in to them. He taken a chew of tobacco and he stomped out of the house. What was in his heart was as nigh to bitterness as ever had been there. It come to him then, like a thousand times afore, that they always got a man at a disadvantage, on account of they never lack words.

Well, sir, a man reckons that the old woman knowed she was bested when the old man slammed the kitchen door, but first off she dried her eyes, like women will, and put some wood in the stove against time she was going to need the oven. She clicked her store teeth, too, every once in a while—but all the time she was a-listening. She was a-listening because she knowed right well that poor Blinker wasn't more than a step from the kitchen stoop. And after a bit the old woman heard the old man say, "Whoa!" There the old fool was, with the bay mare and the stoneboat, alongside of the old dog.

She looked out and give him a look that ought to have wilted him in his tracks, but he give her a glare like ice on a duckpond, right back. "The old fool!" she was a-thinking. Might as well have taken the old dog in his two arms and carried him to wherever it was—but, no, the old fool was sot on a Christian funeral. The tears come up to her eyes again, but still the old woman was riled as could be, and she couldn't make no allowances for him. It was so un-Christian. All she said was:

"I declare, if you've a mind for to make an old fool of yourself, like a heathen in darkness, you might as well change your shirt! Come in here, this minute!" The old man, he taken Blinker up in his arms, and he laid the old dog down on the stoneboat, and gentle, there on the new straw, and stooped and picked off a burr, before he turned to give his old woman so much as a look. He glared at her then, like before, and breshed by into the kitchen. She might have put her hand on his arm, easy—but she couldn't bring herself to do it. She watched him stomp into their bedroom, right off the kitchen, and she seen that when he come out the old man had on a clean shirt. It wasn't the shirt she'd have chose—but at least, she seen, it was fitting. He give her never a look when he went past her and out of the kitchen door—and, a-listening, she heerd the old man say, "Giddap, Dolly! Easy, girl!" The stoneboat was a-grating on the gravel.

Soul alone in her kitchen, the old woman began for to mix a batch of lazyman's biscuit—the old man was uncommon fond of it—but all the while she knowed that her heart wasn't in it. Seemed like there come betwixt her and the dough, bat her eyes as she did, pictures of Blinker and the old man—and some of them pictures was of Blinker when he was skeercely more than a gangling pup, and of the old man when he was still so supple he could put one hand on the top fence rail and clear her.

It wasn't biscuit dough she seen, there in her kitchen on the upper fork: it was Blinker barking at the foot of the lone spruce in the meadow, whilst the old man he circled the tree—and him in his prime then, the best man on the river—with the Harpers Ferry musket cocked for a shot at a silver-gray that Blinker had treed. She seen Blinker leaping; she heerd the musket; she seen the squirrel tumbling, over and over; she seen the old man in his prime. And then she seemed to see Blinker with one flank raked open by a cougar, and still a-laughing, and the old man—he wasn't old then—with one foot on the long, lanky cat.

She seen them two a-going for the cows together, as many the time, and of a sudden her eyes they blurred till the dough wasn't there any more—and the old woman, she jerked back from the table, for her mind was made up, and she taken off her apron and went straight into their bedroom. The old woman was in such a hurry a body might have suspected she had for to catch the stage at the Corners. She come out of the bedroom with her hat on, the pink roses bobbing, and she made for the kitchen door. She had a book under one arm, and when her favorite rocker got in the way she flang it clean across the kitchen. As folks used to tell it, up and down the river, the old woman was in a hurry. But she'd time for to break off one stalk of wallflower, there by the stoop.

He had stopped the bay mare back of the henhouse, where there was a considerable stand of honeysuckle, and the raw black earth, with fishworms in it, was throwed back in a heap. And Blinker wasn't on the stoneboat no longer, so the old woman judged that the old dog must be in his everlasting grave. Back of the henhouse and under the honeysuckle, where the old dog used for to sun himself. The old man, his eyes lifted and shut tight as could be, he seemed for to be a-praying, with his whiskers a-waggling. For the old woman heerd him say, plain enough, as she come a-hurrying up:

"And, Lord, what You got to remember is that Blinker was a danged good dog! Dagnab me, if he wasn't! Wherefore, Lord——"

But right there his old woman shoved the old man over a ways—she had a sharp elbow—and "Amen, Lord," she says, and "You tarnation old fool!" she says, and she makes him take half of the hymnbook. She had the page open at the place. The old man opened his eyes and squinted, but he taken his half of the book, like he was used to, and she chosen the hymn mighty well, though at first she had thought of singing "Old Hundred," on account of it says to serve Him with mirth—like Blinker always done. But she changed her mind, and the place she had the book open was at "Beulah Land." So them two sang—she did, and he trailed her—the old man and the old woman, back of the henhouse, whilst the words went away across the crick and the river:

O Beulah land, sweet Beulah land,
As on thy highest mount I stand,
I look away across the sea,
Where mansions are prepared for me——

Then the old woman, she leant over and dropped in the wallflower and she seen Blinker for the last time—a-laying there on the straw at the bottom like he was sleeping. The old man, he taken up the spade and he done what he had for to do, and times he was thinking of Blinker, and times he was thinking that the old woman's voice still was like a girl's. Happened it was along toward evening, and there was a sliver of young moon in the sky. His old woman, she taken a glance at the new moon, and she might have been a-thinking of times they walked in the mowing together, for what she said was, half to herself, "Yander's a hunter's moon." She meant that there'd be quite a dry spell. That there was too bad, for the old man he bridled to hear it. He tossed in the last turf and he flang down the shovel.

"Hell's fire, old woman!" the old man, he snorted. "You taken leave of your right senses? That there moon is wet as ary moon ever I see!" Then they was at it, like always, over and over, a-jowering and a-jawing again. Him and her was like that.

A TREE. A ROCK. A CLOUD

By Carson McCullers

From *Harper's Bazaar*

CARSON McCULLERS

at twenty-six has won an outstanding place for herself among American fiction writers. She was born Carson Smith, February 19, 1917, in Columbus, Georgia, of Scotch and French Huguenot ancestry. She studied music, hoping to become a concert pianist. She began writing at sixteen, after an illness which put an end to her musical ambitions, and has been writing ever since. She went to New York, did various odd jobs, and studied at night.

When she was nineteen Story *accepted two of her stories, and her first novel, published when she was twenty-three,* The Heart Is a Lonely Hunter, *set the literary world back on its heels. No one believed a young girl had written it. Her second novel, published the following year,* Reflections in a Golden Eye, *appeared serially in* Harper's Bazaar, *and attracted an equal amount of attention. She was represented with a story, "The Jockey," from the* New Yorker, *in the 1942* O. Henry. *She was married to Reeves McCullers in 1937, and was awarded a fellowship to the Bread Loaf Writers' Conference, in Middlebury, Vermont, in the summer of 1940. Last year, while working on her third novel, she was awarded a Guggenheim Fellowship. She is at present at Yaddo, writing and working.*

It was raining that morning, and still very dark. When the boy reached the streetcar café he had almost finished his route and he went in for a cup of coffee. The place was an all-night café owned by a bitter and stingy man called Leo. After the raw, empty street the café seemed friendly and bright: along the counter there were a couple of soldiers, three spinners from the cotton mill, and in a corner a man who sat hunched over with his nose and half his face down in a beer mug. The boy wore a helmet such as aviators wear. When he went into the café he unbuckled the chin strap and raised the right flap up over his pink little ear; often as he drank his coffee someone would speak to him in a friendly way. But this morning Leo did not look into his face and none of the men were talking. He paid and was leaving the café when a voice called out to him:

"Son! Hey, son!"

He turned back and the man in the corner was crooking his finger and nodding to him. He had brought his face out of the beer mug and he seemed suddenly very happy. The man was long and pale, with a big nose and faded orange hair.

"Hey, son!"

The boy went toward him. He was an undersized boy of about twelve, with one shoulder drawn higher than the other because of the weight of the paper sack. His face was shallow, freckled, and his eyes were round child eyes.

"Yeah, mister?"

The man laid one hand on the paper boy's shoulder, then grasped the boy's chin and turned his face slowly from one side to the other. The boy shrank back uneasily.

"Say! What's the big idea?"

The boy's voice was shrill; inside the café it was suddenly very quiet.

The man said slowly: "I love you."

All along the counter the men laughed. The boy, who had scowled and sidled away, did not know what to do. He looked over the counter at Leo, and Leo watched him with a weary, brittle jeer. The boy tried to laugh also. But the man was serious and sad.

"I did not mean to tease you, son," he said. "Sit down and have a beer with me. There is something I have to explain."

Cautiously, out of the corner of his eye, the paper boy questioned the men along the counter to see what he should do. But they had gone back to their beer or their breakfast and did not notice him. Leo put a cup of coffee on the counter and a little jug of cream.

"He is a minor," Leo said.

The paper boy slid himself up onto the stool. His ear beneath the upturned flap of the helmet was very small and red. The man was nodding at him soberly. "It is important," he said. Then he reached in his hip pocket and brought out something which he held up in the palm of his hand for the boy to see.

"Look very carefully," he said.

The boy stared, but there was nothing to look at very carefully. The man held in his big, grimy palm a photograph. It was the face of a woman, but blurred, so that only the hat and the dress she was wearing stood out clearly.

"See?" the man asked.

The boy nodded and the man placed another picture in his palm. The woman was standing on a beach in a bathing suit. The suit made her stomach very big, and that was the main thing you noticed.

"Got a good look?" He leaned over closer and finally asked: "You ever seen her before?"

The boy sat motionless, staring slantwise at the man. "Not so I know of."

"Very well." The man blew on the photographs and put them back into his pocket. "That was my wife."

"Dead?" the boy asked.

Slowly the man shook his head. He pursed his lips as though about to whistle and answered in a long-drawn way: "Nuuu——" he said. "I will explain."

The beer on the counter before the man was in a large brown mug.

He did not pick it up to drink. Instead he bent down and, putting his face over the rim, he rested there for a moment. Then with both hands he tilted the mug and sipped.

"Some night you'll go to sleep with your big nose in a mug and drown," said Leo. "Prominent transient drowns in beer. That would be a cute death."

The paper boy tried to signal to Leo. While the man was not looking he screwed up his face and worked his mouth to question soundlessly: "Drunk?" But Leo only raised his eyebrows and turned away to put some pink strips of bacon on the grill. The man pushed the mug away from him, straightened himself, and folded his loose crooked hands on the counter. His face was sad as he looked at the paper boy. He did not blink, but from time to time the lids closed down with delicate gravity over his pale green eyes. It was nearing dawn and the boy shifted the weight of the paper sack.

"I am talking about love," the man said. "With me it is a science."

The boy half slid down from the stool. But the man raised his forefinger, and there was something about him that held the boy and would not let him go away.

"Twelve years ago I married the woman in the photograph. She was my wife for one year, nine months, three days, and two nights. I loved her. Yes . . ." He tightened his blurred, rambling voice and said again: "I loved her. I thought also that she loved me. I was a railroad engineer. She had all home comforts and luxuries. It never crept into my brain that she was not satisfied. But do you know what happened?"

"Mgneeow!" said Leo.

The man did not take his eyes from the boy's face. "She left me. I came in one night and the house was empty and she was gone. She left me."

"With a fellow?" the boy asked.

Gently the man placed his palm down on the counter. "Why naturally, son. A woman does not run off like that alone."

The café was quiet, the soft rain black and endless in the street outside. Leo pressed down the frying bacon with the prongs of his long fork: "So you have been chasing the floozy for eleven years. You frazzled old rascal!"

For the first time the man glanced at Leo. "Please don't be vulgar. Besides, I was not speaking to you." He turned back to the boy and said in a trusting and secretive undertone: "Let's not pay any attention to him. O.K.?"

The paper boy nodded doubtfully.

"It was like this," the man continued. "I am a person who feels many things. All my life one thing after another has impressed me. Moonlight. The leg of a pretty girl. One thing after another. But the point is that when I had enjoyed anything there was a peculiar sensation as though it was laying around loose in me. Nothing seemed to finish itself up or fit in with the other things. Women? I had my portion of them. The same. Afterward laying around loose in me. I was a man who had never loved."

Very slowly he closed his eyelids, and the gesture was like a curtain drawn at the end of a scene in a play. When he spoke again his voice was excited and the words came fast—the lobes of his large, loose ears seemed to tremble.

"Then I met this woman. I was fifty-one years old and she always said she was thirty. I met her at a filling station and we were married within three days. And do you know what it was like? I just can't tell you. All I had ever felt was gathered together around this woman. Nothing lay around loose in me any more but was finished up by her."

The man stopped suddenly and stroked his long nose. His voice sank down to a steady and reproachful undertone: "I'm not explaining this right. What happened was this. There were these beautiful feelings and loose little pleasures inside me. And this woman was something like an assembly line for my soul. I run these little pieces of myself through her and I come out complete. Now do you follow me?"

"What was her name?" the boy asked.

"Oh," he said. "I called her Dodo. But that is immaterial."

"Did you try to make her come back?"

The man did not seem to hear. "Under the circumstances you can imagine how I felt when she left me."

Leo took the bacon from the grill and folded two strips of it between a bun. He had a gray face, with slitted eyes, and a pinched nose saddled by faint blue shadows. One of the mill workers signaled for more coffee and Leo poured it. He did not give refills on coffee free. The spinner ate breakfast there every morning, but the better Leo knew his customers the stingier he treated them. He nibbled his own bun as though he grudged it to himself.

"And you never got hold of her again?"

The boy did not know what to think of the man, and his child's face was uncertain with mingled curiosity and doubt. He was new on the paper route; it was still strange to him to be out in the town in the black, queer early morning.

"Yes," the man said. "I took a number of steps to get her back. I went around trying to locate her. I went to Tulsa where she had folks. And to Mobile. I went to every town she had ever mentioned to me, and I hunted down every man she had formerly been connected with. Tulsa, Atlanta, Chicago, Cheehaw, Memphis . . . For the better part of two years I chased around the country trying to lay hold of her."

"But the pair of them had vanished from the face of the earth!" said Leo.

"Don't listen to him," the man said confidentially. "And also just forget those two years. They are not important. What matters is that around the third year a curious thing begun to happen to me."

"What?" the boy asked.

The man leaned down and tilted his mug to take a sip of beer. But as he hovered over the mug his nostrils fluttered slightly; he sniffed the staleness of the beer and did not drink. "Love is a curious thing to begin with. At first I thought only of getting her back. It was a kind of mania. But then as time went on I tried to remember her. But do you know what happened?"

"No," the boy said.

"When I laid myself down on a bed and tried to think about her my mind became a blank. I couldn't see her. I would take out her pictures and look. No good. Nothing doing. A blank. Can you imagine it?"

"Say, Mack!" Leo called down the counter. "Can you imagine this bozo's mind a blank!"

Slowly, as though fanning away flies, the man waved his hand. His green eyes were concentrated and fixed on the shallow little face of the paper boy.

"But a sudden piece of glass on a sidewalk. Or a nickel tune in a music box. A shadow on a wall at night. And I would remember. It might happen in a street and I would cry or bang my head against a lamppost. You follow me?"

"A piece of glass . . ." the boy said.

"Anything. I would walk around and I had no power of how and when to remember her. You think you can put up a kind of shield. But remembering don't come to a man face forward—it corners around sideways. I was at the mercy of everything I saw and heard. Suddenly instead of me combing the countryside to find her she begun to chase me around in my very soul. *She* chasing *me,* mind you! And in my soul."

The boy asked finally: "What part of the country were you in then?"

"Ooh," the man groaned. "I was a sick mortal. It was like smallpox. I confess, son, that I boozed. I fornicated. I committed any sin that suddenly appealed to me. I am loath to confess it but I will do so. When I recall that period it is all curdled in my mind, it was so terrible."

The man leaned his head down and tapped his forehead on the counter. For a few seconds he stayed bowed over in this position, the back of his stringy neck covered with orange furze, his hands with their long warped fingers held palm to palm in an attitude of prayer. Then the man straightened himself; he was smiling and suddenly his face was bright and tremulous and old.

"It was in the fifth year that it happened," he said. "And with it I started my science."

Leo's mouth jerked with a pale, quick grin. "Well, none of we boys are getting any younger," he said. Then with sudden anger he balled up a dishcloth he was holding and threw it down hard on the floor. "You draggle-tailed old Romeo!"

"What happened?" the boy asked.

The old man's voice was high and clear: "Peace," he answered.

"Huh?"

"It is hard to explain scientifically, son," he said. "I guess the

logical explanation is that she and I had fleed around from each other for so long that finally we just got tangled up together and lay down and quit. Peace. A queer and beautiful blankness. It was spring in Portland and the rain came every afternoon. All evening I just stayed there on my bed in the dark. And that is how the science come to me."

The windows in the streetcar were pale blue with light. The two soldiers paid for their beers and opened the door—one of the soldiers combed his hair and wiped off his muddy puttees before they went outside. The three mill workers bent silently over their breakfasts. Leo's clock was ticking on the wall.

"It is this. And listen carefully. I meditated on love and reasoned it out. I realized what is wrong with us. Men fall in love for the first time. And what do they fall in love with?"

The boy's soft mouth was partly open and he did not answer.

"A woman," the old man said. "Without science, with nothing to go by, they undertake the most dangerous and sacred experience in God's earth. They fall in love with a woman. Is that correct, son?"

"Yeah," the boy said faintly.

"They start at the wrong end of love. They begin at the climax. Can you wonder it is so miserable? Do you know how men should love?"

The old man reached over and grasped the boy by the collar of his leather jacket. He gave him a gentle little shake and his green eyes gazed down unblinking and grave.

"Son, do you know how love should be begun?"

The boy sat small and listening and still. Slowly he shook his head. The old man leaned closer and whispered:

"A tree. A rock. A cloud."

It was still raining outside in the street: a mild, gray, endless rain. The mill whistle blew for the six-o'clock shift and the three spinners paid and went away. There was no one in the café but Leo, the old man, and the little paper boy.

"The weather was like this in Portland," he said. "At the time my science was begun. I meditated and I started very cautious. I would pick up something from the street and take it home with me. I bought a goldfish and I concentrated on the goldfish and I loved it. I

12

graduated from one thing to another. Day by day I was getting this technique. On the road from Portland to San Diego——"

"Aw shut up!" screamed Leo suddenly. "Shut up! Shut up!"

The old man still held the collar of the boy's jacket; he was trembling and his face was earnest and bright and wild. "For six years now I have gone around by myself and built up my science. And now I am a master, son. I can love anything. No longer do I have to think about it even. I see a street full of people and a beautiful light comes in me. I watch a bird in the sky. Or I meet a traveler on the road. Everything, son. And anybody. All strangers and all loved! Do you realize what a science like mine can mean?"

The boy held himself stiffly, his hands curled tight around the counter edge. Finally he asked: "Did you ever really find that lady?"

"What? What say, son?"

"I mean," the boy asked timidly, "have you fallen in love with a woman again?"

The old man loosened his grasp on the boy's collar. He turned away and for the first time his green eyes had a vague and scattered look. He lifted the mug from the counter, drank down the yellow beer. His head was shaking slowly from side to side. Then finally he answered: "No, son. You see, that is the last step in my science. I go cautious. And I am not quite ready yet."

"Well!" said Leo. "Well well well!"

The old man stood in the open doorway. "Remember," he said. Framed there in the gray damp light of the early morning, he looked shrunken and seedy and frail. But his smile was bright. "Remember I love you," he said with a last nod. And the door closed quietly behind him.

The boy did not speak for a long time. He pulled down the bangs on his forehead and slid his grimy little forefinger around the rim of his empty cup. Then without looking at Leo he finally asked:

"Was he drunk?"

"No," said Leo shortly.

The boy raised his clear voice higher. "Then was he a dope fiend?"

"No."

The boy looked up at Leo, and his flat little face was desperate, his voice urgent and shrill. "Was he crazy? Do you think he was a lunatic?" The paper boy's voice dropped suddenly with doubt. "Leo? Or not?"

But Leo would not answer him. Leo had run a night café for fourteen years, and he held himself to be a critic of craziness. There were the town characters and also the transients who roamed in from the night. He knew the manias of all of them. But he did not want to satisfy the questions of the waiting child. He tightened his pale face and was silent.

So the boy pulled down the right flap of his helmet and as he turned to leave he made the only comment that seemed safe to him, the only remark that could not be laughed down and despised:

"He sure has done a lot of traveling."

KNIFE-LIKE, FLOWER-LIKE, LIKE NOTHING AT ALL IN THE WORLD

By William Saroyan

From *Harper's Bazaar*

WILLIAM SAROYAN

has appeared frequently in the O. Henry Memorial Award Prize Stories. *His first story to appear in a magazine of national circulation,* Story, *was in the 1934* O. Henry, *"The Daring Young Man on the Flying Trapeze," and won a special prize for the best short-short story that year. It was the title story in his first published book of short stories, which was brought out that fall. In 1935 the* O. Henry *included his story, "Five Ripe Pears," from the* Yale Review; *the 1938 volume contained "The Summer of the Beautiful White Horse," from* Esquire; *and in the 1940 book another story from* Story, *"The Three Swimmers and the Educated Grocer," was used.*

This brilliant young author and playwright was born in California, August 31, 1908, of Armenian parents. His rise, after he came into prominence in 1934, was rapid. To say people did not agree about his stories is understatement. The audience left his first and very short play, My Heart's in the Highlands, *presented at the Guild Theater in New York in 1939, with mingled feelings. His succeeding ones fared better. They were* The Time of Your Life, *which received the Pulitzer Prize in 1940 and carried with it an award of $1,000 which Saroyan refused,* Love's Old Sweet Song, *and* The Beautiful People. *Mr. Saroyan uses all his experience in his writing. His work for the Postal Telegraph, both as a messenger boy and later as local manager of the San Francisco office, is apparent in his most recent success,* The Human Comedy, *a book published this year and distributed by the Book-of-the-Month Club. It was also made into a successful movie. Another of his books,* My Name Is Aram, *was a Book-of-the-Month Club choice.*

HE'LL BE AROUND any minute now, Max said. I give you my word. He'll be here.

The little man at the table nodded as Max spoke, and Max said to himself as he wiped the bar, What's he want to see a guy like Pete for?

A good-looking woman came in and ordered a scotch and soda, and while he was getting the drink Max went on talking to the little man.

It's none of my business, he said, but what do you want to see Pete for?

I beg your pardon? the lady said.

Oh, Max said. Excuse me, lady. I was talking to the little fellow at the table over there. (Little fellow at the table? Max repeated to himself. What the hell kind of talk is that?)

He's a friend of mine, the lady said.

No, no, Max said quickly. I was talking to that little gentleman over there. (Little gentleman? Why couldn't I leave out the *little* part of it?)

Well, the lady said, even so. He's a friend of mine.

Who? Max said.

Pete, the lady said.

The little man got up from the table and came over to the bar. He studied the woman carefully, trying at the same time to smile.

What's this? Max thought.

I'm his father, the little man said.

The woman turned and looked down at the little man. It seemed to Max that she didn't think very much of him, or that he, Max, didn't understand anything. (I'm a lousy judge of character, Max decided.)

His father? the woman said.

Yes, the little man said. Peter Morgan.

My name is Ethel Beede, the woman said. The way she said the last name Max knew it had an extra "e" in it somewhere and that, most likely, as he put it, she stank. She didn't exactly stink, but she was probably no good.

Peter Morgan is my son's name, the little man said. My name is Henry.

How do you do, the woman said.

Thank you, the little man said. I came here tonight to see Pete. He hasn't been home in two weeks. Pete's always been dissatisfied, and almost anything at all out of the ordinary throws him off balance.

The woman looked at the little man almost a full minute without speaking.

Max couldn't figure it out.

Pete showed up every night sometime between midnight and two, but he was always alone. Tonight his father shows up at a little after ten, and a little after eleven a woman almost old enough to be Pete's mother shows up too.

Your son, the woman said at last, is a very interesting young man.

I've known him all his life, the little man said quietly. I imagine he's *fascinating* to people who haven't.

I'm quite interested in his ambition, the woman said.

That's very kind of you, the little man said. What ambition is that?

I understand he wants to be an actor, the woman said.

He has a number of ambitions, the little man said. I'm sure you know how old he is.

He said he was twenty-one, the woman said.

He's not quite seventeen, the little man said.

Wait a minute, Max said very loudly. Not quite seventeen? He's been coming in here drinking every night for two weeks now. I can't serve drinks to minors. It's against the law. I thought he was twenty-two or twenty-three.

No, the little man said. He's not quite seventeen. He'll be seventeen August 21. He was born in 1925.

The little man waited a moment for the woman to speak. He hoped the woman would go away and give him a chance to sit down and talk with Pete alone, but the woman didn't seem to want to go.

He's not quite seventeen, the little man said again.

I heard you, the woman said.

Pete is the kind of guy who expects a great deal all the time, the little man said. Have you been giving him money?

The woman was not upset by this question, as Max expected her to be.

Yes, she said.

You're married, the little man said.

I beg your pardon, the woman said.

Well, to put it another way, the little man said, you have children, haven't you?

I have a daughter nineteen years old, the woman said, and another seven years old. Give me another scotch and soda.

Max made another drink for the lady. The little man wasn't drinking.

Your husband is a wealthy man, Pete's father said.

I am wealthy, the woman said. My husbands have all been—poor.

You want to adopt Pete? the little man said.

I *beg* your pardon, the woman said this time. She was really burned up now. Well, what do you know about that? Max thought. A crazy good-looking punk like Pete—well, for the love of Mike.

I only want to warn you, the little man said, that my son will make you unhappy, no matter what you intend to do. I want you to know that you won't hurt *him*. I think he's capable of doing anything. I think he could do something very great or something very strange. I think he could murder almost anybody and not feel guilty. He's very sensitive too. I'm sure you don't know him as well as I do. I want him to take his time and after a while find out for himself what he wants to do. He's restless and bored and pretty angry deeply. I think he can do anything.

I'm afraid I don't understand, the woman said.

I'm very fond of Pete, the little man said. Maybe it's because he's not like me or his mother or any of his brothers and sisters. We're all very fond of him, but *me* most of all. Pete's ashamed of me. I'll tell you that. At the same time I think he likes me more than he likes any other person in the world. I'm sure you don't intend to marry Pete.

Well, for crying out loud, Max thought. The people you run into in a little bar.

You're about twenty years older than Pete, the little man went on.

I told you I have a nineteen-year-old daughter, the woman said.

Then I suppose you *do* want to adopt him, the little man said.

We're going to be married day after tomorrow, the woman said.

What the hell is this? Max asked himself. Pete going to marry this high-tone society dame? That crazy kid who looked like a cross between a movie gangster and a ballet dancer? Who walked swiftly and dramatically, as if he were in a play? Who talked loudly and said the funniest things in the world? Who threw money around as if it were buttons? Going to marry this overfed dame?

I see, the little man said quietly.

He looked at the woman a moment.

I see, he said again.

We're very much in love, the woman said. She was deeply hurt. Even Max could tell that. Well, as far as Max was concerned, if she *had* to marry somebody she could pick out somebody her size, somebody like himself.

Oh-oh, Max thought suddenly. One of these two ought to get out of here in a hurry. That kid will be coming in here any minute now.

He'll be coming in here any minute now, Max said. He wiped the bar as he spoke, so the remark wouldn't be too bald, or whatever it was. Too naked or whatever it was.

Yes, I know, the little man and the woman said at the same time.

We're going to be married, the woman said again.

I've always encouraged Pete to do whatever he's felt like doing, the little man said. I'll pretend I didn't know, and after it's over I'll convince his mother not to interfere too.

You're very kind, the woman said.

She was irritated and it seemed to Max a little ashamed.

I'm thinking of Pete, the little man said.

He turned and walked out of the place without another word. Max got busy with some glasses at the other end of the bar.

Give me another scotch and soda, the woman said.

She was sore and ashamed and she looked pretty ugly all of a sudden. At first she had seemed rather beautiful, or at least striking, but now all of a sudden when Max looked at her she looked awful. I guess a crazy kid like Pete must be wonderful company for a woman like that, Max thought. I guess it means a lot to her. Max put her drink down in front of her and went over to the phonograph and put in a nickel.

When the record ended Max put in another nickel. The kid ought to be in any minute now. He kept looking toward the door and feeling uncomfortable. The woman kept trying not to look toward the door. Max kept putting nickels in the phonograph and looking toward the door.

At two o'clock he said, It's closing time.

The woman paid for nine scotch and sodas and began to go. Near the door she turned around and came back.

That's right, lady, Max said to himself. I'm not seventeen and I don't walk like a dancer and I'm not the funniest young punk in the world, but I'm not so bad. I'm only forty-eight. Let's talk this thing over. If you've got to marry somebody, marry a guy your size. Marry me.

Max leaned over the bar toward the lady. She opened her handbag. Nuts, Max thought. The woman crumpled a bill in her hand and, shaking Max's hand, she left the bill in it and turned to go. At the door she stopped again and Max said to himself, Come on, lady. Think this thing over. You're tight and I'm big and—discreet too. The woman came over to Max again.

We're very much in love with one another, she said. (I'll say we are, Max said. Lady, you've got no idea how much in love with one another we are. Just say the good word.)

Lady, Max said. He felt silly.

The woman moved closer to him, waiting.

Lady, Max said.

Yes? the woman said.

I'm sorry, Max said. This is the first night in two weeks that he's not been in.

It's all right, the woman said.

Can I help you to a cab? Max said.

My car's outside, the lady said.

I'd be glad to drive you home, Max said. I mean——

My chauffeur's in the car, the woman said.

The woman went out before Max had a chance to get around the bar and open the door for her. He went to the door and locked it and while he did so he saw the chauffeur open the door of the car, help the woman in, and then drive away.

Max stood at the door about three minutes, thinking. What's the matter with *me?* he thought. He returned to the bar and put away everything for the night. He put on his coat and then poured himself a little drink, which he sipped thoughtfully.

The door rattled and he didn't even think of hollering out, Closed.

The door rattled again and then he heard the kid shout, Hey, Max! Let me in a minute.

Max turned toward the door. It would be good to see Pete again, after all this stuff. He went to the door and opened it and the kid came in, the same as on any other night.

Where the hell you been? Max asked.

Max, the kid said. Something's happened. Give me a drink.

Max poured him a drink. Pete swallowed the drink and smiled. Max, he said, I'm in love.

Yeah, I know, Max said. He was a little burned up now.

You know? Pete said. I just met her tonight.

Met who? Max said.

Max, I met the most beautiful girl in the world. She's just a kid, but she's wonderful. She's innocent and simple and—well, by God, I'm not ashamed to say it—wonderful.

You said wonderful before, Max said.

She's fourteen years old, Pete said. Where do you think I found her?

Max began to think.

In a movie? he said.

No, Pete said. I went home instead of keeping an appointment. (Pete busted out laughing.) So I decided to stop at the florist's on the corner and take the folks some flowers. I found her in the florist's. She's his daughter. Half Irish, half Italian. Beautiful. Quiet. Lonely. I bought the flowers and took them home and sat around talking, waiting for my father to come home. He'd gone back to the office to do some overtime. So after a while I went back to the florist's and met her father and her mother and asked them if I could take her to the neighborhood movie. After the movie I took her home and I've been walking around town ever since.

I see, Max said. That's swell.

How've things been? Pete said.

Oh, so-so, Max said.

Anybody been around? Pete said.

A few people I don't know, Max said.

Any interesting barroom talk? Pete said.

Some, Max said.

I'm going to open a bar myself someday, Pete said. I like to see all kinds of people and hear them talk.

Is that so? Max said.

Yeah, Pete said. The variety, Max. All the different people alive. All the different faces. All the different ways of talking. I like to listen to the way they *laugh,* especially. Do you know how *she* laughs?

No, Max said.

Like an angel, Pete said. It breaks my heart. It makes me sadder than anything in the world. I'm in love with her, but the only trouble is the world's full of them.

That's right, Max said.

That's the only trouble, Pete said. There are so many of them.

There sure are plenty of them, Max said.

They're all over the place, Pete said. Anywhere you go. This one was in the florist's, right in my block. Think of all the other blocks. All the other cities. The hundreds of thousands of them.

Yeah, Max said. He felt old and grateful for a little place of his own and easy working hours and easy work and a place to sleep and an old indifference about the hundreds of thousands of them.

Yeah, he said. That's right, Pete.

Pete swallowed another drink and tossed a dollar on the bar.

On me tonight, Max said.

Thanks, Pete said. He began to go. See you tomor—— he began to say. He stopped. I may not be around again for a while, he said. It's about three miles from here to my neighborhood.

O.K., Max said.

So long, Pete said.

Max watched him walk away swiftly, like somebody in a hell of a big play. Max put on his hat and let himself out and locked the door, peeking in to see how it looked without him inside. It looked O.K. He began to walk slowly around the corner.

WHITE FOR THE LIVING

By Margarita G. Smith

From *Mademoiselle*

MARGARITA G. SMITH

was born August 2, 1922, in Columbus, Georgia. Her older sister is Carson McCullers. "White for the Living" is her first published story. In June of this year she was graduated from the University of Miami with a Bachelor of Arts degree. She was a member of "Who's Who Among Students in American Universities and Colleges." Miss Smith says she has never had a conventional course in journalism or in writing, but has studied these subjects by reading as much as she could and by writing and experimenting whenever she had the time. During her senior year at college she was on the College Board of Mademoiselle *magazine, which published her story. She did little work on her college newspaper and confesses that her contributions to the yearbook consisted almost entirely of candid-camera shots. She writes: "At home now for a while, anyway, I am having a long-awaited chance to polish up some stories I never had an opportunity to finish at the dormitory. Like every other beginning author I, too, am sweating away on my 'great American novel,' which I am naïvely but nevertheless thoroughly convinced is pretty terrific."*

SHELBY LOOKED FORWARD to Sundays, and she had two good reasons. In the first place her Pa gave her a quarter, a nickel for Sunday school and the other twenty cents just for nothing. Now the other reason would be more difficult for her to explain, for it was not figured up in nickels and dimes, but it amounted to the fact that she liked the sanctimonious feeling it gave her, and she enjoyed her sabbatical journey to the elegant downtown church.

All in all, every Sunday was a good day, both lucrative and holy. And special Sundays were cause for excitement as gifts were distributed. At Christmas there were red mesh stockings holding hard sugary candy and straight little corked-mouthed Santa Clauses; at Easter there were dyed eggs and jelly beans. Last Thanksgiving, she remembered remorsefully, was not so profitable since they had only cut out paper turkeys, but for Flag Day a big fat lady with a mustache and men's shoes stood in the church square after Sunday school and distributed pale, small, cheesecloth flags. She had stayed for church that day and had even taken Communion with the joined members, and after everybody had milled out she had gone down every pew picking up the flags that had been left. She took them all home and stuck them in the coke bottles that lined the petunia border on either side of the walk in front of her house.

Now on Mother's Day Shelby and her Pa were walking briskly toward town: Shelby to Sunday school and her Pa for his beer, as was their weekly custom. Shelby was glad her Pa went with her to get the beer. It made him feel guilty to be spending money that way, and that is why she got the extra twenty cents.

"Pa," she asked cautiously, "what do they do extra for Mother's Day?"

You could see the old man didn't understand what she meant. "What do you mean, 'extra,' Kitten?"

"You know, 'extra.' It ain't poppies they give you, but I 'member something."

"No." The old man became thoughtful and shifted the toothpick to the other side of his mouth. "Poppies is for Poppy Day, and they sell them downtown. You wear real flowers on Mother's Day. Iffen your Ma's aliving, you wear a red flower. Iffen she's dead, you belong to wear a white one." His face had a sad, distant look.

Shelby didn't want him to know she was really interested in getting anything at Sunday school, and she decided not to ask him if he knew whether the church gave the flowers away. She took two or three little nervous skips to catch up with him.

"Pa," she said wistfully, "you know, I been had a hankering after some sweet potatoes. The kind with the marshmallows on the top and the raisins and all sorts of good things on the insides, like we had at Aunt Jo's that time."

Shelby knew already what the answer to this desire would be. "You git you some, Kitten. I don't keer for none. I ain't had a taste for no sweet potatoes since we lived off 'em one year when I was a boy." Any chance reference to this dish brought forth this statement as well as his next, which Shelby had just come to recognize as a joke. "All us was so pore that us chillun wore gunny sacks on weekdays and flour sacks for dress-up on Sunday." The joke sounded so pore-folksy and pitiful that Shelby could not enjoy it, and she laughed only slightly from the front of her throat.

They hurried along. At the end of the block the old man would turn the corner. He reached in his pocket for a twenty-five-cent piece. She always watched this maneuver anxiously, but she managed to look surprised.

"For me? But, Pa, I don't need but a nickel for the collection." Every time she said this she held her breath for fear he would only give her what she needed.

"Well," he said gently, "you'll need some for a little spending money. You're a right good little Kitten around the house."

They parted at the hill, and Shelby slackened her pace. She walked slowly so that she would not be sweaty when she arrived, and folks would think that she had either come in a car or ridden a bus. She dared not wipe her neck and arms with her wilted handkerchief square. Her mother checked the same one out and in each week like a hotel key. She stopped by the drugstore to get the quarter changed in order to have some money to clank around in her pocketbook. Then as the pink brick building loomed into sight she had the familiar uplifted inner surging and she hummed softly to herself, "We shall come rejoicing, bringing in the sheaves." She liked to sing, especially in church.

Now Shelby had a hard walk each week to come downtown to Sunday school, but it was worth it. Her house was only three doors from the narrow white frame tabernacle called THE CHURCH OF GOD WHICH THE ANGEL OF PHILADELPHIA IS OVER. The name annoyed her considerably, for certainly Philadelphia was not in Georgia. It was such a plain church, and besides they never gave away favors. She opened her pocketbook and, keeping the mirror on the inside of her purse, studied herself to see whether she looked fresh before she turned in.

The church was quiet when she reached it. All the members had dispersed to their respective classrooms. Shelby tiptoed by a room full of men Bible students and carefully lowered her head. Her own Primary Department was crowded. She sidled in apologetically and eased into one of the empty seats by a skinny little boy streaked with some powdery substance on all visible parts of his body. It made his eyes look deep set and sick. He turned to her when she sat down and whispered behind his hand, "I've got poison oak. Mother let me come though because my brother always says a piece on Mother's Day." Shelby cringed over to the end of her chair and close on to the redhead's next her.

Miss Benson was going around the room asking each child separately what he had done the past week to help his mother. She had asked each one except the boy with the poison oak and Shelby.

"Frank, son," the teacher continued in her soft Sunday-school voice, "tell us how you were Mother's Little Helper."

"I've been to camp, and Mother she just came to get me yesterday when they wrote her I was sick, then she took me to the doctor and he said I was to go to bed, and I haven't had time to do anything this week. But I generally do though." He added the last as a sage afterthought.

"I'm sure you do. And we all hope you will be well and strong soon.

And, Shelby"—she was completing the circle—"you help your mother all the time. Just tell us some one little thing you did around the house this week."

Shelby fixed her eyes stolidly just above the picture of the boy Jesus. There was a prolonged silence. Her eyes became soft with full, shiny tears.

The kind teacher was distressed. "Why, Shelby, my dear, I had no idea! How thoughtless of me. If I had only known! You never told me—oh, my poor, dear child."

A bell rang. "It's time for the program," Miss Benson gasped thankfully. "Little People, let's see how quietly we can go to the other room. And Shelby, you are going to sit by me, and Frank, you can have the other side." A hurried collection was gathered, and Shelby forgot to jangle her nickels. All the children filed out to go to the one big room.

Shelby had worried considerably for fear there was to be nothing different about Mother's Day. But now her fears were allayed. She liked sympathy, and today she was getting more than her Christian share. She was even going to have a side of Miss Benson. As the children filed into the big room there were two women on either side of the door to give out flowers. One to dole out the red, and the other the white. Miss Benson led Shelby to the card table where the white roses rested in shoe boxes lined with wax paper. The women shook their heads and exchanged grieved expressions. They selected the handsomest blossom to pin on Shelby and smiled at her encouragingly.

Inside, Shelby felt her importance as she sat by Miss Benson on the hard bench. The woman took the child's hand periodically and held it briefly until both palms were clammy with perspiration, or patted her head affectionately. "Such pretty, pretty curls," she whispered emotionally.

In front was a piano, a table, and stern Mr. Worster. Shelby resented Mr. Worster for many things. Every time he came to lecture to them his voice was hard and steady, and he asked all who were not going to smoke or to drink to stand up, and in the face of God to declare it. She never wanted to stand up because she longed for the day when she would be a grown lady, a spy probably, and she would most certainly be obliged to smoke in that capacity. Also Mr. Worster was long on the preaching and short on the singing, and Shelby did like to sing.

Today, however, even Mr. Worster was kindly. He spoke tremulously of his gray-haired mother, her Bible and her plum sauce. At length he introduced the precocious little man to recite the immortal *Mother o' Mine*. Frank moved to the edge of his chair, his black eyes darting from the speaker to the audience in order to decide how it was being received: it was his sissy brother with a coat to match his pants. And when the piece was done, Mr. Worster, overcome, announced that today they could sing whatever hymns they wished.

"Let's sing 'Bringing in the Sheaves,'" Shelby whispered to Miss Benson.

The woman patted her on the head and stood up. "Mr. Worster," she said in a clear but reverent voice, "this little lady wants to sing 'Bringing in the Sheaves.'" All the grown people looked sadly at Shelby, and seemed to be saying, "And so young too. And did you ever see such pretty curls?" Her face was brave and sad, and because she wore a white flower they sang all four verses. After that they had two more songs and a final prayer for mothers, children, and motherless children, and adjourned.

"Good-by, Shelby, good-by," all the children said wistfully.

"We will all see you next Sunday, won't we?" Miss Benson coaxed.

"Yes'm, I'll be here. Iffen I'm living," she gulped, "and nothing happen. Good-by. Good-by."

Shelby walked slowly home, her head hung on her chest. She took no notice of anything—she was thinking. Today had been a fine day. It was nice to have everybody feel sorry for you. She passed by THE CHURCH OF GOD WHICH THE ANGEL OF PHILADELPHIA IS OVER. She looked in curiously. Church was going on. "I'm sure going to ax me somebody where is Philadelphia," she determined. She was glad she had not stayed to church; she knew that the preacher would make up for the laxity of Mr. Worster.

She unpinned the white flower, drew in a long, deep smell with her nose buried in the center petals. Her eyes registered the fixed, clear hardness of the glass buttons on a teddy bear, then they darted swiftly, spurting out electric sparks. She ran past the next three houses, jumped over the petunia bed, and bounded up the steps.

"Ma, Ma," she sang out joyously, "I brung you something." A slow, gray woman came from the back room. "I brung you a present, a flower." Her good deed for the week, only—she thought suddenly, regretfully—she couldn't tell Miss Benson about it. She deposited the white rose, already browning from the sun and her heavy breath, and the Sunday handkerchief on the table.

"SHE SHALL HAVE MUSIC"

By Austin Strong

From the *Atlantic Monthly*

AUSTIN STRONG

was born in San Francisco, April 18, 1881. His grandmother married Robert Louis Stevenson, so as a small boy Mr. Strong lived at Vailima, Samoa, in the South Seas, and had for a companion, tutor, and guardian the famous writer. His mother was Stevenson's favorite amanuensis. He is a graduate of Wellington College, New Zealand, and studied landscape architecture. Until 1905 he was a landscape architect, and he laid out Cornwall Park, in Auckland, New Zealand.

Then he began writing plays and launched on an entirely different career. His first two, The Exile *and* The Little Father of the Wilderness, *were written in collaboration with Lloyd Osbourne, and produced early in this century. Others were* The Toymaker of Nüremburg, *an adaptation from the French of Madame Rostand's play,* Le Bon Petit Diable*—produced by Belasco as* A Good Little Devil, *starring Mary Pickford*—Three Wise Fools, *and* Seventh Heaven, *his most famous play, later made into a moving picture. Years ago he wrote a one-act play,* The Drums of Oudh, *which has been acted all over the world and has been called "the standby of the military, its martial note has resounded in all the barracks of the English-speaking world."*

Mr. Strong is married, and he lives in a charming 1731 house in Quince Street, Nantucket Island. His friends call this man "who played with Stevenson and laughed with Barrie" the "Commodore." He has only recently been writing short stories.

I HEARD with an inward ping of pleasure the whistle of the paddle-wheel steamer warning us that she was swinging her enormous bustle around Brant Point.

The clock in the Unitarian Church began striking the hour.

"The boat's late," I said.

My companion said nothing, but sat beside me upright as an exclamation point, remote as a portrait.

Though we saw him here every morning in his accustomed chair in the Captains' Room, we knew little about him save that he had traveled widely and that he had a native eloquence if he could be induced to talk. Now he had "rounded Brant Point" for good, to end his days in peace on Nantucket Island where he was born.

I smiled as I listened to the deep-toned bell booming circles of sound over the huddled roofs of the gray town. This bronze beauty is not only a Portuguese but a papist, blessed by no less a dignitary than the patriarch of Lisbon. It was bought in that city at the beginning of the last century by a public-spirited sea captain and set up in the gold-capped tower of the South Church, where for over a hundred years this good Catholic has called the freethinking and tolerant Protestants to their non-conforming meetings.

"Yes sir, she's half an hour late," I said again, but Mr. Bolling had inherited from his Quaker forebears the gift of silence. His thin face was aquiline and his aristocratic nose discouraged familiarity. His hands rested neatly folded upon his gold-headed Malacca cane through which ran a tasseled cord; his gold-rimmed eyeglasses hung from a black silk ribbon; his linen was immaculate, always freshly laundered, creaking with starch.

Hoping to lure him into conversation, I said facetiously: "There's a star-face for you, Mr. Bolling!"

I pointed my pipe at a flaming thing in a skirt cut high above her knees, who teetered past our windows on high heels, her hair bobbed boy-fashion, a cigarette between her lips.

Mr. Bolling began banging on the floor with his cane. He turned and held me with a blazing eye, then spoke in a slow, cultivated voice, each word delivered with precision as if he enjoyed the taste of every syllable.

"What's the fun of being a woman if one can't be feminine. These be-bottomed strutters aren't women—they're newts!"

I sat up with interest.

"Tell me, Mr. Bolling, did you ever see a really beautiful woman?"

By a lucky chance I struck a gusher. He gave his panama a tilt, leaned far back, placed a neatly shod foot on the railing, and became someone entirely different: someone warm, expansive, eloquent. He came out from his cell of silence like an escaping Trappist as he stared through the windows at the sunlit square.

"It happened right here on Main Street, up there in front of Ashley's Store, 'Parker's Corner' in my day. You won't believe this when I tell you that right now my heart skips a beat as I recall when I first saw her rounding the head of the square like a brand-new frigate with all sails drawing, flags and pennants flying! My, my, it was a picture! You just couldn't keep your mind where it ought to be when she went by. I don't know how to put it, but even in broad daylight her skin seemed luminous, as if she carried a lamp within her. She came from some enchanted land to dwell among us sober folk who lived in Nantucket under the drab Quaker discipline.

"Though I was a boy of twelve and she a grown woman, I fell in love with her, and don't you believe a boy can't fall in love at twelve. It was very real with me—so real in fact that I would race ahead of her to wait on the corners just to watch her go by, refreshing the whole street with her beauty. There was something magical about her, for when you caught a look from her eyes something inside of you melted away. Never was there a kinder glance. It came to you slowly from under long eyelashes, just for you, for your very own, finding its way to your heart's core, and there it would lie for the rest of the day curled up and warm like some secret good news. I was not alone in my adoration, for the whole town loved her—men, women, children, dogs, off-Islanders, and all hands round!

"Her hair was reddish gold that flashed back the sunlight like a ship's binnacle. I tell you it was so golden you could lose a twenty-dollar gold piece in it and have a hard time finding it. And there was nothing sexless about her like these slab-sided pullets you see on Main Street. No sir, there was no mistaking that she was a woman. She had a small waist, little feet, and a shapely bosom, round and firm, from which rose a lovely neck. She wore earrings, sir, the like of which I've never seen before nor since: tiny sprays of wheat exquisitely fashioned out of pure gold to curve up and around the lobes of her ears. My, my, they were just joy and rapture to behold, and did the things to you they were designed to do. Now you won't believe this, but they were the first earrings I ever saw on a woman, for only the sailors wore them in our Quaker town where most of the women were forced to imprison their beauty within muslin caps or those hideous gray poke bonnets.

"She lived opposite us with a sick father, a retired widower, who had left Nantucket in his youth and established a business in Montevideo where he spent most of his life. After his wife's death he returned with his daughter to end his days like most of us on this precious 'elbow of sand.' Our houses were opposite each other on the same street near the edge of the town where the moors begin. I would get up early on Sunday mornings just to watch her come out of the house to go to church. Occasionally a priest would come from the mainland by the packet to celebrate Mass for the few Catholics who lived here in those days. It was a sight to see her come out of her front door carrying a thick brassbound prayerbook and a rosary of gold beads twisted around her wrist. She wore black lace mittens and a soft mantilla over her hair. I would listen for the crisp rustle of her ruffled black silk dress which stood stiffly around her like a bell.

"We heard that her mother was Spanish and a gold-head like her daughter. I can testify that a fair-haired Castilian makes for a loveliness indescribable. I only saw it once again, and that was in Paris when I watched the Empress Eugénie driving by in the Bois de Boulogne.

"We never saw her father, for his illness kept him a prisoner in the house, but we knew that he was difficult and that she was having a sad time nursing him, though you would never guess from seeing her that there was a thing on her mind but laughter from the joy of living.

"Yes sir, it's a glorious thing to be a beautiful woman, but you've got to know how to be one, and she did, full and bye, you know what I mean—she carried it! Though she was naturally lovely she had something extra, an inward grace I suppose you'd call it. Well, whatever it was, it captured and enraptured the Islanders, bringing color and brightness into their lonely lives. And let me tell you it was lonely around here in those days. Imagine three quarters of the menfolk scattered all over the seven oceans for years at a time. It was hard on the women left behind and she knew it. But she wasn't soft, for that wouldn't have gone down with our shrewd people. She had a straight back, tough as hickory, which her Nantucket forebears had given her, and a whiplash humor which acted like a strong tonic on the lonely and the anxious. That's why no woman was ever known to be jealous of her.

"Yes, it's a funny thing, come to think of it, that though the Quakers on our island were very strict and frowned on color and beauty in any form, they somehow never frowned on her—nobody could. She was accepted by the people like one of those strange, beautiful birds the sailors brought back from the tropics, and they let her go free and unhindered. Life was dull as fog for most of us—no theaters, games, or parties, and lights out at curfew. She sensed the dreariness of our lives and unconsciously took it upon herself to cheer us; and, believe me, she did it in the most enchanting way.

"The gods, in an expansive mood, gave her a voice. Each note had a life of its own and rose from her throat full, clear, and round. I knew instinctively it was something rare, for whenever she sang she stole your thoughts away—far away to uncharted places. Naturally we children went plumb crazy about her and would waylay her after school, surrounding and pressing her close in a giggling, squirming circle, holding her prisoner until she sang herself free.

"She sang us South American love songs and gay ballads while dignified ship captains with tall hats and reefer coats stopped to lean on whalebone canes, and drivers in low-slung wagons loaded with barrels of whale oil fresh from wild sea battles eased their horses to the curb and listened; doors opened a crack on Petticoat Row;

windows were pushed up in houses opposite; the street sweeper rested on his broom, while even the Quakers in their mouse-colored clothes slowed their pace as they walked discreetly by with downcast eyes.

"Then one day we were stunned by the news which exploded in our faces. She was going to marry a Nantucket Quaker! Everyone groaned and there was much talk on Main Street. Somehow it seemed all wrong and wicked that such beauty was condemned to the prison of a disciplined life.

"Our bird of paradise was trapped in a cage. As for me, it was my first meeting with jealousy. Such hatred filled me against that inoffensive, placid young Quaker that it still frightens me to recall its intensity. I cannot remember much about him, for my fury kept him out of focus, but I know that I would have gladly done away with him if I had known how. No one on the island understood what she had in common with him, for it seemed like the union of ice and fire, but there was no doubt that she loved him with all the splendor of her heart.

"After her father's death her Quaker took her to the Meeting House on First Day, where she sat in a gay flowered dress among the dove-gray women, while he joined the menfolk across the aisle. After an hour's silence she was brought before the elders and other weighty members and instructed for her Certificate of Membership into the Society of Friends. It must have been a wrench for her to forswear her allegiance to her own church, with all her love of color and beauty, and surrender herself to the plain life where loveliness was anathema. But she did it. Yes sir, she went over to them hook, line, and sinker.

"She stood up there among them like a Jacqueminot rose in a cabbage patch and was solemnly warned against 'vain and frothy conversation,' of the snares and vanities of adornment and the wearing of 'Babylonian garments.' She was instructed to speak the plain Scripture language of *thee* and *thou* and to learn all the Queries and Advices, and told that vocal music was forbidden as 'it articulates ideas which may convey poison to the mind and tends to seduce the thoughts of youth which makes no selection, but learns all that falls in their way.' She was gravely warned that her singing must cease forever and through the discipline of silence she must 'keep down the willings and the runnings.'

"Well, sir, the poor girl promised them everything, and she was duly signed up and delivered to a life as dull as stale porridge. Lord, I shall never forget the night before her wedding. I couldn't sleep for heartache, and sat like a silly coof at the open window of my attic room staring at the stars which hung close down over the island. I remember everything about that night: the sound of the heavy surf on the South Shore, the faint gaggle of a skein of wild geese high overhead on their long, strong flight to the Carolinas, a moon that was trying to turn night into day. Have you ever noticed how the moonlight changes the gold on the South Church into a misty silver? I remember how still everything was; the whole world held its breath as if aware something ominous was going to happen.

"A dog barked over 'Egypt' way and was promptly silenced. I knew the night was a weather breeder, for I could just hear, faint as conscience, the foreboding sound of the bell buoy occasionally tolling outside the eastern jetty.

"I heard the click of a latch. Then a hooded figure slipped out of the back door of the house opposite and headed straight for the open moors. I knew it was she. In an instant I was down the stairs and out of the house, fast after her. But I found she was hard to keep up with, for she was young and strong and swift, while I was a short-legged youngster. I followed her until my breath hurt me and my feet were full of pain. Then to my dismay I lost sight of her.

"I began to walk vaguely toward the center of the moors, hoping against hope to find her. I must have gone some distance, for a blister fastened on my heel like a wasp and forced me to limp. Tired, sore, and frightened by the loneliness, I turned to go home, when I heard singing coming in faint wisps, high over the distant booming of the surf. I followed the sound for a long way until I came to a sunken bowl in the moors, and there I saw her at the bottom standing straight and still as a statue with her pale face to the moon.

"I sat down on the edge of the bowl, fascinated. She had thrown off her cloak, which made a pool of black at her feet, and stood dressed in scarlet brocade covered with bright leaves of gold; a high tortoiseshell comb held a mantilla above her head, and there was fresh arbutus at her waist and in her hair. As I had never seen jewels in my life before, I fancied I saw a magic ring of light around her neck and a star at each ear.

"She sang as I never hope to hear a mortal sing again. I lay curled up in a tight ball against the cold and listened as she sang and sang through the night, while I floated in and out of sleep until finally the cold roused me and made me flap my arms to keep warm. Still she sang and still I listened, until the first hint of dawn came to warn her.

"At the end she became inspired and sang like someone possessed. It's funny how children sense things. I knew I was looking at something I should not be seeing. It was her farewell forever to her singing and to her freedom. I've heard of a swan song, but I guess I'm one of the few who ever heard it from a human being. When I tried to rise to go away and leave her to herself I slipped on the edge and rolled ignominiously down the bowl to her feet. My sudden appearance struck her off her guard. She knelt, held me tight in her strong arms, gave a great dry gasp, then rose and, gripping my hand hard, she led me off over the moors for home.

"To ease my limping she put her arm about me, helping me over the rough places. I forgot the pain, for it was pure bliss to feel her so close. I can still recall the good scent of her—of sandalwood, fresh linen, and young health. When we reached the edge of the town she knelt, wiped my eyes, and after straightening my clothes she kissed me tenderly, and for no reason at all we both wept. She turned and ran into her house—the most beautiful woman that ever was made.

"I never saw her again. I saw the dead thing they made of her, for I went to her wedding the next day at the Friends' Meeting House. It was awful to sit there for over an hour trying to guess by the backs of the bonnets which one was hers. I tell you it was solemn. We all sat in stillness in a plain wooden house painted white, with the sun pouring in at the many-paned windows; the only sound was the faint twittering of birds outside, and it made you realize that the Quakers don't need cathedrals, high altars, or lofty rose windows; their silence creates something august and awe-inspiring.

"Presently two men chosen as the groomsmen came forward and the young Quaker stood up pink and clean, and I must admit he looked very handsome as he stood there in quiet dignity, dressed in a new gray suit with a fresh linen stock at his throat. I craned my neck to look at the bride. To my dismay I did not recognize her. Her golden crown was gone, hidden behind a gray poke bonnet, her lithe young figure made clumsy by heavy clothes. They had made her just another gray counterpart of their drab and monotonous selves. I caught a fleeting glimpse under her bonnet of a waxen cheek as she rose to join hands with her young bridegroom. Then, according to the custom of the Friends, they married themselves to each other.

"He spoke in such a low voice I could not catch his words, but presently her voice rang out and I heard it for the last time; she spoke and the place was filled with the magic and warmth of her.

"'In the presence of the Lord and this Assembly,' she said, 'I take thee to be my husband, promising with divine assistance to be unto thee a loving and faithful wife until death shall separate us.'

"I did not wait as the two groomsmen brought the marriage certificate on the table to be signed, but slipped out and went behind the Meeting House where, like a puppy, I was sick upon the grass."

Mr. Bolling removed his foot from the railing, fell silent, and showed signs of retiring within his cell.

"What happened then?" I asked, tapping the ashes from my pipe.

"Oh, she disappeared right here in our midst. The Friends lived so close among themselves they seemed to shut unseen doors on the life around them. It was nothing you could put your finger on; we'd pass them in the street, buy things in their shops, go to school to them; they were good, kind, and gentle, and yet they were away from us and seemed to live behind a glass wall.

"Boylike, I soon forgot all about her. I went to Boston, married, seldom came to Nantucket. Life changed, many people left the island, and she and her husband drifted off with many of the Friends who migrated to 'America.' Years afterwards I met an old Quaker lady in Philadelphia who was a distinguished Greek professor in a girls' college. Tiny, round, and pink, she was the spit and image of Benjamin Franklin. She fooled you on first sight, for you thought 'Here's a dear little charmer' until you met her penetrating gaze head on. It was something of a shock when you realized you stood completely unmasked as two quiet gray eyes examined you with interest and dry humor.

"She became quite animated, however, when she heard I came originally from the island of Nantucket, and fairly melted when she found that I had known the Quakeress from South America. She sat for some time in silence and then told me the end of the story with a depth of feeling surprising in a Friend.

" 'She came to our town in Pennsylvania,' she said, 'with her tall young husband, and I can bear witness that she came to us like the clear-eyed daughter of Zeus, Athene herself. None of us had imagined that human beauty could reach such inspired perfection; truly "a girl beautiful as an immortal in nature and form." They lived in a fine house, for her husband prospered and they had a few precious years together, filled with happiness, when tragedy came out of a sky without menace and struck her down: her only son, their high hope, was born dead. Her husband soon followed, carried off by an epidemic, and she was left completely bereft of human ties.

" 'She lived on in our town and clung to our faith. She came to all our meetings, but was never moved by the Spirit to rise and speak; but drifted in and out of our lives remote and alone. She was still radiant to look upon, but she was a puzzle and a heartache to us. The Quakers are a wise people, with knowledge of human suffering, but she baffled us; we could not understand how so strong a character could break, and it was some time before we realized that she was not altogether with us. We were moved by the sight of her, for it was like looking at an exquisite crystal goblet with a crack in it.

" 'Then a very strange and beautiful thing happened. It was at a Quarterly Meeting when many Friends came from far and near with important elders and visiting overseers. Our Meeting House was filled to overflowing and we had a particularly long silence that morning, deep and centered down, when to the surprise of us all the poor lovely thing rose in our midst and removed her bonnet. A pin caught in the ribbon, freeing her hair, spilling gold over her shoulders, and we saw that she was even more beautiful than we had thought. She turned, and smiled on us one by one; then, lifting up her voice, she began to sing.

" 'There was no consternation. No one moved. We sat in deep meditation while she filled the Meeting House with celestial music. She sang and she sang, a glorious Latin hymn of praise which lifted us plain, humble Quakers to the very gates of Heaven itself. After the meeting she was gently brought before the overseers and asked why she had thus disobeyed the Friends' advice against music in any form, and she replied like an honest child: "I had a concern."

" 'The elders withdrew to wrestle with the problem and they pondered for many hours. Finally, to their everlasting credit, they brought in their verdict:

" ' "WHEREAS, *It being the decision of this Quarterly Meeting of the Religious Society of Friends, and whereas she was moved by a concern beyond human jurisdiction; therefore, be it* Resolved, *That she be allowed, whenever and wherever the Spirit doth move her, to lift up her voice and sing to the everlasting glory of God.*" ' "

The good Catholic bell in the tower of the Unitarian Church began booming the noon hour. We both slowly rose and left the Captains' Room in silence.

DEATH AND MY UNCLE FELIX

By Alison Stuart

From *Mademoiselle*

ALISON STUART

was born in Princeton, New Jersey, November 2, 1918. She attended Miss Fine's School, also the Shipley School in Bryn Mawr, and was graduated in 1941 from Sarah Lawrence College. She says she wrote "Death and My Uncle Felix" during her senior year there. Her first published story, "The Yoodeler," appeared in Harper's Bazaar *and was included in the* O. Henry Memorial Award Prize Stories of 1942. *Her story "Sunday Liberty" was one of the four winners in the short-story contest held by* Mademoiselle *this year.*

Miss Stuart married Ensign Paul Norton, U.S.N., in May 1942, and is living at present in Miami, Florida, where her husband is stationed at the Submarine Chaser Training Center. Before the war she traveled in Europe during the summer and spent part of several winters in a northern Vermont village. She is continuing her writing.

My uncle felix was small and sorrowful, and in Triana the gypsies nicknamed him El Milagro—Felix the Miracle. He moved as lightly as the swallows which dipped in the brown river near the bridge, and sometimes, to appear taller on the street, he walked almost on tiptoe. *Hombre,* he was a great matador, my uncle Felix, with all his smallness and sadness. But not once did he let me go to the bullfights.

In those years before the Republic there were many great bullfighters: Soldadito, Niño de Aragón, and of course Felix El Milagro. I believed that Uncle Felix was the greatest of them all. I believed this with the stubbornness of a child, and my brother Manolo believed it too, although he was no longer a child, but nineteen years old and a *banderillero* for Uncle Felix.

We all lived together in the house with the big court on the Calle de la Buena Fortuna: my father, who was Uncle Felix's sword handler, my mother, Manolo, Uncle Felix, and I. Manolo told me that Uncle Felix had bought our house with much money. "He is very rich, little sister," Manolo said. "He is so rich that he could pave the Street of Good Fortune down to the river with gold pieces, shining in the sun."

I thought that Manolo spoke with some exaggeration. I hoped that Uncle Felix would not pave the street with gold, because I liked it as it was, narrow and steep, twisting like a rope between the houses. I liked to look up between the blue or white walls of the houses and see the high sky. When the sirocco blew, the smells from the river were most evil.

Uncle Felix told me when I was very young that he also liked the Street of Good Fortune. "It is good," he said, "to live there. It is perhaps fortunate." We were walking in the spring morning down to the corner, and Uncle Felix held me by the hand. The damp fog drifted along beside us, and no one was on the street.

"You do not think I am superstitious, Consuelo, about the good fortune?"

I did not know what superstitious meant but I knew what Uncle Felix wanted me to say, so I said, "No, Uncle Felix."

"That's it," he said. "No, I am not superstitious like that Soldadito who is half crazy to begin with, so that if he sees a one-eyed man or a woman with a squint he makes the Sign of the Horns so that he may not be caught by a bull on the next windy day."

We walked along for a moment in silence. Uncle Felix's footsteps made no sound on the sidewalk near me. I asked, "Are you afraid of the wind, Uncle Felix?"

He replied, "The wind blows across the straits here and carries hot, evil smells from the river. On a day with wind, one must pour water from the jug on the edge of his cape and scuff it in the sand to make it heavy. Then it swings clumsily, tiring the wrists, but even so, in a gust of wind it is hard to control."

"Is Soldadito more afraid of the wind than you are?" I asked.

"What do you mean?" he said. "I am not afraid of the wind, nor of anything which Soldadito fears. He is only an ignorant gypsy." We stood a moment on the corner before turning back. The mist was beginning to clear, and sunlight slanted between the tiled roofs. Uncle Felix smiled at me. "An ignorant gypsy," he repeated, "but a great matador—perhaps the greatest of us all."

At home we met my mother coming out of her small chapel room. She was very religious, and it seemed to me that she prayed nearly all day. Her face was as pale as some white flower, and I loved her because she was like a kind stranger in our house. Uncle Felix went to her and kissed her very formally, as befitted brother to sister, before he walked out to the court.

"What do you pray for, Mamacita?" I said. "Do you pray for me?"

"Sometimes," she answered, "when you are stubborn and rebellious. When you splash in the fountain and get your white dress wet."

"Do you pray for Uncle Felix?"

"Sometimes I do," she said. I waited for her to say more, but she was silent. Standing beside her in the dark stone hall, I asked a question which I knew at the moment I should not ask.

"Mamá, Uncle Felix will not die, will he?"

"Why do you ask me, Consuelo? Who has been saying things to you?"

"No one. But I think he is afraid of the wind. Manolo thinks that even Soldadito is a little afraid of it, but never Uncle Felix. 'Those who are not sometimes afraid,' he said, 'are those who are not acquainted with death.' "

"Manolo never said that," my mother told me. "It was your uncle Felix."

She smiled sadly. "Manolo is a bullfighter, not a mystic. Your uncle, unhappily, is both. It is a rare and unfortunate combination."

She shook her head. "No, Consuelo, you must not think such things. Uncle Felix is not going to die."

I believed what she said and I was very happy.

They used to come back to the Street of Good Fortune, my father, Manolo and Uncle Felix, after long summer months of bullfights in the north. Late some afternoon they came, still in their bullfighting clothes, for they drove all night when the last fight of the season was over, and their gold-encrusted jackets were tarnished with dust, and gray dust was in their hair. Uncle Felix's eyes were bloodshot, and my father's chin was shadowed with black stubble.

I was always allowed to stay up later than usual the night they came home. We sat around the dark mahogany table in the dining room, and I watched Manolo while he cracked nuts from the bowl in the middle of the table. He smiled, showing his white teeth.

"Oye, little sister," he said, "I was good at Pamplona this year—brilliant, the papers said. And Uncle Felix, you should have seen him—one afternoon the crowd carried him on their shoulders all over town."

"Manolo is good with the sticks," said Uncle Felix. "And stylish too." He sighed then, deeply. "Soldadito was in Pamplona too."

My father half rose from the table and pounded it with his fist. "Soldadito!" he shouted. "That crazy gypsy! He looks like a puppet strung together with wire. He has no style."

"He has much style," Uncle Felix said. "With the straight charging bulls he has a great tragic style like Legartijo."

"Caray!" shouted my father, and clapped his hand over his mouth

lest my mother should hear him swear. *"Que va!"* he said more quietly, "Soldadito is a vulgar gypsy." My father was an obstinate little man with a rare knowledge of the bulls, everyone said. I do not think that God or the Devil could have made him change his mind.

Manolo said gloomily, "The crowd likes Soldadito because he is a fool and takes chances. He is a gypsy clown."

Uncle Felix did not seem to be listening. He looked very small, sitting across the table from me. There was a paleness beneath his brown skin that gave him a fragile, chinalike appearance. "Uncle Felix," I said. But he only shook his head and smiled with an inner sorrow. "He is great, the gypsy clown," he said softly. "He is most well acquainted with death, and I—I am not." He left the dining room without another word.

My father shrugged. "Consuelo," he said suddenly, "go to bed now. It's late."

I kissed my father and Manolo good night, then I walked reluctantly down the long hall. As I passed the carved door of the chapel room I hesitated. Perhaps I thought that my mother was in the chapel; anyway, I felt that someone was there. I pushed open the heavy door slowly, so it would not creak, and peered into the dim room.

All the candles on the altar table were burning, and shadows wavered on the walls and over the blue and white wooden statue of the Virgin. And then I noticed Uncle Felix, in a dark corner, swinging his heavy bullfighting cape in a slow semicircle around him. His head was down as I watched him pivot on his heels, swinging the cape a little ahead of him, the big cape billowing out in the air, and the candle flames flickering. He turned quickly, bringing his right hand close to his hip so the cape wound high and flat like a disk around him. Then he saw me and stood motionless. The cape fell into limp folds, a lifeless thing.

For a moment I did not say anything, because I had seen him practice before in front of the mirror in the hall. But here there was no mirror; only shadows and the cold smell of stone floor. I said, "Uncle Felix, how can you practice here without a mirror?"

He looked at me. "Come here, Consuelo," he said. The candle flames burned brightly now the air was not stirred by the cape. "I am not practicing," Uncle Felix said, "I am remembering. I am remembering Pamplona."

I saw that his face was white and wet with sweat in the candlelight. "You would not know from what Manolo says, but Soldadito is a great matador."

I forgot that it was a chapel, and I turned and spat hard upon the floor. I had seen the Triana gypsies, who loved Uncle Felix, spit when someone mentioned Soldadito, although he was of their own people. Uncle Felix shook his head. "No, Soldadito is truly great."

"You are great, Uncle Felix."

"Yes, my little angel," he said. "I *must* be great, because Soldadito is great. But I would not be great without him."

He smiled his shy, embarrassed smile. "In Pamplona, you know, I was better than Soldadito, so much better that he swore at his *cuadrilla* in a jealous fury. Yet that afternoon I felt death close to me, close to my sword hand. But it did not touch me, and it was neither my friend nor my enemy."

I did not like all this talk of death. Death was an evil word, and my father and Manolo never uttered it. Manolo crossed himself when he heard it in the street. *La muerte,* why did Uncle Felix say it to me?

"Uncle Felix, Mamacita said you were not going to die."

He dropped the cape and put his hands on my shoulders. "No," he said, "she is right. I know she is right." His voice was very unhappy. "Consuelo," he said, "look at me. You must never see Manolo and me with the bulls. You do not know what death is: it is a strange and miraculous thing, and children must not see it. Look at me with your solemn gray eyes; you would not be afraid to look at anything that way, but you must not see us in the ring, because then death is a part of us. It has never been a part of you, my little one."

I began to understand. But I thought of Manolo with his quick smile. "Manolo is alive," I said. "Very alive."

"Yes," he answered. "Manolo forgets death, but I cannot. I am not afraid, yet I cannot understand it, and it is always with me."

"Now, Uncle Felix?" I asked. "Not *now?"*

"No," he replied, holding me tightly by the shoulders, "not now. Not now because you are here. You do not know death." He straightened up then, pleased and a little embarrassed with what he had said. "I speak nonsense," he said suddenly. *"Locuras.* Run away now, Consuelo. You must forget all this. Death is an ugly word, and you must forget it, Consuelito."

"Yes," I said, "I will forget it, Uncle Felix."

I walked out of the dim chapel room without looking behind me. But although I had not understood much of our talk, I did not soon forget it.

The next afternoon the air was motionless and the sun shone glaringly on our tiled roof.

It was late before Uncle Felix came down to the court, rubbing his eyes in the sunlight, for he had been upstairs asleep. He pulled off his rope-soled shoes and sat beside me on the edge of the fountain, dangling his feet in the water. We made a game of rescuing some of the insects which floated unhappily on the water. Uncle Felix was much quicker at catching the floating bugs than I. He scooped them up with one hand and shook them on the stones of the court to dry.

He said, "The season in the north is all over, and I have only one more fight. This Sunday—a benefit in Seville."

"Then we will go on a picnic?" I said. Every year we all celebrated the end of the season by hiring a big wagon on the outskirts of town and driving up the river into the gray, rolling country.

"Cómo no?" he said. "Of course we'll go. To the same place, near those olive orchards of Martinez, where we can sit in the shade and see the river sparkling in the sun and the flocks of goats on the hill." I gazed at my feet, white and wavering under the water of the fountain.

"We'll have more to eat than ever," said Uncle Felix, "loaves and loaves of bread, bunches of onions, cheese and your father's favorite big sausages." I closed my eyes tight in rapture, and at that moment the iron gate on the street slammed, the echo reverberating through the court. As I opened my eyes Manolo came running across the court toward us, his black hair blowing on his forehead. He was panting heavily. "I came," he said, "from the café. You do not know—Uncle Felix, Soldadito was killed in Malaga this afternoon."

"Ay, Manolo," I said, and my feet grew suddenly cold in the water.

"The news just came," Manolo blurted. "They telephoned from Malaga. There was a wind. The cape blew against him, and the bull caught him against the *barrera*. No one could do anything—it happened so fast." Manolo crossed himself, and his hand was trembling.

For a long time Uncle Felix did not speak. His face was more sorrowful than I had ever seen it. "So now,"he said slowly, "so finally death has taken sides with Soldadito."

Manolo and I stared at him stupidly, for we did not know what to say. Uncle Felix slid off the edge of the fountain, leaned down and picked up his shoes. He walked across the court into the house on tiptoe, carrying his shoes. He looked very small indeed.

Uncle Felix went to Madrid for Soldadito's funeral, which was held impressively in the rain. The newspapers showed pictures of the long procession winding down the Gran Vía, where the fronts of buildings and lampposts were draped in black. It was a great state occasion, my mother told me as she stood at the dining-room window watching the rain—"José Rafael Fuentes," she murmured, "Soldadito, a simple-minded gypsy, is buried like a king. Death is a great friend to bullfighters, Consuelo, if they only knew it."

On Sunday morning Uncle Felix came home because he had to fight in the benefit that afternoon. I did not see him, for he went straight to his room and slept until only an hour before the fight. I saw Manolo, who had also been to Madrid, and my father, and they patted my head in a kindly and detached way. I knew from their sober faces that they were hoping for good bulls. They always hoped for good bulls in Seville, because that was their town.

My mother made me sit upstairs in her room. She said I was not to bother Manolo and Uncle Felix as they waited, silently, in the hall downstairs, for my father to drive up outside with the rest of the *cuadrilla*. I stayed by myself until after I heard the cheers from the passers-by when Uncle Felix ran across the sidewalk and climbed into the car. I watched from Mother's window as the black, shining automobile disappeared slowly down the narrow street. For the first time that I could remember, I was afraid for Uncle Felix.

Much later, when the air was cool with the sharp coolness of a late autumn afternoon, I went down into the court. I sat on the edge of the fountain and trailed one hand in the water. Mother was in the chapel, praying as she always did during a bullfight. I wanted to pray that Uncle Felix would have good bulls but I could not keep my mind on prayers. I began to listen for them to come back—so many times they had come back from across the river, with people cheering and clinging to the running board of the car. Crowds would surround the house and climb on the iron grille of the gate like monkeys, while Uncle Felix stood in the hall, bowing, smiling, perhaps pointing shyly at the front of his jacket, where a bull's horn had ripped off the gold embroidery and made a ragged tear in the brocade underneath.

"Blessed Virgin, make him be great this afternoon," I murmured. But the words seemed to have no meaning. I felt sad and alone, and my heart was like a stone with all its weight.

Then the iron gate on the street slammed so sharply that I was startled. I heard someone coming along the hall in the house, and the gate closed a second time more quietly. I slid off the edge of the fountain. "Uncle Felix!" I shouted. "Uncle Felix." My voice sounded high and strange.

My father hurried into the court, carrying the leather sword case. He would not have seen me if I had not shouted, "Papá!" Manolo was right behind him and pushed past us both without saying a word. "Papá," I said, "what is the matter? Where is my uncle Felix?"

My father stopped reluctantly. "He's here, Consuelo. Let me alone."

"But what's the matter?" I repeated. "Papá, what is it?"

"Nothing," said my father. "Uncle Felix would not kill the bulls, that's all. Would not go near them. He was *afraid*. Uncle Felix was afraid."

"What happened?" I asked, the words sticking to my tongue.

"What should happen? Uncle Felix would not leave the *barrera,* would not go into the ring. He would not listen to Manolo and me. 'No, no,' he kept saying, and he hid his face in his hands and would not look at us. And finally Niño de Aragón had to kill his bulls for him." My father's shoulders sagged, but he kept his old stubbornness. "It was something strange," he said. "He will be all right again. Uncle Felix is great—he will be all right next time." He hurried across the court and into the other part of the house.

I stood motionless, not hearing the small trickle of the water running in the fountain. And then I felt that Uncle Felix was standing beside me. I had not heard his footsteps but I knew he was there.

I turned around, *"Ay,* Uncle Felix."

He stood very straight beside the fountain and spoke quietly. "Soldadito was a great fighter, and I also was great. Greater than he, for whatever he could do, I could do it better. I always worked closer to the bulls, everyone saw it. And, Consuelo, he had no respect for death, as I did. He had no respect for anything—not even for me, El Milagro." His eyes shone with sorrow, and he said, "But Soldadito has won, because death was on his side. I could do whatever Soldadito could do; I could follow wherever he led with his gypsy insolence. But now he is dead, I cannot follow. *No puedo seguirle."*

He looked at me; the tears were slowly running down his face. "I do not want to die," he said unsteadily. "Consuelo, I do not want to die."

"No, Uncle Felix," I said.

"Death is a great friend," he said, "to a bullfighter; I know that. I was not afraid of it while Soldadito was alive. But now that Soldadito is dead, I do not want to die." He wiped his eyes hard with the backs of his hands. Then with dignity he pulled a handkerchief from the pocket of his gold jacket and wiped his hands. "But you believe that I am great, don't you, my little one?"

"I believe you are, Uncle Felix."

"Yes," he said. "It was only this time. I will be great again—El Milagro. It is only"—and his voice was very soft—"it is only that I do not want to die."

I gazed into the smooth silver water of the fountain. Uncle Felix did not want to die, and I wished I were dead. I wished it but I knew I would not die, nor Uncle Felix either, for a long time.

"You believe it, don't you, Consuelito, that I will be great again?"

I did not look up from the fountain. I knew it was a lie as I answered. "Yes, Uncle Felix. You do not need death on your side. You will be great—without it."

THE CANE IN THE CORRIDOR

By James Thurber

From the *New Yorker*

JAMES THURBER

was born December 8, 1894, in Columbus, Ohio. His middle name is Grover, which he does not use. He began to write at the age of ten, and started drawing when he was fourteen. He attended Ohio State University, and left to become a code clerk in the State Department from 1918 to 1920, first in Washington, then in the American Embassy in Paris. As a child he lost the sight of one eye, which meant he was barred from active service in World War I. He was a newspaperman on the Columbus Dispatch, *the Paris edition of the Chicago* Tribune, *and the New York* Evening Post. *After writing some sketches for the* New Yorker *he was hired as managing editor.*

His first book was written with E. B. White, also of the New Yorker, *as a parody of the heavy tomes, then being published, taking sex seriously. It was called* Is Sex Necessary? *and sold forty thousand copies to an audience appreciative of its hilarious satire and fed to the teeth with the books it parodied. Mr. Thurber added his own humorous drawings to the book, which helped make it a success. He is the author of eight other books and a very successful play,* The Male Animal, *written with Elliott Nugent, with whom he went to Ohio State University. It was produced in 1940 and later made into an equally successful movie. A book of his drawings will appear this fall,* Men, Women and Dogs, *as well as a book for children,* Many Moons.

"FUNNY THING about postoperative mental states," said Joe Fletcher, rocking the big brandy glass between the palms of his hands and studying the brown tides reflectively. "They take all kinds of curious turns."

George Minturn moved restlessly in his chair, making a new pattern of his long legs. "Let's go to Barney's," he said. "Let's go to Barney's now."

Mrs. Minturn walked over and emptied an ashtray into the fireplace as eloquently as if she were winding the clock. "It's much too late," she said. "I'm sure everybody we'd want to see has left there and gone home to bed."

Minturn finished his brandy and poured out some more.

"You remember Reginald Gardiner's imitation of wallpaper," continued Fletcher, "in which he presented a visual design as making a pattern of sound? Many postoperative cases make those interesting transferences. I know one man who kept drawing on a piece of paper what the ringing of a telephone *looks* like."

"I don't want to hear about him," said Minturn.

Fletcher drank the last of his brandy and held up his glass; after a moment his host walked over and poured in a little more.

Mrs. Minturn found herself finishing her own drink and getting another one, although she seldom touched anything after dinner. "Here's to the Washington Bridge," she said. "Here's to some big dam or other. Let's talk about some big dam. After all, you're an engineer, Joe."

Fletcher lighted a cigarette, holding his brandy glass between his knees. "Which brings up an interesting point," he said. "I mean, if occupational experience gives a special shape and color to the patient's perceptions, then the theory that it is not really a hallucination but a deeper insight into reality probably falls down. For instance, if the number eighteen clangs for one patient and whistles for another—say for George here——"

Minturn spilled ashes on the lapel of his dinner coat and rubbed them into it. "I don't want to hear any numbers," he said thickly. "I don't want to hear any more about it."

His wife, who had been trying to get Fletcher's eye but couldn't, since he continued to study his brandy, spoke up sharply. "George is just getting over a frightful cold," she said, "and he's pretty easily shaken. He would worry frightfully about people, but he doesn't dare think about them. They upset him so." Fletcher did look at her now, and smiled. She realized she had not said what she had meant to say. Something oblique but cleverly phrased and nicely pointed had got lost on its way to her tongue. "You think you're so darn smart," she said.

Minturn got up and began to pace. The brandy had run out. He sat down and lighted a cigarette.

"Of course the people that doctors refer to as squashes," pursued Fletcher, "the invertebrates, you might say, just lie there like vegetables. It is the high-strung cases that manifest the interesting—manifestations. As you just said, Nancy, you think you're so darn smart. I mean, hospitalization moves the mind toward a false simplification. A man gets the idea that he can hold processes in his hand, the way I'm holding this glass. He lies there, you might say, pulling the easy little meanings out of life as simply as if they were daisy petals."

"Daisy petals," said Minturn. "Where's brandy? Why isn't there any more brandy?"

"He gets the idea," Fletcher went on, "that he knows as much about life as Alfred North Whitehead or Carson McCullers."

Minturn said, "Oh God."

"Carson McCullers makes George nervous," said Mrs. Minturn, "and you know it."

"I ask you to remember I have scarcely seen you people since Carson McCullers began to write," said Fletcher stiffly. "I know *Sanctuary* upset George so he had to go away to the mountains. I *do* know that."

"He didn't go away to the mountains at all," said Mrs. Minturn. "So you *don't* know that."

"I want to go away to the mountains now," said Minturn. He began pacing around again, picking up things.

"There's more brandy in the kitchen, darling," said Mrs. Minturn. "In the kitchen," she repeated as he started upstairs.

"Oh," said Minturn. He went out to the kitchen.

Mrs. Minturn went over to Fletcher and stood looking down at him. "It's very sweet of you, Joe, to keep harping on hospitals and sick people and mental states," she said. "I know why you're doing it. You're doing it because George didn't come to see you when you were in the hospital. You know very well that George is too sensitive to visit people in the hospital."

Fletcher stood up too. "Is that why *you* didn't come to see me?" he asked. She was taller than he was. He sat down again.

"Yes, it was, if you want to know so much," she said. "George would have sensed it and he would have worried about you all the time. As it was, he *did* worry about you all the time. But he can't stand things the way you can. You know how sensitive he's always been."

Fletcher tried to drink out of his empty glass. "He wasn't so goddam sensitive when we were both with the Cleveland Telephone Company. He wasn't so goddam sensitive then. No, he was practically a regular guy."

Mrs. Minturn drew herself up a little higher. "It is just quite possible, perhaps," she said, "that you were just not quite perceptious at that time." She went slowly back to her chair and sat down as Minturn came in with a bottle of brandy and a corkscrew.

"Here," he said, handing them to Fletcher. Fletcher put down his glass, inserted the corkscrew accurately into the center of the cork, twisted it competently, and pulled out the cork. "Wonderful thing, technology," said Minturn, "wonderful thing, wonderful thing. I want a drink." Fletcher poured a great splash of brandy into his host's glass and another into his own.

"He doesn't happen to mean he *believes* in it," said Mrs. Minturn. "The trouble with you is you can't tell when a person is allusive even."

"You're thinking of Technocracy," Fletcher told her, taking her glass and pouring a small quantity of brandy into it with studious precision.

"Maybe," said Mrs. Minturn darkly, "and just maybe not."

"Why can't we go home now? Why can't we go home now, Nancy?" said Minturn from deep down in his chair.

"We *are* home, dear," said Mrs. Minturn. She turned to Fletcher. "Anybody that thinks I can't appreciate a game that two can play at is definitely," said Mrs. Minturn, hiccuping, "crazy." She held her breath and tried counting ten slowly.

"Why don't you try bending over and drinking out of the opposite side of your glass?" asked Fletcher.

Minturn sat up a little in his chair.

"Don't have to say things like that," he said severely.

To compensate for her hiccups, Mrs. Minturn assumed a posture of strained dignity. Minturn slid farther down into his chair. They both watched Fletcher, who had set the brandy revolving in his glass and was studying it. He took a sip of his drink. "It is a common misconception," he said, "that postoperative mental states disappear on the patient's advent from the hospital. Out of the hospital, they might recur at any time, and some pretty strange phenomena could happen —as in the case of the hospitalization of a friend."

"If you're just trying to get George down, it's not going to be of the least consequence. I can assure you of that," said Mrs. Minturn. "He's stronger than you are in lots of more important ways."

"Phenomena," said Minturn.

"I'm talking of what *I* might do, not of what George might do," said Fletcher, "in case you consider the manifestation what you choose to call weakness."

"Well," said Mrs. Minturn, "I certainly do—that and meanness."

"I want to see Mrs. Trimingham," said Minturn. "I want to go to Bermuda."

"I suppose it would be too much to say that you can't very well disprove what I'm saying till I say it," said Fletcher.

"No, it wouldn't," said Mrs. Minturn. "I don't see why we can't talk about the Grand Coolidge Dam, or something." She laughed. "That's really frightfully funny. It really is." She laughed again.

Minturn had closed his eyes, but he opened them again. "Can't say I do," he said. "Can't say I do."

Fletcher went over and splashed some more brandy into Minturn's glass. "Let us say that George is lying in the hospital," he said. "Now, because of a recurring phenomena, I call on him every day."

"That's cheap," said Mrs. Minturn, "and that's pompous."

"It's no more pompous than it is predictable," said Fletcher sharply. "It's a condition. It just so happens that it might take the turn of me calling on George every day, from the time he goes in until he gets out."

"You can't do that," said George. "There's such a thing as the law."

"Of course he can't," said Mrs. Minturn. "Besides, George is not going to the hospital."

"I'm not going to the hospital," said Minturn.

"Everybody goes to the hospital sooner or later," said Fletcher. His voice was rising.

"Nine hundred million people don't," said Mrs. Minturn, "all the time."

"I'm stating a pathological case!" shouted Fletcher. "Hypothetical. George has been lying there in that bed for six weeks!"

"No," said Minturn.

"You ought to be ashamed of yourself," said Mrs. Minturn.

"Why?" asked Fletcher. "I'm not saying there is anything the matter with him. He's convalescing, but he can't get up."

"Why can't I get up?" asked Minturn.

"Because you're too weak. You have no more strength than a house mouse. You feel as if you were coming apart like a cheap croquet mallet. If you tried to stand, your knees would bend the wrong way, like a flamingo's."

"I want to go home," mumbled Minturn.

"You *are* home," said his wife.

"He means from the hospital," Fletcher told her, "in the corridors of which, by the way, you hear my cane tapping practically all the time."

"What are *you* doing there?" said Minturn thickly.

"I come to see you every day," said Fletcher. "I have been to see you every day since you got there." He had been moving around the room, and now he went back and sat down.

"Can't stand you calling on me every day," said Minturn. He finished his drink and poured a new one with some effort.

"Don't worry about it, George," said Mrs. Minturn. "We'll take you to the Mayo brothers or someplace, and he'll never find out about it."

"I don't want to go to the Mayo brothers," said Minturn.

Fletcher sat forward in his chair. "And what's more," he said, "I bring you very strange things. That's part of it. That's part of the phenomena. I bring you puzzles that won't work, linked nails that won't come apart, pigs in clover in which the little balls are glued to the bottom of the box. I bring you mystery novels in Yiddish, and artificial flowers made of wire and beads, and horehound candy."

"Terrible, terrible rat," said Mrs. Minturn, "terrible rat Fletcher."

"Police find something to do about that," said Minturn. "Such a thing as law and order. Such a thing as malpractice."

"And licorice whips," continued Fletcher, "and the complete files of *Physical Culture* for 1931, and matchboxes that go broo-oo-oo, broo-oo-oo."

"Broo," said Minturn. "I want to go to Twenty-One."

"Terrible, terrible, terrible rat," said Mrs. Minturn.

"I see," said Fletcher. "You don't even feel sorry for poor old tap-tap. Tap, tap, tap, tap, tap."

"What's that?" said Minturn.

"That's my cane in the corridor," said Fletcher. "You are lying there, trying to unwrassle something I have brought you, when, tap, tap, tap, here I come again."

"Terrible rat, go home," said Mrs. Minturn.

Fletcher bowed to her gravely. "I'm going," he said. "It constitutes the first occasion on which I have ever been ejected from this or any other house, but that is as it should be, I presume."

"Don't throw anybody out," said Minturn. "Tap, tap, tap," he added.

Halfway to the hall door Fletcher turned. "That's right, laugh," he said. "Tap, tap, tap, tap, tap, then."

"Tap, tap, tap," said Minturn from far down near the floor. A new attack of hiccups kept Mrs. Minturn speechless, but she stood up as her guest went out into the hall. Minturn was still saying, "Tap, tap," and Mrs. Minturn was hiccuping, as Fletcher found his hat and coat and went out the front door into the melting snow, looking for a taxi.

THE OLD SHE 'GATOR

By Peggy von der Goltz

From *Story*

PEGGY VON DER GOLTZ

was born January 5, 1900, in Mount Sterling, Kentucky, and comes from a family of pioneers. She went to a number of Southern private schools and attended St. Walburga's in New York. She is married, and her hobby is all kinds of animals. She established the first free clinic for birds in New York. She bred dogs for a time on a Long Island farm, but after they sold the farm and moved back to New York they found they had so many pets there was no room for them all in an apartment. The solution was to open a pet shop. Fish interest her, and she has written a number of stories about Old One Eye, the sunfish. She wrote the first paper on the behavior of fishes, "which offered proof, acceptable to scientists and laymen alike, that fishes can and do think."

Her first novel, McCaw, The Story of a Parrot, *was published in 1937. She is the author of* Our Pets, *a popular booklet, and at present is working on a cat book and a historical novel, both to be published by Simon & Schuster.*

Spring come on in a rush. Evathing was frost pinched and peaked one day, and next morning spring come struttin through the swamp, high-bosomed and hip-switchety as a fly-up-the-creek gal on Saturday night. The cypresses quick put on peart green flutins to cover up their bony limbs. Ferns and flags and rushes come a rollin and a pushin and a piercin through the ground. Mockin birds begun to sass each other. Snakes clumb out of hidey holes. And three of my ducks turned up missing.

I paid hard cash for them ducks.

Maw was pullin paper chinkin out of window frames when I come in, stompin mad. "What's the old she 'gator stole this time?" Maw says, easy's if she's askin how's the collards comin.

"Three ducks," I says. "Just three ducks I laid out three mortal dollars for." "Maybe 'twas chicken snakes," she says, "or weasels, or some feist done it."

"Snakes and weasels and dogs don't leave 'gator tracks," I says. "That old she 'gator's near wore a slick from the swamp up to the yard." I taken down my shotgun and loaded her up with buckshot. "I'm a goin after that pesky 'gator right now."

"In broad daylight?" Maw says. "Well—don't fergit to bury the head and rot out the teeth; 'gator teeth fetches a dollar thutty cents a pound. Shoot her through the head so's not to spoil the belly hide. And mind you fetch home the tail to smoke."

"Yes, ma'am," I says, "and I'll save out the claws to make Least Baby a play toy, if so be you'll leave me go afore the old she 'gator's warmed up and frisky."

Old Baby begins to holler he wants a live baby 'gator for a play dollie, and I got to stop and tell him the' won't be baby 'gators till full summertime. Old Baby's risin six and peart as a tin whistle, he wants to know why's evathing.

Well, I went on back through the piney woods, blue-vi'let starred where they dipped into the live-oak grove where my hogs was rootin. The big red sow was tromplin a rattler, hackin him into hash and gruntin something fearful, whilst ten fat pigs jest turnin into shoats was squealin and runnin around. Then the oak grove give into palmetto and the palmetto squished into swamp, and all the way I could make out 'gator tracks, claw marks on the sides, and slicked-down body draggins in between.

I go on till I spy black water with cypress knees stickin up; then I set sideways down on a stump and wait. I see middlin 'gators and a big garfish and a old snappin turtle makin out it's a moss-covered log and the white things wigglin in its mouth is worms—how a critter so almighty slow as a snappin turtle ever thought to grow its own fish bait is a wonder before the Lord. I see moccasin snakes, fat and lazy and certain death, layin on the water. I hear buck deer thumpin ground and pontoon rabbits goin hippety-hop. But I don't see the old she 'gator.

I set till the sun sunk into a bucket of fire; then, thinks I, I'll go home and eat my supper and come back with a light tonight. I stand up—and there on the bank, bold against the sundown, is a 'gator ten foot long if it's a inch. I jerk up my gun, fire, and slip smack-plunk into the water. I claw out, cussin but thinkin I got the biggest 'gator in the county.

Well, I ain't. Either the 'gator took off wounded and got away, or else I missed. How a man could miss at three, four yards I don't know. But the 'gator's gone. She's left a remembrance, though, on the bank—a nice, fat pig, dead as a coffin nail.

It's black dark when I get home, the wettest, eternal maddest man you're apt to see. I set down and clean my gun first off so's it won't rust.

Maw says, "We et; but the's side meat and peas and poke greens warmin, so dry yourself."

"I slipped," I says. "These here store shoes betrayed my feet. But I'll git that old she 'gator this night."

"Air's chilled some," Maw says. "How you goin to find her if she's holed up?"

So I stayed home. I'd a gone whether or no, but I didn't aim to come home empty-handed in front of Maw. Next morning another shoat turned up missing.

Jim Pearsall's missin stock too, so the first warm night me and Jim go out, jest as the bullbats sail overhead and the whippoorwills begun to whistle and old peppy frog's sayin jug-o-rum, jug-o-rum, and the moon, purty as a little yaller boat tips over the cypress trees. Jim poles the boat. I wear the carbide lamp on my head, turnin and watchin, holdin the shotgun ready.

I swing my head this way and that, shining deer come down to drink and young 'gators with red eyes close together and all manner of wuthless critters. The lamp shined bullfrogs enough to sink the boat. But we was out for 'gator, for a old she 'gator ten foot long with yaller eyes set wide apart.

Of a sudden Jim says, "Shine down! Quick!"

I done so, and yaller eyes glimmed back, big as goose eggs, right in front of us. I heerd Jim draw the pole up so's to stick the 'gator soon's I shoot. I sighted betwixt the eyes, jerked the trigger. My gun misfired.

I loaded again, them big eyes watchin me. But jest as I upped the gun, they sunk, not fast but slow and calcalatin.

We set for a hour at least. We poled on and got two 'gators, one six foot long, one goin on seven. Jim was right tickled. I was some put out.

But I kept my counsel. I buried the head and salted down the belly hide of the one I kept. I hung the tail in the smokehouse, hopin Maw would think it was the old she 'gator—I was plumb mortified to say it wasn't.

Maw come out and taken a look at the 'gator tail and she says, "Hm." That's all—jest *"Hm."*

That day my drake turned up missing.

The two ducks I had left wasn't broody, so Maw set what duck eggs we had under a hen. Like Maw says, the only way to git us another drake is to hatch him.

Next new moon me and Jim go out again, a polin and a shinin and a watchin for 'gator slicks. Bull 'gators was a bellowin like stampeded cattle in a big breeze of wind with thunder rollin over all. It's strange to think that sich a uproar and a poundin, sich a drum-beatin, hell-bent, noise o' battle fury could be a love song. But it is. It's guitar tunes and jook-box music to she 'gators in the swamp.

We come upon a slick where some big 'gator's heaved itself in and out of water so many times the bank shines like a leaky oil barrel's been rolled along it. We set.

Finely bull 'gators began to roar again. A whoppin 'gator skeedaddles by the boat, goin fast, head long as your arm and acrost your chest, eyes yaller, teeth out-stickin—one satisfaction the Lord taken from 'gators in not givin them no lips, they can't lick their chops. This 'gator streaks over to a big cypress stump where two bulls is singin. It switches itself, kinda cute. I know of a sudden that's the old she 'gator—out of range.

One bull roars lovin in her face and smacks her with his tail. She lights into him for fair, then moseys toward the other bull. This other one noses all around her, then he bellows at her and gives her one almighty smack. She rolls over and the boat rocks so me and Jim have got to hold on. She comes back switchin her tail and singin low like she 'gators do.

The first bull swings between and grabs the one she likes, hangs on, a lashing and a twistin. They heave and thrash and bellow, dive and come up again. The she 'gator backs water and watches. They go round and round like a half-ton fluttermill, roilin the water, crashin and bangin. Me and Jim scrabble onto shore and pull our boat up. The bulls wallow and they roll, they r'ar and fall back. They wheeze and blow and puff. The swamp's dead still but for the snortin, splashin 'gators. You can hear teeth crunch on flesh and livin bone.

They bang into a stump and bones crack, clean's a rifleshot. Then we hear a cracklin crunchin, see one bull jerk, hear his teeth snap empty. He wallows round. The black water is streaky red. Me and Jim is splashed all over. They grapple again and heave and grunt and turn and turn, until one bull rolls belly up and sinks into the blood-streaked water.

The other bull's afloat. He slews round, splashin, and we see one forefoot is tore off, jagged, gushin blood. He arches hisself like he's tryin to see, but a 'gator can't bend its neck. He shakes hisself and the water heaves like a washtub. Then he butts the old she 'gator and they swim off together.

"Well," Jim says, "whyn't you shoot?"

"I forgot," I says. "I pure forgot."

We poked around and raised the dead 'gator. Its hide was tore to smithereens, but Jim taken the tail to smoke. I taken nothing and said nothing.

Next day nothing turned up missing. I knowed why that was but Maw didn't know.

" 'Gators or no 'gators, you're goin to hoe up the garden patch," Maw says. "One thing, 'gators don't relish garden sass."

I hoed the garden patch and set out the yams and my tobacco plants that had gone kind of pindlin from settin too long. Old Baby tagged after me all the time, askin when was summertime and when I was gain to fetch him home a baby 'gator. The moon changed and still nothin turned up missing. But I was in a sweat wonderin when the old she 'gator'd git her courtin done and come back. Wait long enough and somethin happens: the hen Maw set on duck eggs turned up missin, and the eggs near about to hatch. That meant the two ducks I had left was wuthless onless I laid out hard cash for a drake.

Then it come on to rain. It rained so hard a mortal man couldn't get through the swamp. Time it did clear up full summer was upon us, and my trigger finger begun to itch. Maw knowed it some way.

"You're not goin a-nigh that swamp," she says. "It's hard luck."

The next morning a fat shoat turned up missing, and then another one.

Now, a man can live without ducks, he can make shift without chickens, but even the Good Book says that man cannot live by bread alone—and no more he can by hominy without hog. But I don't fuss with Maw—Maw's taken a notion that huntin the old she 'gator fetches us bad luck. Maw allows she don't take stock in hoodoo, but when ary woman allows it's better to leave your stock be stole than hunt down a confounded thieving varmint, I say it's edgin onto conjure talk.

Still, I don't fuss with Maw. I let on I'm goin giggin after frogs. Old Baby hollers he wants to go with me—Old Baby is a little dickens. I say he ain't growed up enough. But Maw, that's babied all our young'uns long's she could, says, "Take Old Baby along—he's got to learn swamp ways some time. But look out for snakes and 'gators."

We set off about an hour short of sundown. I taken the carbide lamp, my skinning knife, the frog gig, and my shotgun. Old Baby toted a lard pail to put the frog's legs in. It was hot as Tophet in the swamp, and still as holdin your breath, the same kind of still.

"When the sun goes down," I tell Old Baby, "the frogs pop out; then I'll shine 'em with my light, and stick 'em with my gig, and shuck 'em with my knife, and put 'em in the bucket."

Old Baby says, "I want me a baby 'gator for a play dollie."

I says, "You don't want no 'gator for nothin—big boy like you!"

"I do," he says. "I want a 'gator for a play dollie, and it will grow up to be a old she 'gator and eat ducks, hens, shoats—mules—and evathing."

"Then hush," I says, "and look!"

He hushed. Layin on the bank before us was the old she 'gator. She's gruntin, "Umpf! Umpf!" so busy she don't hear us. And when she grunts, the's cheeps like little biddies callin to a hen. The cheeps come from her nest that's a mound a piece back from the water. It's big as a cord of wood, made out of sweet flags and bulrushes and goose grass and such that she's piled up and trompled down to rot, and whilst it rotted it gave off heat enough to hatch the eggs. The eggs is hatchin now, so she goes, "Umpf! Umpf!" and the babies go, "Cheep! Cheep!"

Old Baby's still as a heathen idol, and I wisht I'd had the wit to leave him home, for a she 'gator with new-hatched young'uns is techy as a mule in flytime, and twicet as dangerous. A she 'gator is the lowliest critter there be, I reckon, that cherishes its young'uns. I figger I'll leave Old Baby see the little 'gators come down to water, then I'll give the old one both barrels and be shet of her for all time.

She heaves herself up and goes up to the nest, so I know the last egg has hatched. She claws into the nest, the young'uns cheepin to split your ears. They come racin out, forty, fifty little 'gators, long as your hand, brown with yaller dapples. Cunning, feisty little varmints, they go scamperin to the water.

I hear Old Baby suck his breath, and he shoots out, grabs a 'gator baby, and yells, "Lookey, Paw!" I see the old she 'gator bow herself, but in a wink she lets go her tail. Old Baby shoots up in the air, his mouth still open, spraddled out like a dead frog. He drops into a fern patch, lays still.

I went crazy mad. I blazed away both barrels, dropped the gig, throwed the gun at the old she 'gator, and jumped her. She's spurtin blood but not bad hurt. I lit on her back and drawed my knife and jabbed and jabbed. She run for the water, me ridin her, bracin my feet—but what could a man do against six hundred pounds of foamin 'gator?

We plunged into the water. I drove the knife into her neck, hung onto the hilt, and went under. She rolled, tryin to scrape me off, her tail a lashin and a thrashin. My breath come hard. My chest was on fire. Hot pokers stuck my eyeballs. They say drownin's easy. It ain't.

She rolled over on the bottom, the mud soft as feathers, chokin, killin. I jest barely held on. She shot up, r'ared. All but drownded, I slipped, grabbed, got her again. She begin to spin and thrash, the water all red around us and foamin into fury. I got her around the neck and hooked my legs under her and hung on, knowing if once I lost my holt I was gone for certain. Between the spinnin and the thrashin I could see some, but what I seen was crazy. I seen Old Baby standin on the bank—and Old Baby was dead, the she 'gator kilt him. I thought I was dead too and in the Bad Place, consarned forever to fight a old she 'gator because I lied to Maw and taken Old Baby to his death. All the time I could hear myself yellin, and see the swamp spin round like I was a top, and hear the jolts when we cracked into stumps and cypress knees; but I couldn't feel a thing. I see the bank come close, heard my leg rake the roots. Then the 'gator jolted, humped herself, let out a sort a grunt, and sagged under me. Old Baby was dancin around, jabbin at the 'gator with the frog gig. I wanted to tell him to git away, but I couldn't. Besides, Old Baby was dead.

Next I knowed Old Baby was scoopin water in the lard can and throwin it at me and yellin, "Paw, wake up!" I grabbed a holt of him and shaken him till I knowed he wan't a spirit. He jest had his wind knocked out. Then I clumb off the old she 'gator. My leg was hurt bad, but the old she 'gator was plum riddled with buckshot and knife cuts and the jabbins Old Baby put in with the frog gig—he'd jabbed me too, but I never let on.

The she 'gator'd come to rest on the mud shelf she built for her young'uns to play on and eat wigglers whilst they growed up, and there I skunt her. I reckoned the hide and teeth would fetch enough to buy me some more ducks I could keep in peace. Yet I couldn't help but recollect that the old she 'gator was a bold and cunning critter, a mighty enemy if she was a varmint—only trouble was her and me both wanted to eat off the same hog, and 'twas my hog. I set so long a thinkin that a little 'gator come scalawaggin between my feet and I catched it for Old Baby.

PECOS BILL AND THE WILLFUL COYOTE

By William C. White

From *Story*

WILLIAM C. WHITE

was born in 1903 in Reading, Pennsylvania, where his father was a Presbyterian minister. After receiving his Bachelor of Arts at Princeton University, in 1923, he was instructor in modern European history at the University of Pennsylvania, where he took his Master of Arts degree in 1925. He taught for several years at the Friends' School, in Wilmington, Delaware, and was awarded the Penfield Fellowship for study abroad by the University of Pennsylvania. From 1926 to 1929 he lived in Moscow and also traveled in Siberia and the Caucasus. In 1930 he was foreign correspondent for the New York Evening Post *and* Public Ledger *Syndicate in Berlin and Warsaw. He speaks and reads Russian, Polish, German, and French, and on his return from abroad in 1930 lectured on modern Europe for the Pond Bureau. His articles on Europe have appeared in the* Atlantic, Harper's, Asia, *New York* Times, Esquire, Readers' Digest, *the* New Yorker, *and other magazines. Since 1936 he has been writing short stories, which have been published in the* Saturday Evening Post, Collier's, *and other national magazines. He has sold stories to the movies, written scenarios for MGM, and is the author of four books and two juvenile books. More recently he was in England for the Office of War Information, for which organization he is still working.*

THE GREAT LEGENDARY cowboy of Texas, Pecos Bill, used to sing of himself,

Oh, I'm wild and woolly
And full of fleas,
Ain't never been curried
Below the knees.

I'm a wild she-wolf
From Bitter Creek
And it's my night
To h-o-w-l!

No one of the many stories tells precisely what happened to him at the end of his career. They don't tell because no one knows except Panhandle Pete who was there and he wouldn't talk until just recently.

Here, for the first time, is Pete's story.

There were a lot of things Pecos Bill used to like, Pete says, and liquor and women and the smell of sagebrush and the way the prairie looked in spring and shooting and riding and singing and the taste of beef broiled over a little outdoor fire were just a few of the things he liked. But I guess what he liked best was hunting coyotes. Ever since he'd been a small boy he'd chased coyotes, trapped coyotes, shot coyotes, thrown rocks at coyotes, and run them ragged on foot until they dropped, with their tongues hanging out. "They're smart animules," Bill always said. "It's a test of a man's intelligence to outthink 'em."

As Bill got older and his wind wasn't so good any more he had to give up chasing coyotes, that is, until Baby came along.

I was with him the night he ran into Baby and I'll never forget it. We were riding along forty miles south of El Paso on as nice a night as I ever saw. The stars were out and it was bright. There was even a piece of moon. That was what made it so funny. We were riding along and Bill was singing,

> *"Beat the drums lowly and play your fifes slowly,*
> *Play the dead march as you drag me along.*
> *Take me to the graveyard and lay a sod o'er me.*
> *For I'm a poor cowboy and I know I done wrong."*

Pecos Bill always sang that song when he was feeling extra happy.

All of a sudden he says, "That's funny!"

"What's funny?"

"There, on that ridge, that thunderstorm coming up."

I looked and saw a black cloud coming up all right, but the stars and the moon were still shining.

"Never saw a thunderstorm on a star-bright night," Bill said. "I'd call that almost a first-class miracle."

Something flashed on the ridge and Bill said, "It's lightning all right." We rode on faster. Bill stopped sudden. "That's funny!"

"What's funny?"

"Did you hear any thunder after that lightning?"

"Nope." I said that because I didn't hear any thunder and we were close enough to the storm to hear it if there was any thunder. "Nope, I didn't hear any."

"Look! Lightning again and no thunder!" Bill shook his head. "I believe in miracles, but only one at a time. A thunderstorm so close with lightning and no thunder, that's almost a first-class miracle."

We rode closer and suddenly we heard a sound. I guess you'd call it laughter, but it was child's laughter and a woman's laughter and a waterfall's laughter, mixed with a horse's neigh and the noise of a tin can full of pebbles, and the roar of a lot of cowboys howling at a joke. It sounded like "Hayheehaw! Haiharhoo! Hearhoiheh!" and ended with "Huh, huh, huh!" delicate, like a skeptical baby.

"A laughing thunderstorm," Bill said, angry, "would be a third miracle. Hell, that's a coyote and the lightning is his eyes flashing!"

The black cloud raised a head and we could see right enough it was a coyote and the biggest one I ever saw and no one ever saw a bigger one. It was easy to tell it was a female because she walked dainty. She was so big she'd have to lie on her side and bend her neck out of shape to nibble at sagebrush. She must have heard us, for the next thing she came at us, just like a thunderstorm that got up on its heels and began chasing you. She went by in such a rush, the air around was chilly for the next half hour. Bill didn't have a chance to draw his gun and fire. All he said was "Oh, Baby!"

That's how Baby got her name!

"Baby!" Bill repeated.

Somewhere, off in the distance, in the next county or maybe over in New Mexico, we heard the "Hayheehaw" and so on and then the final "Huh, huh, huh!"

Bill was awful thoughtful for a while. "I'm going to hunt that baby and get her if it's the last thing I do. Baby! There's a coyote's coyote!"

Me and Bill hunted Baby all that year and all the next and the year after that and the year after that too. Maybe there were even more years but those are all I remember. It was a long time.

Hunting Baby wasn't hard. She was always obliging and willing to hang around and be hunted. We chased her over most of Texas. When we couldn't find her on dark nights she'd let out that laugh of hers, particularly the "Huh, huh, huh" part, and off we'd go. Other times her eyes would flash in the distance and there we'd go again. Sometimes that fooled us—more than fifty times we saw flashes like that and went off hell for leather and found that what we were chasing on the horizon was really a thunderstorm or a twister. Of course, when it thundered, then we knew it wasn't Baby. Half the times Baby'd have been lying low, watching us make fools of ourselves. As we turned back soaking wet we'd hear her "Huh, huh, huh!" off in the other direction. Other times we could get on her trail by waiting till she went to a water hole. She had a thirst like a desert and could drink a hole dry with the noise of a rusty pump. Some nights when we thought we'd lost her, her tracks would help us. They were always deep round holes and you couldn't miss 'em. It's getting off my story, but it was those tracks that helped develop West Texas—they were so deep they caught a lot of rain water and held it through dry spells and the grass grew thick around 'em. A lot of cattlemen today still use those tracks for water holes.

It wasn't hunting Baby that was tough, it was bagging her. In five years Pecos Bill must have had a thousand shots at her, from all distances from a hundred feet to a mile, and he shot at her with lead and iron and silver and a couple of times with a shotgun full of scrap iron. Nothing took any effect. Sometimes the stuff we fired hit Baby's sides and bounced back at us. Once we had to hide under a mesquite thicket for an hour while it rained railroad scrap all around us. As a six-inch piece of steel rail hit Bill on the neck he said, "We just won't try that one again. It's like being hunted by a coyote and shot at."

Other times when Baby was feeling frisky she didn't bother to bounce bullets back at us. She just timed the shot so that as it came to her she leaped up in the air and the bullets went right under her. Then she'd land with a smack you could hear a long way off and sometimes the earth would crack under her. Half the arroyos, those little canyons, in West Texas is from where Baby landed after those jumps. She'd have probably started up a couple of earthquakes in any country not so tough as West Texas.

"That Baby!" Bill would say after missing her once again. He sounded awful proud. "She's just willful! Plumb willful!"

I guess it got to be a game with Baby, because no matter what we tried to do, her laugh never changed or got angry or snarly. Some nights when Bill didn't feel like going out after her Baby'd hang around and there was a kind of disappointment in her laugh, like a kid you promised ice cream for supper he didn't get.

I know it got to be a game with Bill and I never saw him so happy. Of course from time to time we'd take a job to get enough money to try out some new scheme Bill had thought up for getting Baby. That was all he did think about, night after night. He figured out all kinds of baits and snares and deevices, but none of 'em worked. He figured out every kind of trap. After Baby picked up one of 'em and heaved it in the air with her hind foot and it landed on Bill and me and kept us pinned down for five days, we gave up traps. Even that didn't make Bill sore. He laughed and shook his head. "That Baby! She's smart." That was the way he was talking about her. Sometimes when he saw Baby running in the moonlight he'd say, "Look at the way that moonlight shines her gray fur! I bet you never saw anything prettier." And when she'd run fast Bill'd say, "I bet that's the fastest animule there is!" The way he'd talk, you might have thought Bill was raising a child to show off at the State Fair.

One idea Bill had almost did get Baby. The idea was to chase her into the middle of Randall County, which we did, and then to run barbed wire right around the boundaries of the county, which we did. We used all the barbed wire in West Texas doing it and we strung it right. When we got done, stringing it over trees and poles and houses, I never saw such a mess of barbed wire. There wasn't a hole in it big enough for a rattlesnake to crawl through and we ran it so high that not even Baby could jump over it. There we had Baby penned up right and all we had to do now was to wait until she got too weak to move. That wouldn't take too long because we'd been having a drought and the water holes were as dry as sun-bleached bones. And Baby was always thirsty.

We must have waited outside that barbed wire a couple of weeks and all the time Bill kept saying, "We got her this time all right, we got her! She won't be willful no more!" And Bill would jump around excited like a colt in a loco patch. "When man matches his intelligence with animules," Bill would say, "man must win. That's natchural!" Every night we heard Baby crying inside there behind the wire like she was trying to find a way out and getting madder and madder. The more she cried the more Bill grinned and yelled, "We got her this time!"

Then one night when we were watching there was a new sound behind the wire, a soft "Plop, plop, plop!"

"What's that mean?" Bill asked, nervous. "Sounds like she was throwing mud pies." Then he guessed it. "Baby's digging, that's what it is. She's trying to dig her way out and she's throwing up dirt!" He looked half proud as he said, "I knew she'd figure out something to do." He looked half mad as he said, "That won't get her nowhere. We'll surround the fence and when her head shows we'll wallop her."

So Bill called out all the people from Potter, Armstrong, Swisher, and Deaf Smith counties, the ones around Randall. They were glad to stand watch because they're always glad to take a crack at anyone or anything coming from Randall County.

Three days and three nights we waited, and the "Plop, plop, plop" continued but it got fainter and fainter as Baby dug deeper. "This time we got her sure," Bill said. He patrolled the fence day and night with a paddle made from a wagon tongue.

About midnight we heard a new kind of noise. It began as a hiss and turned into a roar and the earth shook and half the people around the fence ran like hell. The roar got louder and right then I felt rain in my face. It felt like rain, it was wet, but when I got some on my hand it had a funny smell.

In the midst of the loud roaring we heard a funny noise. It was "Hayheehaw," and the rest of it and then "Huh, huh, huh!" It sounded awful frightened, but it wasn't coming from back of the fence, it was coming from somewhere behind us.

"That's Baby!" Bill started to jump. "And she's out, she's gotten out!" I never saw a man so mad but he wasn't so mad he couldn't say, "She's that smart, that Baby."

It was beginning to rain even harder. "How'd she get out?"

"Blew out," Bill said. "That's not rain, it's oil. It's got the same smell as the stuff I used to rub on my stiff joints. She dug to hit a pocket and a gusher blew her out."

Way off in the distance, running like a breeze toward Mexico, we heard Baby. "That scared her," Bill said rueful. "She ought to know I didn't mean to have it happen like that. She's scared. She won't come back."

His laugh was awful faint. "She must be over the Rio Grande by now."

Bill nodded. "I didn't think she'd take it like that." He sounded all choked up and he went to his horse and rode off like mad toward Amarillo.

It took me four days to find him. When I caught up with him he was in Amarillo at the Unweaned Calf bar. He wasn't alone, either. Somewhere he'd picked up a girl whose name was Kankakee Katie. I ain't much for women myself—I never learned how to tell a good one from a bad one and I've never been sure there's any real difference. Katie was a big blonde and, from the way she was lapping up pulque, a pretty fair forager. She was comforting Bill and that was what mattered. I heard he'd been crying for three days when he got to town. Now he sat gloomy-like and all he'd say was "Baby!"

"Who's this Baby you're muling over?" Katie asked him.

He just shook his head.

"I never heard a man make as much fuss over me," Katie said like it annoyed her.

Bill just says "Baby," dreamy-like.

"It's awful bad manners," Katie said, "to keep grieving over one lady when you're in the company of another."

"Baby was no lady," Bill said.

"What was she, a hellcat?"

Bill shook his head. "A coyote!"

"That's no way to talk about her," Katie said, like she had to defend her sex. "What was she, blonde or brunette?"

"Gray," Bill said, "gray like early morning. Baby!"

Katie lapped up some more pulque. "I think you're loco but I tell you, I could go for a man who'd say 'Katie' the way you say 'Baby.'"

Bill reached for the bottle and began to cry at the same time and when he cries it's like the first freshets coming down an arroyo in spring.

"Katie," I said, "he's really upset about a coyote." I told her about Baby and how Bill was afraid she was gone for good.

"He's grieving like that over a four-footed, long-haired, howling animal?" I didn't know whether Katie was going to laugh or upset the table. She didn't do either. She began to cry. "I never thought I'd meet such a tenderhearted person in all my life. Bill reminds me of my mother—she was tenderhearted like that too." And she cried as hard as Bill.

Bill blinked and smiled at me. "Pete, here's what I need—sympathy and a chance to forget Baby." As he pounded his fist on the table the walls of the Unweaned Calf shook and the barkeep looked scared. "Katie, if you'll have me, I'm yours. How's for marrying me and lighting out and we'll get a little ranch and raise cattle?"

Katie didn't know whether she was being kidded or not. Then she hit the table with her fist and the walls shook even harder, and down to the floor dropped a little guy who was standing at the bar but not holding on tight. "Pardner," Katie said, "I heard about marriage and I always wanted to try it. It's a deal!" She stopped crying and dried her eyes on her shirtwaist sleeve. "We'll get a ranch house and we'll paper the walls with the pages of a mail-order catalogue and make everything snug." Then she looked worried. "Nope, it's only a dream."

Bill's face got black. "When I make a promise it's a promise."

Katie shook her head. "What about Baby? I know men better than anything in the world except maybe women. Sooner or later you'll get the old hankering to go after Baby and then not even a good woman's love or a forty-foot fence could hold you."

"I told you I was through with Baby," Bill roared, and he made such a noise the little guy at the bar hit the floor again.

"A man's a man and a woman's a fool for forgetting it," Katie said, almost ready to cry again. "I just can't risk having my heart broken over a coyote." She finished off the bottle of pulque. "Nope, we'll stay friends, Bill, and I'll be a sister to you."

"I'll be consternated!" Bill yelled. "I believe you're jealous of Baby!"

"A lady has a right to her feelings, such as she feels," Katie said, wiping her eyes on her shirtwaist sleeve. "I'll tell you what to do, Bill. I ain't going to have no coyote come between us. You bring me Baby's hide and I'll marry you."

Bill just sat back in his chair.

"Besides, it'd be convenient to have," Katie said. "If Baby's as big as you say we could use the hide for a parlor rug and have some lap over in the dining room and what's left we could stuff chinks with."

"I can't do that," Bill said promptly. "I've been trying for years with no luck."

"You don't sound like you even wanted to get it," Katie said with a pout.

"Sure I want to get it, but how?"

"You talk like you're glad a coyote's smarter than Pecos Bill."

"That's enough." Bill banged the table and half the bottles on the bar fell down. "It's a bargain. I'll get it."

"Right now?"

"Right now!"

"Then I'll go off and hunt up a wedding dress and some shoes," Katie said. "You bring the hide back here and we'll have the hottest wedding there ever was in Amarillo." She headed for the door, like a barn being carried off in a spring flood.

Bill didn't say anything for quite a while. He picked up the pulque bottle and found it was empty. He asked, "Got any ideas, Pete?"

"About Katie?" I shook my head.

"About getting Baby. I can't let the little woman down."

He stood up and started to the bar. "Let's have a drink and start thinking."

When Bill asked the barkeep for pulque the barkeep shook his head. "You finished the last bottle. I haven't got a drop."

"Then gimme whisky."

"On top of pulque?" The barkeep looked astonished and the little man beside the bar fell to the floor and lay there.

"What's wrong with that?" Bill asked, getting hot.

"You mix my drinks like that, they'll take the hide off you." But the barkeep poured out whisky. "However, it's your hide."

Bill swung around like he was boiling mad. "What did you say?"

"I said if you mix my drinks they'll take the hide off you!"

"Yeep!" Bill brought a fist down on the bar and cracked the top plank. "We got it!" He slugged down the whisky. "We got it!"

I thought he was crazy. "Got what?"

He pounded me on the back and I bounced toward the front door. "Hurry out, Pete, and get two big water tanks!"

Well, I came back to the bar with the tanks, and when I got there Bill had every bottle off the shelves and he was opening them so fast the popping of corks sounded like gunfire. From somewhere he had got fifty gallons of pulque, and that went into the tanks first. Then he poured in all the whisky in the place.

He was awful enthusiastic. "We'll mix up a drink for Baby that'll take her hide off sure. There's been a drought in this Dust Bowl, and we'll pick up a good dry water hole, fill it up with this mixture, and see what Baby does."

In the tanks went twenty gallons of rum, three cases of bourbon, seven bottles of gin, and a bottle of soda water. The barkeep came up from the cellar with another armful of bottles. One of them had a funny shape.

"What's that?" Bill asked.

"Something called 'Cream dess Violets.' A salesman give it to me."

"Put it in!"

"Here's Liquor dess Peaches."

"Put it in!"

In went cherry brandy, a bottle of bitters, and a gallon of Dago red. Bill didn't look satisfied. "Got anything else in bottles?"

The barkeep, who was baldheaded, handed over a flask of hair tonic.

Bill stuck his finger in the soup and licked it. "Tastes pretty nearly right. What else you got?"

The barkeep offered a bottle of catsup and that went in.

Again Bill sampled the results. "Almost right? Got anything else in a bottle?"

"Some perfume called Eau d'Amour I was saving for my wife."

"Put it in!"

Bill stuck his finger in once more. "That's perfect! It ought to take the hide off a cactus!"

Three teams of horses and ten men and the biggest dray in the county drew the tanks out to the water hole that Bill had decided to use. He had to hope the odor would attract Baby, wherever she was. The mixture from one tank went into the hole with a splash, and the odor it gave off knocked seven men to the ground. I felt a little dizzy myself, but Bill was too excited to notice anything. Twenty-one lizards who lived around that hole ran to it, took one small drink, and twenty of them lay on their backs with their toes turned up. The twenty-first just vanished in a small explosion.

After the men revived they started to move the second tank to the hole but Bill stopped them. "Hold it! Baby may not come here before this stuff dries up, and we'd better save the other tank for another night. We never could mix this drink again the same way."

With the hole half filled we drove off a piece and waited. We waited a long while and we tried to keep Bill quiet but he was pretty nervous. Most of the time he said, "I hope she comes." Sometimes he said, "This is a dirty trick to play on Baby!" Even from a mile away the water hole smelled like an old barroom on Sunday morning. Bill walked up and down saying, "I wonder where Baby is, I wonder what Katie's doing, I wonder if Baby is coming, I wonder if Katie is getting ready," until he sounded all mixed up, as if he was expecting Katie to turn up at the water hole while Baby got ready for a wedding.

Every so often there would be little explosions at the water hole and Bill said, "That must be jack rabbits coming in for a drink! Boy, if only Baby'd come."

Then we heard a funny noise off in the distance, the noise of a rush of a big wind. Bill knew what it was and he yelled, "It's Baby! She's sniffing!" A minute later, over the horizon, came the black shadow that was Baby, running full speed. She came so fast that she had to stop herself at the water hole by braking with her front feet and threw up a sandstorm that blacked out El Paso three days later. We were too excited to pay any attention.

We saw the shadow stand by the hole and we watched Baby lower her head. We heard one more sniff, like a tornado taking a deep breath, and then there was an explosion and a roar that knocked us flat. Bill stood up first. "That got her!" He began jumping. "That got her!" And he started to the hole with all of us running like mad.

Bill beat us all there, and when we caught up to him he said, "I'm consternated! Look at this!" There lay Baby's hide, thick, gray, tangled, and matted, but there was nothing of Baby inside it. Bill didn't know what to do or think. He just stood scratching his head. "I didn't think it would work as good as that." He shook his head. "Well, I got her at last!" His voice sounded funny. Then he said, "Load as much of the hide as you can on the wagon and drag the rest. We'll get back to town and see Katie."

We put a lot of the hide on the wagon and it was piled up like a hayrick. On the way back to town Bill remembered the unused tank of the mixture. "I'm going to bottle and sell it," he said. "It'll be a wonderful thing for knocking off warts and freckles."

We pulled up in front of the Unweaned Calf and Bill yelled, "Hey, Katie!" He was feeling pretty good again. "Hey, Katie, come out and see what I got!"

A flock of barflies rushed out but no Katie, and Bill began to grumble. "Look at the trouble you go to, just for a woman, and then she's off primping herself and too busy to come look." He decided to wait for her and invited everyone in for a drink. By this time fifty guys were going up and down the street boasting how they caught the coyote by putting whisky on her tail.

The barkeep had renewed his stock from somewhere and Bill ordered drinks all around. After twenty minutes he began to yell, "Hey, Katie!"

The barkeep gave him a funny look. "You mean that blonde you were talking to yesterday?"

"Yeah, what about her?"

"Last night a cowhand comes in with a couple hundred dollars and said he was going up to San Antone. Katie said she always wanted to see San Antone so she goes with him. They left about midnight!"

Well, Bill stowed the hide and the tank of mixture away in a shed and he said, "Let's get out of this country, Pete." We went over to New Mexico for a time, punching cattle, but it wasn't the same Bill. He was thoughtful and silent and he never sang any more. He never talked about Baby, either. Then we drifted back to El Paso again and got a job at the One Legged M Ranch. Bill worked hard but his heart wasn't in his work. At night he used to leave our shack and go out and sit somewheres by himself and he got sore if I offered to go along. When he did talk he was pretty gloomy. "I'm getting old," he'd say. "I think we ought to go out to Californy for our last days. That's where rich Texans and poor Texi-cans go before they die. They sit in the sun, I heard, and eat oranges."

Once he said, "I done wrong killing Baby. I shouldn'ta done it. I was so happy when she was around to chase, I didn't know how happy I was."

I couldn't get him interested in roping or riding or liquor or shooting. As for women, when the sister of the owner of the One Legged M came for a visit Bill ran off and hid in the hills for a week.

He came back with a funny look on his face and he wouldn't talk. But that night he said, "Come along with me."

We walked a mile from the ranch buildings. Bill said mysteriously, "Hear anything?"

All I heard was a lot of crickets and maybe a lizard in the grass. I asked, "Where?"

"Over there, back of that hill."

I listened again and I heard a cow in heat and a horse neighing. "I don't hear nothing special."

Bill wasn't even listening to me. He was grinning like a kid. "I can hear her, coming nearer." He shook his head. "She sounds mighty lonesome tonight, mighty lonesome." He repeated, "So lonesome, that 'Huh, huh, huh!' "

I knew who he was talking about. I just chewed on a piece of grass and said nothing.

"You sure you don't hear nothing?" Bill asked.

"I got a cold." I tried to hide what I was thinking about Bill. "I don't hear nothing so good."

The next day I found Bill in the bunkhouse packing his kit. "I'm going back to Amarillo," he said and he wouldn't explain why. "I just got an idea, that's all."

He did explain on the way back. "Baby's still hanging around waiting for me, Pete. I know it." He glared at me. "You think I'm crazy."

I shook my head mighty quick. "Different people hear different things."

"The reason we can't see her is because she has no hide," Bill said like he'd thought it out. "Did you ever see a coyote without a hide?"

"Nope, I never did."

"No one ever did, and that proves it. If a coyote's going to be seen he just has to have a hide!"

We rode on quite a spell and I didn't have a word to say.

Then Bill said, "When we get to Amarillo, I'm going after Baby."

I almost fell off my horse, and it wasn't the horse's fault. "How will you do that?"

Bill didn't say. We came into town and he went to the shed where he stored all the stuff after he got Baby's hide. It was still there but except to pat it once, he wasn't interested in it. He went right to the tank of mixture and pounded it.

It sounded as empty as a dry well.

"It's gone and I can't even mix it again," Bill said, and he sounded heartbroken. "I figured that maybe if I drank some of it, it'd put me in the same shape as Baby. Then I could have gone after her."

I just shook my head. I couldn't say a word.

Bill began to fuss around the tank. With the top off he lowered himself inside. Then I heard him yell, "Get a cup, Pete! There's just a little bit left here."

I got him a cup and he fished up one cupful and even for that he had to scrape bottom. When he came from the tank he was grinning from ear lobe to ear lobe. I was pretty worried but I figured he knew what he was doing.

"You going to drink this now?"

"No sir," Bill said with a lot of pride. "I'm going to drink it fit and proper." And with that he began to sing

"Oh, I'm wild and woolly
And full of fleas,
Ain't never been curried
Below the knees!"

I tried to argue with him all the way to the Unweaned Calf, but his mind was made up. He just kept singing. He told the barkeep, "This time I brought my own liquor."

The barkeep looked suspicious. "How about a chaser?"

"I hope I'll never need a chaser," Bill said with a pleasant laugh. He looked around the room and saw about twenty people. "Come on, folks, gather round and I'll show you something you can tell your grandchildren." He raised the cup, but I was feeling too bad to watch close.

Before he tastes it he sings

"Take me to the graveyard and lay a sod o'er me,
For I'm a poor cowboy and I know I done wrong!"

When I heard that I knew he was extra happy again.

"Pete!" he said to me. "You've been a good friend. When you find someone like Baby, don't treat her bad!"

Then he takes a good long swig from the cup.

There's a sort of flash and explosion, not loud but gentle like, and when I look up, Bill's gone. Completely gone and not a sign of him! Then, and the men who were in the Unweaned Calf at that moment will swear to it, drunk or sober, we heard a gentle fluttering sound. Down from the ceiling like falling leaves came the clothes Bill had been wearing, his shirt, his hat, his pants, his boots, and the hand-carved belt he was so proud of. For a second they stood by themselves, just as if Bill was inside 'em, then they collapsed to the floor.

And that was the end of Pecos Bill, as far as anyone knew.

I hung around town for a couple of days but I was awful lonesome, so I went back to my job at the One Legged M, feeling like a lost calf. I worked extra hard by day so I'd be good and tired at nights, but even then I couldn't sleep.

One night I got up and walked out to where Bill and me used to sit. I was there in the quiet and I just couldn't forget Bill. The only noise I heard was a couple of lizards in the grass.

Now, I ain't going to swear to this because I never heard it again, but as I was sitting there that night a wind came up sudden and it got real cold. The grass began to move or I thought it did. And right behind me I heard "Heyheehaw!" and so on and then "Huh, huh, huh!" Maybe it could have been the wind in the trees, but there weren't any trees and anyway, where did that sudden wind come from? A minute later I swear I heard Bill's voice, as happy as a little child, laughing, "That Baby! She's just willful!" It sounded as if he was chasing along behind, doing what he liked to do most in all this world.

But I couldn't see a thing.

I would even think that I had dreamed it, except that the next morning Bert Simmons, who owns the One Legged M, called us outside and we followed him behind the barn. The ground there used to be as level and smooth as a piece of harness strap, but this morning there was a brand new arroyo, fifty feet deep and running for a quarter mile, just like a big crack in the earth. It was the sort of crack we used to see when Bill and me shot and Baby jumped in the air to duck and then landed hard.

Well, I'm sure that wasn't the finish of the whole thing although I never again heard a sound like Baby or saw any traces. But I've been reading in the newspapers about those California earthquakes and I remember what Bill used to say about wanting to finish his days in California. No one knows what causes those earthquakes, I hear, but I got my own ideas ever since I heard that California was a sort of soft place, nowhere near as tough as West Texas and a whole lot more brittle.

APPENDIX

List of American magazines publishing short stories which were consulted in choosing stories for this volume:

Accent. Box 102, University Station, Urbana, Ill.

American Hebrew (The). Florence Lindemann, man. ed. 48 W. 48th St., New York City.

American Magazine (The). Sumner Blossom, ed. Crowell-Collier Pub. Co., 250 Park Ave., New York City.

American Mercury (The). Eugene Lyons, ed. 570 Lexington Ave., New York City.

American Prefaces. Paul Engle, ed. University Hall, Iowa City, Iowa. (Publication suspended with Summer 1943 issue.)

Atlantic (The). Edward Weeks, ed. 8 Arlington St., Boston, Mass.

Blue Book. Donald Kennicott, ed. The McCall Corp., 230 Park Ave., New York City.

Collier's Weekly. Charles Colebaugh, ed. Crowell-Collier Pub. Co., 250 Park Ave., New York City.

Columbia. John Donahue, ed. Knights of Columbus, 45 Wall St., New Haven, Conn.

Common Ground. M. Margaret Anderson, ed. 222 Fourth Ave., New York City.

Coronet. Arnold Gingrich, ed. 919 N. Michigan Ave., Chicago, Ill.

Cosmopolitan. Frances Whiting, ed. Hearst Magazines, Inc., 57th St. & 8th Ave., New York City.

Country Gentleman. Robert H. Reed, ed. Curtis Pub. Co., Independence Sq., Philadelphia, Pa.

Crisis (The). Roy Wilkins, ed. 69 Fifth Ave., New York City.

Decade of Short Stories. Lee Lukes, ed. 2952 Belden Ave., Chicago, Ill.

Decision. Klaus Mann, ed. Decision, Inc., 125 E. 23d St., New York City.

Direction. M. Tjader Harris, ed. Direction, Inc., Darien, Conn.

Elks' Magazine (The). Coles Phillips, man. ed. 50 E. 42nd St., New York City.

Esquire. Arnold Gingrich, ed. 919 N. Michigan Ave., Chicago, Ill.

Everywoman's. Joan Ranson, ed. 1790 Broadway, New York City.

Fantasy: A Literary Quarterly. Stanley Dehler Mayer, ed. 930 Heberton Ave., Pittsburgh, Pa.

Glamour. Elizabeth Penrose, ed. Jane Maxwell Smith, fiction ed. Condé Nast Publications, 420 Lexington Ave., New York City.

Good Housekeeping. Herbert R. Mayes, ed. Hearst Magazines, Inc., 57th St. & 8th Ave., New York City.

Harper's Bazaar. Carmel Snow, ed. Mrs. Mary Louise Aswell, fiction ed. 572 Madison Ave., New York City.

Harper's Magazine. Frederick Lewis Allen, ed. Harper & Bros., 49 E. 33d St., New York City.

Holland's: The Magazine of the South. J. Tom Mann, ed. Texas Farm & Ranch Co., 3306 Main St., Dallas, Texas.

Household Magazine (The). Nelson Antrim Crawford, ed. 8th & Jackson Sts., Topeka, Kans.

Kansas Magazine (The). Russell I. Thackrey, ed. Kansas State College, Manhattan, Kans.

Kenyon Review (The). John Crowe Ransom, ed. Kenyon College, pub., Gambier, Ohio.

Ladies' Home Journal. Bruce Gould, Beatrice Blackmar Gould, eds. Curtis Pub. Co., Independence Sq., Philadelphia, Pa.

Liberty. Paul Hunter, pub. 122 E. 42nd St., New York City.

Mademoiselle. Betsy Talbot Blackwell, ed. Marian Ives, fiction ed. 1 E. 57th St., New York City.

Matrix. Joseph Moskovitz, ed. 1500 W. Nedro Ave., Philadelphia, Pa.

McCall's Magazine. Otis L. Wiese, ed. Constance Smith, fiction ed. The McCall Corp., 230 Park Ave., New York City.

New Anvil (The). Jack Conroy, ed. 3569 Cottage Grove Ave., Chicago, Ill.

New Masses. Joseph North, ed. 104 E. 9th St., New York City.

New Mexico Quarterly Review. Dudley Wynn, ed. The University of New Mexico, Albuquerque, N. M.

New Yorker (The). Harold Ross, ed. 25 W. 43rd St., New York City.

Opportunity: Journal of Negro Life. Dutton Ferguson, man. ed. National Urban League, 1133 Broadway, Room 826, New York City.

Partisan Review. Dwight MacDonald, et al., eds. 45 Astor Place, New York City.

Poise. Rev. Francis E. Benz, man. ed. 25 Groveland Terrace, Minneapolis, Minn.

Redbook Magazine. Edwin Balmer, ed. The McCall Corp., 230 Park Ave., New York City.

Rocky Mountain Review. Ray B. West, Jr., ed. Box 38, Weber College, Ogden, Utah.

Saturday Evening Post (The). Ben Hibbs, ed. Curtis Pub. Co., Independence Sq., Philadelphia, Pa.

Scholastic: The American High School Weekly. Maurice R. Robinson, ed. 220 E. 42nd St., New York City.

South Today. Lillian E. Smith, Paula Snelling, eds. Clayton, Ga.

Southern Literary Messenger (The). F. Meredith Dietz, ed. 109 E. Cary St., Richmond, Va.

Southwest Review. George Bond, et al., eds. University Press, pub. Southern Methodist University, Dallas, Texas.

Story: The Magazine of the Short Story. Whit Burnett, ed. 432 Fourth Ave., New York City.

Tanager (The). Henry Alden, ed. P. O. Box 66, Grinnell College, Grinnell, Iowa.

This Week. William I. Nichols, ed. Mary Day Winn, fiction ed. United Newspapers Magazine Corp., 420 Lexington Ave., New York City.

Tomorrow. Eileen J. Garrett, ed. Dorothy Pace, fiction ed. 11 E. 44th St., New York City.

Twice a Year. Dorothy Norman, ed. 509 Madison Ave., New York City.

University Review (The). Clarence R. Decker, ed. The University of Kansas City, Kansas City, Mo.

Virginia Quarterly Review (The). Archibald Bolling Shepperson, ed. University of Virginia, 1 West Range, Charlottesville, Va.

Woman's Home Companion. William A. H. Birnie, ed. Eileen Lange, fiction ed. Crowell-Collier Pub. Co., 250 Park Ave., New York City

Woman's Day. Betty Finnin, fiction ed. 19 W. 44th St., New York City.

Writer's Forum (The). Paul H. Rohmann, man. ed. The Antioch Press, Yellow Springs, Ohio.

Yale Literary Magazine (The). Yale University, Box 243-A, Yale Station, New Haven, Conn.

Yale Review (The). Helen MacAfee, man. ed. P. O. Box 1729, New Haven, Conn.

Yankee. Benjamin M. Rice, ed. Yankee, Inc., Dublin, N. H.

List of Prize Stories in O. HENRY MEMORIAL AWARD PRIZE STORIES *1919 to 1943 Inclusive*

1919—1st. ENGLAND TO AMERICA, Margaret Prescott Montague
2nd. FOR THEY KNOW NOT WHAT THEY DO, Wilbur Daniel Steele

1920—1st. EACH IN HIS GENERATION, Maxwell Struthers Burt
2nd. CONTACT, Frances Noyes Hart

1921—1st. THE HEART OF LITTLE SHIKARA, Edison Marshall
2nd. THE MAN WHO CURSED THE LILIES, Charles Tenney Jackson
(Special prize for best work in 1919, 1920, 1921)
THE MARRIAGE IN KAIRWAN, Wilbur Daniel Steele

1922—1st. SNAKE DOCTOR, Irvin S. Cobb
2nd. INNOCENCE, Rose Wilder Lane
SS. GOLD-MOUNTED GUNS, F. R. Buckley

1923—1st. PRELUDE, Edgar Valentine Smith
2nd. A FRIEND OF NAPOLEON, Richard Connell
SS. TOWERS OF FAME, Elizabeth Irons Folson

1924—1st. THE SPRING FLIGHT, Inez Haynes Irwin
2nd. MARGARET BLAKE, Chester T. Crowell
SS. RACHEL AND HER CHILDREN, Frances Newman

1925—1st. MRS. BISBEE'S PRINCESS, Julian Street
2nd. SPLENDID WITH SWORDS, Wythe Williams
SS. PAPAGO WEDDING, Mary Austin

1926—1st. BUBBLES, Wilbur Daniel Steele
2nd. DEATH IN THE WOODS, Sherwood Anderson
SS. COMMAND, Albert Richard Wetjen

1927—1st. CHILD OF GOD, Roark Bradford
2nd. THE KILLERS, Ernest Hemingway
SS. THE SCARLET WOMAN, Louis Bromfield

1928—1st. THE PARROT, Walter Duranty
2nd. THE PECULIAR TREASURE OF KINGS, Marjory Stoneman Douglas
SS. BRIDAL POND, Zona Gale

1929—1st. BIG BLONDE, Dorothy Parker
2nd. THE HOMESICK LADIES, Sidney Howard
SS. HIM AND HER, Katharine Brush

1930—1st. DRESSING-UP, W. R. Burnett
1st. NEITHER JEW NOR GREEK, William M. John
2nd. THE SACRIFICE OF MAIDENS, Elizabeth Madox Roberts
SS. CORONER'S INQUEST, Marc Connelly

1931—1st. (no prize) CAN'T CROSS JORDAN BY MYSELF, Wilbur Daniel Steele
2nd. (1st money) ONE HEAD WELL DONE, John D. Swain
3rd. (2nd money) THE FIVE MINUTE GIRL, Mary Hastings Bradley
SS. HAUNTED GROUND, Oliver La Farge

1932—1st. An End to Dreams, Stephen Vincent Benét
2nd. Farewell to Cuba, James Gould Cozzens
SS. A Trip to Czardis, Edwin Granberry

1933—1st. Gal Young Un, Marjorie Kinnan Rawlings
2nd. The Frill, Pearl S. Buck
SS. To the Invader, Nancy Hale

1934—1st. No More Trouble for Jedwick, Louis Paul
2nd. Old Red, Caroline Gordon
SS. The Daring Young Man on the Flying Trapeze, William Saroyan

1935—1st. The White Horses of Vienna, Kay Boyle
2nd. The Home Place, Dorothy Thomas
SS. John the Six, Josephine W. Johnson

1936—1st. Total Stranger, James Gould Cozzens
2nd. Suite 2049, Sally Benson
SS. A Sum in Addition, William March

1937—1st. The Devil and Daniel Webster, Stephen Vincent Benét
2nd. To Those Who Wait, Elick Moll
3rd. The Fury, Robert M. Coates

1938—1st. The Happiest Man on Earth, Albert Maltz
2nd. Fire and Cloud, Richard Wright
3rd. The Promise, John Steinbeck

1939—1st. Barn Burning, William Faulkner
2nd. Bat Flight, James Still
3rd. Calves, David Cornel de Jong

1940—1st. Freedom's a Hard-Bought Thing, Stephen Vincent Benét
2nd. Don't Get Me Wrong, Roderick Lull
3rd. The Kill, Edward Havill

1941—1st. Defeat, Kay Boyle
2nd. A Worn Path, Eudora Welty
3rd. Eighteenth Summer, Hallie Southgate Abbet
Special Prize for a "First" Story. The Visit, Andy Logan

1942—1st. The Wide Net, Eudora Welty
2nd. Two Rivers, Wallace Stegner
3rd. Windwagon Smith, Wilbur Schramm
Special Prize for a "First" Story. A Long Way To Go, Jeanne E. Wylie

1943—1st. Livvie Is Back, Eudora Welty
2nd. The Knot Hole, Dorothy Canfield
3rd. The Fishermen of Patzcuaro, William Fifield
Special Prize for a "First" Story. The Little Black Boys, Clara Laidlaw